SILENT NIGHT

When the nightmare came, it wasn't her daughter's, but her own.

She awoke in terror, pushing at an invisible weight on her chest, fighting for breath. Her ears seemed to ring from a crash of cannons. She looked wildly around her in the darkness.

The night was silent. No artillery boomed. No vague, dark shapes threatened to snatch her breath. Whimpering overrode the ringing in her ears. She started to go to Lexie, then sank back on the bed. The sounds had been her own.

An owl hooted as if protesting some disturbance of his nocturnal pleasures.

When dawn lit the darkness, Nicki was still awake. . . .

Also by Trish Macdonald Skillman

SOMEONE TO WATCH OVER

BURIED
SECRETS

TRISH MACDONALD
SKILLMAN

A Dell Book

Published by
Dell Publishing
a division of
Bantam Doubleday Dell Publishing Group, Inc.
1540 Broadway
New York, New York 10036

ISBN: 0-440-21742-3

Printed in the United States of America

Published simultaneously in Canada

July 1995

10 9 8 7 6 5 4 3 2 1

RAD

ACKNOWLEDGMENTS

The author wishes to thank Jerry Weiss, Ph.D., for his patient advice and assistance in the creation of this book. Any errors or deviations from accepted psychological approaches contained within are mine alone. Hypnotic regression is a complex process and should be explored only with the help and guidance of a qualified professional.

Special thanks to Carla W. Smith for sharing memories of her radical youth and her experience with troubled children; to Donna Gimarc for revision advice; to Danielle Clemens for editorial insight; and as always, to Jerry, for his encouragement and love.

Trumpeter Lake and the characters in this book are fictitious. Resemblance to existing locations or actual persons, living or dead, is purely coincidental.

For RaBecca Michelle Bartee

*May your childhood memories be happy ones—
and may each remain forever vivid in your heart.*

—Love, Nana

THE HEARSE SONG

Have you ever thought as the hearse goes by,
That you might be the next to die?
They'll wrap you up in a big black sheet,
Then dig a hole about six feet deep.

They'll take you out and lower you down,
And the men with shovels will gather round.
They'll throw in dirt and they'll throw in rocks.
And they won't give a damn if they break the box.

Then the worms'll crawl in and the worms'll crawl out.
They'll crawl in thin and they'll crawl out stout.
First your eyes drop out, then your teeth fall in,
While the worms crawl over your mouth and chin.

The worms crawl in, then the worms crawl out.
The worms play pinochle on your snout.
They invite their friends and their friends' friends too,
You'll be chewed all to hell when they're through with you.

Version of an American ballad
popular with WWII servicemen,
Author Unknown

1

The city transit bus pulled away, trailing a cloud of thick smoke and diesel fumes. Nicki covered her nose and mouth and turned in the opposite direction, up San Jacinto. Within half a block her blouse clung to her skin, a damp cotton sauna in the blistering five o'clock June heat. Near Crockett Boulevard, in sight of the large house on the opposite corner, her feet began to drag.

Morgan Westacott had built his two-story mansion in 1909, paying workers with oily bills from his first wildcat strike. Long since abandoned by his scattered heirs for the splendor and safety of the suburbs, the residence's latest owner had partitioned the house a year ago into six units, seven counting Nicki's tiny apartment above the carriage house.

Three young men, sweat glistening on their bare chests, lounged along the porch railing, dark bottles of St. Pauli Girl beer dangling from their fingers. One flipped a glowing cigarette butt onto a patch of dried grass beside the steps and turned to twist the dial of the ghetto blaster behind him. The sensuous voice of Luther Vandross was replaced by jarring waves of music that pulsated across the wide street,

harsh words condemning authority, urging violence
and abuse against cops and whites and women.

Two out of three.

A shiver rippled down Nicki's back, chilling the
trickle of perspiration between her shoulder blades.
She pushed the thought aside, lifted her chin, and
concentrated on her goal, a modest frame house
halfway down the block.

"Hey, mama, ain't you gonna come home fo' supper?" one of the men, the one called Odell, shouted
above the driving music. Derisive hoots from the
others drowned out the radio's angry voice.

Nicki quickened her pace, grateful the width of
Crockett was between her and her tormentors. Six
months ago the street would have been filled with
activity—little girls playing hopscotch or jacks,
young boys plotting mischief, old women tending
flower beds. Now the sidewalks were deserted.

The music switched to another beat, this one
sensuous and swaying, the lyrics openly sexual.

"Skinny mama like her gotta have a hunger for
somethin'," another man said. Odell leaped down
from the porch rail and began pacing Nicki's steps
on his side of the street.

"Why you always messin' with that uppity white
trash?" a teenage girl in tank top and cheek-
revealing shorts called down from the second-floor
balcony.

"'Cause Ah's partial to white meat, li'l sister,"
Odell said loudly.

Nicki stumbled on some broken pavement but
managed to keep her balance. Odell mimicked her
awkward recovery. Somewhere in the depths of the
house a child's wail interrupted the ensuing hyster-
ics from the others. Spouting a string of profanity,
the teenage girl disappeared inside.

A bright turquoise Firebird with pavement-hugging frame turned the far corner. The beat from the speakers in the back window answered the boom box on the porch, drowning the rumble of supercharged engine. Nicki's pursuer loped back toward his place on the porch. As it drew beside her, the car stopped.

"Hey, mama. What's happenin'?" the man in the passenger seat asked. When Nicki increased her pace to cross behind the car, the driver shifted into reverse and blocked her escape.

A door slammed, and a sturdy woman in tan shorts and white blouse swung down from the porch of the frame house. One brown hand on her waist, she shaded her eyes with the other, directing a fiery glare at the unmoving vehicle.

"Best quit playin' them games, 'less you wanna be talkin' to the Man, you hear?" she shouted at the Firebird's occupants.

The driver flashed an obscene gesture, shifted gears, and cruised to the curb in front of Odell and his companions. Nicki hurried forward and crossed to meet the woman.

"Ellis gets home, he'll have somethin' to say to that trash 'bout runnin' their filthy mouths 'round decent folk."

"Let it go, MarLynn. It'd just get worse," Nicki said. Her eyes probed those of the black woman. "How is she?"

"Got her colorin' some after lunch. 'Bout used up the black and red crayons. Laid down 'round four or so. Finally nodded off, not more'n twenty minutes ago."

"No bad dreams?"

"Not so's you'd notice. Child feels safer in daylight, I reckon. 'Sides, Russell, he watchin' her like a guardian angel."

"We could all use one of those," Nicki murmured, glancing back at the activity around the Firebird. "I'm sure that was the car in the alley that night."

"Wouldn't doubt that. Fools in that house got more brass than sense. Just look at 'em! Pushin' that crap in broad daylight now. Ellis's gonna have to go down to the station. Phone ain't gettin' us nowhere."

She ushered Nicki inside. Out of the Texas sun the temperature dropped substantially, aided by the air conditioner in the living room window. Mar-Lynn led her toward the kitchen at the back of the two-bedroom house, placing a finger to her lips as they passed her grandchildren's room. Nicki stuck her head around the partially closed door and stared at the huddled form on the lower bunk bed.

Her five-year-old daughter lay curled in a fetal position, her left thumb resting against her lower lip. MarLynn, or maybe Russell, had tucked a ripple-patterned afghan around the sleeping child. Nicki felt her chest constrict in anguish. Even as a baby, Lexie had rarely sucked her thumb.

Russell had assumed a protective position on the floor beside the bed, his dark eyes fastened on the book in his lap. The curtains were closed, but he'd twisted until an escaping shaft of sunlight illuminated his page. He raised his head, smiled a greeting, then returned to his story. Nicki couldn't remember seeing the eight-year-old without a book, usually a volume intended for older readers, like the one currently holding his attention.

She pulled the door to and joined MarLynn, accepting a glass of iced tea with a tight smile. A second window unit battled for supremacy against the heat from the sunlight reflecting off the counters of the spotless kitchen. The deep pot simmering on the stove filled the room with the scent of peppers and garlic. Nicki's empty stomach lurched violently.

"I reckon I'll be settin' that child a spell longer," MarLynn said, settling herself across the table.

"Is it that obvious?"

"Child, don't never try makin' a livin' playin' cards."

"Renee always gave me a hard time about wearing my feelings on my sleeve."

"Humph. Hard time's 'bout all that fancy mama o' yours gave you, rest her soul. Well, let's hear it."

"The apartments were terrible . . . rats in the garbage cans, old men sleeping it off on the sidewalk. The neighborhoods made Crockett look like one of the country club drives. The landlady at the only halfway-decent place seemed nice enough, but she wouldn't even discuss paying out the deposit."

"What'd the welfare say?"

"I don't qualify. Not for AFDC . . . not even for food stamps."

"Single girl like you with that baby in there, must be some kinda help somewheres. You doin' more 'n most. You got a job."

"Making twenty dollars a month above the assistance level."

MarLynn poked at the ice in her glass and fished out the lemon wedge. Nicki closed her eyes and let the humming air conditioner lull her thoughts, overriding the frightening visions that had become her constant companions.

"You tell 'em 'bout your mama's bills? An' the ones for that child's sickness?"

She nodded, opening her eyes. Mist blurred the

familiar face before her. MarLynn reached out, covering Nicki's pale, trembling fingers with calloused brown hands.

"All these lawyers runnin' 'round, seems there oughta be somethin' a body could do."

Nicki bit her lip against the tears.

"I could file bankruptcy, but NorTex National's hypersensitive about public image. Three creditors filed suit for nonpayment against one of the tellers last year. They let him go the day the judgments came back. Besides, the last thing I need's another lawyer hounding me."

"You get another letter?"

Nicki nodded.

"Read this one?"

"No. I threw it away. Like the last two."

"Don't seem like the problem's goin' away, child," MarLynn said, getting up to stir the contents of the pot.

"Renee didn't know anyone up north."

Nicki finished her tea and got up to dump the ice in the sink and rinse her glass. The stream of water splashed across the countertop. She reached for a kitchen towel.

The droning window unit muted the sound of MarLynn's seven-year-old granddaughter Sharraye and the two little girls from across the alley jumping rope in the backyard. A week ago Lexie would have been in their midst, adding her giggles to their carefree laughter. A vision of light glinting off a metal blade flashed through Nicki's memory, bringing a wave of nausea.

"Ever think this lawyer might be from your daddy's people?"

Nicki released her death grip on the towel and shook her head. The possibility had crossed her mind and quickly been dismissed. She had barely enough strength to pursue a single goal these days. Confronting the existence of someone from Renee's shadowy past took a backseat to the need to get Lexie away from the violence that surrounded them. She wasn't the only one wanting out. Ellis and MarLynn had been trying to buy a place in a safer neighborhood for almost six months.

"You goin' back to work tomorrow?"

"They made me take a week's vacation. I'll go looking again in the morning."

"That child ain't gonna sleep long as you stay in that place. That old couch in there ain't too bad. Slept on it lots o' times when our boys was home. Laid awake lots o' nights on it too . . . when Raye-Ann was runnin' wild. Ellis be home 'fore too long. He'll walk you to get your things."

"I can't stay here," Nicki said, retrieving her purse from beneath her chair. "I've got to get to the laundry and back before dark. I haven't been since Lexie . . . since that night."

"Child, you got things need washin', you do 'em here. That way, Ellis can see you home after dark . . . you still insist on refusin' my good hospitality."

Nicki wrapped her arms around the older woman.

"I'd never have survived this without you and Ellis."

"Folks survive what they have to in this world, honey. Me and Ellis done owned this house 'most eighteen years. Place ain't been home for a long time. Shoulda moved on years ago, while it was still worth somethin'. Trouble is, folks never think this kinda thing's gonna happen to their street. Can't afford to get out, now."

She opened the back door.

"You set on goin', you best scoot on down the alley. Come back that way, too. Strange cars been drivin' by off an' on all day. I 'spect Ellis made pest enough of hisself, callin' 'bout that trash. Might be they do somethin' 'fore too long."

Nicki slipped through the back gate and made her way toward the Westacott carriage house, past old Mrs. Lansky's with its boarded windows and dead garden patch. At eighty-seven, after six break-ins, Miriam Lansky had finally abandoned her dream of dying in her own bed and allowed her grandchildren to move her to a retirement home. The next two houses had similar histories. The arrival of the crack merchants on the corner had driven away most of the good, honest people who'd raised their families on Crockett Boulevard.

The teenage mother from the second floor was sprawled in a lounge chair on the concrete slab that had replaced the mansion's backyard. An old pecan tree beside the carriage house shaded the tabloid newspaper in her lap. Juice from an orange Popsicle dripped down her arm and onto the fraying outdoor carpet, faded long ago from bright green to dull gray. Her child hung in a baby swing at her feet, chortling to himself. Once in a while the girl gave the swing an erratic push with one foot.

The baby watched Nicki's approach with solemn eyes, then broke into a wide, toothless grin. Nicki smiled back as she climbed the wooden outside stairs to the two-room apartment above the carriage house. The girl ignored her presence.

Inside, a twenty-inch box fan on the kitchen counter whirred ineffectively, rearranging stagnant air trapped by locked windows. Nicki bolted the door and fastened the safety chain before stepping out of her limp skirt and blouse and carefully removing her panty hose. She slipped into jeans and her last clean shirt. The jeans hung low on her hips, reminding her of the meals she'd skipped in recent days.

She pulled out the Jell-O mold she'd made that morning. Cherry. Russell and Sharraye's favorite, as well as Lexie's. Not much of a dinner contribution, but it would have to do, she told herself. No meager offering could hope to repay all she owed Ellis and MarLynn Hill.

The phone rang as she rummaged in the deep closet for the last of the dirty clothes. She tucked the receiver under her chin and stretched out the cord, chasing one of Lexie's socks behind the hamper.

"I'm bringing Jell-O," she said without greeting. "If you've already fixed a salad, we can call it dessert."

"Excuse me?" an unfamiliar male voice asked.

"Sorry. I thought you were someone else."

The elusive sock had wedged itself between the wall and a stack of puzzles. She crawled deeper into the closet.

"What flavor?"

"I beg your pardon?"

"Strawberry and cherry are all right. Raspberry's better. Actually, almost anything's fine, except maybe lemon. I think it's the color."

Nicki abandoned the sock and scowled at the phone.

"Who *is* this?"

"My name's Reed Jordan, Miss Prevot. I'm the attorney whose letters you've been ignoring."

The Michigan lawyer. Nicki shoved the puzzle boxes away from the wall and retrieved the errant sock, cramming it into the pillowcase with the other dirty clothes. Damn. She didn't have time for this.

"How did you get this number? It's unlisted."

"I talked to the bank's personnel department."

Which said volumes about NorTex National's public image, Nicki thought darkly.

"Actually, the regular secretary wasn't there. When I explained to the temp that I was your attorney . . ."

"My attorney?" Nicki flung the pillowcase on the bed and returned to the closet to restack the puzzles. "Look, Mr. Jordan, I've never retained your services. I haven't the vaguest idea why you're hounding me, but if it's about Renee's charge accounts, I placed all that in the hands of a counseling service three years ago. You'll have to speak to someone there."

"I can only assume you didn't read my last letter."

Screeching tires on Crockett Boulevard and an answering squall of rubber from the alley below made Nicki lower the phone. Muffled shouts from the main house followed the sound of slamming doors. She felt the hair rise along her arms.

In the yard the baby began to cry. His mother's rising shrieks drew Nicki toward the front room. The phone cord and the sound of heavy feet scrambling up the stairway halted her advance. Someone rattled the knob and pounded her door.

"Open the fuckin' door!"

Nicki backed away, hugging the hallway wall. A handkerchief-wrapped fist crashed through the front window, raining shards of glass across the couch. The couch where Lexie was usually curled up about now, "reading" memorized stories to her stuffed animals as Nicki fixed their dinner. From the phone the lawyer's insistent demands to be told what was going on echoed Nicki's own thoughts.

A face appeared at the fist hole . . . the man called Odell, an angry scowl making his features more menacing than usual. The weapon he clutched to his bare chest frightened Nicki more than his expression.

"Go away!"

"Uh-uh, mama. The Man's after my ass."

He slashed at the remaining glass with the gun and swung one long leg over the sill. Outside, a voice shouted his name, demanding surrender. Odell responded with his gun. The explosion rattled the glasses in the dish drainer. An acrid smell filled the apartment. Nicki flung the phone to the floor and ran. Outside, someone answered Odell's fire. Somewhere inside the apartment, glass shattered again.

She dived into the closet, pulling the door closed behind her.

2

The brief bursts of gunfire continued. Odell's voice cried out, and something heavy clattered to the floor. As quickly as it had started, the shooting ceased. More feet pounded the wooden stairs, and a crash, like the splintering of wood, preceded harsh shouts of violent language. The voices moved back outside. Nicki huddled in the darkness, shivering despite the oppressive heat. Perspiration tracked down her back as silence descended. She closed her eyes.

An icy fear pushed upward from deep within her. Panic, more frightening than the escalating confrontations with Odell, more terrifying than any nightmare she could remember, oozed like a chemical reaction through her body. She whimpered as tentacles of forgotten horror tightened, knotting her muscles.

Mommy!

Her mouth opened, but the word remained unsaid.

Hide, baby. Hide till I come for you.

The command flitted through her swirling thoughts and was gone, forgotten as quickly as it had come. The voices outside had returned, quieter now, calmer.

Policemen . . . talking back and forth, opening cabinet doors, laughing, exchanging raunchy comments, crunching broken glass beneath their feet. Nicki opened her mouth to call out. No sound emerged. The anxiety spread to her lungs and for an instant she was certain she'd ceased to breathe.

Footsteps converged outside the closet door. Whispered conversation, then the knob rattled and the door was flung open. Nicki crossed her arms over her face to block the sudden glare of late-afternoon sun from the bedroom window. She gulped deep breaths of air to clear the dizziness from her head, embracing the relief that accompanied the return of light.

A man with blond hair reached toward her, and the panic flared again.

I never told!

"Found her," the man called over his shoulder as he pulled her from the closet. Bushy eyebrows creased his sunburned face like chalk marks, accenting his scowling features. He stood up, leaving Nicki huddled on the bedroom floor.

The feeling of relief returned. Nicki looked about her, her battered senses taking in the familiar surroundings as if for the first time. A second man, this one with Hispanic features and a weary expression, holstered the gun in his hand and motioned her to her feet. Both men wore jeans and black T-shirts and, despite the heat, navy-blue nylon jackets. When the first one turned, Nicki could see PO-LICE spelled out in six-inch white letters across his back.

She tried to rise. Cramped from the twisted position she'd assumed in the slanted depth of the closet, her legs collapsed beneath her. The blond man grasped her wrists and jerked her up.

The touch of his hands seem to reawaken the feelings of panic. Aware of how strange her reaction must seem to someone who only wanted to help her, Nicki tried to murmur her thanks. Again, the words seemed frozen somewhere between her mind and her vocal cords.

What's happening to me?

"How'd you get mixed up in this?" the blond policeman asked.

Her silence seemed to anger him. The need to communicate intensified as he shoved her roughly against the wall and twisted her arms behind her. Metal snapped around her wrists.

"Wanna tell us about your boyfriend? Might go easier if you help us."

Boyfriend? Oh, my God!

The blond cop was tearing the sheets from one of the twin beds—Lexie's bed—prodding bulges in the mattress, poking his fingers through the worn spots in her stuffed animals, squeezing their insides, then tossing them onto the floor. Nicki bit her lip. The Hispanic cop began reciting the familiar TV litany.

Remain silent? Of course she didn't want to remain silent.

You're making a mistake! Stop destroying Lexie's things!

The words screamed in her mind, but her voice remained mute.

"I hope you have explanations for what's going on here."

The comment came from a slender, sandy-haired man in a rumpled business suit. He towered over the uniformed black woman who'd escorted him into the room. The blond officer, now trashing Nicki's corner of the room, raised his head and glared at the newcomers.

"Says he's her attorney," the woman said. "Name's Jordan. Collier frisked him. He's clean."

"Sure got here fast, Counselor. Odell must be doing even better than we guessed, keepin' a retainer on such a tight leash," the blond man said.

The lawyer scanned the room. Angry gray-green eyes settled on Nicki and softened for an instant. His expression hardened once more, he turned back to the Hispanic policeman.

"He your lawyer?" the officer asked.

Afraid to trust her voice, she nodded silently. Jordan's solemn expression never changed, but something almost like amusement flickered in his eyes. She felt herself flush.

"Detective . . . ?"

"Luis Rodriguez." He jerked his head in his partner's direction. "Rod Goree."

"Detective Rodriguez, I assume your search warrant covers this building as well as the main house or you wouldn't be here."

"Oh, yeah," Goree said.

"Ms. Prevot has no connection with the tenants in the main house . . . or their illegal activities."

"That so?" Goree grinned at his partner. "Well, pardon us, Counselor, but your *other* client says the lady's been warmin' his bed in exchange for her daily nose candy. Locked him out 'cause he cut her off."

Nicki managed to gasp.

"You're treading thin ground, Detective. Ms. Prevot's the only client I represent here, and she doesn't use drugs. I can see false arrest and harassment charges forming as we speak."

"Bullshit!"

Activity in the hall behind Jordan increased. The woman officer returned, this time leading an even taller man with massive shoulders and short, kinky hair as black as his weathered face. He wore the dark gray uniform of a local security firm.

"Claims he's gotta talk to Rodriguez," the woman explained to Goree's unspoken question.

"Shit! Who handled the invites for this bust?"

"Ellis," Rodriguez said, nodding at the man. "Hope none of your kin are part of this mess."

"One sacrifice is enough, Luis. My boys live clean and do honest folks' work." He pointed at Nicki. "Just like she does."

"Jeez, who's gonna waltz in next? Mother Teresa?"

"Shut up, Rod." Rodriguez studied the older man before him. "Let her go."

"Damn it, Luis."

"Odell's had a pure mean streak since the day he drew breath. Just as soon lie to hurt as to save his hide. Ellis Hill's been a church deacon since before your mama stopped wipin' your butt. Got no reason to think he's lyin. Let her go."

Goree, muttering under his breath, unlocked the cuffs.

"If you need a statement, I'll be happy to bring my client to the station . . . in the morning. I think she's been terrorized enough for one day."

Rodriguez nodded. Ellis Hill wrapped his well-muscled arm around Nicki. Moving on shaky legs, she let him lead her down the hall. Reed Jordan and the two policemen followed. Her first glimpse of the front of the apartment buckled her knees. Jordan added his support to Ellis's, seemingly unintimidated by the older man's greater size.

The front door hung on one hinge, the dangling chain lock swinging gently. A second window had been smashed, leaving the room open to crosscurrents of hot outside air. One of the living room lamps lay on the floor beside the couch, surprisingly undamaged, but uncongealing Jell-O dripped from the shattered glass mold onto the kitchen tile. Darker crimson splatters dotted the cream-colored throw rug inside the door.

"Got some plywood at the house," Ellis said, retrieving Nicki's purse from beside the couch and ushering her through the chaos. "Get my boys to help board things up."

Nicki nodded, still afraid to trust her voice. Outside, the baby swing lay on its side. The black policewoman was trying to take a statement from the young mother. The teenager slouched in the back-porch doorway, clutching her whimpering child, her fingers toying with the bandage above his tiny eyebrow. She glared at the female officer, stuck out her lower lip, and refused to respond to the questions.

Odell sat in the back of an ambulance, his hands cuffed in front of him. An EMT was wrapping gauze around his left upper arm while a uniformed officer stood watch. The prisoner looked up at Nicki and grinned.

"Shoulda been nicer to me, mama. Mighta kept yore skinny ass outta trouble. I be out in a bit. Likely be real hungry, too. You gonna be around?"

Nicki drew back against Ellis. Rodriguez walked over and slammed the ambulance door, silencing Odell's laughter.

"He's right about makin' bail," the detective said. "You'd be safer sleepin' elsewhere tonight."

"She can stay with us. Her girl's there now."

"No," Nicki cried out, relieved to realize she'd spoken aloud. She repeated the word, softer this time. "Ellis, I'm sorry, but I can't stay on this street another night."

"I'm at the Sheraton," Reed Jordan broke in. "Let me book a room for you and your daughter."

"I can't . . . I don't have that kind of money."

The ambulance backed down the driveway onto Crockett. The once-deserted block was suddenly alive with onlookers. People stood in little knots along the street, whispering to one another, pointing at the mansion and the carriage house. Nicki felt as if they could see beneath her clothing. Instinctively she crossed her arms as if protecting her nakedness. The lawyer's hand on her shoulder made her jump.

"Let me take care of your hotel. It's important I talk to you. I promise you'll feel better once you understand why I'm here. We can talk in the lobby if you'd prefer."

He was certainly persistent, even for a lawyer, Nicki thought. And he'd come so far. That realization was more than a little frightening. MarLynn was right. The problem wasn't going to go away. Still . . . she shook her head.

"I'm driving a rental, but I'd be glad to pay for a taxi, both ways . . . if you'd feel better having Mr. Hill check it out."

"I've got a car," Ellis said. Nicki stared at the black man's face. He shrugged. "Public building. Seems safe enough."

She bit her lip, thinking of Lexie. Maybe a decent night's sleep was worth listening to Reed Jordan pitch whatever it was he was selling. *He has nice eyes,* she thought, shocked to realize a simple offer of kindness could invoke a long-dormant emotional response.

"No connecting doors," she said.

"Separate floors if you want." Amusement flickered again in the gray-green eyes. He glanced back at the apartment. "Need anything out of there?"

She stared at the gaping windows. Most of their clothes were scattered across the bedroom floor where Detective Goree had emptied the pillowcase looking for drugs. Even the memory of Lexie's pathetic stuffed animals seemed tainted by this newest form of violence. The thought of returning, even for toothbrushes and a nightgown, made her shudder.

"MarLynn keeps a few of Lexie's things at the house. We can make do for one night."

"Then I'll meet you in the lobby," he said, checking the heavy gold watch on his left wrist. "In about half an hour?"

Nicki glanced at her own cheap watch. Shocked to find it was barely six, she nodded agreement, then turned her eyes toward the middle of the block.

Sharraye and Russell were perched on the front steps. MarLynn hovered above them, her arms dark against the skin of the child she held. Nicki left the men standing on the sidewalk in front of the Westacott mansion and began walking, breaking into a run in midstride, urged forward by an overwhelming need to touch her daughter's frightened face.

▬▬▬ 3 ▬▬▬

Reed forced himself to stop pacing and folded his body into one of the uncomfortably low lobby chairs where he could watch the Sheraton's porticoed entrance. He wasn't sure what he'd expected when, after weeks of unacknowledged correspondence, he'd decided to complete his business in person, but it hadn't been the fragile creature he'd found.

Relieved to learn his unwilling client had survived the raid uninjured, he'd steeled himself for a confrontation. He'd expected to find her as fiery face-to-face as she'd been on the phone, furiously protesting her innocence, not mutely standing by while Rodriguez and Goree trashed her home. Only his offer to pay for a hotel had broken her passive silence.

Despite the report, he really knew very little about the woman, even less about her background. Could he have guessed wrong about her drug usage?

No, he decided, her green-flecked hazel eyes had been clear, not glazed by chemicals.

He removed his tie, wishing he'd taken time to change. Nicole Prevot had gotten to him, he realized. Or rather, those eyes had. They dominated her face, forcing you to ignore the sharp, angular features and square jawline, the too-straight nose and childlike sprinkling of freckles. Like windows to her soul, those eyes had exposed bewilderment and vulnerability and . . . just for an instant . . . something else.

Fear?

Reed closed his own eyes, summoning the memory. Not fear. The emotion he'd glimpsed in that flash of a second had been terror. Terror so raw his instinct had been to protect, to wrap his arms about her and never let go. He felt himself color and ducked his head, though no one was watching.

Slow down before you overdose on testosterone, he told himself. *It's unprofessional, sitting here fantasizing about a beautiful client—especially one whose life's about to be turned upside down. A few billable hours and she'll be just a memory, a haunting one, perhaps, but a memory nonetheless.*

An older-model Buick pulled up in front of the doors, and Nicole Prevot got out, turning back to lift her daughter to the sidewalk. Reed pushed himself up from the depths of the chair but remained where he was, watching, slightly hidden by a potted palm. Nicki conferred a moment with Ellis Hill, then waved him on, straightened her shoulders, and took the little girl's hand.

Alexandra Prevot, Lexie, her mother had called her, stared solemnly about the atrium lobby with large, dark eyes. Nicki's child resembled her only slightly. Same long legs and slender build, but Lexie's tiny features were less irregular, the jawline softer, the snub nose upturned. Her hair, a shade darker than Nicki's, had a decidedly red cast. Reed would have expected a burn-and-peel complexion, but her skin was tanned.

The blond highlights in Nicki's thick cascade of hair presumably came from some paternal influence. His photo of Renee Prevot showed ebony tresses and pale, almost chalky coloring. Where had her grandchild gotten auburn hair? From her own father, Reed realized, wondering how a man could abandon a woman like Nicki and never acknowledge their child . . . unless he already had a family. Nicki didn't strike him as the type to become involved with a married man. Still, that might explain why she'd never pursued child support through the courts.

Lexie clung tightly to her mother's hand as Nicki paused to locate the front desk amid the tropical setting. Reed stepped forward, timing his arrival beside her with the desk clerk's awareness of their presence.

"Ms. Prevot would like her card key, room four-oh-two," he said. Turning to face a startled Nicki, he lowered his voice. "I'm in three-eleven. Is that far enough?"

She ignored the question, slipping the entry card into the pocket of her jeans and stepping back. Lexie followed her lead, retreating behind her mother's legs. Reed dropped to one knee and held out his hand.

"Hi. I'm Reed. You must be Lexie."

Eyes wide, she looked up at her mother. Nicki placed her arm reassuringly across Lexie's shoulders and nodded. Without a word, Lexie put her hand in his, a butterfly's touch against his palm, quickly withdrawn.

"Would you like to see your room?" Lexie nodded. He took Nicki's elbow and steered her toward the glass-walled elevator. "Have you eaten?"

"Lexie had something at MarLynn's. I thought I'd

get some crackers or something from a vending machine later."

"Uh-uh. I made a reservation for the dining room. Our business requires a full stomach." Nicki's complexion paled. "Relax, I promised you'd feel better after we talk, remember?"

He held the elevator doors open. Lexie walked in and circled the enclosure, one hand trailing along the gold-toned handrail. She grinned up at her mother, then pressed her nose against the glass as they began to ascend.

"How did you get to my apartment so quickly?" Nicki asked, still eyeing him with suspicion.

"I was at a pay phone three streets away. I could hear enough of your conversation with Odell to know you had a problem. I got there as quickly as I could talk my way through the police barricade, but I'm glad Mr. Hill came along. My Michigan bar credentials wouldn't have impressed Rodriguez for very long."

"Ellis is head of security at the bank. MarLynn, his wife, offered to watch Lexie after my day-care center raised their rates. Then when my apartment complex hit me with a rent increase, she and Ellis helped me find a cheaper place."

"Cheaper, but not very safe."

"Things were different when we first moved in. The family in the main house had been there for years."

"Mommy," Lexie whispered, tugging Nicki's pant leg.

Reed caught his breath at the look Nicki gave her daughter. What would it be like to have her look at him like that? he wondered, reminding himself to breathe.

"What, sweetie?" She followed Lexie's pointing

finger to the indoor pool at the far end of the atrium below.

"Do you know how to swim?" Reed asked.

Lexie nodded.

"We spent so much time in the pool at our old complex, I'm afraid people thought we were fish."

"Dolphins, Mommy," Lexie corrected shyly. " 'Cause they talk to each other, like we do."

"MarLynn discourages TV watching, but the kids love that Spielberg show with the dolphin and the submarine," Nicki explained. The elevator stopped moving.

He showed her how to use the plastic card key, then waited in the hall until Nicki had flipped on the lights and scanned the expensive two-room suite. To his surprise, she grabbed Lexie's hand and rejoined him, letting the door snap shut behind them. She fixed him with an acid stare.

"Mr. Jordan, I don't know what it is you want from me, but my . . ." She glanced at her daughter. "My *attention* can't be bought, no matter what impression you may have gotten during that episode at my apartment. Nothing you might want to say to me justifies a two-hundred-dollar-a-night hotel suite."

He took the card key from her and reinserted it in the lock.

"Look, Ms. Prevot . . . Nicki. I spent most of my day in the air, part of it in a cabin about the size of your front room. The air-conditioning in my rental car wilted as soon as the temperature hit a hundred and three. Then it took me two hours to track down someone I came twelve hundred miles to see only to find her caught in the crosshair of a firefight.

"The last thing I can remember eating was a dried-out croissant and an unidentifiable lump masquerading as cheese. And that was before the nice little blue-haired matron in the next seat volunteered a blow-by-blow description of her gall bladder surgery. I'm tired and hungry, and the last thing on my mind is seducing a client, especially a reluctant one, even if she is beautiful. Call me an idiot, but I thought a little luxury might be a welcome relief from the hell you just went through."

He stopped. Lexie was watching him with saucer-shaped eyes. Nicki looked chastised. Her altered expression melted his anger.

"Look, I'm sorry. People usually ignore me when I get this way. My mother always says I'd achieve the same results lying on the floor and kicking my heels. I've been tempted a few times, but my brother assures me it never worked when we were kids."

He pushed the door open and held out the card.

"Indulge me while we both unwind. Lexie should be able to find room for something from the dessert cart. I saw a terrific-looking brownie concoction when I made the reservation. I promise I'll explain all this after dinner. If you still don't feel comfortable then, I'll put you in a cab back to the Hills'. Fair enough?"

Nicki looked into the suite and bit her lip. Lexie stood on tiptoes and tugged her mother's hand.

"Please, Mommy? I really like brownies."

Reed suppressed a grin.

"Take a few minutes to get settled, then meet me in the restaurant. Past the front desk, on the left."

She was still standing by the open door when the solid elevator doors hissed shut.

Nicki paused in the restaurant doorway, vividly aware of the other patrons' business attire. Lexie's shorts might be excused, but she felt glaringly out of place in her own worn jeans and simple knit shirt.

"Relax, this is Texas, not Fifth Avenue," Reed Jordan murmured at her elbow, waving the maître d' away and leading her to a corner booth. Lexie, hugging a large stuffed gray rabbit, scooted across the bench to the booster seat already in place and propped her companion beside her.

"Thank you for Mr. Flops," she said solemnly, her shining eyes betraying her delight.

"I'm glad you like him. That's a terrific name."

" 'Cause they don't stand up," she explained, lifting the rabbit's pink-lined ears. She let them go, giggling when they flopped back to either side of his grinning, stitched-on face.

"Thank you for the toothbrushes, too," Nicki murmured. "But the T-shirts weren't necessary."

"I've never found sleeping in my clothes very restful. You don't have to wear them."

Nicki felt herself bristle, then relax as the lawyer's face reflected obvious embarrassment. Why did she insist on taking everything the wrong way? she wondered. Renee, whose excessive devotion to lacy lingerie and haute couture had often embarrassed Nicki, had called her a prude for insisting on nightclothes in even the hottest weather. She'd slept nude only once in her life, in freezing temperatures with snow on the ground . . . and Alan beside her. She turned away, struggling to hide an unexpected surge of emotion.

"I'm sorry I ignored your letters, Mr. Jordan."

"It's Reed. Please?"

"All right . . . Reed. I had no right to react the way I did on the phone this afternoon. I'm sure you're just trying to do your job, but all this is very confusing."

"Dinner first, explanations later."

The couple in the next booth got up to leave. Both wore T-shirts and jeans. Nicki felt a little better. She studied the menu, appalled at the prices of even the children's dinners.

"Relax, Nicki. You can buy next time."

"I hope you like thirty-nine-cent tacos."

"Do they have turkey sam'wiches?" Lexie interrupted, bringing their attention back to more important topics.

Her daughter's sudden appetite shocked Nicki, almost as much as the realization she herself was hungry. She rejected Reed's suggestion of a steak and ordered shrimp scampi. Lexie got her turkey sandwich, as well as a monstrous ice-cream-and-hot-fudge-topped brownie that she polished off completely as both adults watched in awe.

After dinner Reed produced a child's swimsuit he'd picked up in the hotel gift shop on his way to dinner. Nicki's protests weakened against Lexie's excited pleas. Some things were more important than pride, Nicki decided, watching her daughter and another little girl play in the pool's shallow end. Besides, she was too mellowed from the meal and the peaceful surroundings to put up much of an argument.

"When you smile at Lexie, your whole face changes," Reed told her, returning from his room with a briefcase and settling beside her at the poolside table. He'd changed into khaki-colored Dockers slacks and a knit Ralph Lauren shirt that reinforced the impression of quiet wealth Nicki had assumed when she realized his gold watch was definitely not a Timex.

"My biggest character flaw. Renee insisted ladies never exposed their feelings."

"Only a fool would accuse you of not being a lady." He smiled. "I'd say a southern lady, but your accent's wrong. How long have you lived in Texas?"

"All my life. But Ah declare, you Yankees are all alike. 'Spectin' us southern gals to drip honey ever' time we open our little old mouths," Nicki drawled, clamping her hand over her lips even as the words gushed forth.

What had gotten into her? she thought in dismay. Flirting with a man she barely knew like some nineteenth-century belle. She must be having some sort of delayed reaction to all that had happened. Reed Jordan's gray-green eyes reflected his amusement at her obvious embarrassment.

"Actually, Renee was a stickler for proper diction," she murmured, trying to regain her dignity. "I'm afraid it rubbed off. I find myself correcting Lexie the same way."

"I guess we all harbor a stereotype image or two. Would you believe some people think correspondence from a lawyer means they're in trouble?" His grin faded as he placed the briefcase on the table between them. "Ready?"

She nodded. He handed her a bank statement. Nicki glanced briefly at the figures, then shifted her gaze to the data at the top of the page. She drew in her breath sharply.

"This is in my name, my Social Security number."

Reed leaned back in the wrought-iron chair and grinned.

Nicki stared at the account's nearly five-thousand-dollar balance.

"The initial deposits at the first of the month

were from municipal bond interest. There'll be more due the first of July, as well as quarterly dividends on the stocks and mutual funds."

He handed her another statement, this one from a national brokerage firm.

"My God." The papers fluttered to the table. She tucked her hands beneath her arms to stop their trembling. "If this is your idea of some sort of twisted joke . . ."

"It's not."

"But how? Where did it come from? There must be thousands of dollars' worth of shares listed here."

"Three hundred fifty-six thousand, four hundred and eighty dollars and a few odd cents. As of Friday's bell, that is. I didn't have time to check the financial network before dinner."

"That's over a quarter of a million dollars!" Nicki glanced around her, reassuring herself that Lexie was still paddling about the pool. A ficus leaf dropped from an overhanging tree and skittered across the glass table. She picked it up. The leaf felt real. The table felt real. She wasn't dreaming.

"It must belong to another Nicole Prevot."

"With the same Social Security number?"

"Where did it come from?" she repeated.

"I haven't the slightest idea."

Nicki stared at him in disbelief. He shrugged and turned his hands palms up.

"You're serious."

"The statements, along with my instructions, came from a New York law firm about eight names long. I got a six-year-old address, information to verify your identification, and a sizable, prepaid fee. When I tried calling New York, I got the royal runaround."

Nicki closed her eyes, took a deep breath, then looked at Reed Jordan again.

"This is insane. People just don't give away a quarter of a million dollars. Why me? And why you? Why not some lawyer in Dallas or Austin or even San Antonio?"

"My firm's in Rockwall, a small town southeast of Grand Rapids. Since the mid-seventies, we've managed, or rather my late partner managed, a local property for an absentee owner, a New York holding company. We kept the roof repaired, made sure the pipes didn't freeze, saw that the grass got cut and the dock didn't wash away. When Dick died last fall, I took over the account.

"At the end of April, along with our monthly retainer, I got a letter from the trustee for the holding company, another multiname New York law firm, directing me to transfer title of the property to one Nicole Prevot, same six-year-old Texas address."

"You said they sent information to identify me."

"Copies of your high school diploma, registration receipts for the year and a half you spent at UT Austin, a sketchy physical description—which failed to do you justice, and this." He slid a black-and-white photo of a woman in a miniskirt across the table. A younger version of a familiar face smiled up at Nicki.

"Renee."

"Your mother?" She nodded. "The print's been retouched. It's obvious her image was superimposed on a new background. The original was taken outdoors. You can see leaves, there, where her arm's bent. And look closely at her left shoulder. Those are fingertips. Another person's been blocked out."

Ever think this lawyer might be from your daddy's people?

"Mom . . . mie?"

Lexie stood shivering beside the table, her teeth chattering.

Nicki, her thoughts swirling, wrapped her daughter in the towel Reed had carried down from his room.

"I've got to get her into bed."

Reed carried his briefcase and Mr. Flops. He took the card key when she offered it and opened the door. Nicki pushed past him into the suite, motioning him to follow.

"Give me a few minutes. Then we can talk."

Lexie was yawning. Nicki rubbed her hair dry and helped her into the oversize child's T-shirt Reed had had the gift shop send up. The hem hung below Lexie's knees. Nicki tucked Mr. Flops beside her and pulled the covers up.

"Which light do you want on?"

"That one," she said, pointing to the bathroom.

"Do you think you can go to sleep?"

"Uh-huh. I like it here. Can we stay forever?"

"Not forever, baby."

Large frightened brown eyes looked up at her.

"Do we have to go home?"

Lexie's face swam before her. Nicki knelt by the bed and hugged her daughter tightly.

"No, sweetie. We don't ever have to go back there."

"Good."

Nicki turned out the bedside lamp and crossed the room.

"Mommy?"

"Yes, Lexie?"

"Don't shut the door."

"I won't, baby. Go to sleep. I'll be right outside."

"She's really out this time," Nicki said for the third time.

Reed studied her pinched expression.

"Has she always had trouble sleeping?"

Hands clasped in her lap, the knuckles white, Nicki bowed her head. Her hair fell across her cheek, shading her features.

"Last Friday . . . Lexie woke up about three A.M. There's a security light on a pole at the back of the property. She heard something in the alley and climbed onto a chair to see what was happening. Her screams woke me.

"When I got to the window, Odell's buddies were shoving a man into the back of a Firebird. The man's white shirt was covered with blood. Odell was standing beneath the window, grinning, playing with a knife, turning and twisting the blade so it caught the light. For a minute I couldn't move."

She unlocked her fingers and pushed her hair from her face with a trembling hand.

" 'Chill out, mama,' he called up at me. 'Li'l Red's jest havin' nightmares. Nightmares ain't real, you dig. You tell her that an' she be jest fine.' Lexie was clinging to me, sobbing."

"Did you call the police?"

Her jaw tightened and her eyes turned cold.

"I slammed the window and shoved the dresser in front of the bedroom door. Then I spent the rest of the night trying to calm my child. Over the weekend and today, I've been looking for an apartment I could afford in a different neighborhood."

"And now the problem's solved," Reed said softly.

Her eyes betrayed her confusion.

"I don't want to wake up in the morning and find this is all a hoax. If it's real, help me understand. There must be a way to find out where the money came from."

Reed picked up the photograph.

"From her clothes, I'd guess the picture was taken in the late sixties, maybe early seventies. Have you ever before seen it, or one like it?"

"No. Renee didn't like having her picture taken. She hated clutter. No mementos, no personal papers. Bank statements got tossed as soon as she got them, bills and receipts the same way. Even my grade school drawings and report cards disappeared after a few days."

"What do you know about your father?"

She looked away, her lips pressed into a thin line.

"Renee never talked about him. The first time I remember asking I must have been about eight. She said he'd died in Vietnam. She got so flustered, I dropped the subject until seventh grade when we were studying the war. Then I asked her what battle my father had died in. She looked at me like I'd lost my mind and said he'd never been to Vietnam, he'd fled to Canada to escape the draft and died in an accident."

"Did she ever tell you his name or say how she met him?"

"No. Renee never talked about the past . . . to anyone."

"Why do you call her Renee instead of Mother?"

She flushed and lowered her voice.

"Renee traveled a lot while I was growing up. Wanderlust, boredom, itchy feet . . . I don't know what it was. I'd come home from school, and the latest housekeeper would tell me she was off again.

"One summer, she took me with her. I must have been about nine, and I think we were between housekeepers. We spent a month at Corpus Christi. I never understood why she decided to go to the beach. She hated being in the sun, said it made her complexion splotchy. If she wanted to swim, she went down to the condo's pool in the evening."

She looked away again, her voice drifting off. Reed cleared his throat. Nicki shook her head as if erasing a memory.

"Renee told me not to call her Mommy anymore, that it sounded babyish. Then I heard her telling someone I was her little sister. I felt so confused, I didn't question the lie. The beach wasn't very crowded for some reason, but there was a bunch of guys living in the beach house next door. When I got a little older, I understood."

"Did Renee have a job?"

"No," she said absently, coloring when his meaning sank in. "She liked men and I'll admit she had relationships with more than one or two, but she didn't take money from them."

"The lifestyle you describe suggests otherwise. Someone must have paid the bills."

"When I was sixteen, I got my first part-time job. Renee laughed and told me there was no reason for me to work. If I needed a bigger allowance, all I had to do was ask. I told her I didn't like the idea of her boyfriends paying for my clothes and things. She was really offended that I'd suggested such a thing. I got a big lecture about the difference between sexual freedom and selling yourself."

"Not the usual family values discussion mothers have with their teenage daughters," Reed said dryly.

"No one ever accused Renee of being a perfect

mother. I demanded an explanation for where our money came from. She hemmed and hawed and then said my father had left some kind of monthly annuity. There was supposed to be a final lump sum payment due on my twenty-first birthday."

"The day she died," Reed murmured, remembering the brief notation at the bottom of the report.

"She was driving back from her regular shopping trip to Dallas. Usually she flew both ways, but she'd . . . *we'd* bought a sports car, and she was drinking champagne. Celebrating her independence from motherhood, I suppose. She lost control, overshot an exit ramp, and plowed into a gasoline truck that was servicing a station's underground tanks."

"I'm sorry," Reed said softly. Nicki turned back to him, her eyes clearly angry, not grieved.

"For the first week, I was numb. Then the charge statements started pouring in. Thousands of dollars, much of it for things incinerated in the crash. The regular bank deposits had stopped. I couldn't find any information in Renee's things about them *or* the big payment she'd mentioned. I'd signed the account applications . . . and the one for the car. She'd told me it was the new lease on the condo. I couldn't sleep. I cried constantly. Nothing I ate stayed down, so I called the doctor."

"Morning sickness," Reed murmured, mentally connecting dates from the report.

"Renee hadn't bothered to tell our insurance agent about the car. My test results and the bill from the auto dealership came the same day. I quit school, moved into an efficiency, and sold Renee's jewelry and most of our furniture. The bank offered me extra hours, then full time after Lexie was born. We were scraping by until she had a bout with pneumonia three years ago."

"What about Lexie's father?" He would have snatched the question back if it would have erased her anguished expression.

"Alan was killed three weeks before Renee, in a skiing accident . . . the morning after we decided to get married."

Reed was silent. Lexie cried out in her sleep and Nicki went to check on her. He looked at his watch. Almost midnight. Nicki returned, pulling the bedroom door partially closed.

"Do you have any idea what you're going to do?"

"Right now my head's swimming. For the last three days, all I've thought about is moving Lexie somewhere she won't be afraid to look out her bedroom window."

"Michigan's beautiful in summer. Green grass, clear water, open spaces for a child to run and play. Friendly neighbors."

"The Rockwall Chamber of Commerce must love you."

"Actually, your place is on Trumpeter Lake. If you spent the summer there, we could do some digging into the property's history. From the conflicting stories your mother gave you, I'm betting the house is connected to your father in some way."

He watched a wistful yearning grow where apprehension already battled indecision in the revealing hazel eyes.

"Everything's happening too fast. I can't think anymore."

The ringing of the phone prevented further discussion. Nicki ran to pick it up before Lexie woke. Her fingers whitened around the receiver. The blood drained from her face and she started to crumple.

He jumped up, but she waved him away, leaning

against the wall for support instead. She replaced the receiver slowly.

"That was Detective Rodriguez. Odell made bail two hours ago, but he's been rearrested."

"On what charge?"

"Arson. He set the carriage house on fire. Everything Lexie and I had was in that apartment. And now it's gone."

▗▖▗▖▗▖▗▖▗▖ 4 ▗▖▗▖▗▖▗▖▗▖

"**F**unny how them folks we been dickerin' with since last year got in such an all-fired hurry to sell," MarLynn said as Ellis parked the Buick. "Last time we made an offer, they swore they'd never come down that last few thousand."

Nicki murmured something about people deciding to get on with their lives and busied herself retying the bow in Lexie's hair. The bright blue ribbon matched the beads in Sharraye's black braids. The two little girls climbed out of the car and stood side by side, their fingers locked together.

"Humph. This old body might be slowin' down some, but there ain't nothin' wrong with my head, child. Or my eyes. You ain't looked at me straight all week."

"Let it be, woman," Ellis said over the raised trunk. "Russell, take this carry-on. I got the big one."

"Just don't feel right, that's all. Like takin' charity."

Nicki took the older woman's hands in hers and stared into her face. Ellis herded the children toward the airport terminal.

"I'm looking at you straight, MarLynn, and I'm

telling you there's a difference between charity and a gift from a friend."

"Mighty big gift," the older woman sniffed.

"I'd do more if I thought you'd let me. Please don't let that stubborn pride of yours ruin my pleasure. Russell and Sharraye deserve a safe childhood as much as Lexie. You and Ellis work hard to protect them from the life that killed their mother. This is just another part of that."

"RayeAnn loved them babies. Thing was, she loved that damned crack more. Don't worry, child. I ain't fool enough to turn down nothin' might help keep them babies on the right path. But I gotta ask one thing."

Nicki raised her eyebrows in a question.

"You 'member me and Ellis now and again and let us know how things is goin'?"

"I won't forget you." Tears pricked her eyes as she embraced her friend. "I promised myself I wasn't going to cry."

"That place up north's gotta be some part o' your people, child. If it is and it feels like home, you plant your roots deep." She shook a finger in Nicki's face. "But if it ain't all you're hopin' for, you skedaddle on back to us, you hear?"

"Look, Mommy. What's that?"

Nicki sighed and stuffed the in-flight magazine back in the seat pocket.

"We're climbing through the clouds, sweetie."

The skies had been clear on the commuter flight into Dallas. Reed Jordan had been right . . . the first plane's cabin had held fewer than twenty passengers. After a few nervous minutes, Lexie's questions had centered on the patchwork fields and miniature figures far below them. The current plane was larger, demanding explanations of lights, air vents, and call buttons.

Lexie tugged at the seat belt that encircled both her and Mr. Flops, squirming to peer at the businessmen in the row behind them. Nicki unlatched the tray table and pulled a pad of paper and a box of colored pencils from the carry-on beneath her daughter's seat.

"Draw me a picture."

"Of what?"

"Of the house Reed told us about."

Lexie chewed on her lower lip, then bent over the paper. Nicki leaned back and began making a mental list of the things they would have to buy in Grand Rapids before driving to the lake on Saturday. The first item would be a car. Someone was dropping Reed at the airport to meet them, but Nicki had no intention of relying on rental vehicles for transportation.

She'd shopped only for bare necessities in the eleven days since the fire, seeing no reason to replace household goods until she got to Michigan. Moving into a house she already owned made sense, she reminded herself once again, fighting off a nagging uneasiness. She should be relaxed and happy, but everything seemed to be moving too fast.

She'd verified Reed Jordan's credentials and signed signature cards for her accounts the morning after the apartment had been destroyed. The investment firm had accepted, without question, her faxed instructions to convert a block of her holdings to cash. After Reed talked to a senior vice-president at the Michigan bank where her funds were on deposit, a credit application had been rushed through, and a card in Nicki's name had arrived by express mail two days later.

Renee's debts and Lexie's hospital bill had been paid, and she still had an unbelievable amount of money left from the liquidated stocks. And enough income from the rest that she could postpone finding another job or making a decision about returning to school until fall. She tilted her seat back and closed her eyes.

"Orange juice, please."

Nicki struggled awake to find the flight attendant leaning across to place a tray on Lexie's table.

"Lexie and I've been having a lovely conversation. I'm sorry I disturbed you."

"You didn't. I needed to come back to earth anyway."

Lexie giggled.

"That's silly, Mommy. We're still up in the air."

"She's precious," the stewardess murmured, leaving a snack tray and a second juice for Nicki and moving to the next row.

"Wanna see?" Lexie held up her drawing.

Nicki opened Lexie's crackers and cheese and nibbled a grape from her own tray.

"This is the house. And the big trees. And you know what the blue is?"

"The lake?"

"Uh-huh. She said it was sky," Lexie whispered, pointing at the attendant hurrying by with another stack of trays.

"It's very good."

Lexie's conception of their new house and the lake filled the left side of the paper, a half dozen trees the right. Nicki frowned. Lexie's proportions were better than her usual efforts, but something in the picture seemed out of sync. A ridiculous feeling to have about a place she'd never seen, she decided.

"These are squirrels," Lexie announced, pointing to several brown splotches in the trees and on the ground. "Mich'gan's got lots of animals. Russell looked it up in the 'cyclopedia. I want our trees to have squirrels."

"Squirrels love acorns."

"Are our trees acorn trees?"

"I don't know. The trees that make acorns are called oaks."

Nicki's frown deepened. Reed had mentioned the shade trees in the property's side yard, but hadn't been specific. They could as easily be pine or maple, yet some inner sense insisted they wouldn't be.

"Will they find us in Mich'gan, Mommy?"

Nicki didn't need to ask who "they" were.

"No, honey, we'll be safe in Michigan. No one's going to be after us there."

"That's good, 'cause squirrels don't like scary people."

Reed helped Lexie fasten her seat belt, then climbed in the passenger's side of the Blazer. The salesman smiled and waved.

"I figured a sports car, maybe a small sedan," Reed told Nicki as she checked the mirrors.

"I liked the four-wheel drive."

"Sounds like you're thinking ahead to winter," he said, trying not to sound eager.

She ignored his implied question and started the engine.

"Which way?"

"Left about five miles to south M37. Sure you don't want to hit another mall on the way out of town? I think there's still room for another sack or two," he said, glancing over his shoulder and winking at Lexie. Nicki's purchases filled most of the space behind the second seat.

"You told me things were twenty-five or thirty years old. Linens disintegrate if they aren't stored properly, vacuum cleaners fall apart, toasters rust, replacement parts become scarce. We still need cleaning supplies, a mop and broom . . ."

"Whoa." He held up his hands. "I was only teasing."

Nicki grinned.

"I guess I did get a little carried away."

"You're entitled."

"When are we gonna eat?" Lexie whined.

"Dinner's going to be late. We still have to buy groceries. You'll have to make do with those crackers in my purse."

Reed glanced at Lexie and lowered his voice. "Have you given any thought to my suggestion?"

"About a housekeeper?" He nodded. Nicki shook her head. "I can't believe we really need one."

"A huge downstairs living area, four bedrooms, a sleeping porch, and two baths on the second floor. You can't handle all that alone. I had the utilities turned on and a superficial cleaning done, but the place needs more than that. No one's summered there for a decade or more. The porches are due for repainting this year, the kitchen's out-of-date . . ."

"Next you're going to tell me there's an outhouse and we have to haul our water from the lake."

"Nothing like that. It's really a great place. Just a little behind the times. Besides, if you want to learn about the previous owners, you'll need to be neighborly, especially with some of the longtime residents. That means entertaining."

Despite the glare of the late-afternoon sun he could see the stricken expression on her face.

"Nothing fancy," he added hurriedly. "Everything's pretty relaxed, but a housekeeper could make things a lot easier."

"We'll see. How far is it to the house?"

"Rockwall's about eighteen miles. We can pick your food up there. Then it's only fourteen more miles to the lake."

"There aren't any grocery stores closer than that?"

"The convenience store at the crossroads has been there in one form or another since the thirties, but most people drive to Rockwall for the big items."

"Mommy," Lexie's voice interrupted. "What's an outhouse?"

Nicki managed to explain through her laughter without losing control of the Blazer. Reed settled back, content to provide directions and watch the shadows lengthen. Darkness fell quickly around the lake, the sun disappearing behind the dusky tree line like a sugar cookie dipped in cocoa. Nicki worried aloud that it might be dark by the time they reached the lake. He reassured her that enough daylight would remain to see the house.

Lexie began singing a *Sesame Street* song Reed remembered from his own childhood. Nicki hummed along, her voice a pleasant addition to the singsong rhyme. He gazed out the window to hide a contented smile.

As the road curved around the tree-lined lake, Nicki caught glimpses of well-kept homes and cottages and beyond them the blue water of the lake itself. Eagerness and excitement swept aside her initial uneasiness. *This is our home now,* she thought, a bit awed by the tranquil setting. A sense of peace settled about her. She and Lexie could feel safe again here.

Following Reed's directions, she slowed for the last turn. The road angled downward a short distance, toward the lake.

"The hillside on the left is part of your property. The Tarleton family owns the undeveloped section to our right," Reed told her. "And here's your house."

"Squirrels, Mommy! We've got squirrels!"

Nicki pulled into the hard-packed-gravel driveway beside Reed's blue Cutlass. Lexie thrust Mr. Flops at her mother and bounded around the corner of the house in pursuit of the scampering animals. Reed followed her, the house keys in his hand. Nicki trailed behind them, clutching the stuffed rabbit.

Even in deepening twilight the lake was beautiful. The last rays of sun shimmered on the water. A passing powerboat sent a row of whitecaps to join the gentle waves already lapping the shore. In the distance, brightly colored triangular shapes skimmed the surface on the opposite side of the lake. *Sailboats,* Nicki thought, feeling an inexplicable satisfaction.

A breeze rustled through the trees. Above her the squirrels chattered back and forth. Birds called to one another. Her foot sent a small object skittering across the flagstone path. Nicki bent to pick it up. An acorn. From one of the oaks in the yard.

The yard and the trees were to the left of the house, not the right as Lexie had drawn them.

Nicki's grip tightened on the flop-eared bunny, her fingers meeting through his pillowy tummy. *I knew,* she thought, shivering. *They were wrong, and I knew.*

5

The film finished rewinding, trailing off to a flap, flap, flap as the loose end tapped the reel. With a groan he raised a hand from his lap to wipe his brow. He switched off the projector's motor and sat in semidarkness. The machine's lamp cast a circle on the pulldown screen at the far end of the narrow room. Dust motes jitterbugged in the stream of light.

The older stuff always brought back those precious early years of discovery, he thought. He pushed himself up from the leather sofa, switched on the lights, and replaced the film in its metal cylinder. The wall clock chimed softly. Ten thirty. He'd forgotten to eat.

Setting the alarm system, he slipped from the room and slid the sound-insulated panel into place. The rosewood swirls meshed seamlessly. He smiled, delighted as always by the room's invisibility. The maid had left a plate of sushi in the refrigerator. He poured a glass of Chablis, exchanged his stained trousers for a short kimono, and walked from the darkened house to the lake.

A night bird flew squawking from the shore toward another dock as he dropped the robe and entered the water. Goose bumps rose along his skin, cleansing the lingering traces of the past, shocking his thoughts back to the present. The lake lay calm in the moonlight before him, unblemished by ripples from passing craft. This was his favorite time, his moment to savor the present, plan his tomorrow . . . and choose the next film.

Sasaki wanted a copy of the lotus-eaters tape. They might just cut a deal . . . if the wizened old Jap had something special to trade. Something really pristine, without the current emphasis on slash and gore.

He stroked expertly toward deep water and flipped on his back, floating silently, allowing the current to caress his body and wash him gently back toward shore. The old film had been all he remembered. An image from his thirteenth summer surfaced, deepening the smile on his lips—Midge, scampering in the shallows, Kathy and Cordelia rushing to cover her nakedness with a beach towel.

Somewhere to his left, a fish broke the surface with a splash. Laughter from a car traveling the upper road drifted across the water. He scowled and rolled over. Teenagers, returning from an outing, probably high on booze or drugs, too stupid to understand the true essence of the forbidden.

Ought to invite them to the movies. His smile returned.

The air felt chilly on his shoulders. A breeze had risen. He scanned the shoreline. Most houses were already dark. Residents on this side of the lake kept sensible hours. No youthful renters this summer to host wild, late-night parties. No toddling progeny to protest reasonable bedtimes. A pity in a way, but much, much safer.

A child's cry broke the silence, sending him thrashing about in the water, seeking the source. A light appeared in a second-floor window of the last house to his left . . . the house beside the Tarleton land. The old, silent house that had stood empty in recent years, the grounds maintained, but the windows curtained and shuttered, the unchanged interior rejected by a self-indulgent generation demanding the latest electronic marvels and *House Beautiful* settings.

A woman's silhouette crossed the lighted square. The window darkened again, leaving a dull glow to reassure him he hadn't been imagining someone's presence. A hall light, he wondered? To banish a child's disturbing dreams?

He swam into the shadows of his own dock. Another noise broke the silence—a chair scraping across the floor of the second-floor porch. Clouds were moving in. One of the brief nightly squalls was on its way. The haze drifted across the moon, deepening the blackness of the night. He rose quietly from the water and crossed the neighboring yards. Despite the chill air raking his naked body, he felt engulfed by warmth.

A family in *that* house. The cry had been decidedly feminine. A little girl moving about those rooms again, scampering across the grass, giggling, exploring . . . sleeping each night only houses away. Did she wear a frilly nightie or just her panties when she slept?

Suddenly the summer looked much more promising. He turned to slip away. A new sound stopped his movement. A woman humming an almost forgotten tune. He was suddenly bathed in cold sweat, his earlier warmth fleeing with each successive note.

It couldn't be.

Think, dammit. Nothing really ever changed.

Kids watched the same drivel year after year. Parents had the same moronic songs drilled into their brains. A coincidence, that's all it was.

Still . . . that lilting tone, the way the voice rose on the final note at the end of each line? Rubbish! The whole idea was preposterous. More than that. Impossible.

The humming ceased, and silence returned, broken only by the rising wind. He waited a moment, shivering now, his chattering teeth thunderous in his own ears. The concert didn't resume. The moon broke from the clouds, forcing him to dodge from shadow to shadow. He retrieved the kimono and wrapped himself in its silken depths, but shudders continued to rack his body.

Inside the house he poured a second glass of wine, tossing it down hurriedly, willing the fire to return the warmth to his flesh. Reason reasserted itself. The past was buried. Out of millions of voices, hundreds, probably thousands sounded alike.

He poured a third glass of the Chablis and nibbled the sushi. Quite excellent, really. Almost as good as at that little sake bar in Singapore. He crossed to the stereo system and flipped on something inane, pipes and flutes with seashore sounds in the background. Anything to erase the memory of the ludicrous TV prattle the woman had been humming.

A child. A little girl. But how old? More than a toddler, the cry had been too strong for a baby.

The squall hit with a sudden crack of lightning. Standing in the dark, staring out the expanse of floor-to-ceiling windows, he watched the wind roil the lake and batter leaves from the willow beside the dock. Rain slashed against the glass, added ac-

companiment to the babel from the stereo. He
sipped the wine and finished the sushi, wiping his
fingers on the linen napkin the maid had folded
into the delicate shape of a bird.

Had the storm frightened the child in the end
house? he wondered. He massaged the tightening
tendons in his neck.

This could be a special summer . . . if he were
careful. If he were very, very careful.

6

Reluctantly Nicki abandoned her dream. She stretched, wrapping her fingers contentedly around the rungs of the headboard on the narrow metal bed. Wakefulness clouded the fantasy's details. She fought to hold on to them.

Renee had been making pancakes. Little ones, like giant golden coins circling her child-size plate, and bigger ones stacked three high on two larger plates. Renee, whose idea of cooking had usually involved foil-covered rectangles or plastic-topped circles. The thought of her mother even rising for breakfast was hysterical. Nicki had been in charge of meals for as far back as she could remember.

Something had awakened her, she realized. A sound. She opened her eyes.

Confused for an instant by the near-total darkness, she pushed herself to a sitting position. Nearby, birds were holding a noisy convention. She could hear waves slapping against the seawall and, farther out, a speedboat smacking the surface of the lake . . . the sound that had disturbed her sleep? She shook her head and let her eyes adjust. Light etched thin lines around each section of the screened-in sleeping porch.

The blinds. She'd lowered them when the storm

hit. The heavy canvas had been a green cocoon, keeping them safe and dry while thunder and lightning crashed. So complete had been the protective illusion that Lexie had finally drifted to sleep without a single, frightened whimper.

Nicki slipped quietly from beneath the covers and past the two empty beds on her right to the section of heavy shade facing the undeveloped acreage next door. Hand over hand, she tugged the thick cord. The blind rolled upward, letting in the light of a cool, clear morning and the rain-washed scent of dripping foliage and damp earth.

Nature reigned free over the Tarleton property. Fallen limbs, tangled vines, and overgrown bushes shared space with a variety of trees. The virgin woods would enchant an inquisitive five-year-old. She was relieved to see a high, ivy-covered chain-link fence prevented the vegetation from encroaching on the grassy strip she assumed marked her own property line.

She crisscrossed the shade's cord back and forth between the prongs of the wall cleat. A frayed section of the line chafed her palm. She ran her fingers over the torn threads. The break looked old. How long had it been like that? she wondered. Had others who'd slept on this porch noticed the break?

Had one of them been her father?

If her father had once slept in one of these four sturdy metal beds, did her current ownership imply that he hadn't died in Vietnam or on some lonely Canadian highway? Did it mean he'd been alive all this time? That Renee's lies had only recently become truth? If so, why all this now? Why not years ago . . . ?

She closed her eyes, willing deep-buried anger to force a stinging moisture away. Renee *had* cared for her in some bewildering way, despite her slap-dash attempts at single parenthood. But she hadn't really loved her—not the way a mother should. Not the way Nicki loved Lexie.

All those years when knowing she had a father would have meant so much. Why had Renee refused to acknowledge his existence or provide even the barest details? If this place was his heritage to her, why hadn't he come forward when she needed him? She'd been running a race with poverty too long not to value the comfort of material wealth. But it wasn't the money she'd coveted. Contact with another human being, someone else who was a part of her, would have been just as precious.

Sometimes she felt as if she always lost the people she'd cared for when she needed them most. First Alan, slipping out at daylight to dare an advanced ski run when everyone insisted he wasn't ready. Their intimate time together had been so brief. Would he have been as reckless with their future if he'd known those few hours had created another life?

Yes, Nicki thought, nothing would have changed. Alan's passion for stretching limitations, the exact opposite of her own cautious approach to life, had been what attracted her in the first place. To him, seizing the moment was everything.

She'd still been adjusting to her pain and loss weeks later when Renee drove herself to a fiery death. And since then? Did the money and this house mean she'd recently lost someone else? Someone she never knew existed? The possibility taunted her, demanding an answer like one of Lexie's persistent questions.

Lexie. The one constant in her life.

A muffled sound, the same one that had awakened her, broke her reverie and made her whip around.

Light from the now-uncovered section of the sleeping porch revealed her daughter's empty bed, the covers wadded in a lumpy knot. The chair Nicki had dragged onto the porch the night before still blocked one of the twin doorways, the one between Lexie's and her own rumpled bed. Panic forced a cry from her throat.

The muffled sound was repeated, drawing her gaze to a Lexie-size bulge in one of the blinds that faced the lake. The bulge giggled again. Nicki grabbed another cord and reeled the shade open noisily, haphazardly locking the line to the cleat.

"Shh," Lexie whispered, putting a finger to her lips. On the lawn below, a young rabbit froze in mid-hop, nose testing the air, then loped into the woods through a dip under the fence.

"You scared him," Lexie wailed, looking at Nicki accusingly.

"You scared *me,* young lady."

"We were just watching the bunny."

She held up Mr. Flops. The rabbit's face grinned up at Nicki, its expression a comic contrast to her daughter's pout. Nicki sighed and sank down next to them.

"What else have you seen?"

"Nothin'," Lexie said, her lower lip protruding.

"Not even that guy sleeping on our dock steps?"

"A turtle!"

"And that's a blue jay scolding our squirrels from the top of that little pine tree."

Lexie began discovering other delights.

"What makes the funny circles?"

"A fish is catching his breakfast."

"Fish go fishing?"

"No, silly. They just kiss the water and catch a juicy bug. Like this."

Nicki adopted an exaggerated pucker and moved her lips. Lexie mimicked her. Mother and daughter leaned closer to each other until both collapsed in a giggling heap.

"I think the fish have the right idea. I'm hungry."

"Do we have bugs?" Lexie asked, still giggling.

"No, but we have everything we need to make French toast."

"Maple syrup?"

"*And* strawberry syrup."

"Yea!"

"Can we eat on the glass table?"

"Sure," Nicki said, slicing a baguette into thick rounds. "We should protect the glass, though. See if there's a tablecloth in one of those drawers, the ones next to where we found the silverware last night."

Patiently, she explained about melon ballers, egg slicers, spiral canapé tools, and other mysterious discoveries while Lexie rummaged through drawers. Nicki stuck her head in the freezer section of the ancient refrigerator. Either the appliance had been overwhelmed by a full load of groceries or the margarine she'd bought was much softer than her regular brand. No, the oozing carton of ice cream had been brick hard last night. The refrigerator would have to be replaced, and soon.

"Can we use these big napkins?"

Nicki shut the freezer door firmly and turned to look at the quilted rectangles of faded-blue cloth Lexie was holding.

"Those are place mats, not napkins."

"Can we use them? Please, please," Lexie asked, hopping from one foot to the other.

"What makes them so special?"

"Baby ducks."

"Let's see."

Lexie turned the place mats around to reveal a mottled brown duck with orange-and-brown bill marching across a slash of sand. Seven fluffy ducklings trailed behind her. Watching from a stand of cattails was father duck, his green head and white neck ring identifying his family as mallards.

"Mommy? Your face is all funny."

Nicki shook her head.

"The place mats are fine, Lexie. Go on and set the table."

Lexie walked slowly from the kitchen, glancing over her shoulder when she reached the door. Nicki forced a reassuring smile and turned back to her cooking. She wasn't about to explain she'd already seen the place mats . . . beneath a plate of coin-size pancakes in her early morning dream.

She busied herself soaking bread and heating the electric skillet she'd found on the pantry shelf the night before. Reed had shown her how to light the pilot beneath the cracked grids on the old gas stove, but she was used to electric burners. The unfamiliar equipment made her feel awkward and, strangely, a bit afraid. She'd replace the other kitchen appliances along with the struggling refrigerator, she decided.

Lexie came back for silverware, making additional trips for plates and juice and the bottles of syrup. Nicki screwed her mouth into the fish shape and winked, producing a new round of giggles. Her startled reaction to the place mats had been forgotten.

A sliver of finish chipped as she placed the mixing bowl in the porcelain sink. Why stop with appliances, she thought with abandon. Modernization certainly wouldn't hurt the house's resale value. The expense wouldn't be a problem. She shook her head in amazement. Only weeks ago choosing between riding the bus to work or walking three miles in the Texas heat to save an extra dollar for groceries had been a major decision. But she was rich now. Well, at least very well-off.

And maybe a little crazy? How else could she explain the strange sense of false reality that had surrounded her ever since she'd pulled into the drive last night?

She'd watched TV shows about people moving into old houses and suddenly experiencing premonitions or developing precognitive powers. So-called psychic experts claimed ghosts or melancholy spirits of those who'd died in the houses were reaching out, trying to send messages to loved ones left behind or identify the perpetrators of their violent deaths.

Nicki drew in her breath. The last slice of egg-soaked bread landed awkwardly against the rim of the skillet. Splattered coating sizzled, unnoticed, down the outside edge.

Had someone been murdered in this house?

"Raspberries," she muttered, invoking a childhood swearword of frustration. There were simple explanations for everything.

Reed had described the side yard more clearly than she'd remembered, that was all. She'd had other things on her mind. Forgetting insignificant details was understandable. And she must have opened the drawer with the place mats when she was looking for a spatula the night before. Wishful thinking had added the homey touch to the idyllic fantasy she'd conjured up in her sleep.

She scraped the splattered coating from the outer edge of the skillet and began stacking the crusty rounds on a plate.

"Almost ready," she called, lowering her voice when she realized Lexie was hovering in the doorway, a smirk on her face. "Did you get last night's milk glasses out of the drainer?"

"Uh-huh."

"What about ones for juice?"

Lexie shook her head. Nicki flipped the remaining toast.

"Try the cabinets next to the sink."

Lexie shoved the step stool against the counter.

"Big glasses?"

"No, the little ones with oranges around the rim."

The spatula with the last slice of toast froze halfway to the plate. More dream trivia? She'd checked several cupboards last night, but couldn't remember seeing the glasses she'd just described.

Lexie had crawled across the counter to a corner cabinet.

"Here they are."

So much for the powers of recall, Nicki thought, glancing at the already familiar design of tiny oranges and green leaves. She picked up the milk carton and the plate of toast.

"My tummy's growling, sweetie. Lead me to the syrup."

Lexie, carrying the juice glasses, skipped up the hallway to the open entry, past the staircase and the front door and onto the L-shaped downstairs porch. She stopped beside the white wrought-iron

table that occupied the short leg of the L and
turned, a grin lighting her face.

Nicki paused, one foot still on the braided-sisal
rug in the entryway. Lexie had positioned the place
mats opposite one another on the long sides of the
table. Mr. Flops had been accorded a place of
honor on the chair at the near end. Between the
two place settings was a set of wooden decoys,
painted the colors of the mallard and his mate.

"Perfect," she managed to say. Surely this would
have been a part of her dream, if her sleep had been
uninterrupted.

"They were on the shelf beneath the funny window."

"That's a pass-through from the kitchen to the
living room/dining room. So we don't have to carry
things around."

"Oh." Lexie forked two pieces of toast onto her
plate. "Can I have strawberry?"

"*May* I have strawberry," Nicki said automatically. "You've already used maple."

"Just on one piece."

Nicki shook her head and passed the second bot-
tle. The change of scene had certainly improved
both their appetites. She'd made more French toast
than she and Lexie would ever eat. Maybe she
should have invited Reed to breakfast. After carrying in the results of yesterday's shopping spree, he'd
declined to join them for supper, saying he needed
to get home. She wondered suddenly if he'd had a
late date.

"Why's your face red?"

She looked into the big brown eyes that missed
so little.

"I'm just a little warm, sweetie."

"I opened the windows. By myself. Wanna see?" She hopped down and ran to one of the vertical glass panels. "You just turn this handle, but it's kinda hard."

"We'll buy a spray that makes them turn easier."

Despite the abundance of food, they finished every bite. Nicki was putting the last of the dishes into the sink when Lexie raced in, demanded that her mother follow her, and dashed out again. Envisioning a spill, Nicki snatched up a dishrag, but the only thing on the table were the place mats and the sweat rings from the juice pitcher and the syrup bottles.

Lexie, on her knees on a chair by the front windows, whipped around at the sound of footsteps and put a finger to her lips.

"Hurry," she whispered.

Nicki knelt beside her. A mother duck was swimming slowly toward the end of the dock, followed by a string of downy pearls.

"See? Like our big napkins."

"Did you see the daddy duck?" Nicki asked softly.

"Uh-uh. I think he's at work."

"Harvesting bugs, no doubt. How many babies are there?"

"One, two, three, four, five, six, seven. Seven babies."

"No, eight. See? There's a straggler."

Momma duck swerved back along her strung-out children. Lexie slapped her hands over her mouth as the indignant parent quacked her errant offspring back into line and led her family out of sight beyond the dock.

"He's a bad baby," she said solemnly.

"She's trying to protect him. Mommies worry

when their children don't mind. Eight babies are a lot to keep track of."

"That's why you've only got one, right?"

Nicki wrapped her in a bear hug.

"I'd have three or four, funny face, if they could all be just like you."

"Even when I'm bad?"

"Especially when you're bad."

"I gotta go pee," Lexie said, grabbing herself and racing for the half bath in the downstairs hall.

"Slow down. And tie your tennies, so you don't trip."

Nicki nodded and finished clearing the table. She removed the mats and wiped the glass, pausing to stare at the sun-faded plastic flowers in the wrought-iron holder that hung between the table legs. The dull bouquet looked wrong. There should be a clay pot with growing flowers, she thought. Something bright and cheerful.

Red 'raniums.

She frowned. Where on earth had that come from? She hadn't used that childhood shorthand since . . . since she couldn't remember when. Renee had never had a green thumb. Digging in the dirt wasn't one of Nicki's favorite pastimes either. She shivered, thinking she'd rather tackle a dusty house or a grimy oven than disturb the creatures that lurked in a plot of soil.

"It broke."

Lexie stood in the doorway, holding up a two-inch section of shoelace. Nicki gave the table a last wipe.

"Run upstairs and get those red sandals we bought yesterday. They're in the bedroom where you started out last night."

"The one with the can'py?"

"They're on the floor in the closet. When you get back, we'll go exploring."

The next sound Nicki heard was the hollow echo of her child's feet pounding up the stairs.

7

"Don't jump on that," Nicki warned, grabbing Lexie's hand and steering her around a wooden square sunk in the lawn.

"Why not?"

"Because it's protecting a sprinkler head. If it fell in, you could hurt yourself. Or break the spigot."

She knelt and stuck her finger in a hole in the eight-inch block. A curious sense of mischief accompanied the gesture.

"I'll show you what it looks like, but it's not something to play with."

"What's it do?"

"It waters the grass."

"Like MarLynn, with the hose."

"This doesn't use a hose, just underground pipes connecting each sprinkler to the water. There's a control box"—she turned toward the house, her eyes involuntarily settling on a black box partially hidden by shrubbery—"by the garage door."

"How'd you know that?"

"Mommies know lots of things little girls don't," Nicki told her, covering a frown as she replaced the cover. How indeed?

"Don't need to water after a rain," a man's voice called from the flagstone walk.

Nicki stood up and turned around. Lexie rose too, sliding automatically behind her mother, attaching herself to the waist of Nicki's shorts by one hand.

A scowling man with leathery skin and a weathered face studied them through watery blue eyes. He wore tennis shoes, khaki shorts, and a tank shirt that revealed muscular arms and a vigorous patch of gray chest hair. A darker growth formed a thin line above his upper lip. The logo on his battered fishing hat matched the s & s SERVICES stenciled on the door of a Ford pickup parked at the edge of the road.

"I had no intention of turning it on," Nicki said. "I was explaining how it worked."

"Been workin' fine more'n forty years. Your folks rentin' hereabouts?"

Moving closer, he tapped the cover in place with his foot. Lexie molded herself to her mother's leg, tremors of anxiety radiating from her body. Nicki placed a protective hand on her shoulder.

"I own this house."

The man slid a pair of glasses from the case clipped to his belt and put them on. His expression changed to embarrassment.

"I'm real sorry, mam. Truth is, we been havin' some vandalism 'round the lake a ways. Mischief more'n any real damage. Figure it's teenagers from the rent houses. You lookin' so young and all, thought you might be one of 'em. Didn't see your young'un when I come up."

He extended a work-worn hand.

"Name's Bob Stockton. Wind blowed a couple of aluminum skiffs into a window at the marina last night. I come by here to check for damage. Been doin' yard work and such on this place for Dick

Yancy. For Reed Jordan, now that Dick's passed on. He didn't say nothin' 'bout new people last time we talked."

At the mention of the lawyer's name, Lexie's tremors ceased.

"Reed's my friend," she said, taking a cautious step away from Nicki.

The man glanced down at her, a smile softening his features. He dropped to one knee and reached for her hand.

"Reckon I wouldn't mind bein' friends with a pretty little thing like you myself. Most young'uns call me Old Bob."

"My name's Lexie," she told him, withdrawing her hand to retreat behind Nicki once more.

Stockton stood up.

"Tuesday's my regular day for your place. I'll clean up these leaves the storm blowed down then, less your husband's plannin' to hire somebody else."

"You can continue to care for the yard, Mr. Stockton."

He opened his mouth, then closed it again and nodded, withholding whatever comment he'd been about to make.

"Shop's across from the marina, but I live just up the shore a ways. You have any problems, I'm in the book. Folks this side of the lake tend to look out for each other."

Lexie relaxed her death grip on her mother's waistband as he turned to go, but Nicki called him back.

"Did you know the previous owners?"

"Trust, or some such thing, owned it last, far as I know."

"I meant before that?"

"Nah. Dad knew ever'body ever owned along this stretch o' lake. Started the business back in the thirties. Expected me to go in with him, but I figured I ought'a see the world first. Got as far as Jay-pan, back in forty-five. Come running back home to a nice, safe factory job. Durned assembly line gave me ulcers. After Mom passed on, I started helpin' Dad out on weekends. Turned out he knew more'n I thought. Froze my pension and took charge of things a year later."

"Is your father living?"

"Still kickin' up a storm. Out in Sun City. Told me the last time I called he'd been dating a 'younger' woman. She's seventy-four. He's eighty-three."

He reached over and ruffled Lexie's hair affectionately.

"You take care, little one."

Nicki watched him trudge back to his truck.

"I wanna go swimming," Lexie said, tugging Nicki's arm.

"It's better to wait awhile after we eat. Let's see what's on the hillside first." She gave Lexie a gentle push. "Race you to the road."

Trumpeter *Road,* the main route from Rockwall, completely circled the lake. According to Reed, residents along Nicki's particular stretch of shoreline referred to the highway as Upper T. Trumpeter *Lane,* a secondary blacktop drive known as Lower T, doubled back from Nicki's property, dead-ending at the convenience store and marina.

Lower T split Nicki's land in two, the house and yard on the lakeside, the equally large section of hillside between the two roads. Grass walkways and randomly placed stone steps set into each of four

gently rising terraces led to the tennis court Reed
had pointed out the night before. A hodgepodge
of flower and vegetable gardens occupied several
levels.

Lexie skipped ahead to bury her face in some
lilylike blooms on the first tier. Nicki remained at
the bottom of the path, oddly unsettled by her
daughter's fascination with the foliage. A woman's
voice counting cadence made her turn her head. A
petite, elderly woman in walking shoes and pink
terry-cloth romper slowed her pace and crossed the
road to join her.

"Your little girl's a born gardener. Had a sister
the same way. Couldn't pass a bud or a blossom
without pruning or weeding or sniffing. Gwyn
Chamberlin," she said, offering her hand. "You
must be Nicole. Reed mentioned we were finally
getting some young blood around here. Admitted
you were pretty, but, as usual, he understated the
facts. Just like a lawyer."

Nicki took the papery hand, surprised by the
strength of the woman's grip, and called to Lexie to
be introduced. She joined the women eagerly, displaying no trace of the wariness she'd shown in
Bob Stockton's presence.

"Like the daylilies, do you?" Gwyn asked. Lexie
nodded shyly. "So do I. Much prettier than those
somber things they trot out at Easter."

"Do you garden?" Nicki asked.

"Never had the patience." She sniffed. "Doctor's
got me speed walking every morning. A year ago I
was hiking in the Andes and a hip joint gave out.
New one's working fine, but my apple-cheeked
young surgeon won't sign a travel release. So here I
am, tooling along on my Sunday stroll."

Lexie had picked up a stick and was poking

about in a freshly turned patch of soil. Nicki frowned and called to her to stop. Their visitor began jogging in place.

"It's been nice meeting you, Mrs. Chamberlin."

"It's Gwyn. I'm having a dinner party next Friday. You'll come, of course."

"I don't know . . ." Nicki began.

"Reed says you're interested in local history. I've lived here off and on since I was a girl. If anyone knows where all the old skeletons are buried, it's me."

"I'll try to make it."

"You do that. Sixth house from yours," she called over her shoulder as she trotted off, arms swinging. "Drinks at six. And bring an appetite. I've got a marvelous cook."

"Mommy, is that other lady our neighbor, too?"

"What other lady?"

"That one."

Nicki followed the line of Lexie's pointing finger in time to see a figure dive off the end of the dock beside their own.

"I guess so. What do you say we change into our suits?"

Lexie answered by tugging her toward the house.

▬▬ 8 ▬▬

Nicki sat on the second step of the cement-and-stone cutaway that formed a small beach in front of the house and dug her toes in the warm sand. Lexie scampered about in the shallows, chasing minnows and diving for tiny snail shells and waterlogged leaves.

"Watch, Mommy! Watch me!"

She swam about ten feet, then came up sputtering.

"I saw our turtle! He swam away, real fast."

"You opened your eyes?"

"Uh-huh. Can I go out there?"

There was a large wooden raft anchored five or six yards from the end of the dock. The swimmer from the next house had climbed the ladder and now lay on her back, one arm flung across her eyes to block the sun.

"It's awfully far."

"You could carry me, like when I was little. Please."

"Remind me not to feed you so much tomorrow morning," Nicki said, wading into the water.

"Why?"

"You've got entirely too much energy."

She walked backward, pulling Lexie along until

she herself could no longer touch bottom, then flipped over and dog-paddled with Lexie's arms around her neck. Ten feet from the platform, her passenger began to squirm.

"I wanna swim to the ladder."

"Okay, but I'll be right beside you."

The neighbor sat up and reached out to help Lexie up the ladder. Nicki boosted from behind, then followed. Lexie scanned the view in all directions before flopping onto her stomach to peer over the side of the raft.

"That's pretty good swimming for a five-year-old," the woman said.

Lexie flashed a shy smile over her shoulder.

"That's a compliment, Lexie. What do you say?"

"Thank you." She frowned. "How'd you know I'm five?"

"I teach kindergarten in Rockwall. I've seen lots of little girls your age."

"I'm going to kin'ergarten pretty soon. I didn't get to go last time 'cause my birf'day's wrong. Will you be my teacher?"

"I will if you live here this winter. The lake's part of our district." She shaded her eyes with her left hand and smiled at Nicki. "Devon Rheams."

Nicki introduced herself. Devon's slightly thickening body was deeply tanned. Judging from her short, salt-and-pepper hair, Nicki guessed her to be in her mid-forties.

"I was on the phone with my mother when I saw you and Reed carrying things in last night. By the time I got away, it was too late to help. It's going to be nice having another woman nearby."

"Are there many children in the neighborhood?"

"Just Heather and Greg Greenlee's two boys. Seven and four. I had the oldest two years ago. He's a holy terror, but the little one's sweet. They live two houses from me. Greg got a summer grant from Oxford, so their place is closed up, but they'll be back before school starts. The second house beyond them is a rental. The people in there this year had some of their grandkids visiting last week. I think they've got another bunch coming, but not till August."

"I know why we don't go anywhere," Lexie broke in. "There's a red string tied to a big rock. And you know what? The floor's all wavy, like when Mar-Lynn combs out Sharraye's hair."

"Friends back home in Texas," Nicki explained.

Devon and Lexie began discussing anchors and why cables get rusty and how waves leave prints in the sand. Nicki planted her elbows on her knees and propped her chin on her hands, staring back at the shoreline and her new home. The urge to pinch herself was overwhelming. The sudden changes in scenery and lifestyle felt surreal.

Bob Stockton's duties involved more than cutting grass, she decided. Pockets of well-tended flowers added color to the neatly trimmed shrubs and planting areas. Scattered maples and pines softened the overpowering effect of the giant oaks protecting the house from the sun's heat. A circular patch of grass near the water's edge seemed to be struggling to catch up with the rest of the lawn.

I'd plant a tree there instead of grass, Nicki thought. *A weeping willow like the ones beyond Devon's.*

Woodland shaded all the homes lining the shore. Though not crowded together, none boasted a side yard as large as her own. Most had walls of windows facing the lake to take full advantage of the view. Behind her, Devon and Lexie's conversation switched to speculation about a school of fish darting about in the shadows beneath the raft. Nicki counted down to the sixth house.

Larger than Nicki's, Gwyn Chamberlin's home had been built from a similar plan. An open cedar deck had been added across the front beyond the enclosed porch. Three umbrella tables and a large barbecue grill suggested entertaining might be another of the owner's interests . . . in addition to climbing mountains.

If she accepted Gwyn's invitation, Nicki thought, she'd be obligated to reciprocate. The observation was more than a little daunting. She considered the entertainment possibilities of her own property.

The large open spot beneath the oaks would look inviting with a picnic table, and the expanse between the house and lake could use a grouping of lawn chairs. Maybe a lounger or two for reading. She'd seen a folding table propped against the wall in the garage the night before. Topped with a brightly patterned cloth, it would make an adequate buffet table. She could probably manage alone if she stuck to a make-ahead menu. And if her neighbors were used to more formal settings . . .

Waves from a passing powerboat rocked the platform. Lexie squealed, clutching the edge of the raft, then settled back down, fascinated by a water spider surfing the waves. Nicki's gaze swung back to the hillside.

"Devon, do you know who's working in my garden? I thought at first it was the yard man, but it's not."

"That's Del Ferris. See the house with all the glass?"

"The one next to yours?"

"No, that's Clay Verdell's place. The one beyond

that's the Greenlees'. Del's is next. With the angled windows."

"Unusual architecture."

"Wait till you see the inside. Lots of open space, natural materials, strategically placed lighting, minimalist artwork. It's surprisingly restful. He said he needed something less frenzied when he wasn't working."

"What's he do?"

"Fashion photography. He's filmed layouts all over the world . . . Europe, Asia, Hong Kong, Africa."

"Why's he tending my garden?"

"He and Clay and several others have plots on the terraces. Gwyn Chamberlin said Bob Stockton started it. The house hadn't been rented in years and the gardens were a mess. Dick Yancy gave the idea his blessing. He gave some of us tennis privileges, too, since the court was just sitting there unused. Clay and I usually play at least one morning a week."

Nicki continued to stare at the hillside.

"Look, it's no big deal. Everyone will understand if you want to handle things differently now. I'm really surprised Reed didn't explain when he showed you the property."

"I hadn't seen the house before last night."

"I suppose your husband handled everything."

"I'm not married at the moment," Nicki said, searching for a different topic. "I don't play tennis or garden, so it's really not a problem. Do you know Mrs. Chamberlin well?"

"Everyone knows Gwyn."

"She invited me to a dinner party on Friday."

"Oh-oh. I'll bet Reed's the other victim."

"I like Reed," Lexie volunteered, scooting across

the deck on her bottom to join the conversation. Nicki ignored the intrusion and looked at Devon with raised eyebrows.

"I'd better explain. I'll probably have an invitation from her on the phone machine when I go in."

She wrapped her arms around her knees and massaged an untanned strip of skin on her left ring finger.

"Gwyn thinks a year's long enough to mourn the death of a marriage. She's a widow now, but she weathered three divorces herself before she found the right man, so I guess she should know. I hadn't realized I was still in denial until she gave me heck the other day for not having my rings reset."

"I don't understand where Reed fits in."

"Show Gwyn a single woman and she'll find an unattached man somewhere. Clay Verdell's her choice to get me back in circulation. I imagine she's decided Reed's perfect for you."

"Oh, dear. A matchmaker," Nicki murmured, thinking of the arranged dates a determined friend at the bank had set up over the years. Most had considered Lexie extra baggage or assumed a single mother must be seething with suppressed desire. Sexual frustration aside, she preferred to choose her own dates.

"What's a matchmaker?" Lexie asked, poking her head between the two women. Devon leaned back and grinned at Nicki.

"It's an old-fashioned term adults use."

"But what's it mean?"

Nicki looked to Devon for help, but her neighbor was shaking with silent laughter. Beyond Devon, she spotted something bobbing in the water.

"Look, that turtle you saw is swimming right off our little beach. See his head?"

Her attention diverted, Lexie forgot her question. "I wanna go back now."

"I'll come with you," Devon said.

They sidestroked to the end of Nicki's dock, each woman supporting Lexie with the other hand. Lexie raced across the painted planks toward the spot where the turtle's head had last broken the surface. Nicki's admonition not to run succeeded only after a threat of no afternoon swim was added. She and Devon remained at the end of the dock, feet dangling in the water.

"What's this Clay Verdell like?"

"Tall, nice-looking, pretty good shape for fifty-one. He's got gray hair, dark brown eyes, and a really weird rust-colored mustache that wiggles like a caterpillar when he laughs, which he doesn't do nearly often enough. When he thinks no one's looking, he has this sad, contemplative expression . . . it could break your heart."

Gwyn Chamberlin's efforts at kindling romance seemed to be succeeding with at least one of her new neighbors, Nicki mused.

An aluminum rowboat rounded a jutting point of land beyond the Tarleton jungle. The shirtless man pulling the oars rowed steadily in their direction. Glancing over his shoulder, he hailed Devon by name, then turned the boat toward the dock.

"That's Clay," Devon murmured while he was still too far away to overhear.

"What's he think of Gwyn's plotting?"

She shrugged. "It's hard to tell. He's not much of a talker. What little I've learned about him came from Gwyn. He has scars on his legs and a slight limp. She says he served in 'Nam, then stayed over there for a couple of years after his last hitch to work with children. Amerasian kids, I think. When I asked him about it, he changed subjects."

"What kind of work did he do?"

"Counseling, I assume. That's what he did before he moved here. He was an administrator at a hospital for troubled kids—in California. He says he's on sabbatical. You can tell he's got a thing for children. When the grandkids at the rental house got rowdy, Clay took them fishing and wangled permission to tramp the Tarleton woods."

"Has he got kids of his own?"

"He's never been married," she whispered as the rowboat bumped against the dock.

Devon made introductions. Clay Verdell had a deep, quiet voice to match his serious expression. Something about the way his eyes sparkled when he smiled hello made Nicki scramble for a recent memory. Lost in the contemplation, she jumped when Devon touched her arm.

"Sorry. I think the sun's putting me to sleep."

"I just said, with that gorgeous auburn hair, I'll bet your daughter's a daddy's girl," Clay told her.

"Lexie's father died before she was born," Nicki said, without thinking.

Apologies and an awkward silence ensued.

"Nicki's from Texas," Devon said, rescuing the conversation.

"Really. Do you have family in Michigan?"

"No. This just seemed like a safe place to raise a child."

"A thousand miles is a long way to come for security."

"You came over two thousand just to go fishing," Devon chided him.

He studied the tackle box on the floor of the boat.

"Someone once told me this was a wonderful place to be a kid," he said softly. Reaching over the side of the boat, he reeled in a stringer of fish. "It's not bad for trout, either."

He dropped the line back in the water and raised his eyes to the house.

"I didn't know the property was on the market. How'd you find out about it?"

"It's all rather complicated," Nicki said. She looked away, hoping to discourage further inquiry.

Clay's gaze shifted to Lexie, now playing in the shallows.

"I'd like to meet your little one."

Nicki called to Lexie, who raised her eyes from her collection of snail shells, stared at Clay, and then shook her head. As if to avoid a second request, she dived underwater.

"She's a little shy," Nicki apologized.

She bit her lip. Lexie's experience with Odell seemed to have evolved into a distrust of all men. Except Reed Jordan, she realized. The afterthought was somehow comforting.

"I wouldn't worry about it. Kids go through phases. We'll meet another time. Maybe she'd like to go fishing some morning."

"Maybe," Nicki murmured.

He said his good-byes and rowed toward his own dock. Nicki and Devon parted company under the oak trees, and Nicki called to Lexie that it was time to go in. As she gathered their towels, she glanced back at the water.

Clay Verdell had beached his rowboat and unloaded his fishing gear. He stood facing her, staring, as if contemplating the house behind her. His facial expression made her wish she were close enough to see what was reflected in his dark eyes.

"There's grass in my toes," Lexie whined, stamping her feet.

"Come on, there's a footbath by the garage door."

"What's that?"

"I'll show you," Nicki said, leading the way. "Well water gets really cold after it's run awhile, but what's in the pipes will be warm from the sun. You go first."

Once again Nicki felt a sense of bewilderment at the certainty of her knowledge. Rockwall, the nearest municipality, was fourteen miles away. Of course, houses around the lake relied on wells. Anyone would know that . . . except someone like herself who'd never experienced anything but city utilities.

"Did the water have to take nasty stuff, like I did?"

"What?" Nicki asked, wrinkling her forehead.

"To get well."

"No, it didn't. Turn around, funny face."

"That tickles!"

"I'm looking for a switch to turn off the question machine."

Lexie giggled. After a moment, she relinquished the shallow cement basin to her mother and did a jerky one-legged dance, hopping between the flagstones and singing the *Sesame Street* theme as she waited for Nicki to finish.

"Why's he staring at us?"

Nicki's head swung toward Clay Verdell's dock, but the fisherman had disappeared. At the sound of a horn, she turned toward the road. Bob Stockton waved from the window of his truck, then turned onto the short section of road that connected Lower with Upper T. The man working in the hillside garden rose from his knees and brushed loose grass from his clothes. Carrying a wicker basket filled with cut flowers, he started toward his own house without looking up.

"It's cold," Lexie complained through chattering teeth.

"I warned you," Nicki scolded, wrapping her in a towel and scooping her up. "Why'd you get back in?"

"I got more grass."

Nicki tried the narrow garage door and found it locked. Picking her way across the flagstones, she carried Lexie to the front door and set her down.

"Is it time to eat yet?"

"We could go broke filling that bottomless tummy of yours."

"What's going broke?"

"Something we don't have to worry about anymore," Nicki told her with a smile. She turned to survey her property.

On the lake, reflected sun had turned the tranquil surface to a glittering daylight marquee. Above her, birds calling to one another and the chatter of squirrels filled the air. She felt a sudden stab of loneliness, wishing she could share the peace-inspiring view with MarLynn and her family.

In recent years MarLynn had filled the void left as friends from school finished college and married or moved on with their lives. Most of the girls in her department at the bank had been single, preferring the club scene to an inexpensive evening of canasta or Uno. The single mothers she knew had lived far from her own neighborhood, their income augmented, if somewhat infrequently, by child-support payments.

Clay Verdell was right. A thousand miles was a long way. The move had placed an impossible chasm between her and her only confidante. But it had distanced Odell and the nightmares of the past as well, she reminded herself.

Despite the curious sense of déjà vu that had accompanied her arrival, or maybe because of it, she'd been right to come here, she decided. Her lingering misgivings evaporated, replaced by an almost childlike euphoria.

"Bet I can change faster than you can," she taunted Lexie as they entered the house and raced up the stairs.

■■■■■■9■■■■■

He spent a few moments in the garage storing his equipment, carefully replacing each item in its corresponding niche on the pegboard along one wall. The morning's outing had been pleasant, the heat only a minor irritant on his already-sun-darkened skin. Now, in the stagnant air, perspiration dripped into his eyes and trickled down his back. He wiped his forehead, wrinkling his nose at the odors trapped in his hands. Activity had erased the essence of his earlier rituals.

Visions of the child intruded, but he pushed them aside. Thoughts of a leisurely shower hastened his movements.

Cordelia.

The pocket knife in his hand clattered to the floor.

His stepmother would have launched into one of her tirades about wasting water or monopolizing the bathroom or his other myriad sins. Then would have come hugs and kisses and the predictable, apologetic smile. And later still a visit to the tiny, airless room at the back of the family's garage.

A fresh wave of perspiration traced the hollow of his back.

He mustn't think about Cordelia anymore. Those

nights had been revenged, the demons excised. Querulous as ever at the end, the monster who'd invaded his slumber had shriveled, her flesh devoured by the unfiltered cigarettes that had never been far away. Even now, the stench of nicotine that had permeated the very fiber of his life could summon her vivid image.

Motionless air closed about him. Odors of gasoline and cleaning supplies clawed at his memory. He stumbled into the house, abandoned the results of his morning's work in the kitchen sink, and fled to the bathroom.

Needles of scalding water prickled his skin. Clouds of mist cleansed his nostrils and cleared his head. He forced himself to think of the other stirrings Cordelia's ministrations and taunts had awakened in him.

Midge had been six and Kathy an aloof eight to his own eleven when his father had collected him from the home of his mother's latest bed partner and thrust him into the midst of his new family. In the two years before Cordelia had banished him to a tortured military-school existence, he'd absorbed her lessons well . . . and developed his own appetites.

He reached for a towel and came away empty-handed. Dripping water, he stalked down the hall and slammed open the laundry room door. Neatly labeled baskets lined one wall of the organized space. The one marked TOWELS was empty. He found what he sought in the dryer.

"Stupid, slant-eyed bitch!"

Can't trust any of them once they reach puberty, he fumed, jerking out handfuls of thick terry cloth. Anger generated a renewed round of perspiration.

He stored the towels on the open bathroom shelves, then switched on the shower once more.

Thirty minutes later he carried a tray into the front room.

Opaque drapery panels muted the sunlight. Cool, almost chill air circulated throughout the room. He chose a deep leather chair that faced the lake and watched the activity on the water while he ate. By the time he'd finished the individually wrapped sandwiches and delicately seasoned rice-and-grape salad, his anger toward the maid had cooled.

Such exquisite help was impossible to find. Despite offers of a generous salary, the woman still declined exclusive employment. Several times he'd made his distaste of the part-time arrangement clear, but she refused to be swayed.

Best to avoid yet another confrontation. He'd arrange to be out during her next visit. A strongly worded note on the counter would prevent a recurrence of her error with the towels.

He returned to the kitchen and stacked his utensils in the dishwasher. A shiver of anticipation brought a tremor to his hand as he settled back in his chair before the front windows and let his thoughts center on the auburn-haired child.

Much too thin. Perhaps a little too young as well, despite her deceptive height. The softly rounded Midge had been nearly seven by the time he discovered a way to defy Cordelia. His stepmother *had* taught him one thing, he mused. Patience. A little while in the lake's nourishing setting and the little redhead would thrive and blossom. Children always did.

She'd been singing that song again. The acknowledgment raised a prickly sensation along the back of his neck. He mustn't dismiss the mother too easily. The old rumors might not be true. His questions before coming back had been necessarily vague. People had hidden agendas and untold reasons to lie. He knew that better than most. Still, he'd have to be careful. The child had definite possibilities . . . unless the past had returned to haunt him.

He left the leather chair and padded to the back wall, his bare feet leaving no impression on the thick plush carpet. The rosewood panels slid open silently. He deactivated the alarm. Moving the projection table aside, he retrieved a key from a niche beneath the table, then knelt and removed a section of carpet.

The large safe was recessed beneath the floor, anchored in concrete. Access required both the key and a combination, which he recalled from memory. The contents occupied barely half the available space. He thumbed through a folder of grainy snapshots, resisted the temptation to study each one, and removed only three. Several small tins of 16mm film, all but one neatly labeled, lay beneath the folder. His fingers caressed each one, trembling when they touched the unmarked tin.

No need to unleash that particular demon. Not when all he had were uneasy stirrings. Reasonable caution. That was what he was exercising.

He studied the old photos for a long time in the silent room, reaching at one point for a magnifying glass. Finally he replaced the snapshots and secured the safe.

The shadowy images were too obscured by time. The slight similarities between the child in the old pictures and the lake's newest resident could be nothing more than coincidence. How many long-legged, brown-haired children grew into tall, brown-haired adults? The child of the past had been sturdy, almost chubby. The woman was chopstick thin. Only the stupid song bridged the years to link the two.

Paranoid. That's what he'd become since he'd come back. Jumping at shadows, imagining danger where none existed. He no longer looked the same. Even Midge and Kathy had not recognized him when they passed in the hospital corridor. Cordelia had known, instinctively. On her deathbed, beyond speech, his father's fourth wife had still managed to respond with that knowing, unrepentant smirk.

He shook himself. The child in the end house had no connection to the past. As for the mother . . . time would answer his questions.

Time—and the auburn-haired child. Anticipation of seeing her again, of taking her tiny hand in his, made his breath catch in an exquisite agony. He'd have to go back out to chance even a casual glance. More than that would be too much to hope for this soon. He returned the projection table to its original position, aligning the legs precisely with the faint indentations in the carpet, then reset the alarm and went to change.

Such a precious little girl. If she came back out, what would she have on? The bright blue swimsuit with the ruffled vees down the front? Maybe she'd change into one of those little sundresses that were back in style. Midge had worn sundresses. His breath came faster as his own clothes touched his body.

He made himself move slowly and take several deep breaths. Rushing would only summon unwanted attention. Patience and careful timing would bring him what he needed. Timing had always been on his side. He'd watch and wait. With patience, he'd find the perfect time for an encounter. Perfect timing. Perfect child. He stroked his mustache and smiled.

......10 ......

"What's that?" Lexie asked.

"I don't know. Let's go see."

They crossed to an upside-down U-shaped frame in the side yard.

"I think it's an old swing set."

"Where's the slide?"

"I don't think this kind had a slide. The swings are probably around somewhere. If not, we can buy new ones."

A concrete slab near the low hedge that divided Devon's property from their own drew Lexie's attention.

"What's this for?"

Nicki stared at the rectangular outline and felt an almost irresistible urge to touch the pock-marked surface.

"I don't know," she said slowly.

"Hopscotch?" She began hopping the length of the slab on one foot. "Can we buy chalk?"

"It's not for hopscotch."

"Then what's it for?"

"I said I don't know," Nicki snapped.

Lexie's lower lip protruded and the big brown eyes swelled with tears. Nicki dropped to one knee and pulled her close.

"Baby, I'm sorry. I didn't mean to snap at you. Mommy's just feeling like an old grouch."

"Like Oscar on *Sesame Street?*"

"Exactly, except I'm not all green and fuzzy."

"And you don't sleep in the garbage can." Lexie giggled.

They walked toward the edge of the road. A turquoise LeBaron convertible with the top down pulled from the drive beyond Devon's and turned in their direction. Nicki placed a restraining hand on Lexie's shoulder. Instead of passing, the driver slowed to a stop.

"Good afternoon, Mr. Verdell."

Lexie repeated her earlier attempt at becoming a chameleon, hiding behind her mother. Nicki could feel the trembling little body, hot against her own bare legs. She picked Lexie up, then turned back to the car. Lexie buried her face in Nicki's neck, her heartbeat a frantic tom-tom against her mother's breast.

"I wish you'd make it Clay."

He had showered and exchanged his trunks for a crisply ironed white shirt and navy chinos. A subtle scent of after-shave wafted around him. Lexie's arms tightened as Clay studied her a moment before shifting his gaze to Nicki. Again she felt a bewildering twinge of recognition as his dark eyes locked with hers.

"I hope you told your daughter about my fishing invitation," he continued, as if Lexie were invisible. "There's a pair of coves with statue fountains just beyond that little promontory. I saw several baby turtles in one of them last week. There's a family of mallards nesting in the other."

Lexie twisted to uncover one ear, but refused to raise her head. Nicki shifted the weight in her arms. The fingers digging into her back clung tighter. She looked at Clay Verdell helplessly. He smiled and shook his head.

"Maybe when Lexie decides if she'd like to be friends, we could plan an outing. Fix some sandwiches, row over to the coves, and go wading. Sometimes, if you're very quiet, momma duck will let you get really close before she gets nervous."

"I'm sure Lexie would like that . . . in time."

"We can't wait too long. These are a second hatch. Baby ducks grow up very fast."

He shifted the car into gear.

"I forgot to put some things on my housekeeper's shopping list. Can I pick up anything for you while I'm out?"

"We really haven't had much chance to take inventory yet. But thanks for the offer."

With another look at Lexie's back, he winked and drove toward the turn for Upper T. Lexie scrambled down and streaked across the deserted road. Ignoring the gardens, she raced toward the tennis court at the top. Nicki followed at a slower pace. Halfway up the third tier, she glanced back.

The turquoise convertible had stopped just beyond the curve. A small tree blocked her view of the front seat. As she watched, the vehicle pulled away, continuing toward the main road.

The area at the top of the hill was surrounded on three sides by an eight-foot chain-link fence. Dense ivy obscured the court from motorists passing along Upper T and the connecting road. Facing the lake the barrier dropped to half its height, the metal covered with a green vinyl coating instead of foliage. The gate was latched but unlocked, the court deserted.

Nicki sank down on the wide expanse of grass that bordered the court. Lexie investigated the mechanism that controlled the tautness of the net, accepting without protest her mother's admonition not to hang on the webbing. After stepping off every inch of white line, she sprawled across from Nicki. A chipmunk scampered along the fence and disappeared through one of the links. She watched it without comment.

"Lexie."

She continued to stare at the fence.

"Lexie, look at me."

Wide brown eyes brimming with tears met her own.

"Come here." Lexie crept into her lap. "What's wrong?"

"Was that the car in the alley?"

"Of course not!" Nicki stroked a strand of auburn curls. "Is that what you thought when Mr. Verdell stopped?"

Lexie nodded. She hiccuped and wiped her nose on the sleeve of her T-shirt.

"It's the same color."

"Maybe. But this car's a convertible. The one in the alley had a hard top. It's back in Texas. That's a long way from here. Over a thousand miles," she said, echoing Clay Verdell's words. "I promised we'd be safe here. Remember?"

Lexie nodded again. She began raking the grass with her fingers, listlessly tossing cut blades into the air, trying to catch them on her palm.

"Mr. Verdell's our neighbor, like Mrs. Rheams."

"Don't like man neighbors, just girls."

"Ellis was our neighbor. You liked him. And Russell."

"Russell's a little boy."

"Ellis is a man. So's Reed."

"But they're my friends."

Nicki sighed. How did you help a child differentiate between good and evil in this day and age? Somehow she couldn't remember so many gray areas in her own childhood.

"Are you afraid of Mr. Verdell?"

Lexie shrugged.

"What about Mr. Stockton?"

Another rise and fall of the tiny shoulders.

"Honey, we're going to meet a lot of new people here. You can't be afraid of everyone that happens to be a man."

"Why not?"

Nicki frowned. Why not indeed?

"Being scared all the time isn't any fun."

"Do you like men?"

"I like Ellis and some of the men I used to work with, and lots of the boys I knew at school. And I loved your daddy."

Lexie thought about that for a moment.

"Do you like Reed?"

Nicki murmured something noncommittal. Lexie stood up and pressed her face against the gate.

"That man's back."

"Mr. Verdell?" Nicki asked, getting up herself.

"Uh-uh. The man in the garden."

Nicki held out her hand.

"Then I think we should go meet another neighbor."

Del Ferris was a big man. Unlike Bob Stockton and Clay Verdell, his weight tended more toward bulk than muscle. He looked shorter than either man as well, although Nicki couldn't really tell while he was kneeling. What hair he had was white, a bushy semicircle ringing his bronzed dome. A walrus droop of mustache hung over his upper lip.

"Noticed you swimming this morning. How's the water?"

"A little cool after the rain, but the sun was hot."

"Probably not a problem for your youngster with that tan. I'm a rarity like that too. Never burned, even when this mop was more gold than platinum. Del Ferris. And you're . . ."

"Nicki Prevot. My daughter, Lexie."

"Pretty little thing," Ferris noted, returning to his weeding.

Lexie had followed her mother as far as the next-to-last terrace. She'd retrieved the stick she'd been toying with earlier in the day and begun poking about in the same patch of soil. Nicki called to her to stop. Lexie looked up, eyeing Del Ferris warily.

"She's not hurting anything."

"I don't want her digging up someone's seeds."

"Nothing in there yet. Intended to use that section for a late planting. Got busy Saturday morning and never got to it. You and your husband move in yesterday?"

"I'm a widow," Nicki said, surprised how easily the lie slipped out.

"Big house for two people."

"We'll be fine for the summer."

"Place has been vacant for quite a while," he said, shaking the soil from the bulbs of several green onions. Nicki stepped back, away from the flying dirt. "Just renting, I suppose."

"Actually, I bought the house."

A second lie, even easier than the first, reinforcing Devon's and Clay's earlier assumptions about the origins of her ownership. The truth about the circumstances of the property's transfer would be sure to draw unanswerable questions.

Lexie skipped down the last section of rock steps, stopping a few feet away.

"It's nice meeting you, Mr. Ferris. Enjoy your gardening."

"Oh, I will. I've always loved this particular spot. So peaceful and serene. Almost like a cathedral or a churchyard."

Nicki glanced at the woodland about them and the blue sky overhead. She supposed the area did have some resemblance to an open-air church. Del Ferris didn't seem to expect an answer to his remark. He called to Lexie.

"You like digging in the earth?"

She nodded, but kept her distance.

"Feels good, working the soil. Lots of good things come from the ground."

He rooted around in the dirt at the other end of the patch.

"You like carrots?"

Lexie nodded again and took a step closer.

"You rinse this off, you'll find the best-tasting carrot you ever ate." He looked up at Nicki. "Don't believe in chemicals. Nothing in this soil but natural fertilizer."

He held out the carrot. Lexie came close enough to take it, then stepped back. Ferris rocked on his heels and smiled.

"What do you say, Lexie?"

"Can I have another one?"

"Lexie!"

"For the bunny. He likes cawwots, too."

"It's all right. I've got lots of vegetables."

He plucked another root from the earth. Lexie moved even closer and held out her hand. Ferris placed the carrot on her palm with exaggerated ceremony.

"Thank you," she said shyly, looking at Nicki for approval.

"We have a sink full of dishes waiting, young lady. Tell Mr. Ferris good-bye."

"Good-bye, Mr. Ferris."

The neighbor called after them, almost as an afterthought.

"I'll be planting that other section sometime next week. Your girl wants to help, she's welcome."

"Would you like to plant something?" Nicki asked, glancing again at the concrete slab as they passed the swing frame.

Lexie shrugged and ran to wash her carrots beneath the footbath's faucet. She held the dripping vegetables up triumphantly.

"Maybe Mrs. Chamberlin's right about your green thumb."

Lexie looked at her hands, frowning. Nicki stopped laughing long enough to wave in answer to Clay Verdell's returning honk, then urged her daughter toward the door.

"Come on, those dishes aren't going to wash themselves."

Drying her hands on a dish towel, Nicki crossed the front entry to answer the insistent knocking. Devon Rheams stepped back to let her open the screen door.

"Is your phone working?"

"I don't even know if I have one."

"You do. Reed said it was turned on last week.

He called me. He's been trying to get you since early this morning."

"I know where it is." Lexie, wearing only her underpants and carrying Mr. Flops, scampered down the stairs.

"You're supposed to be napping."

"Not sleepy."

She ran between the two women into the main room of the house and slid open a small panel beside the pass-through window.

"See? It's right here."

Nicki stared at the instrument in the recessed niche.

"Maybe the ringer's off," Devon said. She picked the phone up, adjusted the setting, and returned it to its special nook. Instantly the phone rang shrilly. Lexie snatched the receiver from its cradle.

"Prevot res'dence," she said, showing off Mar-Lynn's patient training. "Hi, Reed. Know what? A man gave me two cawwots. One for me and one for our real bunny. I shared mine with Mr. Flops."

She handed the receiver to her mother. Devon waved and slipped out the door. Nicki explained about the phone, then listened quietly, murmuring a few words before hanging up.

Her fingers traced the groove of the sliding panel.

"Do I hav'ta take a nap?"

Nicki remained silent, gnawing her lower lip.

"Do I?"

"No. Reed's coming over. Go get dressed."

Lexie's reaction was less restrained than her own. Reed had said the drive from wherever he'd been calling would take ten minutes. What he'd failed to mention was the identity of the woman he was bringing with him and seemed so anxious for her to meet.

She followed Lexie upstairs to run a brush through her hair and add lipstick to her sun-reddened face.

11

Nicki's concern about Reed's companion evaporated when Lexie led them up the walk. Mildred McCowan was pushing sixty. A fluffy cap of hennaed hair softened the lifelines around her lively green eyes. Her short, compact body looked surprisingly youthful in stirrup pants and print pullover.

"I reminded him short-notice visits were bad manners," she told Nicki, turning affectionate eyes on Reed. "Helen would be after him with a hickory switch, if she were here."

"Helen's my mother," Reed explained. "Mid's been part of our lives for as far back as I can remember. Mom and she were childhood friends."

Lexie, whose idea of dressing had been her swimsuit, hung on Reed's arm, swinging in an arc between the lawyer and Nicki.

"Mommy says I can't go in by myself. Will you watch me?"

"Lexie! Honestly, your manners have gone out the window," Nicki told her, apologizing to her guests.

Reed slipped off his deck shoes and grinned.

"I don't mind. Why don't you give Mid a house tour and join us when you're done."

Through the screened porch, Nicki watched Lexie prance across the grass, chattering nonstop about bunnies and turtles and baby ducks. Her one-man captive audience seemed enchanted.

"That boy can be exasperating sometimes." Mid McCowan sighed. "But he does love children."

"It's mutual, at least with Lexie. And she's not too fond of men right now."

"Because of what you went through before you came here?"

Nicki failed to hide her surprise.

"Reed mentioned your troubles at lunch. I don't think he meant to be so candid. It just slipped out."

Mid ran her hand over the glass-topped table.

"I always remember this porch as a page from one of those *House Beautiful* spreads on gracious living. Bright place settings. Fresh-cut buds in tiny vases. Crystal water goblets, ripe red strawberries spilling from a basket, a pot of real flowers beneath this glass. Isn't it amazing what imagination can create from a few vivid childhood memories?"

"You lived here," Nicki said, her pulse quickening.

"Oh, my, no. I was allowed to tag along with Helen to a party here the summer I was ten. My gram took care of Reed's grandparents' summer place across the lake."

She closed her eyes briefly, as if remembering.

"Daddy brought some emotional baggage home from the war. He'd been gone five years. We kids didn't quite know how to handle the troubled stranger in our midst."

"Delayed stress," Nicki murmured, remembering a feature from a Sunday news magazine. She wondered briefly if her recent spells of confusion could be attributed to a similar reaction. Dealing with Odell certainly ought to be described as trauma.

"Shell shock, they called it back then. Anyway, it was Reed's grandmother's idea I spend the summer with Helen. We were supposed to help with the new baby, but Donnie was such a good little thing, we were usually on our own."

Her face clouded. Nicki, her head swirling with questions, suggested they continue their tour. Lexie and Reed were wading in the shallows, trying to trap minnows in their cupped hands.

Mid exclaimed over the wicker furniture on the leg of the porch that faced the lake. In the combination living room/dining area, she let her hand trail over the back of a faded sofa.

"It's amazing how it still looks the same. Different colors, new upholstery patterns. I don't remember that coffee table, but not much else has changed. Folks with money invest in good things and make them last. My Kenneth taught me that."

"This room's been frozen in time as well," Nicki said, showing her the kitchen. "I'm thinking of donating the appliances to the Smithsonian and remodeling."

"Oh, dear, I see what you mean." Mid ran her hand over a dented section of metal counter trim. "I was so awed by the punch fountain and party decorations, I didn't get beyond the front rooms, not even to ask for the bathroom."

"Do you remember the name of the family who gave the party you attended?"

"Ingram. The party was for one of their sons. Sidney? No, the younger one. James, that was it."

How old had the Ingram boys been the year she was born? Nicki wondered as she led the way upstairs. Well into adulthood certainly. Too old to attract a teenage Renee?

Except for the security it offered, Nicki had never cared for the trappings of wealth, but her mother would probably have been drawn to the Ingrams, she thought. Unlike most of her anti-establishment generation, Renee had appreciated the advantages money brought—travel, jewelry, a fashionable wardrobe.

"The maid's room, of course," Mid said, taking in the slant-ceilinged bedroom above the garage. "Gram's was very similar. I shoved my cot against the angle and pinned Clark Gable's picture above my head. My granddaughter does the same thing now, except the objects of her affection usually have an earring and wear their underwear on the outside."

They finished touring the upstairs and started back down.

"How old's your granddaughter?"

"Steffi's nine . . . going on nineteen. Her brother Matthew's thirteen and into astronomy, so his room's papered with Carl Sagan and star charts and wrinkle-faced aliens. Or it was. KT, my son, carted everyone off to Australia for a year while he sets up a computer system for some ranching interests."

"The children must be excited."

"Yes, but Grandma's not. Since Kenneth died, I've had each child stay at my place in Fort Myers for a month during summer vacation. When Helen learned I'd be alone this year, she insisted I spend the summer with her and Ray here at the lake."

"I haven't met Reed's parents," Nicki said, standing aside to let her guest descend the stairs first.

Lexie met them at the bottom, dripping water and grinning.

"Reed says you gotta come watch me."

She ran back out, letting the screen door slam behind her. Nicki looked at the wet spot on the sisal rug with dismay.

"I'd wager it's survived worse," Mid said.

"I guess we'd better see what she's up to."

Reed let go and took a step backward in the shallow water. Lexie held the handstand for all of three seconds before landing with a splash that drenched his shorts and shirt.

"Told you I could do it, Mommy. Wanna see again?"

"I think we've seen enough," Nicki called from the steps.

Reed waded from the water and stripped off his wet shirt.

"I hope you stop with your top this time," Mid said with mock severity. She was sitting on the top step of the stone cutaway, grinning maliciously.

"Tales from my youthful past are strictly off-limits." Reed said.

"No fair," Nicki protested. "I want to hear this."

Lexie refused her mother's suggestion to take a break and continued her antics in the water.

"She's full of energy today," he said, wringing his shirt and spreading it in the sun to dry.

"Tell me about it," Nicki said. "And about this infamous past of yours."

He felt himself redden.

"Not much to tell. I was about four, I guess. Mom was having a bunch of ladies in and had dressed me up in some kind of scratchy sailor suit and told me to stay out of trouble."

"And out of the lake," Mid added, her eyes twinkling. "The 'bunch of ladies' was the Rockwall garden club."

"Prissy old biddies in silly hats Mom thought she had to impress, and she just said not to get my clothes wet . . ."

"So you went skinny dipping," Nicki finished, laughter lighting her face.

He ducked his head, not so much in embarrassment as to cover his reaction to her laughter.

"Uncle Donnie waded in fully dressed to get me, carried me into the middle of the festivities, bowed to the head biddy, and asked if she'd ever examined that particular specimen of water lily."

"Donnie was eighteen and the best-looking thing old Miss Everman had ever seen," Mid said. "That boy could charm the coldest heart. She just pulled off her lace shawl, draped it over you, and told Donnie she'd never seen one quite that close before."

"I thought she fainted."

"All I know is what Helen told me in her next letter. I think time has slightly embellished the tale."

A bank of clouds moved across the sun, stealing the warmth of the afternoon. Lexie emerged, shivering and ready to go in, already showing petulant signs of her missed nap. Mid, seeking the powder room, walked her to the house, insisting Reed and Nicki stay where they were.

When the two were out of sight, he ran a hand through his damp hair and decided it was probably best to plunge right in.

"I guess Mid told you she spent time around here as a girl."

"We had a nice talk. She said your parents invited her for the summer. I wish you'd brought them with you. I'd like to meet them."

He stared across the lake, avoiding her eyes.

"My parents are staying in Arizona this summer. Dad had unexpected heart surgery in May. I flew out there a month ago. He's doing fine, but they wanted to stay near his doctors."

"Mid doesn't know?"

He raised his eyes.

"I told her after I picked her up."

"Reed! The woman came all the way from Florida."

"The last time Mid talked to Mom, they were packing to come here. KT took off for down under the next day. Mid flew out to San Francisco to see them off, then took a cruise to Alaska. She spent the first part of June tramping around the Northwest and Canada with various tour groups. Mom kept getting a disconnect recording when she tried to leave a message on her machine."

"How awful for everyone."

"It gets worse. Mid called the lake house last week to confirm her arrival. When she got *their* machine, she figured Mom and Dad were out somewhere and left a message. I've been keeping an eye on things, but I didn't check the recorder till this morning. When Mid explained about her condo, the only thing I could think of was you and Lexie."

"What about her condo?" Nicki said, her voice wary.

"She leased it out for the summer."

He took a deep breath and plunged on.

"You need someone to help out, at least until you get settled. Mid needs somewhere to live till the end of summer. She refuses to stay at Mom and Dad's if they're not home, and my place in town's too small."

Nicki's expression reflected her dismay.

"It seemed like a good solution this morning."

"I can't believe you'd even consider asking your mother's best friend to be my housekeeper."

"He didn't exactly ask me. I volunteered," Mid said behind them. She flashed him an exasperated look. "I see you broached the subject with your usual savoir faire, Counselor."

"Guess I blew it, huh?"

"What he's trying to say is that I made such a big to-do about how I'd looked forward to summering at the lake again, he didn't have the heart to simply put me on another plane and wave good-bye. I knew we had a problem when we stopped at my favorite restaurant on the way from the airport. Helen would have had luncheon planned."

"I don't know what to say."

"Say nothing, child. If you want me, I'll stay. If not, I'll make other arrangements. Money's no problem. My Kenneth saw to that."

"I'd love to have you as my guest, I just don't . . ."

"A guest isn't what you need. A place that size calls for a housekeeper. And don't worry about offending my 'genteel' nature. I've been a hard worker all my life. Kenneth and I ran a ranch in the Oklahoma panhandle till some shrewd horse trading during the last oil boom set us up for life. I enjoyed every lazy minute after that, till Kenneth's heart gave out."

Reed watched doubt creep into Nicki's expression.

"Truth is, I've been bored playing rich widow ever since, and I already miss my grandbabies. I'd enjoy helping you fix this place up, cooking your meals, keeping an eye on Lexie. So you decide. A housekeeper in exchange for that little room above the garage . . . or I'll say 'nice meeting you' and be on my way."

"I wouldn't feel right if I didn't pay you," Nicki said.

"*I* wouldn't feel right if you did."

Reed relaxed. Negotiations he could handle.

"Nicki should pay a salary." He held up his hand to silence Mid's protest. "And you should donate it to a good cause."

"If the garden club's still active, you could fund a study of water lilies," Nicki said mischievously.

"Go on and laugh, I can take it. What do you say, ladies?"

"I only see one problem," Nicki said, winking at Mid. "I haven't the slightest idea where to get a photo of Clark Gable."

"I'll make do somehow," Mid told her with a laugh.

Reed looked between the two in bewilderment.

"You may be the architect of this scheme, but we girls have our own secrets," Mid said, linking arms with Nicki and starting back to the house.

He stood in his still-wet shorts, holding his damp shirt, and stared after them. Somehow he had a feeling the garden club episode wouldn't be the only story from the past that came back to haunt him this summer.

⬛⬛⬛⬛⬛ 12 ⬛⬛⬛⬛⬛

"How soon can you start?" Nicki asked the contractor who had appeared Monday morning promptly at eight. She was just beginning to appreciate the advantages of a small town. One phone call from Reed—on a Sunday night, no less—and her remodeling project was under way.

"I'll begin stripping cabinets this morning. Once you decide on appliances and such, I'll get to work on the rest."

"I want to switch to an electric stove."

"No problem. I'll get the gas company to cap the line."

"The refrigerator blocks the traffic pattern where it is now. Could the new one go on the other side of the pantry door?"

"Don't know why not. Used to sit there."

"You know this house?"

"Been in it a time or two."

He tore a page from his notepad and handed it to her.

"That's the building supply in town. You tell Pud Traywick, Joel Lynch said to give you his builder's discount. Best try Wasik's for the fridge and such. Discount place on the highway might be cheaper, but they make it up in delivery charges."

"Thank you for the suggestions. I'm surprised you were able to come so quickly, Mr. Lynch."

"Appreciate if you'd make it Joel," he said, retracting his measuring tape. "This kinda work used to be a sideline. These days, I only take on a job when the spirit moves me. 'Sides, I'm just returning a favor. Reed Jordan untangled some paperwork when I retired a while back."

"What sort of work did you do?"

"Sheriff's department."

"Miz Mid's here," Lexie said from the doorway, careful to keep a safe distance between herself and the paunchy man with thinning gray hair. She and Mrs. McCowan had settled matters of proper address the evening before.

Nicki walked the contractor out through the garage. He nodded to Mid, who declined his offer to carry her suitcases inside, and said he'd be back as soon as he picked up supplies.

"I have to go into Rockwall," Nicki told Mid once her things had been stored in the room above the garage. "I'll try not to be gone too long."

"No rush. Lexie can help me empty kitchen cabinets before the contractor gets back. There's no use cleaning downstairs till he's done, but I can start on the upstairs after lunch. I saw fifth-generation dust bunnies under the beds."

"I didn't see any bunnies in my room," Lexie protested.

Smiling, Nicki started into the garage, but turned back.

"Mid, are geraniums hard to grow?"

"Heavens, no. Any nursery will have them already potted."

"There's a concrete slab next to the swing frame

in the side yard. Do you know what it was used
for?"

"I don't remember anything in the yard except
trees and grass. Those things must have come
later."

Nicki climbed into the Blazer.

"Take your time," Mid called. "With Mr. Lynch
taking over the kitchen, I'm planning sandwiches
for lunch."

Nicki stuffed the nursery receipt into her purse on
top of the warranties from Wasik's and the delivery
order from the building supply. Her head was spinning from decisions . . . white or almond appliances . . . matching fronts or black glass panels
. . . butcher-block or Formica counters . . . con-
tinuous vinyl or tiles for the floor. And who would
have thought there were so many shades of white
paint . . . dotted Swiss, pearly mist, ivory frost
. . . the list was endless.

Thank God the color decision at the nursery had
been a snap, she thought, glancing at the large clay
pot cradled in a box on the seat beside her. Bright
clusters of scarlet petals and green leaves. *Red 'raniums*.

Nearing the turnoff for Upper T, she ran over the
mental list she'd made on the way into town, certain she'd forgotten something. Wasik's, the building supply, the nursery . . .

Lexie's shoelaces. And the lubricant for the
porch-window handles. She'd meant to pick up another loaf of bread, too. Sandwiches might be their
main fare for a while. Joel Lynch had warned the
stove might be out of service for a day or two if the
gas man and the electrician couldn't coordinate
their schedules.

She began watching for the billboard Reed had pointed out as a landmark for Shore Drive, the scenic road that circled the shoreline not accessed by Lower T. The convenience store at the juncture of both county roads would probably have what she needed.

A sign at the three-way intersection read PINE CROSSING—UNINCORPORATED. On an electrical pole, a forest of arrows pointed the way to a bed-and-breakfast, a beauty-and-gift shop, a Best Western motel, a veterinarian, and other points of interest. Motor craft and sailboats with furled masts bobbed at anchor along the marina's E-shaped dock.

Across from the marina, one end of a clapboard duplex advertised a bait-and-tackle business. The other touted lawn care and mower repair. Bob Stockton's S & S SERVICES logo was wood-burned into a redwood plank above the second door.

The grocery, a mishmash of construction, occupied the third side of the Y. A modern facade and a banner of pink neon script that flashed MARQUET'S MARKET did little to camouflage the building's various additions. She found a parking spot in the store's side lot and stepped from the outside humidity into the refreshingly cool interior.

As she entered, the screen brushed a cluster of small brass bells above the door, filling the air with music. Nicki felt a strange surge of childish anticipation at the sound.

Despite the pink neon outside, the store's dim interior projected a mom-and-pop atmosphere. A cluster of old-fashioned pickle barrels held jumbled displays of batteries, poison ivy lotions, and allergy medications. Beyond the barrels, a large chalkboard listed weekly specials. Yellowed photographs in cheap frames lined the wall behind the checkout counter.

The middle-aged man at the register looked up briefly and smiled, then continued ringing up purchases. Nicki slipped a shopping basket over her arm and began browsing.

She found the bread in the second aisle. A brief search uncovered the other items she needed. The aroma of ripening fruit drew her to a row of wooden baskets along the back wall. Shopping here was more fun than at an impersonal chain store, Nicki thought, waiting while a chatty teenage girl weighed her fresh peaches and bright purple plums and scribbled a price in green crayon on the brown paper sacks.

An ancient freezer case had been wedged between the modern meat cooler and the checkout counter. Nicki lifted the scarred plastic cover and bent to scan the offerings.

Frosty icicles pricked her nostrils. Sharp pain streaking behind her eyes accompanied the blast of icy air. She moved aside to allow a woman and her young son to make their selection.

"Lime ones, Mommy. They're my favorites."

The child's words seemed to echo in Nicki's thoughts. Once again she felt the same surreal detachment she'd experienced when she'd pulled into her drive at the lake, as if she were watching the moment from another dimension.

The little boy grinned up at her as his mother let him down. Nicki found herself unable to respond, torn between the need to hold on to reality and an emotional hunger for something she couldn't pin down. She gripped the freezer case, grounding herself against the intense rush of confusing emotion.

As suddenly as it had begun the feeling passed,

leaving her weak-kneed. Still clinging to the case with one hand, she raised the other to her eyes, jerking it away as she touched her face. Her fingers were cold, their tips coated with bits of frost. Shivering, she dropped the freezer's lid.

Where were these weird reactions coming from? Could she have some illness that hadn't shown up during the long-overdue physicals she and Lexie had had before leaving Texas? Nicki wondered vaguely. A lifelong aversion to doctors and hospitals made her push the thought aside. One medical visit a year was still one too many.

Delayed stress. That's all it was, she thought, remembering the magazine article she'd mentioned to Mid. Military personnel weren't its only victims. Lexie's response to the trauma with Odell and the resulting upheaval in their lives had been a sudden aversion to men. It was only natural to have some type of reaction herself. She was tired, stressed out from so many changes in such a short time. And maybe still a little scared. Both she and Lexie just needed time to adjust. She took a deep breath and headed for the busy checkout counter.

The conversation between the shoppers ahead of her ranged from the humidity that lingered from Saturday night's rain to Detroit's chances for the American League pennant. Now and then the bells over the screen door tinkled an arrival or departure. Nicki studied the old photos on the wall as she waited her turn.

The oldest picture, its sepia tones faded and creased with lines, appeared to have been taken in front of an earlier version of the current store. A somber-faced man stood with one foot on the running board of a twenties-era truck. Beside him were two half-grown children and a woman whose white apron did little to hide an obvious pregnancy. Painted on the truck's wooden rails was MARQUET'S PRODUCE—BEST PRICES ON THE LAKE—FREE DELIVERY.

Later photos documented that the owner's competitive streak had passed to the next generation. Nicki smiled at one snapshot of an enterprising business challenging the market's territory. A crudely lettered sign propped on a wooden crate offered LEMMANAID—1¢ A GLASS. The smile on the entrepreneur, a small boy in striped shirt and short pants, revealed missing front teeth. Behind the child, a poster in the store's plate-glass window urged customers to SUPPORT OUR TROOPS. BUY WAR BONDS.

The line moved up, and conversation switched to a local politician's shortcomings. Nicki's eyes strayed back to the remaining pictures.

Sepia and black and white had given way to color prints. In one, taken on the steps of yet another incarnation of the building, a knot of youngsters in the bell-bottoms and tie-dyed shirts of the protest era vied for the camera's attention. She let her eyes slide over the laughing faces, drawn to a preteen girl standing somewhat apart from the others, her arms crossed, a defiant expression creasing her chubby baby face.

Suddenly the photo seemed to telescope outward, the young girl's eyes beseeching Nicki, drawing her into the picture. The girl's features blurred as if dirt had been thrown against the glass but the eyes still pierced Nicki's consciousness. A claustrophobic darkness blurred her peripheral vision. Fighting for breath she turned, stumbling blindly into a soft-drink case as the blackness claimed her.

*   *   *

"Drink. It's okay. It's just water."

"What happened?" Nicki murmured, struggling to sit up. Somehow, she realized, she'd gotten outside. She was lying on the market's raised wooden porch. Several concerned faces peered at her from above. Clay Verdell's was one of them.

"You fainted," Clay said. "When I got to you, your arms and hands were like ice. I carried you out here to warm up."

"Should I call someone? A doctor, maybe?" the man who'd been running the register asked.

Nicki shook her head vehemently, instantly regretting the sudden movement.

"I'll be okay in a minute," she told the store owner.

The man looked dubious.

"Honestly. I'm fine. Please go back to your customers."

"I'll stay with her," Clay assured him.

The other people hovering over her got into their cars or followed the owner back inside.

"This is embarrassing. I can't imagine what came over me."

"Have you had anything to eat today?"

"Some juice." She sipped the water Clay had urged on her.

"That's not food. As thin as you are, it's a wonder you don't pass out on a regular schedule. Let me buy you lunch."

"Mid has sandwiches waiting."

"Mid?"

"My . . . a friend who's helping me with the house."

He looked at her closely, his lips pursed. Nicki looked away. She struggled to get up, suddenly aware her purse must still be inside at the bottom of her shopping basket.

"I have to get my things."

"Stay put. I'll get them."

He was gone before she could protest. She raised her face to catch the sun's warmth. Her rescuer had been right. She felt as if she'd been sleeping in the freezer case. Goose bumps covered her arms despite the fact that she must have been outside several minutes. *What had happened to her in there?*

Clay thought she'd fainted. Had she? What had she been doing just before the world went black? With a growing sense of dismay, she realized she couldn't remember. She had a vague sense of having moved from the ice-cream case to the counter, but after that . . . nothing.

"Here's your purse. And your groceries. Are you up to walking to my car? I'll drive you home."

"There's no need for that. Just let me sit here a bit longer and I'll be fine. What do I owe you for the groceries?"

"Not a thing. I'm growing tomatoes and cucumbers in your garden. One sack of food is cheap rent."

She smiled, warmed by the unaccustomed friendliness of a neighbor who barely knew her name.

"I wouldn't sit here too long," Clay said. "Your Popsicles are probably beginning to melt already."

"I didn't buy Popsicles."

"Sure you did. They were right on top of the produce."

"Raspberries!"

"No. Peaches and plums. The guy at the register checked to be sure they weren't bruised."

"I was referring to the Popsicles."

He opened the grocery sack.

"These are lime. Did you mean to get raspberry?"

"I didn't mean to get them at all. Someone must have put them in my basket by mistake. Raspberries is just something I say when I get mad."

Nicki looked up at his sudden intake of breath. His eyes were guarded.

"It's a nice safe swearword when you've got kids around. They mimic everything you say."

The store owner interrupted the conversation as he returned to check on her. Clay, his voice strangely subdued, held out the frozen treats.

"Someone put these in Mrs. Prevot's basket by mistake," he said.

"I'll be happy to take them back," the merchant told Nicki. "But you put them in the basket yourself. I looked up while you were standing there at the freezer case. I remember thinking you must really like Popsicles. Your face was lit up like a kid's."

Nicki opened her mouth but nothing came out. She reached for the Popsicles and put them back in the sack, a memory of frosty fingertips suddenly fresh in her mind.

"Of course, I just forgot for a moment."

She stood up, relieved to find she still could.

"My . . . friend's waiting lunch."

"Sure you don't want me to drive you?" Clay asked again.

Nicki shook her head, clutching the grocery sack and her purse tightly. She dug the car keys from the pocket of her slacks.

"All right, but take it easy. I'll be right behind you."

Her hands were still trembling as she unlocked the door of the Blazer. Having someone follow her was probably a good idea. It was impossible to predict what strange action she might take next. After all, she'd bought a treat she hadn't craved since childhood . . . in a flavor she couldn't remember buying before.

......13......

He pulled into the garage slowly. Carrying his purchases into the house, he allowed himself a yawn. Sleep had been long in coming the night before. Even the most prized film in his collection hadn't provided the release he sought. The child kept intruding.

Lexie. He said the name aloud, twisting the inflection until the syllables fell naturally from his lips with no hint of the images they produced. And then there was Nicki.

He thought about Nicki's face as she'd carried in her groceries a moment ago. She was obviously hiding something. He'd have to watch her closely till he learned what it was. If the alarm niggling at the back of his mind turned out to be more than a suspicion . . .

If Nicki Prevot turned out to be an impostor, he'd deal with the problem, he told himself as he went to his room to change.

The light on the answering machine beside the bed was blinking furiously. Ignoring it, he carried his things to the laundry, then punched the button and listened. The second message made him stare thoughtfully at the instrument. His fingers strayed to his face, tugging unconsciously at the wiry hairs on his lip.

He stretched naked on the bed and closed his eyes, ignoring the remaining calls. Attending Gwyn's party could be a safe way to learn more about Nicki. Lexie would be with a sitter. Little chance of an unguarded expression revealing his emotion. Once again his fingers tweaked his mustache.

Could he maintain the facade he'd perfected if Nicki let something slip? Some tiny clue that only he would recognize?

Cool air wafted over his body, drying the perspiration that prickled his forehead. Friday was a long way off. Plenty of time to make a decision. He reached out a hand to replay the messages he'd missed.

▪▪▪▪▪▪14▪▪▪▪▪▪

"**W**asik's called. They had a cancellation and wanted to bring the appliances out late this afternoon."

"We need the electrician and the gas company first," Nicki protested, dropping the grocery sack onto the only spot on the dining room table not covered by items from the kitchen cabinets.

Joel Lynch stuck his head through the pass-through.

"Caught the gas man in the neighborhood this morning. Line's already capped. Electrician said he'd be by day after tomorrow. You can plug the fridge into the outlet in the garage for now. I know a couple of husky young fellas I can get to bring it in when we're ready."

"Joel noticed ice cream dripping from the freezer," Mid explained. "He thinks the lower section will be all right till Wasik's delivers. I asked Devon Rheams next door to store the frozen things. She and Lexie just carried the last of them over."

Mid stopped rearranging the items on a large walnut tray and looked more closely at Nicki.

"Are you all right? You look a little pale."

Nicki turned away and began emptying the groceries onto the table. Glimpses of the quiet water glistening in the sunlight on the drive home and the friendly waves from lake residents she passed had buoyed her spirits, putting the market episode into perspective. The closer she'd gotten to her own house, the more trivial the whole thing seemed. Clay Verdell had been right. She really needed to pay more attention to her eating habits.

"I'm just hungry. And a little tired."

"You should have eaten something this morning. Lexie and I made tuna salad for lunch. She insisted we wait for you," Mid said, looking at her watch. "It's after one. I'll put these things away and fix some sandwiches."

She reached for the perishable items on the table. The front screen door slammed, then opened and shut again quietly.

"Popsicles," Lexie squealed, entering the room with Devon. She raced over to examine the box.

Behind them, the contractor cleared his throat.

"I'm 'bout ready to start sanding cabinets. You folks might want to get what you need from the kitchen and move outside for a spell. I've hung plastic in the doorway and taped the pass-through, but it's gonna get pretty dusty."

"Lexie, go up and get your suit on," Mid said. "Devon's going to join us for a picnic. We'll let her put these with the rest of our frozen things and have them after your swim."

She handed the Popsicles to Devon. Lexie continued staring at the picture on the box.

"How come they're green?" she asked.

"Haven't you ever had a lime Popsicle?" Devon asked.

Lexie shook her head.

"Sometimes it's good to try new things," Nicki

said quickly. Lexie shrugged, then raced off to change.

Nicki followed Mid into the ravaged kitchen, startled by the contractor's accomplishments. Every cabinet had been completely stripped of paint. She murmured her surprise to Mid while Joel was getting his sanding equipment from his truck.

"He got back about eight forty-five and started painting some sort of foul-smelling remover on them. A little later three teenagers showed up with rubber gloves and putty knives and went to work. When the whole thing was done, Joel handed each one a receipt for a Sea Doo rental and reminded them they'd be answering to him if they got rowdy. I'll say one thing, the man knows how to deal with kids."

"He'll meet his match in Lexie."

"Oh, you'd be surprised. They had a nice little chat before the crowd showed up," Mid told her. "Long-distance, of course. She hung in the doorway while he manned the paintbrush and fielded all sorts of questions."

Something in the older woman's voice made Nicki glance at her sharply. Mid was staring out the garage door, a bemused smile lighting her eyes. She shook her head and maneuvered around Nicki and the disconnected stove toward the refrigerator.

"You probably think I'm crazy for insisting on an electric stove," Nicki told her. "Everyone always raves about gas."

"I figured you had a bad experience as a child, or your mother went overboard with warnings about pilot lights."

"Renee . . . my mother didn't do much cooking. And I don't think I've ever seen a gas explosion or fire. I'd remember something like that, wouldn't I?"

"Memories like that can fade over time. And some kids find it's easier to forget scary things."

She handed Nicki the tuna salad and a plastic-wrapped plate of vegetables and dip. Grabbing a pitcher of lemonade, she marched into the dining room for the tray, already loaded with the rest of the picnic supplies. Nicki followed, eyeing the pitcher. Lemonade reminded her of something . . .

"My strap's twisted, Mommy," Lexie complained at her elbow.

By the time she'd solved Lexie's problem, the elusive thread of thought had skittered away.

A pair of warring blue jays in one of the oaks drowned out the muted, angry-hornet sound of Joel Lynch's sander. Nicki lay back in one of the lounge chairs Devon had carried over from her patio and sighed. She really needed to buy her own lawn furniture. That is, if she ever found the energy to move. Hunger was certainly no longer a problem. Two sandwiches. She hadn't eaten two helpings of anything in . . . well, in a long time.

Mid had changed into a swimming suit, declaring that her cleaning abilities couldn't compete with the whirlwind being stirred up in the kitchen. She and Lexie were exploring the shallows along the Tarleton shoreline. Devon lay in a second lounger, dozing over a paperback book.

If this is what people mean by living a life of ease, I'm going to savor every minute, Nicki thought. *Anything this peaceful can't last forever.* She closed her eyes.

As if putting thought to action, a motor roared to life nearby.

"Old Bob's doing Del Ferris's place today," Devon

murmured through a yawn. She raised the back of her chair and tossed her book aside.

"People really call him that?"

"Uh-huh. Especially the kids. Except his own, of course."

"He's married?"

"Divorced. It must be . . . I don't know . . . ten, twelve years. His girls haven't visited for ages."

"What happened?"

"I don't think anyone really knows. His wife wasn't from around here. He married late, and she was much younger. The family used to visit his parents every summer when the factory shut down for two weeks . . . before the divorce.

"Rumor is, things got really nasty. The wife didn't want him to have visitation. She married some Grosse Pointe surgeon three months later. Old Bob chucked everything in Detroit soon after that and threw in with his dad. Keeps to himself socially. Gun-shy, I guess. You get that way after a divorce."

"Have you always lived around Rockwall?"

"Pretty much. We spent summers on the lake till I was twelve. After that, we stayed in town year-round."

Nicki caught movement out of the corner of her eye and turned to see Del Ferris climbing the hillside to his garden plot. Her eyes settled on the inverted U-shaped frame in the yard.

"Where did you live when you came to the lake?"

"Rental houses. Mostly the ones down by the marina. The cheap seats, my mother called them. Daddy said it didn't matter if we staked a claim in the bleachers, as long as he could go fishing after work every evening. He was office manager for a CPA firm in Grand Rapids."

"Did you ever rent near here?"

Devon rubbed the untanned circle on her ring finger.

"That last summer we rented the place the Greenlees own now. Mother said she wanted to live like the rich folks did just once in her life. We moved back to town after a month."

Nicki caught the bitter note in Devon's voice and decided not to pursue the issue.

"Do you remember the swing set in this yard? Or the cement slab beside it?"

"I remember a swing. And some other apparatus. A trapeze, maybe."

"Rings," Nicki said, startled to realize she'd translated into words the hazy image that had flashed through her mind.

"That's right. Have you seen a picture of them?"

"Lucky guess," Nicki murmured, shaking her head. She wondered if Devon's question was valid. Renee's life . . . so sterile, so devoid of the trappings most people collected. Had there once been photographs and memorabilia? A past suddenly erased . . . declared as off-limits as any discussion of Nicki's paternal heritage?

"What about the slab?"

"That I don't remember. But there *was* something there."

"What about the people who lived here?"

"The house wasn't occupied that summer. At least not the few weeks we were here. Daddy warned us about trespassing."

She rubbed a finger along her temple.

"I remember now. Old Bob's father caught a bunch of us in the yard and chased us off. We were peering in the windows of the playhouse. The slab must be the old foundation."

A playhouse. With a wooden railing around its miniature porch, Nicki thought suddenly, the image now vivid in her mind. Like a photograph, its colors still as fresh as they must have been so long ago when she first saw it. Before Renee uncluttered their lives.

Mid and Lexie had returned, their hands full of treasures collected during their tour of the undeveloped waterfront.

"Miz Mid says it's from one of the baby ducks," Lexie said, holding out a bit of feathery down. "I'm gonna find a special place to keep it. I'm gonna keep *all* my special things there."

Nicki gathered Lexie in her lap, ignoring the dripping swimsuit. Lexie's concern about the safety of her treasures was understandable. Most of the things she'd held dear lay buried amid the rubble of the gutted apartment. She kissed the top of her daughter's wet hair.

"That's a terrific idea, Lexie. I think everyone should keep their childhood memories in a special place."

Lexie squirmed around as if to crawl off the lounger, then quickly resettled even more tightly in her mother's arms.

"Thought I'd make another payment on my garden rent," Del Ferris said as he held out a plastic sack.

Nicki, wearing her clinging daughter like a second skin, twisted around to thank him and to introduce Mid. The older woman took the vegetables and excused herself to check on the contractor's progress. Lexie watched warily as Del took the chair the housekeeper had just vacated.

"Did your bunny eat the carrot?" he asked her.

"No."

"Maybe you didn't leave it in the right place. Sometimes bunnies have a favorite spot." He reached into the pocket of his tan coveralls. "I brought him another one."

"Thank you." She loosened her death grip on Nicki long enough to take the carrot from his hand.

"Would you like me to help you look for the right spot?"

Lexie bit her lip and leaned forward to check her mother's reaction. Nicki smiled her encouragement.

"Sometimes they like to sit along fences. Like over there," he said, indicating the boundary of the Tarleton land.

Nicki watched the indecision on her daughter's face as she eyed the high fence.

"I'll be right here, Lexie. If you find where he sits, you'll know where to watch for him."

Curiosity won. Lexie scrambled down and followed Del, making an obvious effort to maintain a comfortable distance between them. Devon, silent till now, spoke softly once the pair were engrossed in examining the ground along the fence.

"She really doesn't like men, does she?"

Nicki quietly sketched the history of Lexie's withdrawal.

"She even connected Clay Verdell's car with the one in the alley because they're similar in color."

"Poor baby. It's a shame you weren't able to get away from there sooner."

Nicki ignored the implied question about her lifestyle change. Lexie and Del were bending over a low spot of ground midway down the chain-link barrier, much closer to each other than Nicki would have expected Lexie to allow. After a moment, Lexie scampered back to the semicircle of chairs.

"There's this place? Where the grass is all squished? Mr. Ferris says that's where the bunny sits. 'Cause there's fur."

She paused to take a breath.

"We left the cawwot. Mr. Ferris says if I'm real quiet the bunny might come out when it starts getting dark."

Del murmured something about checking on the progress of his yard and excused himself. Lexie waved a spirited good-bye. Devon sent her to retrieve a checkers set she'd seen in the dining room, and soon both heads were bent over the game board. Nicki settled more comfortably on the lounger and closed her eyes.

Supporting Lexie's body with one hand, Devon waved to Clay with the other. Lexie sensed the movement and opened her eyes.

"Learning to float on your back can be harder than learning to swim. You're doing great. Just relax a little more, I'm not going to let you sink."

Clay entered the water with a clean surface dive and began stroking toward the raft. His powerful arms left minimal wake. Devon concentrated on Lexie's suspended body until he reached the ladder, then raised her eyes as he rose from the water.

He certainly had great legs, she thought, despite the angry scars marring his thighs. And a terrific tan. And a nice little tush. She felt herself flush. Such scandalous musings from a supposedly staid kindergarten teacher. And in the presence of a future student. One thing was clear. Her sexuality hadn't died with her marriage.

"Let's swim out to the raft," she said, lowering Lexie's legs into the water.

Lexie's face lit up, then fell as she noticed Clay. She shook her head. Devon bent until they were face-to-face.

"Lexie, you know I'm your friend." The little girl nodded. "And you know I wouldn't let anyone hurt you."

A second nod, tiny lips pressed tightly together.

"Well, Mr. Verdell's my friend, too, and it makes me sad when my friends can't be friends with each other. Couldn't you try to like him, just a little? He's really nice. And he knows lots of things about animals and fish."

Lexie contemplated the figure on the raft.

"Does he know about bunnies?"

"I'm sure he does. Why don't we ask him?" She held out her hand. "I'll be with you every minute."

Still Lexie hesitated.

"Would you rather wait with your mom? We could play another game of checkers when I come back."

The dark eyes glanced back toward where her mother slept on the lounge chair. She shook her head, then held out her hand.

Nicki sat up with a start, awakened by Lexie's squeals. Masculine laughter boomed across the water. Her mouth dropped as Clay Verdell rose from a crouch, catapulting Lexie from his shoulders into a dive across the open space between himself and Devon. Devon waited until Lexie had surfaced and flung the water from her eyes, then sent her back toward Clay.

The toss was short and this time Lexie forgot to close her mouth. She came up sputtering, reaching out to Clay and wrapping her arms around his neck. He carried her toward shallow water.

"I think that's the signal we've had enough," Devon called, wading after them.

"Nooooo. Once more, please?" Lexie pleaded, bouncing up and down in Clay's arms.

Nicki stared at her daughter in amazement. Devon waved to her to join them.

"Mommy, watch me."

"Okay," Clay told her. "One more for your mom. Then you have to play quietly for a little while so we old folks can catch our breath. Deal?"

"Deal."

Once more Lexie became a guided missile between the two adults. When Devon had returned her to Clay, successfully this time, he pointed toward shore. Lexie frowned, then shrugged and, making a huge production of the action, splashed back toward the cove steps.

"Which one of you cast the spell?" Nicki asked.

"Don't look at me. I just convinced her Clay didn't bite. He's the one who won her over."

"Must have been something to do with the minnows I caught in my hands," Clay said with a grin.

"You *do* have mystical powers."

"It's all in the timing. She's a great kid." He hoisted himself onto the edge of the seawall, leaving his feet dangling in the water. "You look like you're feeling better."

"Mid fixed a great lunch," Nicki said, forestalling Devon's questions with a quick explanation. "I skipped breakfast and got a little dizzy while I was shopping."

Mid came out to tell Nicki that Joel had finished sanding and Wasik's had called to say they'd deliver in about an hour.

"Let's have those Popsicles before they get here," Devon said, eliciting enthusiastic approval from Lexie. She shooed Mid to a chair and ran home to get the treats. Nicki and Clay joined the house-keeper. Lexie allowed Mid to wrap her in a towel, then sprawled on the grass in front of the adults.

Even Mid enjoyed herself when Devon returned.

"I like green ones, Mommy."

Nicki smiled contentedly.

"I'd forgotten how good they were," she said, catching a melting drop with her tongue. "It's like I had a craving and never realized it."

She glanced up to find Clay's dark eyes locked on her face. He looked away, but not before she experienced the same disturbing familiarity she'd felt when they'd first met.

Bob Stockton ambled across the grass from the direction of Del's house and knelt beside Clay. He reached out and tugged a lock of Lexie's wet hair. She dropped her Popsicle stick in the grass, shrugged off her towel, and scrambled back into the lake.

"Skittish little thing," Stockton said, turning back to Clay. "Got my winch working again. Figured I'd tackle that old stump you want out after I finish here tomorrow, if that's okay."

"Sounds fine to me," Clay told him.

When the yardman disappeared, Lexie came out of the water and wandered over to check on the carrot she'd left by the fence.

"Were you as shy as Lexie at that age?" Clay asked suddenly.

"I don't know. I don't remember myself at Lexie's age."

"How old are you in your earliest memories?" he asked.

"Six or seven, I guess. I remember starting school."

"And before that?" Devon asked.

Nicki looked away without answering, suddenly disturbed by the direction of the conversation.

"You must have *some* memories," Clay insisted. "What about learning to roller-skate or ride a bike?"

"I think I remember learning to swim. Renee said I took to water like salmon to a spawning stream."

The conversation with her mother had taken place after a grade-school slumber party. Nicki's classmates had been swapping childhood stories. For the first time, she'd learned that other people had clear pictures of their early years. The realization had sent questions ricocheting about in her head. Voicing them had produced little response . . . only an offhand reference to her early swimming experiences and a disjointed lecture about concentrating on the future instead of the past.

For Renee, who flitted from one thing to another like a nervous butterfly, the abrupt change of subjects was normal. Her emphasis on the future was not. Renee had lived her life in the present. At the time, Nicki had swallowed her disappointment and abandoned her attempts to recall anything from early childhood.

"Do you think you actually remember learning to swim, or just the image created by what you were told?" Clay asked, the intensity of his deep voice breaking into her thoughts.

"I don't know. I've never really thought about it."

"Maybe you should," he said softly.

She wanted to ask why he cared what images her memory had produced or why it seemed so important, but she was suddenly uncomfortable with the discussion. Still aware of his penetrating gaze, she groped for a different subject. Clay himself came to her rescue.

"I had a message on my machine from Gwyn Chamberlin when I got in from the store. She's throwing together one of her dinner parties Friday night."

"I know. She called me this morning," Devon said. "Nicki's going, too."

"I haven't really decided," Nicki protested. "Lexie . . ."

". . . will be fine with me," Mid insisted, joining the conversation. "Gwyn Chamberlin's been the lake's premier hostess for decades. You can't tell her no."

"Besides that, I won't let you miss one of Ichiro Tanaka's performances," Devon said.

"Gwyn's Japanese cook," Clay explained. "Miko, his wife, says he does his best work when he has an audience. She's a part-time housekeeper, mostly for bachelors like me. Claims our places could never be as messy as a house with five kids."

"Her wages pay those kids' tuition to private school. Miko will be there Friday night. She always serves Gwyn's parties."

"I still don't know. All I have is casual clothes."

"Typical female complaint. 'I don't have a *thing* to wear.'"

"Chauvinist," Devon chided. "Where were you when the women's movement began? Another planet?"

"Yes!"

A loud snap accompanied his venomous retort. The three women jerked their heads around. Clay was staring vacantly across the lake, his left index finger tracing a jagged scar on his thigh. Clenched in the whitened knuckles of his other hand were the broken halves of his Popsicle stick.

The clang of a truck's tailgate broke the silence. "That'll be Wasik's," Mid murmured.

Devon whispered to Nicki as Lexie ran up to display a pine cone she'd uncovered.

"There's a new boutique in Rockwall. We'll go shopping."

"Lexie, don't forget what we talked about," Clay said, rising to leave.

Nicki looked at her daughter.

"He's gonna teach me to fish," Lexie announced before racing off to investigate the commotion in the driveway.

Later that evening Reed called to check the progress of the remodeling. His offer to walk her to Gwyn's on Friday evening sounded natural and unforced. She was glad he couldn't see her expression as she hung up the phone.

Every participant in Gwyn's little production seemed to have fallen right in line. The local matchmaker had done her work well. Nicki hoped she could steer the conversation toward a discussion of her home's previous owners and away from any inquiries about the status of her love life.

Exhausted by her water aerobics, Lexie had succumbed to sleep earlier than usual. Mid had remained upstairs after tucking her in. Nicki turned out the lights, suddenly eager to curl into her bed on the sleeping porch and listen to the waves washing the shore. She, too, was asleep in minutes.

▬▬▬▬▬▬15▬▬▬▬▬

"Try this one," Devon said, dangling yet another outfit over the dressing room's swinging door.

"I love the print, but isn't the style kind of . . . dated?"

"So dated it's 'in' again. According to the magazines out front, sixties fashions are hot."

Devon wandered back to the front of the store to scan the jewelry rack. Many of the items marked "exclusive design" were expensive rip-offs of the bead-and-leather creations she'd worn in college years ago.

Funny how so many things reminded her of the past lately. Ever since Nicki had asked about that old playhouse, bits and pieces of those last weeks at the lake had slipped unbidden into her thoughts.

Unlike Nicki's cloudy vision of her childhood, some of her own memories were quite vivid, especially since her divorce. She wondered if her parents' acknowledgment of the death of her marriage had brought back to them the bitter exchange of words that accompanied their own announcement that humid afternoon of her twelfth summer. Her protest that day—that parents had no right to inflict such pain—had resulted in a determination to remain childless, ironically reinforced by a history of female problems and now her own failed marriage.

Fences had been mended over the years, even if her parents' union had not. Still, as intense as the images were, some details of that day remained indistinct, try as she might to summon them. She tossed her head to clear the cobwebs. If they were of any importance, she reasoned, she wouldn't have forgotten them.

"What do you think?"

She turned and caught her breath.

"I think Reed's a goner."

The jumpsuit had a squared neckline, short loose sleeves, and wide palazzo-pant legs that flowed from a slightly raised waist. Tiny jade rosebuds on a beige background brought out the green highlights in Nicki's hazel eyes.

"You don't think it's too . . . hippie-ish for the party?"

"It's almost perfect. You've got the height an outfit like that needs. And you remind me of . . ." She studied Nicki critically. "Michelle Phillips. She wore something a lot like that in a concert once."

"The actress?" Nicki asked, clearly puzzled.

"Lord, I'm definitely showing my age. She used to sing with the Mamas and the Papas. 'California Dreamin'? 'Words of Love'?" She sighed. "You're probably too young. Take my word for it. She looked terrific, and so do you."

"*Almost* perfect?"

"It needs these," Devon said, draping a stand of multicolored beads around Nicki's neck and rummaging for the matching earrings.

The owner, who'd been trying not to hover, accepted Nicki's check and wrapped the purchases in tissue before sliding them into a bag. Outside, Nicki gave Devon a squeeze.

"This was fun. It's been ages since I've been on a shopping spree with a friend. Thanks for coming with me. I didn't mean to keep putting it off till the last minute."

"We don't have to quit now if you still want to shop."

"I'd rather get home and set up the new lawn furniture."

"Good, then Lexie and I'll have time for our swim."

"And I can help Mid finish cleaning upstairs."

"What's your industrious contractor up to this afternoon?"

"Fitting countertops and stripping wallpaper. He told Mid he'd probably be finished by the middle of next week."

"The man certainly doesn't waste time."

"Tell me about it. He shows up at eight o'clock and never leaves before six. If he was as dedicated in his law enforcement career, the crime rate around here must be pretty low." .

"It is. Or at least it *was.*"

Devon grinned, pointing to the expired parking meter and the ticket beneath the wiper blade of Nicki's Blazer. Laughing, Nicki retrieved the ticket and unlocked the vehicle.

"Are the swings in that box or not, Lexie?" Nicki asked.

"No."

"Then they're certainly not up here," Mid announced. She quit swiping at cobwebs and wiped her forehead. "They must be stored on the open rafters in the garage. We'll have to tackle that another day."

Lexie materialized from the shadows of the attic storage area that extended out from Mid's room. She held out a small wooden plaque covered with bits of knotted cord.

"What's this?"

Nicki started to reach for it, but drew her hand back. Lexie looked at Mid.

"It probably belonged to some child who used to live here. Reed's uncle Donnie had one just like it. He had to learn to tie seamen's knots as part of his sailing classes at the country club. The plaque's a certification award."

"It belongs in the green bedroom," Nicki said abruptly.

She led the way past Lexie's room with its canopied bed to the room directly across the hall, hesitating on the threshold.

"There," Nicki said, pointing to an exposed nail. Lexie and Mid pushed into the room. Nicki, still standing in the hall, lowered her trembling finger.

"I cleaned in here and still didn't put it together, Nicki. You're really clever," Mid exclaimed, taking the plaque from Lexie and hooking it over the nail. "See, Lexie? The room has a nautical theme. The mirror frame is a ship's wheel, and the headboard posts are oars."

One of the baths that opened onto the hall had stolen its area from the bedroom, leaving a perfect sleeping alcove beneath the eaves. Nicki's eyes dropped to the bed that completely filled the narrow space. Lexie had crawled across the uncovered mattress to examine the headboard and now lay staring up at the sailor's knots on the adjacent wall.

"Get off the bed, Lexie," Nicki said sharply.

Lexie giggled and flung her head from side to side in refusal.

"I said get off!"

Mid laid a hand on Nicki's arm. Lexie's lower lip trembled as she scooted from the bed.

An irrational feeling of panic kept Nicki from apologizing. Her punishment was the onset of a piercing headache. She raised her hands to massage her throbbing temples.

"If you're going to go swimming with Devon, you better get changed, Lexie," Mid said softly, murmuring a suggestion to Nicki that she lie down for a while.

Nicki glanced back at the unknown seaman's display of craftsmanship as she turned to leave. Realization struck as abruptly as her headache, knotting her insides as tightly as the individual bits of cord.

She couldn't have known about the bedroom's nautical motif—not until Mid pointed it out. Since the night she'd arrived, she'd been unconsciously avoiding that particular bedroom.

"Don't you look pretty," Mid exclaimed as Nicki paused in the kitchen doorway. Joel Lynch looked up from nailing a section of quarter round and smiled his concurrence.

"Thank you. Where's Lexie?"

"Over at Devon's, helping her get ready," Mid said.

"Joel, there's a cement slab in the side yard . . ."

"Used to be a playhouse."

"You remember it?" He nodded. "Could you rebuild it when you finish in here? As a surprise for Lexie?"

"I can probably come up with something."

"I want one just like the original."

The contractor rocked back on his heels. Running a hand through his thinning gray hair, he stared at the floor for a moment, then raised his eyes and regarded Nicki thoughtfully.

"Exactly like the old one?"

She nodded, suddenly embarrassed.

"I'll make some sketches. See if we can agree on the design." He picked up his toolbox and turned to Mid. "Be back about seven."

The housekeeper nodded.

"Joel's wife died two years ago, and his son lives in Denver," Mid told Nicki as they watched the contractor back out the drive. "I asked him to come back this evening and play Parcheesi with Lexie and me. I hope you don't mind."

"I think it's a lovely idea."

"Oh, I almost forgot to show you." She led Nicki back to the kitchen and pointed to the newly stripped wall. "One of the previous owners charted their children's growth."

Ollie, 5½, Pip, 3 yrs, Ollie, age 11.

Nicki's eyes traced the various stages of progress for each child. The dozen or so penciled notations were faded, almost indecipherable in places. A trio of darker lines on the bottom half of the wall drew her attention.

"This writing's different. At least what's left of it is."

"Some of the plaster came off with the wallpaper in places."

Nicki rubbed her finger over one of the partially obliterated notations.

"This looks like an *S*, and that's definitely a *Y*."

"Sammy? Or Sherry?"

"Something shorter."

"Sally, maybe," Mid suggested.

Nicki continued to study the wall.

"Did Joel know any of these people?"

"I started to ask him, and then Lexie . . ."

As if to add further explanation, the front screen door slammed and Lexie called out, asking when Reed was coming.

Nicki felt a stab of anxiety. In recent years she defined a social gathering as a barbecue in the Hills' backyard or ice cream and cake for Lexie's birthday. The nearest she'd come to dinner-party conversation had been lunchtime exchanges with coworkers in NorTex National's break room. She slipped into the hallway bath to check her hair.

She'd swept the sides into a loose ponytail, leaving the rest to cascade down her back and over her shoulders. On a whim, she'd braided the flyaway strands on either side of her face. The result, she decided, looked very sixtyish.

Devon, who'd declared she missed having kids around during summer vacations, had been entertaining Lexie each afternoon while Nicki and Mid washed windows and polished floors on the second floor. Years of disuse translated into layers of dirt and throbbing muscles.

A swim each evening had lessened Nicki's aches and burned a few unwanted calories as well. Since the electrician had shown up on Tuesday, Mid had been cooking the type of meals that must have delighted her Oklahoma ranch hands. The first few pounds had been okay; many more and her new clothes would be too tight.

Exhaustion, yet another by-product of the whirlwind labor, had produced blissful, nightmare-free sleep each night. Whether that, in turn, had prevented a recurrence of the strange episodes of déjà vu, Nicki didn't know and didn't care. It was enough that life had settled into a safe, predictable routine.

Today's brief nap had done more than banish her sudden headache and improve her unusually wasp-ish disposition. If not eager for her command performance before the lake's version of Broadway's Dolly Levi, she at least felt refreshed.

"You look pretty, Mommy."

Lexie stood in the doorway, eyes shining. Ashamed of her earlier temperament, Nicki knelt and hugged her tightly.

"I'm sorry I snapped at you. No housecleaning tomorrow. We'll spend the day together, do something special."

"Reed, too?"

"If he doesn't have plans."

"Did I hear someone mention my name?" a familiar masculine voice called out.

Nicki took one last look in the mirror. Reed's reaction when Lexie pulled her into the entryway suggested she needn't have worried.

"Wow," he said softly.

"You look pretty good yourself," Nicki managed to say, taking in his light blue sports jacket and tan Dockers slacks.

Murmuring something about Parcheesi games requiring proper nourishment, Mid ushered Lexie toward the kitchen. Lexie looked back at her mother wistfully. Nicki blew her a kiss.

"It's only six houses," Reed noted. "I thought we'd walk."

The lake breeze ruffled Nicki's hair as they crossed the lawn. Devon and Clay were standing at the end of Devon's dock, watching a water-skier crisscross the wake of the motorboat pulling him. Reed and Nicki waited for the couple to join them.

Shadows from the willow beside the dock softened the intensity of the sun's fading rays.

Clay was dressed similarly to Reed in a navy blazer, gray slacks, and a dress shirt, open at the neck. His steel-gray hair and slight limp added a distinguished elder-statesman touch. He held Devon's arm companionably as they walked, laughing at something she'd said. The teacher looked youthful in a knee-length split skirt and sleeveless blouse, a linen jacket draped casually about her shoulders.

Reed took Nicki's hand, sending a pleasant chill up her arm as they stepped back into the sunlight. She smiled at the other two partygoers. Clay stumbled momentarily and dropped Devon's arm, then recovered and stared at Nicki.

"I told you you'd have men falling at your feet," Devon said with a laugh, turning to her escort. "Isn't she smashing?"

"Smashing," Clay echoed, his voice barely audible.

"Well, we'd best be off to see the wizard," Reed said.

"The wizard?"

"Ichiro Tanaka, master of the Ginsu, ruler of the blade."

"Emperor of the cutlass," Devon added, giggling. "Chieftain of the chopsticks."

Clay had nothing to add to the banter. Reed led the way along the shore, chatting about the marvels Gwyn's chef was likely to create. As they neared the Greenlees' unoccupied house, a shore bird wading in the shallows rose into the air with a startled cry. Nicki glanced back to track its flight and caught

Clay watching her. He looked away quickly, following the bird's path. Even after they continued on, Nicki could sense his eyes once again riveted on the back of her head.

16

G wyn, wearing bright pink hostess pajamas, welcomed them onto the deck. Electric Japanese lanterns waved gently in the breeze. Miko Tanaka, her black hair piled high, drifted between the cushioned seating areas, unobtrusively taking drink orders.

"Looks like we beat the crowd," Reed said. "Who's missing?"

"The Nielsons, the Cravenses, and Del Ferris. Betsy Nielson had relatives show up unannounced this morning. Dawn Cravens called an hour ago from the emergency room. Reg broke his collarbone roughhousing with that monstrosity they call a dog."

"Six people make a nice party," Devon told her.

"Five. Del called right after Dawn. His twenty-four-hour assignment took two days. He's sitting in an airport, waiting for a flight. I tried to get Joel Lynch to fill in at the last minute, but he already had plans."

"I'm afraid Mid . . . the friend who's helping me with the house . . . got to him first."

Gwyn raised her eyebrows.

"Smart lady, your Mid."

Reed caught Devon and Nicki exchanging

amused looks. Miko brought the drinks, rewarding them with her light tinkling laughter when Clay murmured something in her ear.

"All right, share the joke," Devon told Clay once Miko had left.

"I just asked her how long Ichiro's been holed up in the kitchen with his sharpening steel."

Reed joined the laughter, his reaction tempered somewhat by Nicki's distracted expression. Apprehension about her first social gathering was understandable, but cancellations from the other two couples should have relieved any worries she harbored. Lexie was safely tucked away with Mid. No crack dealers lurked in the shadows. What kept her poised so tensely on the edge of her seat? And why did her gaze keep straying to Clay?

"Relax," he whispered in Nicki's ear.

Her answering smile seemed forced. He shifted his own attention to the other male member of the party. Clay seemed like a decent enough guy. Rather quiet and solitary, but you wouldn't label him antisocial. Of course, he'd only been around a little more than a year.

On the bench seat beside him Nicki shifted position, leaning in to listen to some tale Gwyn was spinning.

She really did look terrific, Reed thought. The braids were a nice touch, and her jewelry and that thing she was wearing . . . the whole look. Like she'd stepped back in time . . . into the decade of Woodstock and love-ins and that flower-power nonsense.

The small talk continued, as did Nicki's nervous glances at Clay.

Clay had been squiring Devon around the last month or so, Reed knew. He couldn't remember ever seeing him with anyone else. And it wasn't as if there weren't other available women out there. He sucked thoughtfully on a chip of ice from his drink. Something about Clay was making Nicki uncomfortable.

Something he'd said or done? A pass maybe. If that was what it was, Nicki obviously hadn't welcomed the overture. She was just beginning to get her life together; still vulnerable, her emotions battered by what had happened in Texas. The last thing she needed was the unwanted attention of some old guy trying to prove he still had it by seducing a younger woman.

Reed slid his arm protectively around the back of the bench railing and dropped his hand lightly on Nicki's shoulder. She jumped at his touch, then turned her head and smiled at him.

"Where was Del off to this time?" Devon asked Gwyn.

"Vancouver. Those formal gardens and flowering window boxes should make wonderful backdrops for a fashion layout. Have you ever been to Canada, Nicki?"

"I'd never been out of Texas till I moved here. Renee . . . my mother often traveled, but I was usually in school."

"Will your mother be visiting this summer?" Gwyn asked.

"She died six years ago."

Clay rose abruptly and crossed the deck to stare toward the lake. Conversation lagged as Miko returned to freshen their drinks.

"We have an unexpected guest," Clay said softly as Miko withdrew once more.

Devon and Gwyn joined him at the rail. Reed

caught Nicki's hand and moved alongside the others, carefully placing himself between her and Clay.

"What is it?" Nicki asked, studying the immense dusty-colored bird wading just offshore.

"A great blue heron," Gwyn said. "Goes fishing about this time every evening.

The huge bird stalked the shallows on spindly legs for several minutes, unperturbed by the audience or the occasional shrieking gull. Finally his awkward movement ceased. Not even a feather quivered. The heron's head darted into the water and instantly reappeared, a struggling fish trapped in his yellowish bill. Spreading his majestic wings, he rose and disappeared into the deepening shadows.

Nicki clapped her hands in delight.

"I wish Lexie could have seen him."

A gong sounded softly. Gwyn ushered them to seats around the massive gas-fired cooking pit where Miko, using a set of tongs, offered all the guests steaming white towels to cleanse their hands. A moment later, she returned and set out a series of small dishes.

Reed grinned as Nicki took her first timid bite of sushi. The others, more familiar with the beautifully sculptured delicacies, dug in with gusto. He helped himself to a crab roll and a bit of the green horseradish that added fire to the traditional appetizers.

"If you really want to expose Lexie to nature, you should take her to Kellogg's," Devon suggested.

"The cereal company?" Nicki asked, clearly confused.

"Same origins, different enterprise," Gwyn told her. "One of the family's philanthropic interests was a bird sanctuary that's now part of Michigan

State University. It's one of the few places you're likely to see a trumpeter these days."

"They were hunted to near-extinction before the turn of the century," Devon explained. "The sanctuary began a restoration project a few years ago."

"Trumpeter swans . . . I thought the lake . . ." Nicki's voice trailed off in embarrassment. Surprisingly, Clay sprang to her defense.

"When I first heard the name, I visualized a statue of Dizzy Gillespie sitting in the harbor. I got teased a lot about that." He turned away to stare across the lake where lights were becoming visible on the far shore.

Miko reappeared with bowls of clear broth enhanced with tiny bits of mushroom and green onion.

"I promised Lexie we'd do something special tomorrow. Is the sanctuary far?"

"About forty minutes," Devon said. "It's down by Gull Lake. I was about Lexie's age the first time my parents took me there."

"Why don't you come with us."

"I'd like to tag along, too. If no one objects."

Reed almost applauded Nicki's success at covering her startled reaction to Clay's self-invitation.

"Why don't we all go? Gwyn?"

Their hostess shook her head.

"I'll settle for hearing Lexie's version of the visit. Next Friday's July first. I thought I'd kick off the long weekend with a neighborhood picnic. We'll include Lexie and your friend Mid in the invitation. 'Course, my little do won't compete with the club bash on the Fourth."

"If your parties don't top the club, it's not because Ichiro isn't trying," Devon said.

Gwyn's cook, in crisply pressed chef's jacket and

matching hat, had joined them silently. His wife followed a few paces behind with a tray containing the various ingredients of their dinner. Reed looked at Nicki and grinned.

Ichiro Tanaka bowed and adjusted the controls on the rectangular cooking surface. Using only a two-tined fork and a combination cleaver-spatula, he slid the contents of various dishes onto the grill. The flat knife began to fly.

Fluffy white rice danced about the griddle. A whole onion spun in the air, landed on the tip of the blade, then plunged back to the cooking surface, disintegrating beneath the onslaught of Ichiro's lightning hands.

Broccoli lost its head. Shrimp mislaid their tails. Zucchini and mushrooms displayed split personalities. When the cleaver finally stopped bobbing and weaving and each guest had been served, Ichiro folded his hands and bowed again. Everyone, including Gwyn, applauded.

The chef beamed his pleasure and adjusted his grill once more. Miko dimmed the lanterns. Pouring a bit of oil on the grill, he added the discarded shrimp tails, and the knife flashed again. Another liquid joined the constantly moving mixture as Ichiro produced a lighter.

Flames shot three feet into the air, lighting the night. Beside him, Reed felt Nicki tremble. Ichiro smothered the fire with a bowl and scraped the charred residue from the grill.

"Enjoy. *Arigato*," he told them, slipping away as Miko brought the lights up again.

"Magnificent," Devon murmured, breaking the silence.

Reed saw Nicki's glazed expression and reached for her hand.

"Hey, you okay?"

In response to his whispered question, her body jerked to rigid attention. She shuddered and turned her head away from the others. After a deep breath, she nodded.

"Isn't he something?" Devon asked.

"I wish somebody had warned me," Nicki murmured.

"His performance is different each time," Clay explained.

Conversation came to a halt while everyone followed the chef's admonishment to "enjoy."

Nicki returned from the powder room after dinner to find Miko once again dimming the lanterns. She and Ichiro bade everyone good-night, leaving the men in charge of the portable bar. Conversation on the deck turned to Gwyn and her travels with her fourth husband.

"Nepal, the Galapagos, the Great Barrier Reef . . . Karl insisted we see it all. Didn't see any reason to mope about after he died. Traveling keeps you young."

"It always wears me out," Devon said with a sigh.

"Makes you appreciate coming home, I'll grant you that. Karl always said, 'When you've grown wise enough, or maybe just ancient enough, your favorite destination becomes the place where you were happiest as a child.' For me, that's right here."

Devon and Reed began comparing childhood memories of the lake. Clay seemed to be listening intently, his fingers locked around a crossed knee. Nicki began to relax. She'd probably imagined his curious fascination with her earlier.

Lights across the water glowed brighter now in the total darkness. The moon was playing hide-and-seek with a bank of cloud cover. Farther down the shore, laughter drifted in from another gathering. Someone's dog barked once, then was silent. Conversation faltered. Nicki turned to Clay.

"I understand you're retired."

"He's too young to retire," Gwyn broke in.

"Actually, I'm on more of a sabbatical. I took some time off . . . to find myself, I suppose you could say."

"I thought that's what your generation did in the sixties," Reed said.

"A few of us flunked that course," Clay said quietly, his expression making it clear the subject was closed.

"I know I'm the stereotypical victim of the generation gap, but I'm glad Karl and I were living abroad during those years. The newspaper reports and letters from home were bad enough. Families we'd known for years split apart. So many bright young minds—wasting their educations, smoking dope and dropping acid, destroying property."

"Down with the establishment," Devon murmured.

"Exactly. And the stupidest things set them off! Pip Sheridan picketed the club one year . . . all because the membership voted to ban bare feet in the dining room. The friend who wrote me about it said no one was surprised. That girl had been fighting authority and championing radical causes since childhood."

"People who want change use whatever form of power is available," Clay said mildly. "Media coverage fueled the frenzy, but the student protests were effective. Good things came out of those years. Changes that were long overdue."

"I won't deny that. Desegregation, women's

rights. All those ridiculous social barriers that needed to come down. I never disagreed with their goals, only the way some of them went about it . . . burning things, planting bombs. I was an early believer in sexual freedom, but making love on the library steps . . . I'm afraid that's where I draw the line."

Nicki caught the twitch of Clay's mustache as he raised a hand to hide a smile. Devon's caterpillar comparison was right on target.

"I didn't protest the war in college," Devon said. "I suppose that makes me a real rebel."

"No, it makes my point. Not everyone believed in burning draft cards and bras," Clay noted.

"But some of the kids who rebelled were so young. The summer Watergate broke, I stayed on campus to begin my graduate work. Mother wrote me about a thirteen-year-old who ran away because she'd been grounded for some minor infraction. When her parents read her diary, it was filled with talk about peace and love and 'being one' with the flower children in San Francisco."

"In my youth you ran away to join the circus. And then only if you were a boy. Not that it didn't cross *my* mind a time or two," Gwyn told them, producing a round of laughter.

"You mentioned someone named Sheridan. Wasn't that one of the families who owned Nicki's house?" Reed asked.

Nicki, who'd been wondering how to redirect conversation, flashed him a grateful smile.

"We found the names Pip and Ollie on a kitchen wall when the contractor stripped the wallpaper."

"Good old Ollie. Now there was a barracuda if I ever knew one."

"Were they brother and sister?" Nicki asked hopefully.

"Olympia and Phillipa Sheridan—their mother spent a year in Greece when she was at an impressionable age. They were sisters, though there were times people wondered if one or the other hadn't been left on the family's doorstep."

Clay crossed to the bar to refresh the drinks.

"They sound like real hell-raisers," he said over his shoulder.

"Ollie was older by eight years. Ambitious as sin and way ahead of her time. The parents had been told they couldn't have another child. Daddy Sheridan had some pretty radical ideas himself for the times. Gossip has it that even before Momma had finished explaining the family's social position to their little darling, Daddy took away her teething ring and shoved an abacus in her crib. The goal was to make her his successor at Sheridan Industries."

"The technology conglomerate," Reed explained to Nicki.

"It started out a little smaller. Grandpa Sheridan was a grain farmer. Made a living supplying Post and Kellogg's, but he loved tinkering with machinery. Patented some thingamabob that had Walt Chrysler and Henry Ford fighting on his doorstep. All of a sudden raising first-generation cornflakes took a backseat to industrial progress."

Gwyn allowed Clay to top off her wineglass, then continued.

"Ollie, always an obedient child, lapped up her parents' teachings. She was well on her way to being a spoiled, eight-year-old intellectual snob . . ."

". . . when along came little sister," Clay murmured.

"Exactly. The new apple of everyone's eye."

"I suppose, being a radical, Ollie's sister wanted to tear the business down."

"Very good, Devon. Put them in the same room and sparks flew. I met them when they bought the lake house in the late forties. Pip was about six or so. Ollie preferred reading stock market reports to keeping an eye on baby sister. She'd been trying to teach Pip to swim, but the child was terrified of the water. Matters came to a head when she tossed Pip off the end of the dock."

"How awful," Devon murmured.

"I think Ollie did it more out of frustration than a desire to injure. Or maybe she'd read somewhere about the sink-or-swim theory of instruction. Either way, Pip nearly drowned before they got her out, and that was the end of the lessons."

Clay tossed down the last of his fifth bourbon and water and returned to the bar. Devon, bathed in the light of a nearby lantern, followed his movements with worried eyes. Nicki wondered briefly whether Gwyn's choice for Devon's affections had a drinking problem. Beside her, Reed slipped his hand over hers.

"Did the Sheridans ever have a son?" she asked, growing impatient with the saga.

"Those two girls were more than enough for one family."

"How many other families have owned the house? Mid spent time here as a girl. She mentioned someone named Ingram."

"Vic and Miriam. Bought the place in the late thirties when it was still basically a farmhouse. Did a lot of structural work, modernized the bathrooms, things like that."

"Mid remembers attending a party for one of their sons."

"That would have been Sid or James."

"Either of them still around?" Reed asked, giving Nicki's hand a squeeze.

"Sid must be about sixty. Last I heard, he was in Atlanta. Jimbo, the younger one, was doing something with cellular phones in Houston. Or maybe it was Dallas."

Nicki returned Reed's squeeze.

"Who came after the Ingrams?" Devon asked, retrieving her empty wineglass from the deck floor. She reached for Clay's tumbler and carefully poured two thirds of its liquid into her own glass. Clay looked at her intently, then smiled and handed her the rest of his unfinished drink. Nicki caught a triumphant glint in Gwyn's eyes at the small exchange.

"The Sheridans rented from the Ingrams for a few summers, then bought them out. In sixty-one the girls' parents died in the crash of their private plane. Pip was seventeen. Ollie got herself named her sister's legal guardian and seized control of the corporation as well. A year or so later, Pip escaped to Berkeley to nurture her radical bent. Ollie sold the place to Morris and Agnes Fitzsimmons in sixty-four."

Two years before I was born, Nicki thought, leaning forward intently. Before she could form the question, Gwyn began again.

"They had two boys, Cullen and Ryan. Fire-engine-red hair and tempers to match, but oh, they loved to tease. Female bodies were dropping like two-week-old rose petals around that dock for a while. If I'd been thirty years younger and not thrice-burned, I'd probably have been one of them. Luckily, someone introduced me to Karl before I could make a fool of myself."

Nicki had to swallow to get the words out.

"How old were Cullen and Ryan Fitzsimmons?"

Gwyn looked at her closely. Nicki, certain she heard the wheels and cogs spinning in her hostess's mind, prayed the shadows would cover her blush.

"Late teens, early twenties when they lived at the lake. Ryan's a priest in the Boston archdiocese now. Morris and Agnes are barely in their seventies, but they're already living in some retirement complex."

"Maybe Nicki would like their address."

Nicki's flush deepened at Clay's words. She knew without looking his dark eyes were fixed on her face.

"Miko left a pot of coffee on a timer," Gwyn said, breaking the awkward silence. "Devon, would you mind . . ."

Devon slid open the patio door and disappeared.

"What about Cullen Fitzsimmons?" Reed asked, ignoring Nicki's warning nudge.

"He never came back from Vietnam," Gwyn said softly.

Nicki stood up abruptly, forgetting Reed's hand was still clasped in hers. If Gwyn noticed them disentangling themselves, she gave no reaction.

"It's late. I really need to get home."

Devon returned with the coffee, but Nicki rejected a plea to stay longer. Clay's intensive gaze and the questions she was sure Gwyn was poised to ask pushed her toward the steps. Reed followed her, as did their hostess.

"If you want to take in the bird sanctuary tomorrow, we'll need to get an early start," Devon called.

"If someone who knows the way will drive, we can take my car," Nicki said, wishing Clay had not invited himself.

"I'll play chauffeur," Reed told her. "Seven thirty?"

Everyone agreed. Gwyn accepted their thanks for the evening but followed them partway down the path, chatting about the landscaping revealed by softly glowing tier lights. As the darkness was about to swallow them, she placed a hand on Nicki's arm and leaned close.

"I'm not going to ask why it's so important, but there's a little more I can tell you about the house. A property management company bought out the Fitzsimmons after Cullen died. By the time Karl and I moved back in 1980, the place had been sitting empty for several years."

"What happened to the Sheridan girls?" Reed asked, keeping his own voice low.

"They're both gone now. Karl and I were still living in Europe when friends wrote that Pip had drowned. I guess she never did learn to swim."

▪▪▪▪▪▪▪17▪▪▪▪▪

Beyond Gwyn's well-maintained, estatelike tract, the ground beneath their feet grew unpredictable. Reed took Nicki's hand, steering her around a bush that loomed suddenly in the darkness. The older couple in the rental house had either gone to bed or were away for the evening. No lights pierced the blackness of the next three houses, reducing to cautious exploration what had been a leisurely stroll earlier in the evening.

Nicki, unexpectedly silent, allowed him to lead the way. Near the weeping willow beside the rental house's dock, she tripped over an exposed root and stumbled into him. Caught off guard, he backed against the tree, drawing her with him.

Instinctively his arms tightened about her. Instead of pushing him away, her hands relaxed against his chest. He bent his head, giving in to the impulse he'd been trying to control all evening. Her lips yielded hesitantly to his, as if she, too, were fighting some inner battle. Reed waged his own internal war against escalating his campaign, afraid of ruining the moment.

Nicki trembled, invoking a memory of earlier in the evening.

"Ichiro's little bonfire frightened you, didn't it?"

She stepped back but left her hand in his.

"I was startled, that's all."

So startled you went into a trance, Reed thought darkly, frustrated by the invisible wall she erected whenever he tried to get close. She'd enjoyed the kiss. Was the barrier her method of discouraging anything more?

"Either of the Fitzsimmons boys could be my father," she said suddenly. "Gwyn mentioned they were redheads. Lexie's hair is auburn. She has to have inherited a recessive gene from somewhere. Alan's hair was dark, and you saw Renee's picture. Pale complexion, black hair."

They began walking again.

"Cullen Fitzsimmons died in Vietnam. Renee told me that's what happened to my father."

"She also claimed he'd fled to Canada, didn't she?"

"That was later. Don't you see? She changed her story to put me off. Renee was seventeen when I was born. Cullen would have been very young too. Gwyn said the boys had lots of girlfriends. What if Renee was one of them?"

"James Ingram lives in Dallas. If *he* were your father, Renee could have kept in touch over the years."

"He'd have been ten or twelve years older than she was."

"Vulnerable to prosecution for seducing an underage girl."

Nicki stopped walking.

"That's an awful stretch," she said doubtfully.

"He'd have had a career by then, maybe a wife and family. Polite society of the Ingrams' generation might have overlooked a summer fling. A scandal would have threatened his lifestyle."

"You're saying he . . . or his family paid for my mother's silence?"

"That annuity she told you about came from somewhere."

She sighed. The moon sought cover once more behind the clouds. Reed slipped his arm around her again, guiding her past the line of evergreens marking the boundary between the rental unit and Del Ferris's side yard.

"But if he's still alive, why the house and money now?"

"Guilty conscience, nostalgia, any number of things."

Another explanation halted his steps once more.

"Of course," he began cautiously, "Ryan Fitzsimmons's entering the priesthood doesn't mean he was celibate in his youth. Maybe his calling grew out of a need for penance. His parents are getting older. They could be having second thoughts about their earlier rejection of their grandchild. Especially if Father Ryan's been counseling them over the years."

"Why not approach me directly then, get to know Lexie? If what you're suggesting's true, she's their *great*-grandchild."

Reed remained silent, but Nicki seemed to read his thoughts. She dropped his hand and drew back. His stomach twisted as the darkness enveloped her outline, creating yet another barrier between them. When she spoke, her voice, though barely a dull whisper, betrayed a pain that far surpassed his own.

"*She's* illegitimate, too."

"That's one of those social changes Gwyn was talking about. People don't make such a fuss about things like that anymore."

"Some people do."

"So what? You turned out fine, and you're raising a pretty terrific kid. This is all speculation, anyway. Whatever happened, it was a long time ago. Why does it matter now who paid Renee to raise you alone?"

"I want to know the truth about myself."

"You sound like Clay," Reed said, sighing. "Okay, as long as we're building scenarios, what about the Sheridans?"

Nicki's laughter eased the tension that had risen between them. She slipped her hand in his once more and walked on.

"Even the most radical woman can't father a child."

"There could have been male cousins. They wouldn't have to have lived in the house, only visited. Gwyn said Ollie valued her social position as much as her ability to read spreadsheets. With all that wealth a hundred thousand here or there to bury skeletons in the family closet would never have been missed."

"That still wouldn't explain my current windfall. What about your mother? Would she remember any of these people?"

"She probably knew some of them, but she's always lived on the other side of the lake. Besides, I was already born when you were conceived. Mom and Dad would have been running around with the young married crowd."

"What about your uncle . . . Donnie, is it? Mid talked as if he would have been young enough to know the Sheridans, and maybe the Fitzsimmons boys, as well."

"Donnie wasn't involved with any of them."

He felt his throat constrict. Why did she persist in digging up the past?

"Not even the radical Pip Sheridan?"

"No."

An awkward silence followed his curt response. Reed took Nicki's arm to steer her away from the shrubbery that outlined Del Ferris's darkened patio.

"How was the dinner party?" a disembodied voice asked.

"Dammit, Del," Reed said, turning toward the invisible speaker, his heart still racing. "You scared the life out of us. I thought you were hung up in an airport somewhere."

"Got in a little while ago. Been sitting here unwinding with a drink, trying to decide if I'd be in danger of drowning if I went for a swim."

"I wouldn't recommend it, especially if you spent your delay in the airport bar," Reed told him.

"Why don't you and Ms. Prevot join me and fill me in on what I missed? I assume Ichiro gave his usual masterful performance."

"Complete with pyrotechnics."

"I really should be getting home," Nicki murmured.

They said their good-nights and moved on.

"I'd forgotten voices carry farther around water," Nicki said, leaning close to speak directly into his ear.

"We'll be okay once we're beyond the Greenlees'."

"Did you know Devon stayed in the Greenlee house once when she was a girl?"

"No, I didn't. The house beside Gwyn's and the place Clay's staying at are the only rental properties along this stretch now. And it takes big bucks to afford either one."

"Clay must come from a wealthy family. He doesn't talk much about himself, does he?"

"No, he doesn't," Reed said. The moon broke from the clouds, making walking easier. He tried to think of a way to prolong the evening.

"What do you know about him?" Nicki asked suddenly.

"Clay? Not much. Why?"

"I don't know. Something about him bothers me."

"If anyone bothers you, you tell me. I'll defend your honor," Reed told her, pulling her into the shadows of the willow in front of Devon's house.

As before, the sagging leaves provided a protective canopy. The second kiss rivaled the first. He pressed her against him, demanding a deeper response.

"Who's going to defend me from you?" she murmured, coming up for air.

"I'm harmless. Ask Mid."

"I just might do that."

At her door he kissed her again, lightly this time, and told her he'd see her in the morning. Her whispered "Psst" made him whip around.

"Can you find more out about the Ingrams and Fitzsimmonses?"

"I'm an attorney, not Sam Spade. If you really want to pursue this, I can hire an investigator."

In the glow from the lamp Mid had left burning, he could see her hesitate. She bit her lip and stared at the ground, looking more like a troubled child than the responsive woman he'd kissed only moments before. Reed felt his resistance crumble. What the hell. It shouldn't be that hard.

"Okay. I'll do some preliminary research. Maybe I can at least eliminate somebody."

Without warning she threw her arms about him. The hug was more reminiscent of Lexie's animated greetings than the sensuous embraces they'd shared walking home.

"While you're digging into things, check out Clay, too," Nicki whispered before stepping back.

He opened his mouth to protest, but she'd already disappeared inside.

In the car he thought about her request as he backed onto Lower T, turning toward the homes they'd just strolled past. Lights burned now in both Devon's and Clay's houses. Only Del's remained in darkness. The older couple couldn't have been far behind Nicki and himself, Reed decided.

Check out Clay too.

Jokes about women's intuition aside, if something about Clay bothered Nicki, the guy deserved close scrutiny.

He shook his head, surprised at his fierce urge to shelter Nicki from even minor distress. From her beginning as an unwilling client in a simple property transfer, Ms. Nicki Prevot had become someone very special to him. Very special indeed.

Nicki snapped off the living room light and moved onto the section of first-floor porch that faced the lake. A cluster of lights on the far shore identified the area Reed had pointed out as the country club. In the distance a low rumbling warned of approaching rain. Moist air, stirred by a rising breeze, swirled about the flower beds. She leaned her forehead against the screen and breathed deeply.

Somewhere on her clothing, the scent of Reed's after-shave lingered. If she closed her eyes, she would be back in his arms, cradled safely in his protective embrace. All the worry and self-doubt would be gone. She sighed. The last time she'd fallen in love and confided her insecurities, the result had been a loss so devastating only Lexie's impending arrival had held her together.

Alan and Renee. Both torn from her life like shutters and shingles in a hurricane gale.

Where did Renee fit into Trumpeter Lake's social life in the turbulent sixties? Nicki wondered. *Was I conceived by an Ingram, or a Fitzsimmons, or just some drop-in visitor who enjoyed a brief fling with Renee and moved on?*

"I need to know," she whispered. "I've always needed to know."

She cranked the windows closed against the approaching rain and went back inside, skirting the familiar shapes of tables and chairs. The house felt a part of her now, she realized . . . except for the room with the nautical theme. That morning's momentary panic replayed in her head.

The sisal rug crunched softly beneath her feet, guiding her across the entryway to the stairs. Her anxiety evaporated as quickly as it had come, replaced by an urgent need to touch her daughter's face.

A plug-in night-light in the upper hallway allowed her to find her way on the stairs. Lexie's canopy bed was empty, as was her bed on the porch. Nicki found her in Mid's room, curled beside the grandmotherly woman.

What would it have been like to have a grandmother? Nicki wondered as she bent to scoop up her child . . . the kind of grandmother who wanted and cared about her?

"Did you have a nice time?" Mid whispered in the semidarkness.

"Yes, I'll tell you about it in the morning. I closed the windows downstairs. It's starting to storm."

Lexie opened her eyes long enough to comprehend the shift in sleeping arrangements, then drifted off again. The deluge hit as Nicki was slipping into her own nightgown. Brief flashes of lightning illuminated the darkness. Instead of rushing to lower the canvas blinds, she sat cross-legged on the bed and watched the rain sheeting onto the surface of the lake and running off the roof's protective overhang.

The cloud cover quickly moved on, taking the lightning with it. Thunder continued to rumble, but farther away. Moonlight on the water revealed the ever-changing concentric circles of the now-gentle drizzle. A bird's cry pierced the night, so like the anguished wail of a child in distress, Nicki stiffened and turned to reassure herself Lexie was all right.

Undisturbed by the squall, Mr. Flops clutched tightly in the crook of one arm, Lexie slept deeply. Her hair was splayed across her pillow. Auburn hair. A Fitzsimmons legacy?

Nicki slid beneath the covers and let the dripping rain lull her to sleep.

18

Safe and dry, he watched the deluge slacken. He'd made the right decision about the party, he realized. All that discussion about previous owners. A smoke screen to cover what was already known? Or a probing to recall the past?

Either way, Nicki's presence was becoming dangerous. Even if she were an innocent stranger, she asked far too many questions. Someone else might remember, might begin to ask *other* questions. Questions with no safe answers.

He drew the curtains and crossed to the hidden room. In his present condition, sleep was impossible. Too many drinks, too little coffee. Neither had succeeded in drowning his growing apprehension. His train of thought brought a smile. Instantly he pushed it away. There would be no enjoyment in discovery.

Or in confronting the past. Much better to think of Lexie.

His fingers toyed with the key, tracing its outline over and over as he sat in the darkness, his eyes closed. His other hand strayed to his lap. At length his body shuddered, leaving the silk kimono damp and clammy against his skin. With a final moan, he flung back his head.

Puny, that's what it is. Never satisfy a woman with it, that's for sure.

Cordelia's voice echoed about him, robbing the moment of its release. He pounded his fist on the projection table. But the long-buried memories remained vividly imprinted, despite his vow to forget.

Not puny, he thought fiercely. *Not with the right stimulus.* What Cordelia had wanted couldn't be coaxed to life for nicotine-stained teeth and sagging breasts. Not even with threats and brutality.

Innocence and purity. That's what had made him a man. He wasn't like his father after his stepsisters' births, dissipated by a weakness for liquor, an indiscriminate youth, and binges of self-pitying bed hopping with whores he was certain could restore his manhood and thus satisfy his shrewish fourth wife.

Were memories of the past as vividly imprinted on Nicki Prevot's mind as on his own? he wondered. He stroked the key he'd clutched so tightly a moment before, then slipped it back in its hiding place.

Better to keep the past buried a little longer. Especially when the future held such promise. Turning on a light, he crossed to the shelves that rose from floor to ceiling the length of the room. His fingers caressed the metal cylinders, pausing on a section labeled FAIRY TALES.

A quick adjustment of the air-conditioning, then the projector whirred to life. Little Red Riding Hood skipped listlessly past an artificial forest, oblivious to the shadowed figure lurking behind the plastic foliage. An off-camera wind machine whipped her cape away from her body. Shivering and suddenly wary, the confused child clutched at the billowing cloth, trying vainly to cover her nakedness.

He snuggled into his chair, satisfied with his choice of material. A quality production. Really excellent for its time.

Another image from long ago intruded on his thoughts, bringing a momentary flash of terror. Swearing, he restarted the film. He wasn't ready to unleash the darker portions of that memory . . . not yet. Not till he was certain. Not till he had no other choice.

Little Red, her glazed eyes clearly frightened now, opened her basket to show the grinning wolf the goodies she was carrying to Grandma.

He wondered if Lexie liked fairy tales.

⁅▪▪▪▪▪▪19▪▪▪▪▪

Lexie tugged on Reed's and Clay's hands, urging them up the trail toward the lagoon. Devon shook her head and grinned. The tension she'd sensed in Nicki the previous night seemed to have evaporated in the crisp morning air. A squirrel scampered across the path, so at ease with the sanctuary's constant parade of visitors he waited until they were a yard away before scurrying into the tree line. Songbirds serenaded his arrival.

Several families with children as eager as Lexie surged past them, obscuring Devon's view of the trio ahead. Beside her, Nicki's steps had slowed. The younger woman had been unusually silent on the ride down, listening intently to her daughter's animated chatter with the two men in the Blazer's front seat, only occasionally glancing at the passing scenery.

Quiet wasn't the way she'd have described Clay this morning, Devon thought as another group hurried around them. His animated mustache had been in constant motion as he told silly jokes, tweaked Lexie's auburn curls, and whispered in her ear to produce yet another round of giggles. His usual studied control had evaporated in the presence of a child.

In the dozen or so times they'd been together, Clay had never relaxed his guard. Not even in recent weeks when he'd held her against him and kissed her good-night. His emotional restraint hung like a curtain between them, shadowing his inner thoughts, distancing them despite any physical closeness.

Last night the curtain had slipped, allowing her a disturbing glimpse of hidden pain. The alcohol was responsible, of course. She'd never known him to take more than one drink. What had set him off? Certainly not the evening's conversation. All the talk had been innocent enough. Some of Gwyn's tales he'd actually seemed to find amusing. And yet . . .

The path widened at the lagoon. Reed was standing at the water's edge, studying the trail map. Clay squatted nearby, surrounded by a knot of children as he pointed out differences between the various duck families paddling across the surface or clustered along the shore. Lexie clung to his side, her hand proudly clasping his.

All he needs is a flute and she'd follow him anywhere, Devon thought, pleased to see Lexie overcoming her fear of men. Despite his reserve with adults, Clay maintained an obvious love affair with kids.

"Have you ever felt as if what's happening had happened before?" Nicki asked quietly, breaking into her thoughts.

Devon looked at her sharply, responding to the strain in her voice.

"Déjà vu. Everyone feels it sometimes."

"More than that. It's like realizing you know something you couldn't possibly know. Like I know this path circles the lagoon and then veers left, around the lake."

"There's a map on the brochure."

"I didn't look at the map," Nicki said.

"Come on, Mommy. You're gonna miss the babies."

Nicki closed her eyes briefly before allowing her daughter to pull her toward the water. Devon followed slowly, disturbed by what she'd seen in Nicki's eyes.

The mallard mother who'd caught Lexie's attention had finished gathering her offspring under her wing and settled herself for a rest. Disappointed, Lexie moved on.

"What's that?" she demanded, stopping abruptly, eyes widening at a bugling call.

"A trumpeter swan," Reed said softly.

A shrieking toddler raced past them, pursued by an older child. Partially obscured by reeds along the bank, the female trumpeter spread her wings and called again. With an answering cry her mate rose into the air from across the lagoon, gliding to a landing that placed him between his family and the gathering crowd. Lexie clapped her hands.

"That had to be a six-foot wingspan," someone whispered.

"More like eight, according to the brochures," Clay offered, moving aside to give a pair of little girls a better view.

They moved on along the bark-chip path to the sanctuary's other treasures, laughing at Lexie's observation that the wood duck's artificial nesting sites looked like mailboxes. A flock of Canadian geese blanketed the shore of the lake itself. Chipmunks and tiny lizards darting across the trail were a constant source of delight.

Any other time Clay's running nature commentary would have fascinated Devon. This morning Nicki held all her attention. Caught up in Lexie's enthusiasm, neither of the men had noticed the young mother's drawn expression or wan complexion.

"Birds of prey to the left, around this bend," Clay announced over his shoulder. "They even have a bald eagle."

"You've been here before," Nicki said sharply.

He turned to meet her gaze, his expression puzzled.

"No. I heard someone mention the eagle as we came in."

"How do you know what's around the corner?" she persisted.

Devon watched the curtain fall as Clay's eyes narrowed.

"I looked at the map before I gave it to Reed." His expression softened, suddenly concerned. "You look pale, Nicki. Do you want to find a bench and sit down?"

"I'm fine. Let's go on."

Clay's eyes swung from Nicki to Devon in an unspoken question. Devon shook her head and motioned him toward where Reed and Lexie waited by the turn for the birds of prey.

"He's got scary eyes," Lexie complained, clinging to Reed as a red-tailed hawk stared back at them from inside his cage.

"Hawks need sharp eyes to find their food," Clay told her.

"Does he think I'm food?"

"I think he'd prefer something smaller, like a mouse," Devon said. "Maybe he's wishing his tail was as pretty a shade of red as your hair."

Lexie thought about that for a moment.

"I don't think he likes it in there."

"Only his body's in the cage. His spirit will always be free," Clay murmured.

Devon heard Nicki's sharp intake of breath and looked up, but Nicki had turned away and was walking rapidly toward the next section of cages.

"This guy's really huge," Reed said as Lexie planted herself in front of the bald eagle.

"I spotted an eagle once a long time ago, riding the currents back in a canyon in California," Clay said. "You rarely see them now. Housing developers have driven them out."

"Hasn't illegal hunting killed off a lot of them?" Reed asked.

"Mommy!"

Lexie's cry brought three heads whipping around. Nicki lay crumpled on the ground, her face a bloodless white. Clay got to her first, scooping her into his arms and carrying her to a grassy area beside the trail.

"What happened?" Nicki asked, opening her eyes. Lexie sat beside her, crying softly.

"You fainted again."

"*Again?*" Reed asked savagely, gripping Clay's shoulder.

"I assumed she'd told you. She passed out at Marquet's Monday."

"She just said she got a little dizzy," Devon protested.

Nicki tried to sit up. Still whimpering, Lexie buried her face in her mother's neck.

"I'm okay, Lexie, honest. I just need to sit here a little while. Sweetie, look at me. Dry your tears."

Reed dropped to the ground beside them.

"Did you mention these 'fainting' spells during that physical you had?" Nicki shook her head. "Why not?"

"I'd never had one before Monday. Besides . . ."

She closed her eyes and pressed her lips together tightly, trying to deny the truth that had been hovering about the fringes of her consciousness since Monday's episode. Reed's hand on her arm forced her to go on.

"I don't think it's anything physical. It feels more emotional . . . like the delayed stress you keep reading about."

She'd said the words. If they decided she was crazy . . . She glanced at Clay. He was looking away, staring down the path at a couple with a little girl about Lexie's age.

"What's the last thing you remember?" Devon asked gently.

Nicki closed her eyes, trying to recapture the moment before everything went black, fighting the same inner chill that had seized her outside the convenience store.

"I was watching the eagle, thinking how fierce looking he was, even in captivity." She frowned and bit her lip. "Reed said something . . ."

". . . about illegal hunting killing off the eagle population," Clay finished.

Nicki stiffened.

"And I had this . . . vision . . . of an eagle lying in a hole. It had been shot with an arrow, and it was staring up at me." She shivered and drew Lexie closer. "Why would I think of something like that?"

"Too many PBS documentaries. Some of those nature things would give Freddy Krueger nightmares," Devon said.

"But I never watch those shows. And this was so

real. I could feel the wind on my face. It ruffled the eagle's feathers. And I could see other birds. Vultures. Circling over us."

In her arms, Lexie whimpered once more.

"Try to forget it," Reed muttered.

"Sometimes it's healthier to remember," Clay said.

He gently pried Lexie from Nicki's arms.

"Come on, little one. Let's you and I walk on a short ways. We can circle around and meet everyone back at the lagoon. Maybe if we're real quiet, we'll spot a deer."

Lexie looked at her mother, clearly torn.

"It's okay, sweetie. You go on. I'll be along in a little bit," Nicki told her.

Lexie allowed Clay to wipe her tears with his handkerchief, then blew her nose and followed reluctantly, one tiny hand in his, the other waving feebly at the trio left behind. Nicki blew her a kiss and turned pleading eyes to Devon.

"I'll go with them," Devon assured her. She stood up, but hesitated. "Did this have anything to do with what we talked about earlier?"

"I don't know."

"There are people you can talk to about this kind of thing."

Nicki felt the heat of panic replacing her earlier chill. She shook her head. Devon eyed her sternly, then hurried to catch up with Clay and Lexie. Nicki watched until the three were out of sight before burying her face in her hands. Immediately Reed's arms were about her. His lips pressed against her hair.

"No one should try to deal with things alone, Nicki. Why don't you tell me what's been going on?

Anything you say is privileged, remember? I'm your lawyer."

"I don't think anyone watching would get that impression." Her attempt at a laugh ended in a hiccup.

"The hell with other people. Talk to me, Nicki."

Sniffling, she pressed her lips together and raised her eyes.

"It began when we pulled into the driveway last week. The house, the grounds, everything looked familiar. I even knew before you unlocked the door that we'd find a canopy bed and a sleeping porch upstairs."

"We talked about the house in your hotel room in Texas."

She shook her head.

"You didn't mention any of those things. Just that it had four bedrooms and needed a lot of work. And you talked a lot about the lake. The night we got here I dreamed about the place mats, and I knew where the juice glasses were, and then on Monday I put the wrong Popsicles in my basket . . ."

Reed loosened his embrace and leaned back to stare at her, his expression puzzled. Nicki sighed. He must be thinking her mental basket was missing a few items of its own. The whole thing sounded preposterous. Maybe she *was* crazy.

"Look, let's just forget it."

"Forget you've passed out twice? What if you take your next swan dive in front of a car? Or behind the wheel of one?"

She bit her lip. He'd voiced her own fears. Damn Odell and his cronies for making her so vulnerable. Why couldn't she put that trauma behind her?

"Devon's right, you know. If this keeps up, you should see a professional."

Nicki jumped up and took several steps away, dusting the seat of her jeans, trying to still her trembling hands.

"Don't shut me out, Nicki."

"Renee said all analysts ever did was ask stupid questions and poke around in your mind, trying to open you up like a soup can. I won't let anyone do that to me."

Reed studied her face intently.

"You make it sound like someone's already tried."

"No!"

Several people on the path glanced at them and hurried on. She forced herself to slow her rapid breathing. The effort had no effect on her racing pulse.

"I came here because I wanted to protect Lexie. She'll never feel safe if some shrink locks me in a padded cell."

"What about you, Nicki? Do you feel safe here?"

"Sometimes," she said softly.

"And the rest of the time?"

"I wonder what connection all this good fortune has with my anonymous father. But you're working on that problem, right?"

Reed opened his mouth to protest. She started walking, anxious to avoid more questions for which she had no answers.

"Come on, I'm okay now, and I'll feel even better when I know Lexie's not fretting about me."

"Wait." He cupped his hands over her shoulder. "You've got a hitchhiker."

He opened his palms to let her view the captured insect.

"A walking-stick," she said, stepping closer.

"I expected you to squeal and make a face."

"When you can't afford cable TV, you have to rely on firsthand nature lessons. Lexie and I spent lots of Saturday afternoons at the library learning about the moths and bugs she and Russell turned up in MarLynn's backyard and flower bushes. I don't think she's ever seen a walking-stick."

"Then it's time she did."

Their prize cradled carefully in Reed's cupped hands, they made their way back toward the lagoon.

Lexie had settled Indian style near the shore, watching the ducks and listlessly stacking bark chips in a pile beside her. Every few minutes she glanced back down the trail.

"What's wrong with Nicki?" Devon asked Clay softly.

He stared at her a moment, the curtain drawn more tightly than ever. She returned his gaze steadily.

"I know you've got a degree in psychology and certification in a lot of related fields as well."

His eyes narrowed.

"That mail they put in my box by mistake last week? It was addressed to Clay Verdell, Ph.D. I recognized some of the other letters after your name, too. I teach, remember? And I've been taking extra psychology courses as well. Even five-year-olds need counseling these days. If someone doesn't help Nicki, Lexie might need some herself."

"Lexie's problems don't go that deep."

"And Nicki's?"

He turned away, following Lexie's watchful gaze.

"Dammit, Clay, you could help her."

"People have to want to be helped."

Devon continued to stare at him.

"I'm an administrator. I haven't treated patients for years."

The explanation sounded lame, especially since his eyes refused to meet hers.

"If she came to you, you'd help her, wouldn't you?"

His protective curtain slipped a bit. He turned away with a shrug.

"Can't you at least ask her about what's bothering her?"

"No, I can't."

"Can't, or won't?"

Any response he might have made was interrupted by Lexie's announcement that Reed and Nicki were coming. Lexie rushed to meet them, exclaiming over something Reed had trapped in his hands. Devon turned back to her companion.

Clay's emotional control had broken, exposing a longing so raw Devon's breath caught in her throat. Immediately his defenses clicked into place once more and he strode forward, his face a mask of casual interest.

Devon remained where she was, stunned by the transformation she'd just witnessed. Clay obviously harbored strong emotions toward their new neighbor. Why wouldn't he use his training and experience to ease her distress?

Pasting a smile on her face to disguise her own confusion, she moved to join the others.

▬▬ 20 ▬▬

Lexie climbed down from the Blazer and held
out her hands.

"Don't hold him too tight," Clay warned,
transferring the walking-stick into her cupped
hands.

Grown-ups could be so silly, she thought. He'd
already said the same thing three times since they'd
left the sanks-wary.

"We really should have left him there," her
mother said.

"He'll make lots of friends in our garden," Lexie
promised, starting toward the road. The insect tickled her hands, urging her forward.

"Don't cross unless one of us is watching," her
mother called after her.

Lexie glanced toward the garden. Mr. Ferris was
kneeling by a patch of freshly turned earth on the
second level. At the sound of her mother's voice, he
looked up and waved.

"I'll see her back across," he called, turning his
eyes to Lexie. "Can you show me what you've got?"

She looked back at her mother and bit her lip.
Even though her mother had said not to be afraid,
Mr. Ferris still felt like a stranger. Russell had al-
ways known who was safe to talk to and who you

should run back in the house to hide from. But Russell wasn't here.

She'd been afraid of Mr. Verdell at first, she reminded herself. 'Cause of his car. But he wasn't like the men in the alley. He was nice. Mr. Ferris was probably nice, too. He'd given her cawwots for the bunny. And he'd shown her where to put them. That had been nice. Maybe Mommy was right. You shouldn't be afraid of people just 'cause they were boys.

"Can I show him?"

"All right, but don't stay long. Mid's fixing a late lunch for everyone. And mind your manners," her mother called after her.

Lexie fought the urge to dash across the road without looking both ways, suddenly glad Mr. Ferris had come down to meet her. The walking-stick had increased its ticklish dance on her palms.

"What have you got?"

"A walking-stick. I gotta let him go 'cause he tickles."

"Let him loose in the flower bed."

She opened her hands and released her captive.

"Will he stay here?"

"Where else would he want to go?"

"Back to the sanks-wary. That's where we got him."

"Did you like the sanctuary?"

She nodded. The walking-stick had settled on the stem of the flowers Mrs. Chamberlin had called daylilies. Lexie wondered what they were called at night.

"Did you see the eagle?"

"Mommy didn't like him. She went to sleep and fell down."

Mr. Ferris didn't say anything for a moment.

Lexie, squatting beside the flower bed, watched the walking-stick disappear into the leaves of the day-lilies. She felt a tug on her hair.

"Let me show you something."

She followed him to the patch of dirt on the second level, wondering why his voice sounded so funny all of a sudden. He knelt and pointed to a row of tiny green plants poking out of the damp earth. Lexie flopped on the grass at the end of the dirt.

"What are they?"

"Herbs. Chives, sage, peppermint. I'm going to plant more of them soon. Want to help?"

She shrugged. A lock of hair fell onto her forehead. Mr. Ferris reached out to brush it away.

"Where'd you get your red hair?"

"I dunno." She scooted around until the garden row was between them and poked at the dirt with her finger.

"I'm going back to the nursery tomorrow for more plants."

Lexie giggled.

"Nurseries are for babies."

"You're not a baby, are you, Lexie?"

She shook her head. He tossed a blade of grass toward her. It landed on the edge of her sandal, tickling her toe. She blew on her foot until the grass fell off.

"Mr. Verdell's gonna take me fishing."

Mr. Ferris made a funny sound. Lexie looked up. The early afternoon sun hurt her eyes, making her squint. Mr. Ferris's back was to the sun. She couldn't see his face.

"Is this fishing expedition planned for tomorrow?"

"Uh-uh. The next day."

"You need bait to go fishing. If you help me to-morrow, we could dig some worms. Would you like that?"

"I dunno."

"Lexie, look at me."

Lexie raised her head, shielding her eyes with her arm.

"You aren't afraid of getting dirty, are you?"

She shook her head.

"Are you afraid of worms?"

Again she shook her head.

"You aren't afraid of me, are you? I just want us to be friends. Like you're friends with Mr. Verdell. There's nothing scary about that, is there?"

"Uh-uh."

"I didn't think so. Why don't you ask your mother about helping me tomorrow? We'll dig your bait and surprise Mr. Verdell. I think he'd like that."

"Okay. Can I go home now?"

"Take my hand. I promised I wouldn't let you cross alone."

Lexie let him walk her across the road. She ran into the house without looking back.

Nicki felt Lexie tug her sleeve. She bent her head to listen to the whispered plea.

"Are you sure?"

"Uh-huh. We're gonna look for the babies," Lexie said, suddenly shy. She hung on the back of Nicki's chair, her knees bent, sandals barely touching the porch floor.

"Clay, are you sure you want to take this monkey fishing?"

"She wants to see the fountains in the coves. I thought we might go wading. Why don't you come with us?" he asked, placing his iced tea glass carefully on the place mat.

Nicki looked out over the lake. She could feel Clay's eyes on her, waiting for an answer.

"We'll see," she told him. "Lexie, help Mid clear the table."

"I wanna go outside."

"After you clear the table. Did Mr. Ferris give you another carrot for the bunny?"

"Uh-uh. Can I help him plant things tomorrow?"

The request took Nicki by surprise. First her eagerness for a fishing trip with Clay, now a plea to spend an afternoon with yet another male. Lexie's fears seemed to be falling by the wayside. She shook off the feeling that the turnaround might have its downside. Getting Lexie beyond her past trauma had been the point of this move in the first place.

"I suppose it's all right."

"What are you going to plant?" Devon asked.

"Peppermints," Lexie told them.

"I like the red-and-white ones that look like pinwheels," Reed murmured.

Her expression perplexed, Lexie looked at each of the laughing adults, shrugged her shoulders with a huge sigh, and, after yet another reminder, began ferrying plates into the kitchen.

Clay and Devon made polite excuses and thanked Mid for an excellent lunch before crossing the side yard toward their own houses. Nicki watched them with a frown. Her neighbors' body language said volumes. Their easy companionship of earlier that morning had somehow been strained during their expedition.

She tried to remember when she'd become aware of an awkwardness between the two. Had it been there before she fainted? She shook her head, trying to clear the cobwebs clouding her memory. Reed's hand on her arm brought her thoughts back to the present.

"Let's go sit on the porch," he murmured.

Nicki was glad to see Mid hustling Lexie upstairs to change for her afternoon swim. The day was barely half over, but she felt exhausted. She sank onto the cushions of the porch sofa.

Reed sat beside her, his body turned toward hers. He took her hand and rubbed her fingers between his own.

"Why didn't you tell me earlier what's been happening to you?" he asked softly.

Nicki shook her head, not trusting her voice.

"You know I care about you, don't you?"

Unexpectedly she felt tears crowding her lashes. Reed pulled her against him. A hint of after-shave and the woodsy scents from a morning outdoors joined the perfume wafting from the flower beds beyond the screens. His arms encircled her as they had at the sanctuary. The embrace felt comforting, no demands, no gentle push to make it something more. It felt safe, Nicki realized.

"I've got to stop blubbering on your shoulder."

"I'm not complaining."

"I feel like I'm on a roller coaster. One minute everything's fine. Lexie's happy. She's getting over her fears. Life's better than it's been in ages . . ."

"And then you have one of these episodes of déjà vu, or you black out."

She nodded.

"And nothing like it ever happened before you came here?"

"No . . . except . . ."

She drew back, chewing her lower lip and staring fixedly at the porch floor.

"Except what?"

"In the apartment, after the police pulled me out of the closet . . . I . . . I couldn't say anything."

"A cop's best weapon can be intimidation."

"It was more than that. I know this sounds ridiculous, but I felt as if something terrible would happen if I remembered and voiced the thoughts in my head."

She wiped her tears with the back of her hand, suddenly feeling foolish.

"These spells I'm having seem connected to the lake, to this house. The episode in the apartment felt just as surreal, but I didn't know about this place then. I can't believe there's any connection."

"You're sure nothing like that ever happened before?"

"Not that I can remember, and I usually have a good memory for things. Except my early childhood."

Reed frowned. He looked so like a little boy trying to puzzle out the answer to a pop quiz. Nicki restrained the impulse to reach out and tousle his hair.

"There's another possibility. Have you ever considered that your mother might have brought you here when you were very small? Maybe even lived here with your father for a time after you were born?"

"I've thought about that. Most of these flashes I get aren't frightening. Some actually make me feel safe and secure. But they're so vague, just bits and pieces of things. And if we lived here long enough for me to remember *things*, why don't I remember people?"

She realized her voice had become strident, her words tumbling over themselves. Reed took her hands again.

"What about voices?" She looked at him blankly. "Have you ever heard voices?"

Nicki nodded slowly.

"I hear a sort of echo, but the words are garbled, nothing that makes any sense." She frowned. "It's so frustrating."

Reed looked concerned. Suddenly the implications of what she'd just described made Nicki pull her hands from his.

"You think I'm having some sort of mental breakdown."

He opened his mouth to protest but she cut him off.

"Everything that's happened has to be stress related. I'm *not* going crazy. Losing Alan and then Renee, trying to cope with her financial mess and raise Lexie by myself . . . I've had drug dealers on my doorstep and police ransacking my apartment and then a . . . a fairy godfather appears like some Disney character and makes it all go away. People's systems have short-circuited under a lot less pressure than that."

"I don't think you're going crazy," Reed said quietly, zeroing in on the fear at the heart of her tirade.

The gray-green eyes stared at her without pity. His sun-reddened face reflected only concern. A lock of sandy-colored hair had fallen across his forehead. Funny, she thought, the red highlights had never seemed so prominent before. The sun must have inflamed his hair as well as his cheeks. Instinctively she reached out as she would to Lexie and smoothed the errant lock, then lowered her hand, suddenly embarrassed.

"I need time to adjust to the changes in my life and to the idea that my father may not have died the way Renee said he had."

"He may still be dead, Nicki. The most logical explanation for the house and the money is an estate settlement. Do you really need the added stress of learning the details right now?"

"I need the truth. Help me find that and I'll be fine."

Lexie's giggle from the doorway sent them into their respective corners of the sofa like guilty teenagers. Nicki held out her arms and the child ran to her, her bare feet thumping softly across the painted wooden floor. The sound echoed in the recesses of Nicki's mind, releasing a small shiver of panic.

But no sudden blackness. And no voices.

She had to fight whatever was happening to her, she realized, burying her face in Lexie's neck. She could not give in to madness, if that was what it was. Nothing, and no one, must ever separate her and this bundle of giggles.

"Miz Mid braided my hair," Lexie told them.

She tossed her head from side to side, swinging the auburn plaits across her face to tickle her nose.

"I wanna swim." She planted herself in front of Reed. "Will you go in with me?"

"I can't this time. I have things to do at home."

Lexie's lower lip threatened to protrude. Nicki pushed it gently back in place with an index finger.

"We can go in as soon as I change," she told her.

The pout re-formed into a grin. Nicki rolled her eyes and got up to walk Reed to the door.

"I'll call you this evening," he murmured, kissing her lightly on the cheek.

Behind them, Lexie giggled again. Reed reached around Nicki and tweaked an auburn braid, then hurried down the flagstone path toward the driveway. Nicki turned to climb the stairs. Lexie, her face an impish mask, waited on the steps. She scooted up each tread on her bottom, slowing Nicki's progress.

"Reed kissed you."

"Sometimes people kiss when they say goodbye."

"Uh-uh," Lexie said, shaking her head. The braids teased her nose again. She rubbed her face with the palm of one hand.

"He kissed you 'cause he likes you."

"And what makes you think that, Miss Know-it-all?"

Lexie shrugged her shoulders and grinned, then twisted around to scamper on up the stairs. Nicki suppressed a smile of her own, her earlier fatigue lifted by the exchange. As she went to find her suit, her steps felt lighter.

"Hi," Devon said, dropping down beside Nicki and dangling her feet in the water. Lexie looked up and grinned but continued to splash about in the shallows beside the dock, trying to trap a minnow in her hands. Nicki slapped her feet against the water, creating tiny ripples that propelled a hand-size piece of floating bark toward shore.

"You look like you're feeling better."

She nodded and leaned back on her arms, tilting her face to catch the sun.

"You had us worried."

"Ummmmm."

Somewhere on the lake, an outboard sputtered to life. The motor's sound faded in the distance and silence returned.

"Clay's a psychologist, you know."

Involuntarily Nicki's eyes flew open. The sun's glare drove them shut again.

"I remember you said he worked with children." She dropped her head to stare across the water. "You're out too far, Lexie. Get back near shore."

Behind them a man's voice called something and another male responded. Both women twisted around. Clay Verdell was crossing the expanse of grass between his own and Del Ferris's dock. Del, in a pair of swim trunks that hung to his knees and did little to camouflage his bulk, waited above the shoreline, holding one end of an overturned aluminum rowboat.

Together the two men flipped the boat and carried it to the water's edge. To Nicki, it looked as if Clay had shouldered most of the burden. Del looped the bright yellow rope that dangled from the narrow end of the craft around a cleat on his dock. Clay said something and shook his head, bending to reattach the line. Del watched closely, one hand absently twisting his drooping mustache. When Clay finished, the pair walked to the end of the dock and stood talking.

Nicki turned back around. Lexie had discovered the piece of floating bark and was using it as a shovel to scoop sand into a mound just above the waterline in the cove. *What she needs is a shovel and pail,* Nicki thought, feeling a twinge of guilt.

By necessity, accumulating toys had never been a priority. Lexie had cherished what playthings Nicki managed to provide and used her imagination to fill in the gaps. Now those dolls and games, as well as her books, had been reduced to ashes.

The few things that had been kept at MarLynn's had cushioned the loss somewhat, as had Reed's gift of Mr. Flops. Swimming and exploring would soon lose their appeal. She'd noticed a toy store in Rockwall. Next week they'd go shopping.

"If you asked him, I think he'd try to help you," Devon said quietly, continuing the conversation.

"I'm not crazy!"

"Even well-adjusted people need help now and then. I saw someone for a while, after my divorce."

Nicki turned her head slowly to look at her neighbor.

"I had all this anger and guilt. Even though my parents' marriage had fallen apart, I thought mine was going to be different. *I* was going to do all the right things."

Devon stared across the water. Embarrassed, Nicki looked back to where Lexie sat scooping water into a hole she'd made in the center of the sand mound.

"I did the right things too. I just did them with the wrong man. Therapy helped me see that." She scrambled to her feet. "At least think about talking to someone. It doesn't have to be Clay."

Nicki watched Devon walk to the end of the dock and dive into the water. A moment later she resurfaced and stroked expertly toward the raft. Nicki glanced toward Del's dock. Clay, his expression indistinct at this distance, had also been watching Devon's progress.

Del had climbed into the rowboat. He sat facing the narrow end of the craft, his hands clutching the oars, his legs thrust awkwardly in front of him. Clay dropped his head and said something, then knelt to steady the boat as Del twisted to face the opposite direction.

Untying the yellow rope, Clay tossed it into the bottom of the boat and gave the craft a shove. He watched Del's slapstick combination of uncoordinated strokes maneuver the vessel in the direction of the marina, then swung his head back toward the raft. Nicki followed his gaze. Devon now lay on her back in the sun, one arm flung across her eyes.

Nicki slipped off the dock into the water. By the time she'd waded to where Lexie played, Clay had crossed to his own property and disappeared. He'd been wearing trunks. If he'd been intending to swim, he'd obviously had second thoughts.

"It keeps leaking out," Lexie complained, pointing to a breach in her sand fortification. "The lake won't stay away."

She sank onto the sand beside her daughter. For the next few minutes they scooped sand into a barrier in a vain attempt to ward off the encroaching water. When Mid came out to suggest a game of checkers, Lexie happily abandoned the project. Nicki grabbed her towel and followed them to the footbath.

Much later Nicki lay in bed, listening to the night. In the yard, crickets were chirping love songs. Deep in the Tarleton wilderness a bullfrog began a steady croaking, and an owl registered his complaint. Waves slapped at the cove as a light breeze ruffled the oaks.

She turned over for what felt like the hundredth time and scowled at the darkness. Her surroundings were peaceful enough. Why wouldn't sleep come? Trying to blank out the night sounds, she let her thoughts wander.

"Raspberries."

The oath whispered across the darkness. The owl posed a question.

"Whooo?"

"Clay Verdell, that's who," Nicki mumbled into the pillow.

As promised, Reed had called during the evening. His Saturday afternoon in the reference section of Rockwall's public library had established Clay's credentials.

"According to the profile article in the trade journal I found," Reed had told her, "Clay graduated from Berkeley in sixty-five. And get this. You think Berkeley in the sixties, you think protest, right?"

Nicki had murmured agreement.

"He enlisted. Served two tours in 'Nam. Well, almost two. He was wounded midway through the second hitch. Got a medical discharge but stayed in Southeast Asia."

The article had gone on to confirm what Gwyn had told Devon about Clay's refugee work. He'd returned in seventy-three, completed his graduate work, and taken a position with a private Berkeley clinic that treated troubled children and adolescents. The profile had been written four years ago, soon after Clay had been named head of the facility's substance-abuse program.

She flipped over once more, squinting into the darkness at Lexie's relaxed shape in the next bed. Reed's advice echoed in her thoughts.

"Clay's got excellent credentials," he'd insisted. "I really think you should talk to him about your blackouts . . . unless you just don't like the guy."

She'd ignored the implied question.

"If he's so great, why did he leave the clinic?"

"I called a guy I went to school with, a neurosurgeon who practices in San Francisco."

"And he knows Clay?"

"No, but he made some calls and phoned me back. Turns out Clay asked for an extended leave of absence about eighteen months ago. The official position is he's on personal leave."

"And the gossip?"

"Lots of guesses, nothing conclusive. He sold his boat and condo and simply dropped out. Like the hippies in the sixties. My friend thinks he probably saw one too many burned-out kid."

She'd promised to think about Reed's suggestion, then changed the subject. Her subconscious must have been listening to her assurance, she mused, shifting onto her back. Clay's face kept intruding on her thoughts. Did she really dislike the man, as Reed had suggested?

Disturbing was a better description for her reaction to Clay, she decided. Despite her initial reserve, she felt drawn to him, as was Lexie. Funny how he'd subdued her child's fears so quickly. Probably all those whispered conferences that seemed to produce so many giggles. Either that or he'd been unobtrusively exercising his professional skills.

Maybe she should consider Reed's and Devon's suggestions, Nicki thought, trying to dismiss her distaste for Clay's vocation. A yawn forced her eyes closed.

What seemed like only moments later, she felt Lexie tugging her arm.

"Mommy, wake up."

Reluctantly Nicki open her eyes, struggling against a tightness in her chest and abdomen, an emptiness that reminded her of the grief that lingered for weeks after Alan's and Renee's deaths.

"What's the matter, sweetie?"

"You were crying."

She raised a hand to her face. Her cheeks were wet. When she turned her head, her pillow felt damp.

"I must have been dreaming."

"A bad dream?"

"Just a sad one," she said, stifling a yawn. Nothing remained of the dream except sadness and a curious sense of loss. Lexie's dark eyes, reflecting the moonlight, peered into hers.

"I could lie down beside you, if you'd like," she said matter-of-factly, repeating words Nicki had said so often.

"I'd like that very much."

Cool little feet slipped beneath the covers and pressed against her thighs. Eyelashes tickled her neck as Lexie's arms slid about her. Whisper-soft breath caressed her throat, and the scent of bubble bath and powder freshened the bed.

Nicki felt herself drifting back toward sleep. A flash of recognition flittered through her mind, escaping into oblivion even as she struggled to recapture the comprehension. Something about Clay when he had looked at her . . .

Sleep won out as warmth from the small body beside her crept into hers. No other dreams disturbed her slumber.

▬▬▬ 21 ▬▬▬

"She'll be fine. You can see them from here. Relax," Devon told Nicki, noting the tension in the young mother's body as they watched Lexie and Del cross the road. They were sitting in the side yard, drinking Mid's fresh-squeezed lemonade, the half-empty pitcher on the low table before them.

"I know I'm overprotective," Nicki said, leaning back in her lounge chair with a sigh.

"With what you've told me about your life the past few months, it's understandable, but all that's over now."

Devon looked up at the sound of a vehicle pulling into her drive. A door slammed and Bob Stockton appeared at the corner of the house. He saw them and crossed the yard.

"Afternoon, Miz Prevot, Miz Rheams. Thought I might start diggin' out that pyracantha."

"Today?" Devon asked doubtfully. She'd asked Bob weeks ago to clean out the dead bushes along the side of her house, but hadn't expected him to do it on a Sunday.

"Get sorta antsy on the weekend. 'Sides, can't hardly fit special jobs like that in, this time of year."

His eyes shifted to the hillside garden where

Lexie and Del were bent over a patch of freshly turned earth.

"Looks like your young'un's havin' fun, Miz Prevot." He turned back to Devon. "What about them bushes?"

"I guess now's as good a time as any." She waited until he was out of earshot, then leaned over and murmured to Nicki, "The man's got to be lonely. I wish he'd find some nice widow."

"You've been around Gwyn too much."

"You're probably right. She's fun though, isn't she? All those stories about the people who used to live around here."

Both women looked up at the sound of yet another vehicle, this one in Nicki's drive. Moments later Joel Lynch appeared.

"Speaking of great stories," Devon whispered. "My cousin's a police dispatcher. According to her, retired cops know all the best dirt."

"Brought those sketches we talked about," Joel told Nicki, nodding a greeting. " 'Less this is a bad time."

"Your timing's perfect. Lexie's planting peppermints."

Joel glanced at the hillside and nodded. He pulled several sheets of graph paper from the folder under his arm and moved the pitcher to spread them on the table.

"That what you're after?"

Devon caught her breath. The structure in the drawing was a duplicate of the playhouse that had captured her attention that last childhood summer she'd spent at the lake.

Nicki studied the sketch for a long moment.

"The porch railings . . ."

Joel switched drawings, exchanging the sketch

that showed perpendicular supports for one with a design of x's formed by crossed boards. Nicki nodded hesitantly.

"And there should be flower boxes, one on either side of the door, beneath the windows. And green shingles."

"Like the original," he said, eyeing Nicki thoughtfully.

"Lexie's going to love it," Devon said.

Mid, even more animated than usual, arrived with extra glasses, insisting Joel stay awhile, prodding him into conversation. Nicki, on the other hand, had little to say.

A speedboat swung into sight around the outcropping of the Tarleton land, its high-powered whine demanding their attention. The sun-bronzed teenager at the wheel swerved the boat erratically between the raft and Nicki's dock. His passengers whooped approval. Joel muttered an oath under his breath.

"Young fools. Lake patrol's gonna have to talk to them 'fore someone gets hurt."

"I always think of the lake as peaceful, but I suppose young people cause a lot of mischief," Mid said.

"In the summer you get boating accidents, keg parties, young studs bloodying noses over some gal in a micro-bikini. Off-season, it's break-ins and vandalism."

"What's the worst thing kids have ever done around here?" Devon asked, thinking as much about some of her own youthful escapades as the vandalism she'd heard Bob Stockton complaining about a few weeks before.

"Coked-up fifteen-year-old ran his runabout full

speed onto the public beach a few years back. Killed a toddler."

"How awful," Mid murmured.

Joel shifted in his chair. He stared along the shoreline, one hand absently stroking his chin.

"Had a runaway years ago that never did turn up. Jenna her name was. Jenna Edgerley."

"My mother wrote me about her," Devon said. "She was awfully young, wasn't she?"

"Looked 'bout ten. Actually, she was thirteen— going on twenty-one, according to the kids I talked to. Street smart, we'd call her now."

"What happened?" Mid asked.

"Girl threw a hissy fit when her folks said she had to go along on a family outing. They let her stay home, but told her she was grounded. When they came back, she was gone, along with her backpack, some clothes, and about eighty dollars in cash."

"How could a child just disappear like that?"

Joel shook his head.

"Happened all the time in the seventies. Her folks went through her things. Found a diary and some clippings about Haight-Ashbury—love-ins and flower power. Someone saw her walking toward the crossroads. We figured she hitched a ride from there."

"That was it? She just vanished?" Mid asked again.

"Backpack and most of the clothes turned up in a Trailways lost-and-found halfway across the country two months later. We ran every lead we got into the ground. Truth is, somewhere between here and that bus station, that little girl ran into more trouble than she could handle."

"Gwyn was telling us about the families who

used to own Nicki's house," Devon said, seeking a less depressing topic. "Do you remember any of them?"

"Played basketball with Sid Ingram in high school."

"What about his brother?" Nicki asked suddenly, leaning forward in the lounge chair.

"Jimmy was more into football. Played for Michigan State in the mid-fifties. Good-looking kid. All the gals thought he hung the moon. Had lots of daddies mumbling about loaded shotguns."

"Did anything like that ever happen?"

Devon glanced at Nicki, surprised by her sudden appetite for gossip.

"Nope. Sid told me when they'd had the mumps, Jimmy's went down. We always figured he was sterile. 'Course, most folks didn't know that. Last I heard he was on his fourth wife and still no kids."

Nicki's shoulders seemed to sag.

"According to Gwyn, one of the girls who lived here was a problem," Devon said, still puzzled by Nicki's reaction.

"That'd be Pip Sheridan. Kept things lively, that's for sure. Reckless enough for any two boys her size. Always sailing that boat of hers after dark or trying some fool stunt on water skis."

"I thought she was afraid of the water," Devon said.

"She was, but she'd tackle just about anything as long as she had a life jacket. Never got near the water without one."

"And yet she drowned," Nicki murmured. Devon looked up sharply.

"Night sailing. Fool woman was almost thirty. Thought she'd have known better by then. Best anyone could tell, she got caught by the boom and knocked overboard. Fastener on her vest was frayed and tore loose . . . in the dark, unconscious like she was . . . never had a chance."

"How sad," Mid murmured.

Devon looked over at Nicki. Her young neighbor had leaned back in her lounger and was contemplating the leaves of the oaks that towered above them.

"Like this?" Lexie asked, looking up from the hole she'd just dug. She liked the little shovel Mr. Ferris had given her to use. If he hadn't talked so much about how each tool had its own special job to do, she might have asked to borrow the shovel to dig sand in the cove.

"That's fine. Now we take a seedling . . ."

He reached behind her for one of the funny little green boxes he said had come from the nursery. His breathing sounded funny, the way people's did when they had a cold. Lexie looked to see if his nose was running. It wasn't. She sat back on her heels, out of the way.

"Hold out your hands."

She did as she was told. Mr. Ferris turned the box upside down and tapped on its bottom. The tiny plant and a handful of dirt plopped into her waiting fingers.

"Put the seedling in the hole, and pack dirt around it. Make sure you cover the roots. Now, tamp it down, like this." He cupped his hands over her fingers and pressed them against the dirt. "That's right. You're going to be a very good gardener."

Lexie looked up and grinned. A lock of her hair fell across her face. She brushed it away and began digging the next hole. When she was done, Mr. Ferris reached around her again for another little box. His body swayed against her for a moment, the way her mother's had right before she fell down in front of the eagle's cage. Startled, Lexie jumped back.

"Sorry," Mr. Ferris murmured, settling back on the grass.

"Are you gonna go to sleep and fall down?"

"You mean like your mother?"

She nodded solemnly. Mr. Ferris tugged on his mustache.

"Lost my balance, that's all."

When they finished the plants, he showed her how to make a little trench for the seeds he'd bought and then cover them up. Planting seeds wasn't as much fun as digging holes. Her attention wandered to a large peanut can in the basket of gardening supplies.

"Are we gonna plant peanuts?"

His laughter made her frown. Grown-ups were always laughing when you asked questions. Sometimes she wanted to tell them they were being rude, but Mommy and MarLynn had told her little girls shouldn't say such things to adults. She wished someone would explain why kids weren't allowed to be rude, but grown-ups were.

"The can's for your worms." He pointed to the opposite end of the garden patch. "Ought to be some good ones down there."

She scooted to the far end of the plot and waited impatiently while Mr. Ferris labeled the planted rows with Popsicle-stick signs. Finally he stacked the empty green boxes in his basket and carried his tools to where she was sitting.

"I want big ones, 'cause I wanna catch really big fish," she told him, poking the little shovel into the dirt.

"Then dig carefully so you don't chop the big ones in two."

She continued more slowly, uncovering a plump reddish-brown worm. Wrinkling her nose, she picked the creature up with two fingers and dropped it into the container. Mr. Ferris beamed his approval. Soon the peanut can held a dozen wriggling worms and several scoops of moist earth.

The afternoon sun had warmed the garden. Lexie leaned back on her heels to swipe at the hair that kept falling into her eyes. When she looked up, Mr. Ferris was staring at her. Little beads of water glistened on the top of his head above his ring of white hair, reminding her of hot dogs when her mother cooked them in the oven. More water dripped from his droopy mustache.

"You have dirt on your face," he told her, digging a handkerchief from his pants. He held her chin in one hand and wiped the dirt away with the other. Lexie squirmed uneasily. His cold seemed to be getting worse. She hoped he wasn't going to sneeze on her. He stopped rubbing her cheek to examine her face, then nodded.

"Much better."

"I'm gonna look for the walking-stick," she said, jumping up to run to the lower level of the garden. After several minutes of searching, she spied the insect under a daylily leaf. Mr. Ferris's shadow fell across the flower bed, blocking the sun.

"He likes it here," she said.

"Lots of plants to eat."

"He won't eat the daylilies will he?"

"He might. You like the daylilies, don't you, Lexie?"

"Uh-huh." She twisted to look up as his shadow drew closer.

"So do I. Of all the flowers in this garden, they're my favorites."

She continued to study the walking-stick.

"You know, sometimes *people* eat flowers," Mr. Ferris said.

Lexie giggled, thinking about a plate of lilies for supper.

"You have to be very careful, though. Some flowers are poisonous. If you eat the wrong ones, you can die."

The walking-stick moved deeper into the flower bed. Lexie scrambled to her feet.

"I wanna go home now, Mr. Ferris."

Mr. Ferris pushed the pesky lock of hair off her forehead.

"My name is Del, Lexie."

"Mommy says it's not polite to call grown-ups by first names."

"You call Mr. Jordan Reed."

"Mommy says that's okay 'cause he's our 'tourney.'"

Mr. Ferris held out his hand as they came to the road. She wiped her dirty palm on her shorts before taking it.

"Maybe we could call each other by secret names," he said.

She looked up at him, blinking against the sun that poked through the leaves of the big trees in the side yard.

"You don't know about secret names, do you? I'll bet your mommy had one when she was a little girl."

"Like what?"

"Oh, probably something like Breeze or Skylark or Freedom. Didn't she ever talk to you about it?"

Lexie shook her head. He touched her cheek.

"Your skin's as soft as a baby bird's. How about Sparrow?"

"I'm not a bird. I'm a bunny." She put her feet together, bent her knees, and hopped up the walk. "Like Mr. Flops."

"Then, my secret name for you will be Bunny. Just remember, you can't tell anyone."

Lexie paused in mid-hop and cocked her head to one side.

"Why not?"

"Because if anyone knew, it wouldn't be our secret anymore."

Behind them, tires crunched on gravel.

"Reed's here," Lexie squealed, running toward the driveway, clutching the can of bait.

"What'cha got?" Reed asked, returning Lexie's welcoming hug.

"Worms." She reached into her peanut can and held up a thick specimen, giggling as the captive curled around her finger.

"That's a nice big one."

"Do you think I'll catch a big fish?"

"I wouldn't be surprised. Hello, Del. Have you been teaching my girl all about the flora and fauna?"

"She's a fast learner. Quick as a bunny, aren't you?" Del asked, winking at Lexie. She turned away, suddenly fascinated by a half-buried acorn in the driveway gravel.

"Mommy's outside," she said, abandoning the acorn and taking Reed's hand.

Hugging the can of bait, she pulled him around the corner of the house. In Devon's side yard Bob Stockton paused whatever activity had brought him out on a Sunday and waved a greeting.

Mid came to meet them. Squeezing Reed's arm in a brief hello, she mumbled something about needing more glasses and went into the house. Nicki, bent over a pitcher of lemonade, straightened and smiled as they approached. She looked much more relaxed this afternoon, Reed thought. None of the tight lines about her mouth. No confusion dimming her expressive eyes.

"Look, Mommy," Lexie called, running forward, the can of bait in her outstretched hand.

One of the square wooden sprinkler covers tilted beneath Lexie's foot, sending her sprawling and the peanut can flying. The contents cascaded over Nicki, catching in the folds of her blouse, filling the glass in her hand with writhing creatures.

Nicki stared at her glass, then flung it away, slapping at her blouse.

"Nooooo!"

The glass shattered against the rim of the metal table. Eyes wild with terror, Nicki backed away, still whimpering, still frantically beating her clothes. Her body swayed. Reed reached out to her as she crumpled to the ground.

"Mommeeee."

The moan was so low Reed wasn't sure he'd heard the word. He cradled Nicki's head in his lap. Suddenly Clay Verdell was beside him. They each took an ice-cold arm and began chafing the warmth back into her body. A worm wriggled from her shirt pocket. Clay flung it in the direction of the table where Del had begun to collect the rest of the captives.

Drawn by Nicki's cry, Bob Stockton had stopped his work to observe the scene in the yard. Devon had knelt by Lexie to examine her scratched knee, trying unsuccessfully to divert her attention from the sight of her mother lying on the ground once again. Joel stood a few feet away, studying Nicki with a concern that mirrored Reed's own.

It was obvious Nicki needed help to deal with whatever was happening to her. Surely now she'd take his advice and talk to someone. Reed glanced at Clay and was surprised to read anger in his expression. He'd have expected a psychologist to show a little more compassion.

Nicki stirred.

"Wh . . . what happened?"

"You had a panic attack," Clay murmured before Reed could respond. Nicki struggled to sit up.

"I'm all dirty."

"You don't remember what happened?" Reed asked.

She shook her head.

"Lexie was running toward me and"—her brow knitted in concentration—"and then I woke up on the ground."

Reed looked at Clay. The older man shook his head.

"Devon, can you take Nicki inside? No, Lexie, you stay here with Reed and me. Your mommy just needs to rest."

"She had sad dreams last night," Lexie said, her tear-stained eyes peering into her mother's. Nicki hugged her.

"That's why I need to lie down for a while today," Nicki said, examining her dirt-streaked blouse. She murmured something about a bath and clean clothes and allowed Devon to walk her to the house.

Mid met them at the door, exchanged a few words, then hurried to comfort Lexie. Bob Stockton had taken up his shovel again, attacking the dead shrubbery with a vengeance. Del handed the peanut can to Lexie, whispered something in her ear, and started across the yard in the direction of his own place.

"The fish ought to leap out of the water for those guys," Clay said gently, kneeling to wipe Lexie's tears with a finger.

"Mommy didn't like them."

Clay stroked her hair.

"You know, my sister doesn't like worms very much either."

"Does she go fishing?"

"Sometimes. When I'm around to bait her hook. Let's go see if any of the big fish are hiding under the dock."

Reed watched as Lexie followed Clay. A murmur of voices behind him made him turn around. Joel and Mid were talking quietly. He joined them.

"Something's troubling that young woman," Joel said, nodding toward the house. "Best keep an eye on her, if I were you."

"That's just what I intend to do," Reed told him, as Mid began collecting the pieces of broken glass.

▬▬▬ 22 ▬▬▬

"**Y**ou're sure you're okay? You didn't touch those brownies. Or much of your dinner, for that matter."

"I'm fine, Mid, really. I just don't have much appetite."

The afternoon's heat had not faded with the sun, but remained to fill the usually pleasant evening hours with a muggy sultriness. Even the ever-present breeze had fled. Overhead, Lexie's bare feet pounded down the hall, and the bathroom door slammed.

"I don't suppose you want to talk about this afternoon."

Nicki stared at her lap and shook her head.

"Well, I've never been one to pry," Mid said, pushing herself up from her chair. "But I'm here if you feel the need."

"Thank you," Nicki said softly.

She climbed the stairs, leaving Mid to putter about the kitchen. Lexie met her in the hall, a damp towel draping her sturdy little body. Nicki helped her into her pajamas, then tucked her in bed.

"You didn't like my worms," Lexie said, her voice an accusation.

"No, I guess I didn't," Nicki murmured, wishing

she could remember the missing moments Devon had described.

"Why do you fall down so much?"

"I don't know."

She smoothed away the damp strands of auburn hair that curled about her daughter's face. Lexie wrinkled her nose.

"Do people eat flowers?"

Nicki smiled, glad to be back to the usual off-the-wall questions that made having a five-year-old such an adventure.

"I suppose in some places they do. Grown-ups sometimes drink dandelion wine. Dandelions are sort of a flower."

"Could I drink dandyline wine?"

"No, you could not."

"Why?"

"Because it would make you very sick, that's why."

"Did you drink some? Is that why you keep falling down?"

Nicki looked at her child in confusion. Where had that connection sprung from.

"No, I did not have any dandyline wine."

Lexie pursed her lips and nodded her head.

"Good, 'cause I don't want you to die."

Before Nicki could choke out a response to that startling statement, Lexie launched off on another tangent.

"Did you have a secret name when you were little?"

"I don't think so. Why?"

"If I told you, it wouldn't be a secret anymore."

She clasped her arms about Nicki's neck and pulled her down for a noisy kiss. The ensuing giggle-fest didn't end until Nicki had snapped out the light and gone to the room with the canopy bed to lay out Lexie's clothes for her early-morning expedition.

A short time later Mid stuck her head in to say good-night.

"I've been thinking over what Joel said about life jackets," Nicki told her. "I think Lexie should wear one tomorrow."

"I saw some in the closet next to the downstairs bath. Would you like me to go see if there's one her size?"

"No, I'll do it. I've decided one of those brownies would taste good after all. You go on to bed."

Downstairs Nicki managed to eat most of a brownie before the thoughts crowding her mind sabotaged her appetite.

A life spent entirely in urban settings couldn't explain her reaction to a few clods of dirt and a couple of worms. The apartment over the carriage house had been empty for a long time before Ellis persuaded the owners to rent it. She and MarLynn had battled dust and spiders, even a scorpion or two, to make the place livable. None of those things had sent her crashing to the floor. Nothing she'd ever experienced had done that to her—until she moved to this house, this place.

From what Devon had told her, she'd lost a block of time during today's blackout. She had no conscious memory of the moments before she passed out. The frequency of these weird episodes seemed to be increasing. Did that, and the lost minutes, mean the problem was getting worse?

She pushed the thought aside and went to look for the life vests Mid had said she'd seen.

The house's architect had used very little of the available space beneath the stairs to create the

closet next to the downstairs bath, but the last owners had filled every inch with lake-related equipment.

A pair of badminton rackets with rotted strings
hung on the back of the door. Metal hooks held
weathered windbreakers, a straw hat with a hole in
its brim, and a rubber bathing cap covered with
pink flowers. Piled haphazardly on the floor were
mildewed lawn furniture cushions, folded director's
chairs with missing seats or backs, and a splintered
canoe paddle.

The life vests were dangling by their straps from
wooden pegs on the right-hand side of the closet.
They looked worn but serviceable. Nicki untangled
the only one small enough for a child and turned it
over to check the fasteners.

P I P. She traced the pale-black letters on the
faded orange vest with a finger. Suddenly she was
struggling against a wave of now-familiar dizziness.
She clung to the doorframe.

To her relief the feeling subsided. The expected
chill never came. Her pounding heart and trembling hands assured her the terror had been real,
not imagined, but this time she'd battled the darkness and won.

Leaning against the closet door, replaying the
thoughts that had flickered through her mind before the panic flared, she tried to figure out what
had triggered the episode. If she could pinpoint the
causes of her anxiety . . .

She carried the vest into the entryway where the
light was better.

P I P. One of the children whose growth was
charted on the kitchen wall. A young woman Gwyn
had described as a radical and whose death Joel

had discussed only hours ago. A death by drowning.

Her concern for Lexie's safety had sent her rummaging through the downstairs closet. Such a simple explanation when she thought about it. Joel's vivid description of Pip's death and her own concern for Lexie must have combined to trigger the attack.

Nicki smoothed the vest's tangled straps and smiled grimly. Pip Sheridan had worn this life jacket as a child, perhaps at the same age as Lexie was now.

She examined the canvas strips that held the metal fasteners to the safety device. The heavy sewing fibers were unbroken. They held firm against her insistent tugging, as did the various other straps. Pip Sheridan had been an adult when foolishness had combined with faulty equipment to cause her death. This vest, this particular vest, had kept her safe as a child. It would protect Lexie as well.

Nicki looped the life jacket over the newel post on the stairs, trying to control her exuberance. She'd faced a terror and explained it away. Eventually similar reasons for the other episodes were sure to come to her. Whatever cosmic connection she had with this house and the lake—a previous visit, once-vivid photos now destroyed—none of it meant she was crazy.

Unable to completely repress her delighted relief, she whirled in a circle, clapping a hand over her mouth to silence a childish squeal. Energy surged through her, bringing a rush of perspiration. She wanted to laugh out loud, to run about the yard and leap into the lake.

And why shouldn't she, she thought, stopping in

mid-spin. Pip Sheridan might have been afraid of water, but Nicki Prevot could swim like a fish. A dolphin, Lexie had said. If she were careful, if she didn't dive or take foolish chances, she should be safe enough swimming out to the raft and back.

She felt deliciously naughty wading into the refreshingly cool water a moment later. The semi-darkness of a crescent moon spurred the heady boldness that had driven her to abandon her clothes on the grass. Alan would have been proud of her recklessness, she thought.

Water slapped against her, gently caressing places usually covered by her suit. She felt her nipples grow taut. Gooseflesh prickled her skin. Swimming nude was swimming free. If the garden club ladies only knew.

"And how are you sleeping tonight, Reed?" she whispered.

Suddenly flushed, she plunged beneath the surface and stroked to the end of the dock, flipping on her back to float silently toward the raft.

Except for Gwyn's landscape lighting and an occasional security lamp, the shoreline was dark. No ground clutter here to mar the view of the sky. The sliver of moon grinned down at her, surrounded by more stars than she could ever remember seeing. A feeling of omniscience washed over her.

Alan had radiated such a power, an aura that had drawn her inside its circle as if in response to some need she hadn't known she had. He'd once told her there was always a moment during each of his endless adventures when he knew he was invincible. Was this what he had felt? This rush of confidence that promised you could do anything—negotiate world peace, feed the hungry, solve the mysteries of the universe?

Well, maybe nothing quite that dramatic. But she could swim across the lake and back, and no one would ever know. Her head bumped the raft, jolting her back to reality. She clung with both hands to the rungs of the ladder.

Swim across the lake—alone—in the darkness? What had given her such an idea?

Some of Pip Sheridan's recklessness must have seeped into the old vest and transmitted itself to her. Someone would know if she tried to traverse the lake. The person whose shore her naked body washed up on would certainly know.

Nicki lay back in the water and closed her eyes. What would it be like to drown? To simply let go and sink beneath the surface? The ultimate blackout.

She snapped upright, shock spreading through her at the direction her thoughts had taken. If anyone read her mind, they'd think she was suicidal. Grasping the top of the ladder, she pulled herself onto the raft and lay on her back, once again studying the night sky. A shape seemed to leap out at her. The Little Dipper, with Polaris at the end of its handle. Ursa Minor. Little Bear.

Polaris? Little Bear? Where had that knowledge sprung from? Space walks and shuttle flights had been deemed more relevant than star placement during her school years. Her exposure to the constellations had consisted of a single reading assignment, a chapter in an eighth-grade science book.

Gems from some forgotten PBS special, she decided, yawning. The raft's gentle rocking inspired a soothing contentment. A shooting star blazed a luminous streak across the night sky. She closed her eyes to make a wish.

When she opened them again, the stars had

shifted position. She shivered. Another blackout? A yawn and the lack of anxiety convinced her she'd fallen asleep. She stretched, rubbing her back across the rough surface of the raft. A sudden freshening breeze caressed her body, arousing a longing and making her moan.

Somewhere upshore a series of splashes summoned images of hungry fish feeding on Lexie's worms. Nicki shivered again. Clay was picking Lexie up very early. At this hour she should be as deeply asleep as her daughter. Tucked in her own bed. Alone.

She slid silently from the raft, welcoming the shock of cool water against her skin. Moments later she gathered her clothes and slipped quietly into the house.

▪▪▪▪▪ **23** ▪▪▪▪▪

The water should have felt refreshing, but the turmoil in his belly produced a heat that refused to be doused. Oblivious to his surroundings he pushed on past the rental unit and beyond the seawall that defined Gwyn Chamberlin's property. It was no use. He could never swim far enough to escape his fear or the danger that lay waiting to destroy him.

Dammit!

He should never have come back to the States. Asia and the Orient were full of kids. Kids you could dare to touch. Kids from families with too many mouths to feed, families eager to sell a child, especially a little girl.

The States were dangerous. But he preferred light-skinned, round-eyed little girls. That was the trouble. Once you allowed yourself to indulge . . .

That weekend in San Jose. The little blonde he'd taken from the nearly deserted playground had been smart, too smart to believe his usual threats to harm her family or her pets. He hated it when they didn't understand his need, when they screamed and fought the way the little blonde had instead of just closing their eyes and letting him love them.

He expected them to cry; it made him sad, but he

understood. Sometimes he cried himself from the joy they'd given him. Such soft, submissive little things, the children he chose to receive his love. Except the little blonde in San Jose. He hadn't wanted to hurt her so badly, but she wouldn't stop screaming. Suppose he'd let her go and she'd seen the stupid newspaper that weekend?

He never should have talked to that damned writer. At the least he should have vetoed the photo. It had seemed safe enough at the time. The rag authorizing the feature usually wouldn't have been something kids might see, but the writer, damn him, had sold reprint rights to some of the California papers.

Catatonic, the reports had said about the child in San Jose in the weeks that followed. But people came out of things like that all the time. The girl had screamed, and the West Coast had become a dangerous place.

He'd had to get away, leave everything. One lousy mistake and twenty years—the carefully constructed persona, the perfect career—everything had been in jeopardy.

It had been that God-awful summer all over again. The rage that had turned to violence, the lies, and the heart-pounding fear of exposure. He clenched his fists and kicked off again.

He should never have come back, especially not to this particular stretch of shoreline. All he'd wanted was a safe haven, a place where he could indulge himself, a base from which to make an occasional, carefully choreographed foray when his need became too great.

Instead, Nicki Prevot had shown up, and he'd found himself reliving that horrible summer. And now he was going to have to *do* something. All because she hadn't wasted away in some sanitarium surrounded by grim-faced, ineffectual men in white coats as he'd been told, but had grown up and come back.

Making friends with Nicki and Lexie had been a calculated risk. That it had paid off was small consolation. Ignoring the pair would have been a far greater risk. No doubt or suspicion remained, only the fear gnawing its way through his bowels.

What if he hadn't witnessed Nicki's latest "spell"? His intestines clenched in renewed agony. He spun around and started back, past the softly illuminated Chamberlin estate. Damn Gwyn. She'd started all this. Dredging up those stories. Piquing Nicki's interest.

Dammit! Why did she have to come back after all this time? Why couldn't she have stayed away? He'd been safe till she came. A shiver traced its way along his spine. He hated the need for violence. But more importantly, he hated the aftermath, the gut-wrenching fear of waiting for discovery.

After Kathy had driven him beyond reason, he'd locked himself in the bathroom and vomited for hours, hugging the porcelain until his father battered down the door and dragged him out to face his accusers. It had been days before he'd kept down food after San Jose.

He never liked to hurt anyone, especially not a child. He loved little girls. Loved everything about them. And Lexie was so exquisite, so much like Midge, his virginal foray into the forbidden. But witnesses were the greatest danger of all. Nicki had proved that . . . and left him no choice.

His heart was thumping wildly. Gasping, he stopped swimming to tread water. Panic flared, growing stronger, writhing from his stomach to his chest to his throat.

Slow, deep breaths, the kind that had always helped when he knew Cordelia would be coming for him. The anxiety receded, only to flare once more. He was back in the airless, cell-like room, and Cordelia was locking the door, backing him against the wall, into the corner, tugging at his pajamas, taunting him, trapping him in a nightmare that never seemed to end.

Puny! That's all you'll ever be, a puny baby with a puny thing between your legs. Now come here and put your head in your stepmomma's lap and do what you can. Maybe this time you'll get it right.

He'd tried, but it was never enough for Cordelia. Never enough to prevent the punishment that followed. He pressed his fist to his mouth and bit his flesh to stifle a cry. The physical pain snapped his thoughts back to the present.

Cordelia had violated his body, stolen his childhood, and derided his masculinity, but she couldn't hurt him anymore. She was where she belonged. In the ground with the snails and the worms. And in the end, if only for a little while, he knew he'd triumphed.

A smile curved his lips at the memory, and the panic receded. Fear, he'd learned, could work two ways. Midge had been his revenge. Cordelia had filled his nights with terror. In between those times he'd become Midge's nightmare.

But it hadn't been enough.

He'd wanted to make Kathy pay as well. Kathy, with her smug superiority and her perfect mimic of Cordelia's deriding voice. Kathy had been a mistake. She'd been too old. Threats that ensured her little sister's silence meant nothing to her. Like the little blonde in San Jose and that terrible summer that haunted him once more, Kathy had fought back. It had been the first time he'd lost control.

If there had been the slightest chance she wouldn't tell when it began, her bruises freed her tongue. And when Kathy had talked, so had Midge.

His father had refused to listen when he tried to explain about Cordelia and the room in the garage, calling him a liar and a pervert and bloodying his mouth. The next morning he'd been sent away, enrolled in boarding school, and consigned to Herr Grossman, a headmaster who'd have felt as much at home training recruits for the next rise of the Third Reich.

Small for his age, bewildered by the harsh discipline, and constantly ridiculed by upperclassmen, he'd withdrawn into a fantasy world. A world where Midge was his to control, Kathy jumped at his command, and no one ever provoked his smoldering wrath. A world that fueled and honed his need.

He'd buried his anger, denying the existence of his violent side until that one terrifying afternoon twenty years ago. Even then, he'd contained the situation. *Until now.*

The air had grown chilly. His legs throbbed with the stress of treading water. He struck out for his own dock, each stroke bringing him closer to the moment when he'd have to face the past. A past that refused to remain buried. Something would have to be done—before Nicki's "spells" revealed too much.

A sound almost like a moan broke the silence. He raised his head to listen. Probably a night bird or an animal stalking its prey deep in the Tarleton woods. The sound was not repeated. His eyes strayed to the darkened house beside the tangled acreage.

Eliminating Nicki meant letting go of Lexie as well. An almost physical pain wrenched at his heart. The child was everything he wanted. Trusting dark eyes and baby-soft skin. Sturdy little legs and the tender promise between them. So like his precious Midge.

He rose from the shallows and waded ashore, unconcerned about being seen or heard. At this hour everyone was asleep. Certainly Lexie would be tucked in her bed.

The breeze caressed his arousal, driving him toward the house and the hidden room. Time was running out, but he knew now what must be done. Somehow he had to find a way to get rid of Nicki and still show Lexie how much he loved her.

24

Mr. Verdell unwrapped the yellow rope from the funny handle on the side of the dock and stepped back.

"Sure you don't want to join us?" he asked.

Lexie looked up hopefully, but her mother shook her head.

"Maybe next time. Have fun. And be careful."

"I'll take good care of her," Mr. Verdell called.

Mommy waved and the dock began to get smaller as the boat pulled away. Lexie twisted around to watch Mr. Verdell row. The bulky vest her mother had made her wear rubbed against her cheek. She pushed it away, frowning down at the black letters printed across the front. Sometimes she knew words if she'd seen them in one of her books . . . the books that had all burned up. She didn't know this word.

"D—L—D. What's that spell?"

"You're looking at it upside down. Those are *P*'s. And the middle letter's an *I*. *P–I–P*."

"*I*'s have dots."

"Not capital *I*'s."

"Oh." She frowned at the word again. "What's it spell?"

"Pip."

She wrinkled her nose. It didn't sound like a real word.

"What's it mean?"

"It's the name of a girl who used to live in your house."

Lexie looked back at the shore. Her house was almost hidden by the big trees and tangled bushes on the point of land where no one lived. She turned back.

"It's a funny name."

"It's a nickname. Like Lexie instead of Alexandra."

"Do you know her?"

"I used to . . . a long time ago."

He stopped pulling on the oars and let the boat drift past the shoreline. In two places the bushes were much thinner, and the water seemed to disappear into the trees.

"Those are the coves I told you about. We'll fish for a while, then come back and explore. Maybe we'll catch momma duck and her hatchlings on the nest."

They rowed on, nodding to the people in the boats they passed—a man in one, two older boys in another, fishing lines already dangling in the water. A woman in a canoe paddled across in front of them and waved a silent greeting. Mr. Verdell murmured that the people with power boats, whose noisy motors might scare the fish, usually didn't like to get up so early.

The funny cloud that had been hanging over the middle of the lake began to go away. She could almost see the other shore.

"I had good luck about here last time," Mr. Verdell said, lifting the oars and dropping them into the boat.

Cold water splattered on her legs, tickling as it ran down. She covered her mouth to hold back a giggle.

Mr. Verdell grinned. He dipped his hand in the water and flicked more water drops over her knees.

She giggled again, not muffling the sound this time, and cupped her own hand over the side of the boat. Her aim was high, and she forgot to open her fingers. The tiny scoop of lake water splashed into Mr. Verdell's face. Little beads of water trickled down his cheeks and dripped from his mustache.

"I didn't mean to . . ."

His laughter was much louder than her giggles. Lexie laughed too, happy he wasn't mad. All at once they were both dipping their hands over the side, shaking water at each other.

Finally Mr. Verdell held up his hands.

"I give up. You win."

He reached behind him and pulled a towel from a bag in the pointy end of the boat. Lexie held up her face to be dried. Leaning forward, he pressed the towel against her skin and squeezed the water from the lock of hair that always fell in her eyes, then tucked it behind her ear. His fingers trailed down her cheek to her chin. She looked up at him, puzzled by the funny look on his face.

Suddenly he dropped his hand and sat back, turning away to stare across the lake. Lexie couldn't see anything special to look at. She wondered if he was mad at her after all.

"Did we scare the fish away?"

His eyes swung back to her face, and he smiled.

"I guess we'll have to bait our hooks and find out."

The peanut can was under the seat. He poked the dirt until a fat worm curled around his finger.

"Want me to bait your hook?" he asked, picking up one of the poles from the bottom of the boat.

"Uh-uh. I want to."

He showed her how on his pole.

"I'd yell a whole lot if you did that to me."

"Worms can't feel things the way people do."

"Oh," she said, not sure she really believed him. Screwing up her face she baited her own hook. Mr. Verdell knew an awful lot of stuff, she decided. Her worm didn't yell either.

The boat drifted slowly, trailing out their lines. A dragonfly skimmed the water, chasing a smaller bug. Lexie's attention wandered.

"What made those?" she asked, touching one of the jagged scars that crisscrossed the skin above Mr. Verdell's knee.

"I was wounded in a war . . . a long time ago."

"Do they hurt?"

"They used to. Now they only hurt when I think about them."

"Oh."

He didn't say anything for a long time, just sat staring at the water, looking very sad.

"Mr. Verdell? Are you mad 'cause I asked?"

"About my scars? No, I'm not mad." He smiled then and reached out to tug on the curl that stubbornly refused to stay put. "I never get mad at little girls."

He reeled in their lines to check their bait, then threw them back out and handed Lexie her pole.

"I don't mind if you call me Clay, Lexie."

"Mommy said I can't. She says it's not"—she thought a moment—"not proper."

"Well, I don't want you to disobey your mother. We'll just have to think of an alternative she'll approve of."

Lexie frowned.

"I could call you Fish Man. It could be your secret name."

"A secret name?"

"That's what people call each other so other people don't know they're talking to each other." Her
frown deepened. At least she thought that's what
Mr. Ferris had meant. When she said it out loud, it
sounded all mixed up.

"So you'd call me Fish Man and I'd call you
something else? Some secret name?"

"Uh-huh."

"What would you like your secret name to be?"

Lexie sighed. She really liked Bunny, but Mr.
Ferris wanted to call her that. Somehow she didn't
think he'd like it if she let Mr. Verdell use it too. A
breeze ruffled her hair. She turned her face up and
closed her eyes against the sun.

"I like the wind and the clouds and the sky."

Mr. Verdell made a funny sound. She opened her
eyes.

"Did you ever hear anyone call someone Sky,
Lexie?"

"I don't think so. Is that what you want to call
me?"

"No, I think Sunshine suits you better. Let's
think of another name for me, too. I don't think I
really look much like a fish, do you? Besides, fish
sometimes smell pretty funny."

Lexie giggled, suddenly remembering the faces
her mother had made when she'd asked about the
circles on the water.

Mr. Verdell put his finger against her lips and
pointed to the twitching tip of her pole. Moments
later, with a little help, her first fish lay flopping in
the bottom of the boat. Lexie threw her arms

around Mr. Verdell in excitement. He returned her
hug, pressing his face into her hair until she wriggled free.

"He's not awful big. Can we can catch some
more? Miz Mid said we can have fish for supper if I
get lots of big ones."

Mr. Verdell seemed to have to hunt for his voice.

"Sunshine, we'll stay here all day if that's what it
takes."

It didn't take all day. Once Mr. Verdell assured
her Miz Mid would be more than satisfied with
their catch, they started back. Lexie watched the
shoreline slide past, the midmorning sun warm on
her face and legs. Mr. Verdell didn't say much, but
now and then she looked up to find him watching
her.

"Know what?" she asked. Mr. Verdell shook his
head. "I didn't used to like you. But now I think
you're nice."

"Thank you. That's about the nicest compliment
any little girl's ever given me."

"Do you know lots of little girls?"

"None with hair as pretty as yours. Did your
daddy have red hair?"

"Mommy says he didn't. He died 'fore I got
born."

"That's very sad."

She shrugged.

He stopped rowing for a while and let the boat
drift. Mr. Verdell was nice. Lexie was glad his car
wasn't the one she'd seen in the alley. She rubbed
her lower lip. Her fingers smelled like the fish
they'd caught.

"Some men outside our window hurt somebody.
And they yelled at me and said nasty words 'cause I
saw."

"Are those men around here now?"

"No," she whispered.

"But you're still afraid?"

She bit her lip. He took her hands and ran his fingers over hers. Lexie felt a tear begin to form in the corner of her eye.

"Sometimes I have bad dreams. The men come into my room and hurt me and hurt Mommy."

"Has that ever really happened?"

"No. Mommy says they're far away. That they can't hurt us 'cause they don't know where we are."

Her tear spilled over. He wiped it away.

"I'll bet you don't have those dreams as often as you did when you first moved here. Do you?"

She shook her head.

"Maybe that's because you don't think about them as much."

"You mean like your scars?"

Mr. Verdell nodded, then picked up the oars again.

"You know an awful lot of stuff."

He smiled.

"I think it's time to check out those coves. And I have a special place I want to show you."

Lexie squirmed around to look toward the approaching shore. Mr. Verdell was awful smart. And he knew lots of fun things to do. She decided maybe she'd make him her best friend. Next to Reed, of course. He was her very best friend.

Much later, when the sun was high overhead and they were rowing back, she sat quietly on the boat's bench seat, one hand trailing in the water, and watched her house grow bigger around the overgrown point of land.

"Did you like her?"

"Who?"

"The girl who lived in our house."

Mr. Verdell looked beyond her. Lexie twisted to look that way too. The only thing she could see was the house. She turned back around.

"Yes, I liked her. She had a crooked little smile and long brown hair. Sometimes she wore it in braids and wove flowers in them. And she loved this lake."

Mr. Verdell's voice sounded funny, and he was talking the way grown-ups sometimes did when they forgot kids were around. Lexie frowned, wishing she hadn't asked about the girl who'd worn her vest. Before she could think of a better question, Mr. Verdell started talking again.

"Pip liked to argue. Especially about politics."

"What's pol'tiks?"

"Grown-up talk, like the news on TV," he said, looking at Lexie as if he'd just remembered she was in the boat.

"Was she fun?"

"Yes. But she was also very foolish."

"As much fun as me?"

He threw back his head and laughed.

"Sunshine, no one's as much fun as you. Look, your mommy's waiting for us."

Lexie twisted to look at the dock and bit her lip.

"I'm not gonna tell anyone about the special place. Not even Mommy."

A small smile turned up the corners of Mr. Verdell's mouth as he nodded slowly.

"Use the back door," Nicki called after Lexie. Barely waiting to hear her exclamations over the results of the fishing expedition, Lexie had raced toward the house, the dripping stringer of fish bouncing against her leg. Nicki turned to Clay.

"Mid's making sandwiches."

"I'll have to beg off. I have an afternoon appointment."

"You'll help us eat your catch tonight, won't you? Devon's bringing a pasta salad, and Mid's made some sort of gooey dessert that must be about a thousand calories a serving."

"I'll be there. We bachelors can't afford to turn down homemade goodies."

Nicki watched him push away from her dock and row toward his own, then followed Lexie inside.

"We're gonna eat spiders, like the fish do," Lexie said, meeting her at the kitchen door with her plate. Mid's sandwich creation, peanut butter on round bread with raisin eyes and cheese-curl legs, looked very much like a spider.

"Yummy. Maybe we should invite the fish to lunch."

"They're coming to supper." Lexie giggled.

"So they are. Let's hurry up and eat. I want you to go shopping with me."

"No!"

Nicki raised her eyebrows. Lexie looked at the floor.

"I don't wanna shop," she whined, lower lip protruding.

"Not even to replace your *Cat in the Hat* books?"

"*Babar* and *Madeleine* too?"

"Everything we can find."

The matter settled, the spider sandwich, and another just like it, quickly disappeared. Fishing was obviously more strenuous than it looked.

On the way into Rockwall, Lexie fell asleep, waking up lethargic and out of sorts, despite her original enthusiasm. Juggling overflowing sacks of *Dr.*

Seuss and other favorites and nearing the end of her own patience, Nicki urged her cranky child toward the car.

"You need a nap, young lady. Get in and buckle up," she said over her shoulder, storing the bags in the rear of the Blazer. She turned back to an empty front seat and a deserted sidewalk. Calling Lexie's name brought no response.

For a moment she was certain her heart had ceased to beat. Then she spotted a small figure peering in a window halfway down the block. Anger flared, pushing aside panic and fear.

"Alexandra Prevot, if you ever scare me like that again, you'll forget how to swim by the time I let you back in the water."

Her forehead still pressed against the glass, Lexie twisted to look up at her mother. Big brown eyes above a pouty frown met Nicki's exasperated gaze.

"I just wanted to look."

Taking in the display of sand buckets and shovels and plastic beach balls, Nicki sighed.

"You just can't run off from me like that. It's not . . ." The word *safe* stuck in her throat. Being safe was the reason they'd come here. Maybe she was overreacting. "It's just not a good idea."

" 'Cause the men in the alley might find us?"

"No, sweetie, that's not it at all. Next time, just tell me when you want to look at something."

"Could I get a shovel? To dig in the sand?"

Penitent dark eyes, heavy with exhaustion, looked up at her.

"I think we can manage a shovel and a bucket. And maybe one of those silly octopus molds as well."

Sleep delayed for yet another moment, Lexie's mood brightened as they went inside. Their store purchases expanded to include a set of dishes—for tea parties with Mr. Flops, a coloring book and crayons, and several puzzles.

"Big Bird," Lexie squealed, snatching the *Sesame Street* character from a display rack as they continued exploring.

"If you want a doll, you'll have to put something else back," Nicki told her, determined that Lexie learn not to take their new financial status for granted.

"He's not a doll. He's a puppet."

Lexie slipped Big Bird on her hand and began an animated conversation with the other characters in the display.

"A puppet," Nicki echoed. "I never knew they came that way." She reached for a different character in a wildly striped shirt, shivering slightly. The store's air-conditioning seemed to be working overtime.

"That's Ernie," Lexie said. "And that one's Bert."

"Bert and Ernie puppets," Nicki murmured.

"Let me get Big Bird," Lexie whined, tugging on Nicki's shirt. "I don't wanna put anything back. I don't have to, do I? Please, please? I won't ask for anything else, I promise. Not for a long, long time. Mommy?"

Nicki shivered again. It was ridiculous to keep a business this cold. The store's electric bill must be horrendous. Lexie repeated her plea.

"All right, you don't have to this time. Now let's pay for these things and go back outside. I need some sunshine."

Lexie ran toward the checkout counter, Big Bird still perched on her hand. Nicki followed with the shopping cart. The middle-aged clerk chattered nonstop while she rang up their purchases.

"If that serviceman doesn't show up soon, I believe I'll melt. Used to work all summer with just open windows and maybe a fan or two. Now we're so used to AC, every time it goes down we think we're suffering."

Nicki looked at the woman closely. Perspiration beaded her forehead. A second clerk, an older man, was wiping his brow. She had to admit the front of the store did seem much warmer than the rear area they'd just left.

"My grandchildren just love these Bert and Ernie puppets. They put on the cutest show with them last Christmas."

Nicki stared in dismay at the trio of puppets.

"Lexie, I said you could have *one* puppet."

"I only got Big Bird. You put Bert and Ernie in there."

Nicki looked down at Lexie. Innocence radiated from the tired little face.

"Of course, I just forgot. Will you take a check?" she asked, suddenly anxious to escape the clerk's puzzled stare.

Driving home with Lexie playing quietly on the seat beside her, Nicki tried to remember placing the extra puppets in the cart. First Popsicles, now children's toys. If she kept doing things like this, she might find herself calling Reed to bail her out of jail for shoplifting.

The thought made her hands tighten on the wheel. She slowed for a flagman where a utility excavation had narrowed the road to a single lane, then stopped as he flashed a dust-covered STOP sign. A bright yellow digging machine backed away from the excavation, repositioned its arm, and opened its maw. Rich dark earth cascaded into a pile beside the road.

"My name's Bert. What's your's?" Lexie chirped, suddenly thrusting a puppet in Nicki's face.

The car lurched forward. Desperately, Nicki fumbled with the gear shift, shoving it into PARK even as she fought the panic clawing her chest.

Oh, God, please. Not while I'm driving.

She tried to focus on the activity outside the car, the flagman's sweaty face and upraised hand, the pavement crumbling beneath a jackhammer's onslaught. Slowly the terror faded, leaving only a dull ache behind her eyes. She laid her forehead against the wheel, too drained to summon tears.

What had awakened the demons this time? Not the stupid puppets, she thought, anger replacing her fear. She'd seen the brightly colored characters before. You couldn't miss them. They were all over the place—on TV, in Lexie's books, prancing around the mall as life-size promotional figures. But not as puppets, she realized. She'd never seen them as puppets.

Or had she?

"Wanna see?"

Nicki turned her head.

"My loose tooth. Wanna see?"

Nicki clutched the wheel to still her suddenly trembling fingers and murmured something about "when we get home." The vague ache in her head flared into a throbbing pain. She shut her eyes, blocking the glare of the sun.

"Mommy, that man's waving at you."

Nicki opened her eyes to the flagman's frantic gyrations. Someone behind her leaned on his horn. She shifted back into gear and followed the construction detour. Beside her, Lexie and her puppet waved happily to the utility crew.

Maybe I am losing my mind, Nicki thought, cautiously winding her way toward the lake. What other explanation could there be when something as innocent as a child's plaything could threaten to send her spinning out of control?

▬▬▬ 25 ▬▬▬

"If that's as good as it looks, I want the recipe," Nicki said, holding the screen door open and taking the pasta salad.

Devon studied Nicki's face.

"Are you feeling better? Mid sounded really worried when I called. She said you came home with a splitting headache."

"I feel fine now. Lexie and I both took long naps."

"I really wish you'd talk to Clay about those blackouts. I know—you don't like doctors—but you like Clay. You know him. It wouldn't be like talking to some stranger. Please promise you'll think about it."

"I promise. Let me put this away and get some tea. Lexie's on the porch." She patted Devon's hand. "I'm fine. Really."

Devon shook her head as Nicki disappeared into the kitchen. Extra makeup and a few words of denial couldn't disguise the shadowy circles rimming Nicki's eyes or the lines of stress that etched her mouth.

Mid's right to worry, Devon thought. *I'm worried. Reed's worried. Clay is too. He'd never admit it, but I've seen it in his eyes.*

"Hello."

Lexie's voice, altered from its natural pitch, made Devon turn. A bright yellow head peeped around the corner of the doorway to the dining porch. The giggle accompanying the repeated greeting was pure Lexie. Devon grinned.

"Big Bird. You look much taller on TV."

"He's not the *real* Big Bird. He's just a puppet. See?"

Lexie offered her newest toy for closer inspection, then tugged Devon toward the porch sofa.

"Mommy took me shopping."

"I guess she did," Devon said, surveying the tower of books and puzzles on the coffee table.

"I got coloring books and crayons. And dishes and a bucket and shovel and an oct-you-puss. For the sand," she explained breathlessly. She picked up a *Cat in the Hat* book. "Will you read this to me?"

"Let's read it together."

She settled on the sofa, Lexie curled beside her. Soon Lexie was reciting whole passages and pointing out words.

"I'll bet you're getting anxious for kindergarten."

"Uh-huh." Lexie twisted to see Devon's face. "Can I call you Devon in kin'ergarten?"

"No. We talked about that, remember? You'll have to call me Mrs. Rheams."

Lexie frowned.

"Tell you what. We'll practice before school starts. It'll be just like learning another new word."

"I learned one today. P–I–P. Pip. It's a girl's name."

"I know."

"Oh," Lexie said, clearly disappointed. She brightened. "Did you know she used to live here?"

"I'd heard that."

Lexie screwed her face into a frown.

"Did you know she had a crooked smile and wore flowers in her hair?"

"No. I didn't know that."

Satisfied she'd won the five-year-old's version of one-upmanship, Lexie returned to the book.

"Lexie, who told you about Pip?"

"Mr. Verdell. He knew her a long time ago. He said she wasn't as fun as me. Did you know he hurt his leg in a war?"

Devon nodded. Tired of the verbal game, Lexie scooted off the sofa to get another book. Devon stared across the expanse of lawn toward the dock beyond her own.

Clay had listened politely to Gwyn's stories about the families who'd owned Nicki's house. Not once had he volunteered that he'd known Pip Sheridan. His usual control had slipped several times that evening, emphasizing the curious undercurrent of tension that had marked the gathering. At the time, she'd blamed his sudden affinity for bourbon and water for the awkwardness she sensed. Now she wondered if the drinking had been the result, rather than the cause, of his distress.

Nicki returned, bearing a pitcher of tea and a plate of fruit and cheese.

"Did you tell Devon about your fish, Lexie?"

"I caught two big ones and three little ones. Mr. Verdell made me put the little ones back, but he gave me his big ones."

"Did you get to see the fountains in the Tarleton coves?" Devon asked, reaching for a glass of tea.

"Uh-huh. One's this really big fish. Water used to come out his mouth, but it doesn't anymore 'cause the 'lectricity's turned off. There's another one of a lady with a funny-looking pitcher. It doesn't work either."

"What else did you see?"

"We went down these trails and I saw a woodpecker and a bunch of squirrels and a big spider web and this funny stump that looked like an old man, and then we went up a different trail to the . . ."

She clapped both hands over her mouth, a stricken expression replacing the enthusiasm she'd shown an instant before.

"Where did the other trail go?" Nicki asked.

"To a special place, but I can't tell. It's a secret."

"Secrets are very important when you're five years old," Devon told Nicki with a wink. "Did you see the ducks?"

"Uh-huh. There's only seven babies now. Like on our place mats. Mr. Verdell said a turtle got the other one," she announced matter-of-factly.

"I think Mid could use your help in the kitchen," Nicki told Lexie quickly, holding firm against the usual whine of "Do I have to?" When Lexie was safely out of hearing, she turned to Devon.

"How could Clay tell her something like that? She'll probably have nightmares tonight."

"Clay's dealt with children for years. I'm sure his explanation wasn't quite so blunt. I wouldn't worry. Kids have a way of putting things in perspective."

Nicki looked unconvinced.

"Why don't you ask him about it? He just crossed the yard to the front door."

Lexie intercepted Clay before Nicki could get to the door, begging him to join her and Mr. Flops and the puppets for a tea party on the stairway landing.

"If you ladies will excuse me, I'll be with you shortly. It seems I forgot a previous engagement."

Nicki had to laugh as she watched him fold his long legs beneath him, accept a graham cracker from the five-inch serving platter, and raise a minuscule cup of tea to his lips. She and Devon retreated to the porch, leaving the pair to their private party.

Tea was still being served a short time later when Nicki returned to check the progress of dinner. Hearing footsteps on the walk and hoping that Reed had accepted her phoned invitation after all, she swung the screen door open in welcome. Del Ferris let the bulky package he was carrying slide to the flagstone steps and smiled.

"Obviously not who you expected. I apologize if I've come at a bad moment."

"No, of course not. I thought you might be Reed."

"Sorry to disappoint you," he said, tugging his mustache. She stood back, inviting him in. He hefted the package again.

"We were about to have dinner. Would you care to . . ."

"Thank you, no. Just wanted to leave this for Lexie. Oh, there she is. Hello, Verdell."

Lexie didn't look up, but Clay returned the greeting. Del tore the wrapping from the package to reveal the aluminum tubing and green-and-white webbing of a child-size lounge chair.

"How nice. Lexie, what do you say?"

Still perched on the stairs, surrounded by her entourage, Lexie murmured a thank-you.

"Looks like you've made some new friends," Del said, kneeling awkwardly to bring himself to the same level as Clay and his hostess. "What are their names?"

"This is Big Bird."

"And those characters in the striped shirts?"

"Bert and Ernie. Mommy bought them."

"Well, sorry I interrupted things. Enjoy your dinner."

He got to his feet, using the newel post for support, and turned to Clay.

"Those tomato plants of yours need staking. Liable to rot if you don't get them tied up soon."

"Thanks for the warning. I'll take a look at them."

Nicki pulled the screen door closed and watched as Del crossed the yard toward the road.

"He's a funny man," Devon said at her elbow, making her start. "Hardly see him for weeks, except in that garden, then out of the blue he comes calling. And with presents, no less. I think you've caught his fancy."

"The gift was for Lexie," Nicki said, moving the lounger away from the door.

"I can understand being taken with *her*," Clay said, scooping Lexie up under one arm. "I'm kind of smitten myself."

Lexie's giggles almost drowned Mid's announcement that dinner was ready.

"I'd ask Mid what went into that dessert, but I'm afraid I'd soon overdose on calories if I learned to make it myself. When it comes to sweets, I don't seem to know where to stop," Devon told Nicki as they cleared the table.

"Tell me about it. Lexie, stop pestering Clay and go pick up the things you left on the stairway."

"Do I have to?"

"You do if you want to play Parcheesi before you go to bed."

The grumbles continued, accompanied now by a pout.

"What happened to that ray of sunshine I took fishing this morning?"

"Don't start till I get back," Lexie called, racing from the room.

"You're right, Devon. The man has a magic touch."

The adults grouped around the dining room table, laying out the Parcheesi board and markers while Lexie carried her toys up to her room. Devon nudged Nicki.

"Ask him."

"Ask me what?" Clay asked, picking up on the exchange.

"I'm worried Lexie might have nightmares about the turtles and the missing duckling."

Clay traced a scratch in the finish of the old table as if carefully choosing his words.

"Children cope better with the truth, especially concerning death. For that matter, so do adults. I gave her a simple explanation about nature's balance. She asked a lot of questions, but I think she understood. If I'm wrong, give me a call and I'll come talk to her again. Even if it's the middle of the night."

Lexie bounced into the room at that moment, already dressed in baby-doll pajamas and fuzzy slippers. She insisted on sitting between Clay and Devon, forcing everyone to change places. By the middle of the second game, she had abandoned her playing piece and crawled into Clay's lap.

"Will you put me to bed?" she asked, wrapping

her arms about his neck and smothering a yawn against his chest.

Mid, who'd gone upstairs to write to her grandchildren after dispensing with the dishes, joined Devon and Nicki as Clay carried Lexie up the stairs.

"Child's got that man wrapped around her finger."

"I can't wait till she's a teenager," Nicki groaned, rolling her eyes. "What's in the envelope?"

"That picture I told you about. The one I packed to give to Helen. I think it was taken around 1965. Reed would have been about five. Helen's older boy and girl must have been at camp."

Nicki studied the little boy leaning against his father's knee in the color picture, thinking that his pristine outfit—a sailor suit with short pants and jaunty white hat—had probably survived about two seconds after the photographer's last shot.

"Who's the good-looking redhead next to Mrs. Jordan?" Devon asked.

"Helen's younger brother Donnie."

Her eyes still fastened on the grinning, freckle-faced young man beside Reed's mother, Nicki laid the picture down and thrust her trembling hands beneath the table, pressing them against her stomach, trying to calm the turmoil threatening to dislodge her supper.

"Where was this taken?" Devon asked.

"In front of Ray and Helen's place across the lake."

Across the lake, Nicki thought. A short drive, an even briefer distance by boat from where they were sitting. Not awfully far for a red-haired young lover to come courting.

Donnie and Renee. Suddenly Reed's handling of the property, his diligence in tracking her down, even his hesitation when he first drew her into his arms made perfect sense. She shivered. What would they be if Donnie were her father, first cousins? Some places had laws about such things. Of course, an attorney would know all about that. And about ways to muddy the trail of property ownership.

"I've never heard you say where Reed's uncle is now," she said, not really trusting her voice.

"He died a few of years after this was taken," Mid said softly, slipping the photo back into the envelope.

"How . . . how did he die?" Nicki asked, not caring that her voice broke, drawing a curious glance from Devon.

"I'd rather you asked Reed about it," she said. "I think I'll turn in. Joel's coming in the morning to finish the trim."

A moment later they heard the sound of Mid's door at the top of the stairs closing firmly. Devon opened her mouth as if to ask a question, placing a hand on Nicki's arm, but Nicki shook her head. The indistinct murmur of Clay's voice and Lexie's muffled giggle floated in from the outside, traveling between the two screened porches.

"You really like that song, don't you?" Mr. Verdell asked as he tucked Lexie and Mr. Flops and Big Bird in bed.

"Uh-huh. Mommy sings it to me if I have bad dreams."

"You're not going to have bad dreams tonight, are you, Sunshine?"

"I'm gonna dream about woodpeckers and fish and our special place." She looked at him solemnly. "I didn't tell anybody."

Mr. Verdell gave her a little squeeze and tugged a lock of her hair. She scooted over so he could sit on the bed. His hand stroked her forehead gently, making her feel all warm and fuzzy. She liked the way he smelled.

"Are you a doctor?"

"I'm a kind of doctor."

"The kind that helps people?"

"All doctors want to help people, Sunshine. I'm the kind who tries to help people feel better about things."

She thought about that for a moment.

"Like when we talked about the men in the alley?"

"Something like that," he said, smiling down at her.

"Can you help my mommy stop falling down so much?"

"It doesn't work quite like that, Lexie. People have to want my help. They have to ask me themselves. And sometimes I'm not the right doctor for them."

"Oh."

He smoothed the covers and tucked them tighter around her.

"How'd you know I was a doctor, Sunshine?"

"I heard Devon and Mommy talking."

"I bet you hear lots of things people don't realize you do."

He kissed her cheek and squeezed her again and then got up. Lexie hugged Big Bird and Mr. Flops, snuggling deeper under the covers. The blanket next to her face smelled like Mr. Verdell.

"You want these guys in there too?"

"I'm gonna let Bert and Ernie sleep with Mommy 'cause they're her favorites." She yawned, fighting to keep her eyes from closing. "When can we go back to our special place?"

"Sometime soon, Sunshine, I promise. Now go to sleep. Sweet dreams."

He turned out the porch light but continued to stand beside the bed. Lexie could see him in the glow from the hall light. She tried to make her eyelids stay open. Mr. Verdell and his smell, lingering on the covers, were the last things she remembered when sleep won out.

Nicki bolted up in bed, disoriented by the darkness and the shrieks that pierced the night. The screams continued, making seconds seem like minutes as she threw off the last vestige of sleep that insisted she must be having a nightmare. But the screams were real and they were coming from Lexie.

She switched on the light, the movement automatic as she moved to the other bed. The shrieking trailed off into a series of gasps and whimpers punctuated by an occasional hiccup.

"Lexie, sweetie, it's okay. You're having a bad dream."

Lexie's trembling little body protested, twisting from side to side in denial, thrashing against her arms. Mid's anxious face appeared in the doorway.

"Is she all right?"

Nicki shook her head.

"I saw him," Lexie whimpered, her voice petulant, her eyes scrunched tightly shut against whatever had invaded her sleep.

Nicki rocked her child in her arms.

"Who do you think you saw, sweetie?"

"A man. He . . . was standing . . . by your bed." The hiccups had overpowered the sobs. Mid murmured something about a glass of water and disappeared.

"Lexie, open your eyes. That's better. Now look around. See? There's nobody here. It was just a bad dream."

"No it . . . wasn't." Her lower lip protruded now, the tear-rimmed eyes threatening to overflow once more. "I saw him."

"Sweetie, there was nobody there."

"There was too!"

Huge tears and even bigger gasps accompanied the frantic insistence. Nicki accepted the water Mid held out and urged Lexie to drink. The sobs subsided and the hiccups trailed off. She tried to return Lexie to her bed.

"Nooooo!"

Nicki looked at Mid in desperation.

"Would you try to go back to sleep if we proved there's no one in the house but just us three?" Mid asked.

Lexie looked up at her warily.

"We could go through each room," Mid explained to Nicki's questioning look.

Nicki forced Lexie to loosen the death grip on her neck.

"Would that make you feel better, Lexie?"

Lexie raised terrified eyes and nodded. Nicki started to rise, but the arms tightened about her once more.

"We'll all go look," Mid suggested.

Switching on lights as they went, they peered under beds and into dark corners, even shining a flashlight into the far reaches of the attic storage area. Lexie managed a tiny smile when Mid's broom attack on a closed shower curtain revealed only an empty bathtub, but her arms remained fastened tightly about her mother's neck.

Mid's cooking was definitely sticking to Lexie's ribs, Nicki thought. Her back had begun to ache.

Downstairs Mid checked the dead bolt while Nicki peered out the long windows beside the front door. Mid flipped on the kitchen light. The side door that led to the clothesline that ran between the house and the Tarleton woods was also secured. At Lexie's insistence, Nicki opened the doors of the Blazer to prove no one was hiding in the vehicle. Not even the garage rafters escaped examination.

When every light in the house was blazing and each dark corner and man-size cabinet had been examined, Nicki turned her head until she could see her daughter's face.

"Now, are you satisfied?"

Lexie nodded.

"I'll get the lights," Mid murmured.

Back in her bed with Nicki curled protectively around her, Lexie finally relaxed in sleep. Exhaustion fought with anger for control of Nicki's thoughts.

Give me a call, even if it's the middle of the night.

She fumed, sending dark sentiments in the direction of Clay's house. Duck-eating turtles and child-snatching men that crept through the night were all the same in the mind of a child with Lexie's imagination.

The soft sound of a door closing somewhere inside the house tapped at the fringes of her consciousness. Mid's using the bathroom, she thought, sleep conquering her irritation at Clay and forcing her eyes closed.

===== 26 =====

A cry echoed somewhere in the black expanse of woodland, sending spasms of terror along his spine. Urine gushed across his pants, recalling bygone shame. He bit back a cry of his own and threw himself against the wall, listening for renewed activity from inside, certain the pounding in his ears must be the report of running feet; the harsh whoosh that surrounded him, the noise of approaching helicopters. Any second, searchlights would flood the narrow space between garage and fence. A disembodied voice would demand that he reveal himself.

Beating wings rustled toward a treetop perch, and an owl hooted the avian equivalent of a satisfied belch. His terror subsided. The pounding diminished to the familiar, if erratic, beat of his heart. The whoosh became his labored breath. There were no footsteps, no hovering helicopter, no blazing light. Only a frightened little boy trapped inside an aging body.

He hugged the clapboard siding, seeking what warmth remained from the heat of the day. The surface gave no comfort. His soiled slacks clung to his body, chilling him, reminding him of long-ago failures. Memory of the claustrophobic minutes of hiding returned to torture him further—that tiny, airless space, so similar to the garage room; the muffled sound of the women's nervous laughter, so like Cordelia's whispered taunts.

Anger flared against the images. Cordelia's face dissolved, replaced by Nicki's angular features, *her* deceptively innocent expression. He pressed a fist to his mouth, smothering a cry of rage as he'd meant to extinguish his tormentor's life.

He began to inch toward the drive, away from the front of the house. She could be sitting in the darkness of the upper porch, waiting, hoping to pinpoint his movement with a flashlight beam. He felt gravel beneath his feet, stepped back onto the closely clipped grass, and sprinted toward the road.

In the safety of a cleansing shower the memory of the dark space flared again. He forced it away with the sting of scalding water. Rage festered and grew as the water flailed his flesh, washing away his shame, absolving his failure.

He'd moved too fast. Panic was as much his enemy as Nicki. But time was running out. Every hour, every returning memory brought exposure nearer.

Damn Nicki! And damn the stupid puppets!

Mommy bought them.

Of course she had. The damn puppets were yet another hint of what was to come. He had to keep trying. Had to find another way. She'd left him no choice.

One way or another Nicki Prevot had to die.

......27......

N icki slipped the skillet into the soapy water
and grabbed a dishcloth to clean a spot of
grease that had dripped onto the floor. A
black smudge a few feet away caught her attention.
She reached out to wipe the smear but drew back
her hand.

The dirt in front of the outside door seemed to
form a wavy pattern against the cream-colored
flooring.

"Mid," she called over her shoulder.

The housekeeper's face appeared in the pass-
through window on the dining room side.

"Didn't you tell me you mopped last night?"

"Sure did. I never could fry fish without splat-
tering grease. That new floor was as slick as an ice
rink."

"Could you come here a minute?"

"Be right there. Lexie, shouldn't you put on some
shoes?"

Lexie ran into the kitchen, heading for the outside door. Nicki held out her arm, but the child
ducked easily beneath it and lunged for the door-
knob. The dirt outline scattered in a dozen directions beneath her bare feet.

"Where do you think you're going?" Nicki asked sharply.

"To get my tennies."

"What are they doing outside?"

"Miz Mid hung them up 'cause they got wet."

"I meant to bring them in before I went to bed," Mid said from the doorway. "They're probably wet again from last night's dew. You'd better wear your red sandals."

"We're gonna watch tennis. I *gotta* wear my tennies."

"Then go see if they're dry."

Lexie charged through the door, slamming it shut behind her.

"You'll have to turn the inner knob or let her back in," Mid told Nicki. "That door has a snap lock."

"It's not a dead bolt?"

"No. I guess whoever installed the locks on the front door and the garage didn't think a kitchen needed a dead bolt. Or maybe they forgot it. Anyway, if the inner knob's turned, when you go out, the door locks behind you."

The pounding of a child-size fist underscored her words.

"I can't get in," Lexie's voice complained through the closed door.

"Could you reach your shoes?" Mid asked when Nicki opened the door.

"It's too high and they're all drippy."

"They'll dry again in an hour or two."

Dragging her feet and mumbling about tennis players on TV not wearing red shoes, Lexie left to find her sandals.

"What did you want me for?" Mid asked.

Nicki looked at the scattered bits of dirt and

shook her head. Whatever pattern she'd imagined she'd seen was gone now. Lexie's nightmare had her questioning her own perceptions. Mid had probably concentrated her mopping on the area around the stove and simply missed the smear near the threshold.

"It doesn't matter. We'd better open the garage. I think that's Joel's truck on the driveway."

The contractor had indeed arrived. He carried in a stack of trim molding and went back for two rolls of wallpaper.

"Should be finished up a little after noon. All except that screen you wanted for this door. Be a lot cooler, cooking in here on hot days once it comes in," he added.

"I'd like you to put a dead-bolt lock on the inside door," Nicki told him. Imaginary intruders aside, a new lock made good sense, she reasoned.

"Meant to suggest that before. Surprised vandals haven't hit this place over the years. All it'd take to spring that lock is a table knife or a piece of thin plastic. Still, with the house being so close to the fence and all, reckon only someone who'd been inside would know the door's even there."

Rubbing her suddenly chilled arms, Nicki stared at the door.

"Worked on that special project this weekend. Got a rush job on a rental unit down by the marina this week, but I ought to be able to get back to it next Saturday. Maybe finish up by Sunday. Need to take another look at that slab, though."

Lexie bounded into the room, insisting she'd seen Devon climbing to the court. She smiled shyly at Joel.

"We're going to watch a tennis match. Why don't you check those measurements before you get started in here," Nicki told him over the top of Lexie's head.

Mid walked with them into the yard. As Nicki had expected, the sound of tennis balls on the paved court drew Lexie's attention. Nicki took her across the road, then returned to where Joel was checking the playhouse slab. The three were talking quietly when Del Ferris came up the road, carrying his gardening tools. He waved a greeting without joining them.

"Fella reminds me a bit of someone," Joel murmured. He shook his head. "Memory's not what it used to be."

"I've got the same complaint," Mid said with a laugh.

"Probably come to me eventually. Usually does."

Nicki left the pair and crossed the road. Lexie, bouncing down each level of stone steps, met her on the second tier.

"Hurry, Mommy. They're already playing."

Nicki listened to the thumping balls. Her anger at Clay over Lexie's nightmare lingered. Still, he and Devon had volunteered to give her a lesson after they were done. If you were going to own a tennis court, the least you could do was learn the game, she reasoned.

"If you get bored, come help me weed," Del called to Lexie from the flower bed where he knelt. He held up a wiggling, earth-covered creature. "Lots of these fellas crawled out to catch the dew this morning, if you need more bait."

Nicki shivered.

"You can come back down if you get tired of watching," she told Lexie. "Just don't cross the road without an adult."

* * *

Mr. Ferris was right, Lexie decided, tossing a piece of clipped grass in the air. Tennis was boring. Devon and Mr. Verdell seemed to be having fun running around, chasing the yellow balls. Most of the time all she could do was sit. Mommy wouldn't let her run onto the court after the balls like she'd seen on TV. If a ball bounced onto the grass, she could toss it back, but that didn't happen very often.

She whispered to Mommy she was going to help Mr. Ferris and climbed back down to the garden.

"Knew that silly game would get old."

Lexie shrugged and wandered over to a plot where a tangle of vinelike plants trailed across the ground. Little green balls that looked like baby apples hid between the leaves.

"What're these?"

Mr. Ferris stopped pulling bits of grass from a flower bed and looked up.

"Tomato vines. Ought to be staked up or caged before they start to rot. Verdell's been too busy fishing to tend to them."

"Tomatoes live in cages?"

"Special ones, like those." He pointed to another plot. "Mine are so full you can't really see them, but they're there."

"I hope Mr. Verdell's don't rot. I like tomatoes."

Mr. Ferris stood up and dusted off the knees of his pants.

"Got extra cages in my garage. S'pose I could loan him some. Want to come along and help carry?"

Lexie glanced up toward the tennis courts. Mommy had said not to cross the road without an adult, but Mr. Ferris was an adult.

"Only take a few minutes. I know Verdell would be glad not to have to make a trip into town."

Lexie followed Mr. Ferris toward his house.

Devon dropped down beside Nicki on the grass.

"That was some workout. Ready for your first lesson?"

"I suppose." Nicki watched Clay tighten the drooping net on the opposite side of the court. "Lexie had a terrible nightmare last night. I'm surprised her screams didn't wake you."

"My sinuses were giving me fits, so I took some prescription medicine. Sometimes it really puts me out. Did you call Clay?"

"I decided he was the problem, not the solution," she murmured as Devon's tennis partner joined them.

Clay picked up Devon's racket.

"Ready, Nicki? After that beating I just took, my age is showing. We'll start out slow. I don't need *two* women around here able to run me into the ground."

Lexie looked around. Mr. Ferris's car filled half of the big garage. Several large metal pans and a row of dark-colored bottles lined a counter that ran the length of the empty side. A heavy black curtain covered the only window.

"What's that?" Lexie asked, pointing at a funny-looking clothesline strung with tiny clips.

"Sometimes I use the garage as a darkroom to develop film. That's where I hang prints while they dry."

"I don't like dark rooms."

"It doesn't get that dark. Let me show you."

Mr. Ferris pushed a button and the garage door

slid down. He reached up and switched on a funny-looking lightbulb, then turned off the overhead light. Most of the garage got real dark except around the counter beneath the bulb. The glowing bulb reminded Lexie of her mother's flashlight when they were searching the house.

"It's scary. I don't like it."

"Didn't mean to frighten you, Bunny." He pushed the button again and the door rolled up, letting in the sunlight.

"Why don't you have the store 'velope your pictures? That's what MarLynn does."

"Taking pictures is how I make my living."

"Like the lady at K mart? MarLynn took me there one time. I gave Mommy my picture for Christmas."

Mr. Ferris smiled.

"My pictures are a little different than that." He picked up a magazine lying on the counter. "This is one I took."

Lexie studied the man and woman on the page he held out. They were standing on a big rock at the beach. Waves crashed all around them and the sky was cloudy, like it was going to rain. The lady wore a long white dress, and her hair was wet. The man stood behind her, his arms around her waist, his head bent as if whispering secrets. Lexie thought he looked a little like Reed.

"I'll bet your mommy would like a new picture of you. What do you think, Bunny? Shall we surprise her?"

Lexie looked back at the road doubtfully. She hadn't told Mommy she was leaving the garden. If Mommy got mad, she might not let her go swimming after lunch.

"Tennis games last a long time. A picture just

takes a minute," Mr. Ferris said. He opened the door into the house and looked back at her.

Mommy had said the K mart picture was her best Christmas present ever. She'd kept it in a frame by her bed. But the picture had burned up. Mommy would probably like a new one, Lexie decided. She followed Mr. Ferris inside.

The room Mr. Ferris called his studio was filled with equipment. Lexie stood by a chair he'd called a settee while he adjusted two big lights that looked like white umbrellas. Getting things right seemed to take a long time. If he didn't hurry up, Lexie thought, the tennis game would be over. Then Mommy would really be mad.

Finally Mr. Ferris stopped fussing and moved behind the camera. Lexie leaned against the settee and tried to smile as big as the lady at K mart had told her to do.

"Don't smile like that. It's not natural."

Lexie stopped smiling and frowned instead. Mr. Ferris left the camera and lifted her onto the settee.

"Cross your legs. No, like an Indian. That's it."

Lexie tugged at her shorts. Sometimes when she and Sharraye sat like this, MarLynn said their panties showed. She didn't think Mommy would like the picture if that happened. Mr. Ferris knelt in front of her, slid his hands under her hips, and scooted her against the back of the settee. His fingers tickled along her legs as he let go. Lexie squirmed away.

"Stop fidgeting. I want to get the right pose. There. That's better."

He patted her knee, straightened her shoulders, and smiled.

"You're a very pretty little girl, you know that, Bunny? I wish we had more time so I could do this right."

Mr. Ferris brushed her hair behind her ear. He was breathing funny again, like his cold had come back. His hand cupped her chin. For a minute Lexie thought he was going to kiss her cheek the way Mr. Verdell had when she'd scratched her leg and started to cry in the woods. She hoped he wouldn't; Mommy made her take nasty-tasting stuff when she caught a cold.

Instead of leaning toward her, Mr. Ferris brushed his fingers across her lips and moved back to the camera.

"Stick out your chin and do this," he told her, puckering his lips as if he knew what she'd been thinking. "That's it. Now, relax your mouth a little. A little more. Perfect."

He took several more quick pictures, saying silly things and making funny faces that made her giggle. They'd been away from the garden an awfully long time, Lexie realized.

"Can we go back now?"

"You haven't paid me for your picture yet."

Lexie frowned. MarLynn had paid the lady at K mart.

"I don't have any money."

"I always get some kind of payment, Bunny." He smiled. "Tell you what. I'll settle for a big hug this time."

Russell always said you had to pay for things, or it was stealing. If she stole something, Lexie thought, Mommy wouldn't *ever* let her go swimming again. She didn't want to hug Mr. Ferris, but she guessed she didn't have a choice—he'd already taken her picture.

Mr. Ferris bent down and gathered her into his arms, lifting her from the settee. His mustache felt scratchy against her face. Lexie squirmed until he put her down.

They went back through the garage to get the to-mato cages.

"I wanna look for the walking-stick," she told him as they started along the road toward the garden.

"I'm afraid you can't do that, Bunny."

"Why?"

"The walking-stick began eating the daylilies."

Lexie looked up. Mr. Ferris was tugging his mustache.

"Did they make him sick?"

"No, he didn't get sick."

"Did you take him back to the sanks-wary?" she asked hopefully.

"I had to destroy him, Bunny, before he did more damage."

Lexie felt a tear forming in the corner of one eye. She was sure Mommy and Reed would have taken the walking-stick back to the sanks-wary if Mr. Ferris had asked. Clutching the cages to her chest, she walked faster, her head down, her lips pressed tightly together to make the tear go away.

"Don't run, Bunny, you might fall on the cages and get hurt. I wouldn't want something like that to happen to you."

Lexie made her feet go slower. Mr. Ferris caught up with her and placed one hand lightly on her shoulder.

"You're not going to spoil your mommy's surprise because I had to destroy the walking-stick, are you, Bunny?"

Lexie shook her head without looking up. Maybe Mr. Ferris would bring the pictures to her house when he got done 'veloping them. She chewed on her lower lip. Mommy had said she shouldn't be afraid of a neighbor just 'cause he was a man. She wasn't really afraid of Mr. Ferris, she told herself, but she didn't like him very much either. Not like she liked Mr. Verdell. *He* would have taken the walking-stick back to the sanks-wary.

Nicki's heart gave a little lurch when she started down from the courts and realized the gardens were deserted. Lexie's shout drew her attention. Her daughter and Del were walking up the road, carrying several cone-shaped wire frames. Lexie called her again. Del stopped fiddling with his mustache and waved.

"Sometimes Del reminds me of someone," Devon murmured, catching up with her.

"Joel Lynch said the same thing this morning," Nicki responded. She hurried to meet Lexie on the lowest terrace.

"You promised to stay in the garden, young lady."

Lexie hung her head and toed a clod of dirt with her sandal.

"Afraid I'm to blame," Del said.

He gestured to where Clay was examining his own garden plot.

"Lexie was worried about Verdell's tomatoes. When I mentioned I had extra cages, she was so eager to go get them, I just didn't think." He tapped Lexie on the shoulder. "We'll have to do better at keeping promises, won't we?"

Lexie nodded without raising her head.

"You were right about my tomatoes," Clay told Del, as he joined the group. "I'm going to have to get busy."

"These should help," Del said, handing him the cages.

"That's neighborly of you, Del. I think I'll set them up before I head for the house."

"I'll help," Devon said.

Nicki thanked the pair again for her lesson and nudged Lexie toward the road. As if to make up for her earlier disobedience, she clung tightly to Nicki's hand as they crossed. Her thoughts on other matters, Nicki barely noticed Lexie's uncharacteristic silence.

Standing in front of the net with Devon's racket in her hand had triggered a memory, drawing her back to a moment in her forgotten childhood. The image of Renee wrapping Nicki's tiny hand around an adult-size racket and guiding her stroke across the net had been vivid. The court's white lines, the vine-covered chain-link that muffled the sound of vehicles passing on Upper T, the scent of lilacs growing on the hillside beyond the fence, even the impression on her palm of the tiny holes in the racket's leather grip—each returned in sharp focus. Only one detail hovered tantalizingly beyond reach.

Who had returned her awkward, childish serve?

The shadowy figure she'd faced at the net remained an enigma. Refusal of the image to coalesce only increased her anxiety. She could feel and smell, could almost taste, that long-ago moment, and still the faceless person in tennis whites would not come into focus.

Why had Renee worked so hard to bury every trace of her childhood, to erase whatever memories might have remained? What terrible thing had driven them from the lake? How had her mother denied her her past so completely?

She'd managed to continue the lesson, but Clay's

intense scrutiny had made it clear he'd sensed her momentary distress. Like her dream about pancakes and place mats, this new memory lingered, adding an urgency to her search for the truth.

Nicki felt as if she were rushing toward some unknown destination, blind and out of control. She needed to do something to solve the puzzle her life had become, not just wait for the next panic attack to add yet another crooked piece.

Had she been the center of a nasty custody dispute? she wondered, immediately rejecting the idea. Renee wouldn't have left her so often with housekeepers she'd barely known, vulnerable to being snatched back, if she'd been involved in a parental kidnapping. Besides, the theory that the money that supported them had come from someone connected to Trumpeter Lake was the only one that made sense.

Fingers dug into her palm, drawing her thoughts back from the answerless void. Her eyes followed Lexie's pointing finger to the turtle on the steps of the dock.

"Is he the one that got the baby duck?"

"I don't know, honey."

Damn Clay Verdell.

"You'd never let anyone get *me*, would you?"

Double damn.

"No, Lexie. I'll always be here to keep you safe."

Lexie kicked at an acorn with the toe of her sandal.

"I wish my daddy hadn't died. Then I'd have two people to keep me safe."

Hearing the echo of her own childhood thoughts was like a knife slicing through Nicki's chest. She scooped Lexie into her arms in a fierce hug.

There was no way to bring Alan back for Lexie,

Nicki thought, but there was nothing to stop her from tackling head-on the problem of her own missing parent. Her jaw tightened. Someone had the solution to that mystery, and if she was right, the snapshot Mid had shown her might have provided the key.

▪▪▪▪▪ 28 ▪▪▪▪▪

"This is more work than I expected. I'm a city boy at heart," Clay said, rearranging vines inside one of the wire cages.

"Just keep thinking about ripe tomatoes and BLTs," Devon told him.

She leaned back on her heels and looked around. They were alone on the hillside. The noonday sun had added another layer to the perspiration of their morning exertion. Warm earth and cut grass and the scent of Del's flowers underscored the peacefulness and serenity of the garden, and yet she felt edgy.

Maybe it was Clay's presence, she thought. The sharing of such a mundane task shouldn't cause unease. But gardening was such a domestic activity. Pruning her mother's roses had been one of the few things her mother and father had continued to share during their last tension-filled year together.

Her parents' breakup had entered Devon's thoughts shortly after she and Clay began to work. Her life until that summer now seemed so idyllic; those days so full of wonder and innocence.

When Clay spoke, she was so absorbed in her reverie that she had to ask him to repeat himself.

"I said, 'a nickel for your thoughts.' Price adjusted for inflation," he explained with a smile.

"I was thinking about the last summer I spent at the lake as a child. It seems like that time belongs to another world."

"How old were you?"

"Twelve, but I was still a baby, really. I looked more like eight or nine—pudgy, flat-chested, baby-faced . . ."

Something snaked through her memory, then slithered away.

"What's the matter?"

She shook her head.

"Nothing. A snip of something I couldn't hang on to. I'm getting as bad as Nicki about childhood memories."

"Twelve can be a painful year."

"It was. My folks broke up, and we quit coming to the lake. My whole world changed. I grew a lot that next year and developed a bustline. Everything happened too fast. It was more than I could handle. I turned into a real hellion for a while."

"What brought all that back?"

"Living on this side of the lake again, I suppose. That and Lexie's innocence. I'd forgotten I was ever that untouched by life." She shaded her eyes to study his face. "Playing therapist, are you?"

"Never crossed my mind."

She stood looking down at Del's riotous flower beds and the neat, symmetrical plantings that reflected Bob Stockton's touch. The English-country-garden designs seemed odd from a rustic personality like Old Bob, she thought, wondering where the yardman was today. Usually he spent Tuesdays at Nicki's, but she couldn't remember hearing his mower all morning.

Clay finished caging the last tomato plant and picked up the can of balls and both rackets. As they crossed the road, Devon thought about how easily she'd abandoned her initial resistance to Gwyn's matchmaking scheme. Clay's determination to mask his emotions intrigued her. No matter how hard he worked to maintain his distance, his voice and his eyes gave away how much he cared about things like kindness and propriety. And people. Clay cared about people.

"Nicki's afraid to open up to a stranger about what she's going through, Clay. Why haven't you offered to help her?"

He looked away, staring at Nicki's house as if seeing through the walls into the heart of its occupant. After a moment he shifted his gaze, studying the toe of his tennis shoe as intently. For an instant, Devon feared she'd pushed the issue beyond the limits of their tenuous friendship.

"I'm not the right therapist for Nicki. Besides, she's not ready to face any truths."

"You mean she's not ready to 'find herself.' "

The remark drew a wry smile.

"Something like that." His face clouded. "Nicki's demons might go away if she left here."

"You can't really mean she should run from her problems?"

"Sometimes ignorance can be less painful than discovering the truth."

The bitterness in his voice wrenched Devon's gaze from Nicki's house to his face.

"Why did you come here, Clay?"

"Like all rats I got tired of the maze."

An automatic response; too simplistic to be the truth.

"You knew Pip Sheridan at Berkeley, didn't you?"

To her surprise he nodded. Somehow she'd expected denial.

"Pip was everything parents of my generation worried about—spontaneous and irreverent, outspoken and rude, a real woman but never a lady—the consummate rebel."

"Sounds like you knew her well."

"As well as anyone could know a rebel behind a cause, I suppose. We met outside the ROTC office." The wry grin flashed again. "*Life* magazine would have loved it—the soldier and the protest leader."

"Rocky ground for a relationship."

"An ongoing skirmish describes it better than relationship. We had some heated discussions over the next couple of years."

"For example?"

The lightheartedness left his voice.

"Pip thought I should burn my draft card. I thought I should do my patriotic duty. The week I graduated, I enlisted."

Clay broke the silence that followed. The bitterness in his voice remained.

"The irony is, she was right about a lot of things. 'Nam nearly destroyed our generation. It made everyone a victim—the Vietnamese who lived it, the Americans who fought it, the people left behind. We were all victims in one way or another."

"Even Pip and her protest friends?" Devon asked softly, afraid to break the spell permitting her to see behind his mask.

"Especially Pip."

Silence stretched again.

"Did you ever see her after you got back?"

"Once. I tried to look her up after my first hitch. She was living in some commune back in the hills.

She slammed the gate in my face and called me a baby-killer."

"That's awful," Devon murmured. She turned away, torn by the naked pain in his expression.

"I heard years later that she regretted saying it the moment it was out of her mouth. But apologizing about her politics wasn't part of Pip's makeup. Someone told me she softened a lot in the years before she died. Her approach, not her beliefs."

"It was Pip who said the lake was a great place to be a child, wasn't it?"

"Yes," he admitted quietly, turning away from the house where Pip Sheridan had once been a child. His face had resumed its emotional mask. Clearly the subject was closed.

Nicki opened the screen door and motioned Clay inside, wondering if her discussion with Devon about Lexie's nightmare had prompted his unexpected afternoon visit.

"Lexie told me about the search you've been conducting."

She hadn't told Devon about their middle-of-the-night security sweep. At the courts Lexie's only exchange with Clay had taken place in Nicki's presence. The nightmare and its aftermath had not been discussed then either. Her confusion must have shown on her face.

"The missing swings? That empty frame out front keeps reminding me I promised her I'd help you tackle the garage."

"Lexie's upstairs, taking a nap."

"Probably better if she's not around to get in the way. Do I need to go back for my ladder?"

"There's an old wooden one hanging on the wall in the garage. I don't know how sturdy it is."

"Let's find out."

The paint-splattered ladder wobbled too much in Nicki's opinion, but Clay insisted it could handle the job at hand. Unfinished rafters extended the length of the garage. Beneath the slant where the roof joined the house, one-by-six boards straddled the beams at random intervals, creating makeshift shelving for an odd assortment of cardboard cartons.

Mid left her supper preparations to lend an extra pair of hands. Together she and Nicki ferried boxes to the floor as Clay lifted them down. Nicki gave the contents of each a quick look, shaking her head over the things people deemed worth saving.

Many of the boxes she stacked along the wall on the unused side of the garage for Bob Stockton to haul away. She had no use for rusty tools or frayed and faded curtains. One or two cartons, whose contents looked intriguing, she set aside to examine more closely on some rainy afternoon. None of the containers yielded the elusive playground equipment.

"Any idea what's up here?" Clay asked, moving the ladder below the last section. The area looked like a graveyard for fishing equipment. Old tarps and nets and minnow buckets were stacked haphazardly in the narrow space, as was a small pile of weathered boards.

"Junk, junk, and more junk," Mid volunteered.

Nicki stepped closer to the ladder.

"Isn't that the end of a chain? There, behind those boots."

"You've got good eyes," Clay told her, balancing himself on the ladder's top step to reach beyond the hip boots into the dark corner. "I think we've got something. Oh-oh. Shit! Look out!"

The warning came too late. As the weight shifted on the make-do shelving, the boards parted, allowing items to tumble through the gap. A large heavy tarp unfolded as if in slow motion, spreading like a blanket over Nicki, jerking her hand from the ladder, driving her to the floor.

Hip boots and tangled chains cascaded after the tarp, unseating Clay as he tried to juggle the onslaught. In seconds he and the remaining items followed the tarp's descent, pinning Nicki's arms, tightening the heavy canvas against her face.

"Dammit. These boards are jammed beneath the front of the car. Hang on, Nicki, we'll get you out in a minute. Mid, I need another hand. Careful. The damn things are full of splinters."

This time the blackness was real. This time it wouldn't go away. Minutes became hours as Nicki struggled against the weight on her chest and her arms, oblivious to Clay's muffled oaths.

No, please. Get it off.

She tried to cry out, to free the words screaming in her head. Canvas filled her mouth, trapping what little air remained from her fall. Terror seized control, seeping outward from her lungs, oozing into her pores like an insatiable malignancy.

Mommeeee! Make him stop!

The roaring words became a warning babble.

Mustn't tell. The worms will get Mommy!

Her chest hurt so bad, and there wasn't any air.

The weight on her arms shifted slightly, then the darkness lifted. A face swam in front of her. She coughed, filling her lungs with precious air. Hands closed firmly about her forearms. Still caught up in the terror, she pulled against their grasp.

"No, please. I didn't. I swear I didn't," she murmured.

The face moved closer; other eyes peered into her own. Familiar eyes. The thought had no time to penetrate her consciousness before her mind embraced the darkness.

"Nicki? Try to sit up. You'll breathe easier."

The words seemed to come from far away. Nicki struggled to a sitting position. She was in the house, on the front-porch sofa. Mid hovered above her; Clay knelt by her side, his usually impassive features strained and anxious.

"How do you feel?"

The concern in his voice touched her strangely.

"What happened to me?" Nicki asked.

Clay described the events in the garage.

"It was more than momentary panic," he concluded. "As some of my young patients would say, you 'freaked out,' Nicki. I can't let you continue like this. I'll ask some colleagues for referrals, get you the names of people in this area . . ."

She shook her head, as much to clear it as to reinforce her verbal denial.

"I don't want a stranger digging about in my mind," Nicki protested, her voice sounding more like Lexie's than her own. She felt emotionally battered, as if she might start weeping at any moment.

Clay opened his mouth as if to protest.

"You're not a stranger," she blurted out.

She felt her face flame as he took her hands, embarrassed by a sudden urge to curl into his arms for a reassuring hug.

"Nicki, I'm not licensed in Michigan. It wouldn't be legal for me to treat you, not to mention the ethical considerations involved." He looked away, out across the lake.

"Devon says you've worked with children. What's

happening to me goes back to my childhood. I'm certain of that."

"All the more reason to find a therapist who's licensed in this state, the kind of person who can work with you for as long as it takes."

"You could be that person. I don't care about legalities and ethics. I already know you."

"You don't know me, Nicki. Not the way you think you do." He held her gaze for a long moment. "I'm sorry. It just wouldn't work."

He dropped her hands and stood up as if to go.

"How come nobody said you were here?" Lexie demanded from the doorway, hands on her hips.

"Hello, Sunshine. Guess what we found in the garage."

"My swing!"

"And some monkey rings, but they're very dirty. I'm going to take them home, clean them up, and then hang them for you."

"Today?" Lexie asked hopefully.

"Probably not."

Her expression fell, then brightened again.

"Are you gonna eat with us?"

"Not tonight," he told Lexie.

Lexie followed him back into the house. Nicki heard their footsteps go first to the garage, then into the kitchen. Clay's step, punctuated by rattling chains, returned alone to the front door. He waved as he passed the porch and crossed the yard.

Devon came out as Clay approached her patio, and they stood chatting for a moment. Afternoon shadows from the willow tree by the dock shaded the pair. Devon glanced in Nicki's direction, then quickly looked away. At that distance the porch screens prevented anyone from seeing inside, but

Nicki could see out, and she could guess at their conversation.

Mid lay in her bed, listening to the silence. Something had awakened her—a sound or movement somewhere in the house. Not like last night, not Lexie's screams, though she had to admit the child's imagination had them all on edge.

The noise, whatever it had been, wasn't repeated, yet she felt instinctively that something wasn't right.

Next you'll be swearing you've been visited by little green men who offered a tour of their saucer, she scolded herself. *Maybe Nicki got up for the bathroom. And maybe you're turning into a Nervous Nelly in your dotage.*

Still, there wouldn't be any harm in checking to see if Nicki was all right. "Won't rest till you're sure your chick's been tucked in safe," her husband had always teased when KT was growing up and had given her some silly reason to fret. Kenneth must be smiling from his grave to see how she'd adopted Nicki and Lexie to fill the void left when KT and the grandchildren moved halfway around the world.

The weather front the radio had warned about was moving in. A strong breeze gusted through the hall from the sleeping porch and up the staircase from the first floor. The weatherman had promised wind but no rain, but how often did he get things right? Maybe she should go down and close the front-porch windows after she checked on everybody.

She trotted down the hall, past the room with the canopy bed and the one with the nautical theme to the two bedrooms behind the sleeping porch.

The breeze was stronger here, whistling through

the doors that provided access to the porch from each room. Lexie had chosen the bed to the left of the left doorway. Nicki's lay between the two openings. Two more beds filled the wider area to the right of the second door.

Clouds had not yet succeeded in obscuring the moon. Mid could make out Lexie's form in the bed on her left. She was curled on her side, relaxed in sleep, her tangled auburn hair veiled across her face. Mid tucked the covers more tightly about the little body and turned to check on Nicki.

Twisted sheets revealed an empty bed.

That must have been what awakened me, Mid thought. Nicki had had trouble sleeping and had gone down for a glass of milk or something to eat. She'd hardly touched her dinner, not surprising after her fright in the garage. With all that had been happening to her, it was no wonder Nicki couldn't sleep.

She started back down the hall. At the stairs she paused, staring down into the darkness. If Nicki was down there, why hadn't she turned on a light? With her mind riled the way it was, sitting around in the dark brooding wasn't a healthy thing to do. Not a healthy thing at all.

Mid went back for her robe and slippers and turned on the stairway light. Halfway down she caught her breath.

The front door stood wide open, the key still protruding on the interior side of the dead-bolt lock. Nicki had insisted a key remain in the lock whenever they were home. The fire that had destroyed her apartment was still fresh in her mind. Joel had shared her concern about the danger of a misplaced key during an emergency and recommended a different type of dead bolt for the kitchen. One that could be opened from inside without a key.

Mid moved to shut the door, then hesitated. Uneasiness made her step outside. She glanced around, chiding herself for foolish notions as she shivered in the cool night air. Movement caught her eye, turning her toward the lake, pulling her farther into the yard. She quickened her steps until she was running, ignoring the acorns and bits of bark beneath the thin soles of her slippers. At the dock she slowed, afraid of startling the ghostly figure huddled at the far end.

The weather front had brought fog with it. Mist hung over the center of the lake. Trailing tentacles stretched toward shore like beckoning fingers. Nicki stood facing the water, clutching herself with her arms, her pale nightgown billowing about her ankles in the breeze.

Mid moved forward cautiously.

"Nicki? Honey, are you all right?"

"I couldn't sleep."

Mid moved a little closer, shivering, though not from the cold. Nicki was leaning into the breeze, gripping the end of the dock with her toes as if poised to dive into the dark water below.

"It's getting chilly. Don't you think you should come in? I could make you some cocoa. Warm you right up."

She reached out to draw Nicki back from the edge. Her hands closed on arms as cold as an Oklahoma-panhandle January morning. Mid wrapped her arms around Nicki's trembling body and pulled her back.

"Why do the people who love me always die?"

The words were whispered so softly Mid almost

missed them. She turned Nicki around and tightened her embrace.

"You mustn't think such things. Lexie loves you, and I love you, and we're not going to die. Reed loves you too. Just doesn't realize it yet," she muttered under her breath.

Mid wished Reed would suddenly materialize out of the fog. She hadn't bargained on playing therapist when the rascal talked her into taking this job. Organizing households and kissing boo-boos she could handle. KT hadn't been a minute's problem in all his thirty-four years. She had no experience counseling a troubled child. And that was what Nicki was, she thought. A frightened little child who couldn't find her way.

She urged Nicki along, hustling her toward the house, away from the water.

"What you need is to crawl back into bed. I'll get another blanket and let the blinds down so it won't be so cold," Mid said, lowering her voice as they reached the upper hall.

She checked to be sure Lexie was still covered, then lowered the heavy canvas blinds and got the extra cover, tucking it around Nicki's still-shivering body. She carried a straight chair from the bedroom onto the porch.

"I'll just sit here till you fall asleep."

From beneath the blankets, Nicki's icy hand sought hers.

"Thank you, Mid. I wish Renee had been like you."

Mid smiled to herself in the darkness at the half-mumbled sentiment as Nicki's eyes closed in sleep. Not much experience as a counselor, but mothering she knew. Maybe that was what Nicki needed after all. To be cared for and loved.

......29......

He stopped the film again and let it rewind. His head was throbbing. His muscles felt like one solid ache, as much from tension as from any of the day's activities. Hours had passed as he sat in the darkness, stopping and rewinding the film.

Rethreading the reel, he started the projector again, letting scenes ruined by cavorting adults play out this time instead of skipping ahead. He fingered the key in his hand, turning it over and over, digging its sharp edges into his palm, devising and rejecting scenarios.

The damn housekeeper was the problem. Killing the old woman wasn't the answer. Accidents happened. People in the throes of depression did terrible things. But no one would believe Mid McCowan, with her hausfrau muscles, had calmly let someone of Nicki's fragile strength hold her head under water. What he needed was one evening without the old biddy asleep in the bed at the top of the stairs. Even a few precious hours would do.

He sat straighter in the chair. The film was nearing the best part. A momentary break, an awkward, skewed shot of sky, and then she was there, climbing onto the swing.

The sturdy brown-haired child began to pump her legs, leaning back in the seat, her eyes on the sky as she rose higher and higher, laughing to herself.

Nicki. Not then, of course. Her name had been changed.

To protect the innocent, he thought darkly. He stopped twisting the key. The child on the screen had abandoned the swing and moved on to the rings. She dangled now upside down, sundress over her head, flaunting her white panties at the hidden camera. He smiled, enjoying the moment, stroking an arousal.

When the scene was over, he rewound the film and put it away. His hand reached for the unmarked canister, then drew back. Not yet. Not till he had a plan would he trust himself to view that particularly damning piece of celluloid.

What he needed right now, he decided, was a swim to work the knots from his muscles so he could sleep. It would have to be a quick dip, he realized as he stepped outside. The wind had picked up; the air was chilly. He scanned the shoreline and caught his breath.

The image had to be an illusion of the fog. He blinked, but the figure remained. The woman on the dock was decidedly real. Decidedly Nicki. His pulse quickened. As he began to creep forward, moving silently from shadow to shadow, another figure emerged from the darkness.

Goddamned bitch!

Anger flared, consuming him, driving him forward, away from the safety of the shadows. He stumbled over an exposed root of Devon's willow and fell to his knees. Wind whipped away his muffled oath. Neither woman turned her head.

He beat his fists on the ground, his anger dissipated by the pain of his fall. To be so close . . . a few seconds and it would have been over. He'd have been free; he'd have been safe.

The housekeeper led Nicki away. He rubbed his eyes, surprised to find his cheeks were wet. Cordelia would be proud of him. Blubbering like a baby. He got painfully to his feet and limped home, his mind swirling, his swim forgotten.

Knowledge could be better than anger, he told himself as he stood under a steaming shower. Nicki had seemed obsessed with the water as she stood alone on the end of the dock. If the lake had beckoned her once, it might do so again.

Patience, he reminded himself. All he needed was a little patience.

⬛⬛⬛ 30 ⬛⬛⬛⬛

"Are you sure you'll be all right?" Mid asked doubtfully.

Nicki pressed the keys to the Blazer into the housekeeper's hand.

"I'm not planning anything foolish. I just want a little time to think. Take Lexie to that city park you've been telling her about. There's bound to be kids there. The only people she's seen since we got here are adults."

"Well, if you're sure. She was awfully excited about lunch at McDonald's."

"I'm sure."

Lexie waved as Mid backed cautiously from the drive. Nicki watched until they were out of sight, then walked back inside.

As the forecasters had promised, last night's front had moved on. The sun was shining, offering its own assurance that muggy July days were fast approaching. Inside the house the air remained cool and crisp. Nicki took a moment to collect her thoughts, then dialed Reed's office.

"I need to see you," she said when he came on the line.

"I've got a client coming in half an hour and a loan closing at one that's probably going to take most of the afternoon. I was about to call and suggest dinner tonight. Would that do?"

Nicki frowned. That wasn't the setting she'd hoped for.

"I want to go some place quiet where we can talk."

"That's easily arranged. See you about seven."

She stood staring at the receiver in her trembling hand for a long moment before she placed it in its cradle. Reed had become more than her attorney, more than a good friend. If what she was thinking proved to be wrong, she might be ruining the only relationship she'd known since Alan. The problem was, she thought with a sigh, the same would be true if her theory was right.

Outside, the tailgate of a truck clanged, and a mower roared to life. Bob Stockton. Soon the fragrance of new-mown grass wafted through the open windows. She wandered about the house for a while, aimlessly picking up items, rearranging a lampshade, straightening a sofa pillow. Finally the house held no more fascination, and she carried her thoughts outside.

"Mornin', Miz Prevot. Sorry I didn't make it yesterday. Personal emergency. Won't happen again."

"I hope your father isn't ill."

"Nothin' like that," the yardman said, his expression closed against further questions.

Old Bob went back to his mowing. Nicki crossed the yard, stopping by the circular patch of grass near the shoreline. The growth looked newer here than elsewhere in the yard, the ground sunken at odd places around the edges. When the yardman stopped his mower to clean some cuttings from the discharge chute, Nicki waved him over.

"Been meanin' to haul some topsoil to fill in

there, now it's settled some," he noted, mopping his brow.

"What caused it?"

"Used to be a willow like the one over at Miz Rheams's. 'Cept yours was bigger. Branches hung clear out over the water."

Nicki had a momentary flash of memory—a canopy of slender leaves almost touching the water, forming a curtain to hide in the shadows. She waited for the moment to pass. Some memories, she'd come to realize, like the one of Renee and herself on the tennis court, were nonthreatening. Their images only startled rather than frightened her.

If she could discover why others brought panic and terror, she thought, she'd be much closer to healing herself. And to knowing the truth about her past.

"What happened to the tree?"

"Storm blew it down, year or so ago. Happens like that sometimes. Willows grow fast enough, but this one was old. Don't usually live that long. Dug the stump up and replanted this spring. Hell of a job, too. Pardon the language."

"Can you plant another one? One with some size?"

He took off his cap and looked at her through lowered lids.

"Big trees cost a bit. Wrong time of year, too," he added.

"I'll pay a reasonable price for a decent-size tree. You decide when to plant it."

He nodded and returned to his mowing.

Nicki picked up a twig that had blown into the yard from Devon's willow and returned to the house. She'd put the file Reed had given her in a bedroom drawer. Now she got it out and studied the black-and-white snapshot.

Reed had been right about some type of plant growing behind the youthful Renee. Despite the attempt to superimpose the figure on a different background, Nicki could clearly make out a cluster of long slender leaves near the crook of her mother's arm. She held the twig from Devon's willow behind her own elbow and stared at her arm in the mirror. The image looked much the same.

Bob Stockton's mower had fallen silent once more. Nicki checked the drive and found his truck was gone. It was almost noon. He'd be back after lunch to finish trimming the yard, but for now the house and grounds were hers alone. She changed into a swimming suit and grabbed a towel.

Her appetite at breakfast had been as lacking as it was at dinner the night before. Now her stomach was protesting the abuse. She stopped long enough to grab a can of soda and make a sandwich, which she wrapped in a napkin and carried outside.

She sat cross-legged on the end of the dock and nibbled her lunch, pinching off bits of bread and dropping them into the water. Minnows and fingerlings congregated below the surface to investigate the offerings. One or two larger fish darted into the fray, disbursing the others, claiming the spoils for themselves.

Survival of the fittest, Nicki thought with irritation. She tossed several larger pieces of bread away from the dock to draw the attention of the bigger fish and scattered the rest for the smaller ones that remained. The feast exhausted, her audience swam off in search of more routine fare. Nicki looked about her.

A few boats were out—power craft crisscrossing

the lake, a rowboat or two of fishermen, a mini-fleet of sails clustered in front of the club on the opposite shore.

The restlessness that had drawn her to this spot in the middle of the night had been somehow connected to those terrible moments beneath the tarp, Nicki realized suddenly.

Drowning must feel a lot like that, she thought. The weight on your chest, the desperate gasping for air, the terror when water rushed in instead . . .

Could she have almost drowned as a child? Wouldn't she still fear the water if she had? Like Pip Sheridan? Maybe she'd never actually lived here before. Maybe she was just some reincarnation of the previous owner.

Voicing that kind of nonsense could get her locked up, she scolded herself. She shook her napkin over the water to distribute the remaining crumbs and started back to the house, suddenly soured on the idea of a swim.

Several oranges rolled across the counter as Mid shoved the grocery sack through the pass-through and snatched up the phone. Outside, Lexie raced past the porch, eager to show her mother some small treasure she'd picked up in the park.

"Prevot residence," Mid said into the phone breathlessly, pushing aside a nagging worry that Nicki might have spent all morning at the end of the dock.

"You gotta be Miz McCowan. Nicki wrote me 'bout you. I'm MarLynn Hill."

"Yes, Mrs. Hill. Nicki's told me about you and your family, too. She misses you a great deal."

"I'm kinda glad you answered 'stead of her. I

been readin' over what she said in her last letter, or more rightly, what she *didn't* say . . ."

Mid kept an eye on the door as she and MarLynn shared their concern.

Mid cupped her hand over the mouthpiece and whispered something as Nicki entered the room, then offered the receiver.

"Your friend MarLynn." Mid steered Lexie toward the kitchen, murmuring something about needing help with the groceries.

Nicki's spirits brightened at the sound of the familiar drawl.

"Been missin' you too, honey. Ellis been livin' with me too long, I 'spect. Said he knew I wouldn't wait till the rates went down to let you know."

"Know what?"

"That Odell got hisself blowed away. Police 'spect some deal went bad. Thought you all might sleep better knowin'. That young'un still doin' okay?"

"Lexie's fine," Nicki murmured, stunned by the relief she felt at the death of another human being.

"How you makin' it, girl? And don't give me that 'ever'thin's fine' nonsense. Miz McCowan and me had a chat 'fore you got on. You tell MarLynn what's troublin' you, you hear?"

That explains the hurried exchange before Mid gave me the phone, Nicki thought, surprisingly unperturbed by the conspiracy. She moved away from the pass-through and lowered her voice.

"I love it here, MarLynn, I really do. All my neighbors are friendly; everyone's pitched in to help us get settled and make us feel at home. It's everything I wanted for Lexie, but . . ."

"But somethin' ain't right."

"I think I lived here a long time ago," she blurted out.

"You mean in another life, like that MacLaine woman?"

"No, not like that. It's just, I don't know, sometimes I wish I'd never left Texas. I feel like I belong here, but I've been having these . . . spells, I guess you'd call them."

"Girl, that's what doctors is for. I know you don't truck with none of that, but could be one of them might could help you understand what's botherin' you."

"There is someone. One of my neighbors, a psychologist."

"Ask me, that's like an arrow pointin' the way. Now you think on what I'm sayin' and you'll see I'm right. That little girl needs her momma. You gotta do whatever it takes to get right with yourself. Comin' back here ain't gonna do that."

"I really miss you, MarLynn."

MarLynn shushed someone else on her end of the line.

"Lord knows I miss you too, honey, but that Miz McCowan, she sounds like a sensible soul. She says there's lots of folks want to help you. You just give 'em a chance, you hear?"

"I hear," Nicki said, managing a smile.

"Good. 'Cause if you don't mind old MarLynn, she's comin' up there and tannin' your britches. And you know I'm big enough to do it, too. Now, put that little one on so these young'uns can have their say and stop pesterin' me to death."

Reed pulled into a parking spot near the door of the club and turned off the motor. Nicki hadn't said a dozen words since he'd picked her up and made no move now to unbuckle her seat belt.

"You'd better tell me what I've done so I can apologize. The club's got a gourmet chef, but neither one of us is going to enjoy our dinner if we don't clear the air."

"I wanted to talk to you alone."

Whatever was troubling her, it must be serious, he decided. She still refused to look at him. He started the car.

"You're going to regret this, you know."

That made her turn her head. He grinned.

"There's no way we'll get this great a parking spot when we come back."

"You may not want to bring me back after we talk."

He glanced at her sharply. She'd turned away again to stare out the side window. Her hands, resting on the purse in her lap, were trembling. He turned down a narrow lane.

"Where are we going?" she asked.

"My parents' place."

Nicki nodded. Other than a brief murmured appreciation for his mother's decorating flare, she offered no conversation as he led her through the house to the open deck that faced the lake.

"Is this alone enough?" She nodded. "Then please tell me what's going on. What have I done?"

"Have you learned anything about the families who owned my house?"

"As a matter of fact, I talked with Morris Fitzsimmons on the phone this morning. He's never heard the name Renee Prevot. Don't look at me like that. Double-oh-seven would have been proud of the cover story I concocted."

"What did you tell him?"

"I explained I'd been hired to locate the heirs of a young woman who'd spent time at Trumpeter Lake in the mid-sixties, and I thought his boys might have known her. He was very eager to help. So was Mrs. Fitzsimmons."

"And?"

Reed frowned.

"Father Ryan spent the entire year you were conceived as an exchange student in Italy. He boarded in a monastery—his parents' effort to dampen what they saw as an overenthusiastic response to the fairer sex. Apparently their strategy worked. He entered the priesthood soon after he returned."

Nicki leaned on the deck railing and stared across the lake. An inside lamp had clicked on in response to a series of timers. Its glow allowed Reed to see her features clearly.

"Their other boy . . . the one who died in Vietnam."

"Cullen got expelled from Notre Dame during his sophomore year for having a girl in his room. The army was willing to overlook his previous sexual shenanigans."

"He must have had leaves during his training."

"Nicki, he shipped out eleven months before you were born."

Her shoulders slumped and her eyes closed.

"I'm still working on the Ingram boys."

"Joel Lynch told us the youngest one, Jimmy, was sterile."

"That leaves us with Sidney."

"Or someone we haven't considered before," Nicki said softly, turning to face him.

"You mean someone connected with the Sheridan family?"

"I mean your mother's younger brother."

"Donnie's not a part of your past, Nicki."

This time it was Reed who turned away. For a long moment neither said anything.

"I had another panic attack yesterday."

He snapped around to look at her.

"This was the worst one yet. For a moment I actually believed I was going to die." She took a deep breath and locked her gaze with his. "Reed, you have to tell me the truth."

He looked at her in bewilderment.

"I think that picture of Renee was taken in front of the willow tree that blew down last year. Those fingers on her shoulder . . . are they Donnie's?"

"No!" He turned away again. "Donnie had nothing to do with you or your mother. Nothing at all."

"But his hair . . . Lexie . . ."

"Lexie got her hair color from someone else, Nicki."

He leaned his elbows on the railing and rubbed his temples. Why couldn't she just let it be?

"Why are you so sure I'm wrong and you're right?"

"Donnie committed suicide when I was seven."

Her gasp was followed by a murmured apology.

He told her the rest of it. When he finished she still hadn't spoken.

"Rockwall likes to think of itself as sophisticated, but it's really a typical small town. In the mid-sixties people around here still lumped gays in the same pot with murderers and rapists. My grandparents had suspected for a long time. They were sad, of course, but Donnie was a pretty terrific person. They would never have rejected him."

"He didn't know that," Nicki said softly.

Reed nodded.

"Gramps would have tossed Donnie's roommate

out on his ear, if he'd come around here waving the pictures he'd found in Donnie's things. Probably sued him for invasion of privacy, as well, reputations be damned. All Donnie could envision was the loss and destruction of the family he loved."

"When did you learn the truth?"

"My parents talked with the three of us kids after the funeral. They didn't try to explain sexual orientation or anything, just that Donnie had had trouble accepting that he was different from other boys. As we got older and asked more pointed questions, they simply filled in the blanks."

"I think I like your mother and father already."

For the first time in several minutes Reed smiled. He reached for her hand. She surprised him by moving into his arms. The scent of perfumed soap clung to her skin, teasing his senses, stirring his already unsettled emotions. There hadn't been anyone special in his life in a very long time. He slid his hand down Nicki's back, molding her body to his.

"If we keep this up, all the good parking spaces will be gone," she whispered huskily, breaking the embrace.

He felt as if a part of him had been wrenched away.

"Nicki . . ."

She placed her fingers on his lips.

"I'm not saying 'no,' Reed. Just 'not yet.' My life's in too much turmoil to make any commitments right now."

The specter of Nicki's problem succeeded in dampening his ardor.

"You need to talk to a professional about what's happening."

"That psychobabble nonsense is for desperate people."

"And *you're* not desperate?"

"Not yet."

"I really don't like those two words."

Her smile melted his resolve.

"How about the two words *let's eat?*"

"Those I can handle."

On the way to the car Nicki took his hand. By the time they walked into the club, Reed felt as if he were seventeen again and on his first big date.

Euphoria lingered, even after the taillights of Reed's car had disappeared. Nicki stood inside the front door, reluctant to turn the key in the dead bolt and begin to unwind. She hadn't felt so alive since she and Alan . . . At least she still had the decency to blush, she thought.

Necking in a car like some fifteen-year-old. She ran her tongue across her lips, still tingling from Reed's last kiss, and suppressed a giggle. There was no way she was going to be able to sleep. Energy was bursting from every pore. Even the sobering realization that her search for paternal identity seemed to have been derailed could not dampen her high spirits.

Or douse her passion.

A cold shower was the usual recommendation. But why opt for such a mundane solution when she had an entire lake at her disposal? She started to slip back outside, but turned and ran lightly upstairs instead. Skinny-dipping wouldn't put out the flame Reed had ignited, Nicki thought, smiling to herself as she changed in the darkness.

The night was clear. No creeping fog. No alcohol-twisted dream. She pushed away the memory of the previous night's confusion as she entered the water.

Anyone out and about would have had visions of sea monsters when they heard her thrashing through the water, but the exercise had succeeded in cooling her passion, Nicki thought as she lay panting on the raft. She picked out Polaris and Ursa Minor above her. Would Lexie be frightened if they swam out in darkness to look at the stars? she wondered. A safer alternative might be to borrow Clay's boat.

Polaris flickered, replaced by a memory so clear her breath caught in her throat.

A dark mast in the moonlight. Wooden decking against her back. Water lapping against the hull, lulling her to sleep. Renee's laughter. Someone's arms carrying her up to bed.

Polaris came back into focus. Nicki sat up and hugged herself, trying to fix each detail in her mind. Nonthreatening flashbacks seemed to be occurring now as often as the blackouts that frightened her. Did that mean eventually everything would come back, and the panic attacks would stop?

Maybe MarLynn had been right, Nicki thought. Talking about her fears with her friend had been comforting. If therapy could help her remember, it was worth considering.

Somewhere a turtle slid from the bank with a splash. Or maybe it had been a fish in search of a midnight snack. The raft rocked gently, bobbing on the hollow barrels that kept it afloat. Nicki yawned. The swim had done its work. She scooted over to the ladder, slid silently into the water, and kicked off.

Annoyance rather than panic was her first reaction when she felt the scratchy touch about her an-

kle. Vegetation from the untended Tarleton shoreline often broke free to float through the water. She
kicked her foot, expecting the vine to slide away.

Instead the weed seemed to tighten as if still attached to the bottom of the lake. Nicki scowled in
the darkness. Nothing grew under the raft. She
tried to draw her leg up to reach the persistent tangle.

Without warning she was dragged under, jerked
back toward the raft. Nicki flailed her arms. Her
left hand struck one of the barrels like the hammer
of a gong. Pain shot through her knuckles, but she
was too busy fighting her way to the surface to feel
the minor discomfort.

She'd managed to close her mouth against the
rushing water, but very little air remained in her
lungs. Gasping for breath, she broke the surface
and clawed at the barrel beside her head.

"Help!"

The cry sounded ridiculous even to her own ears.
No one was awake at this hour. Except for idiots
foolish enough to reject every warning they'd ever
heard about swimming alone.

Again the twisted mass about her ankles was
pulling her down. She stopped fighting and tried to
double up, reaching out to free her feet. Something
floated by her hand. Instead of the knotted leaves or
cordlike vine she expected, her fingers closed on the
rough-textured surface of a rope.

Fear turned to panic as a different sort of pressure shoved her even deeper, almost as if a hand
were forcing her down. She continued to flail her
arms, pushing against anything she came in contact with, fighting for another gasp of air.

The downward pull seemed to suddenly lessen.
Nicki kicked to the surface and screamed again.

"Nicki!"

She tried to turn toward the voice, but the rope around her ankles was tightening again. She was so close to the raft. If she could only grab the ladder.

"Help me!"

An arm tightened about her waist. She twisted, desperate to get away. A voice spoke in her ear.

"If you keep struggling, you'll drown us both."

You'll drown. You'll drown.

The words echoed in Nicki's head even as darkness closed about her.

"She's coming around."

"I'll get a blanket."

"Devon," Nicki murmured, trying to raise her head. Somehow she'd gotten from the water to her neighbor's screened porch.

"She'll be right back," Clay said, sliding his arm behind her back to help her sit up. "I didn't want to panic Mrs. McCowan or Lexie, so I beat down Devon's door instead."

She looked at him in unspoken question.

"Insomnia. I was taking a walk. If I hadn't heard your cries . . . What in the hell did you think you were doing?"

"Taking a swim."

She tried to smile, but his scowl drove any attempt at levity from her thoughts. The memory of her ordeal returned, bringing a chill.

"Somebody tried to drown me."

"Some careless fisherman or boater." He held up a tangle of bright yellow rope. "Damned stuff floats. All anyone has to do is snag it with a pole and fish it out."

Nicki shook her head. The sensation of a force pushing her toward the bottom was still vivid. She voiced the thought as Devon returned. Her two neighbors exchanged a look.

"Nicki, two thirds of the people around here use rope like that to tie up their boats."

"I've got some in the garage," Devon added. "Old Bob used it last year to stake out that little birch beside the house."

"It felt as if someone was pulling on my ankles."

"Nicki, that's crazy. Why would someone want to drown you?"

She looked up at Devon's concerned expression and closed her eyes, fighting renewed panic. Maybe she *was* losing her mind.

"I don't know why. It just felt so real."

Clay took the blanket from Devon, wrapped it about Nicki's shoulders, and took her trembling hands in his own steady ones.

"Right now, in your state of mind, you can't trust your senses." *Or your judgment*, his expression told her. "Your feet got tangled in the rope. You panicked, became disoriented. Up became down; left became right; the rope felt like an enemy."

You can't trust your senses.

And you're not desperate?

Nicki's breath caught in a sob. She clutched Clay's hands.

"Please help me."

"I got the name of a woman psychologist . . ."

"I don't want a stranger." Her eyes pleaded with him.

Clay sighed and looked away. Nicki glanced at Devon. The older woman pressed her lips together tightly and shook her head. Outside, a moth kissed the screen, seeking the light. Finally, Clay nodded.

"You won't regret this," Devon told him, laying her hand on his arm.

"I already do," he murmured, avoiding both women's eyes.

"What happens now?" Nicki asked. She realized she was shaking as if she'd just crossed some invisible abyss with no means of return.

"Now Devon and I walk you home. I have a few things I have to clear up before we can have our first session."

Nicki looked up in alarm.

"Second thoughts already? I can still give you a referral."

"No," she said quickly. "I just thought we'd jump right in. Maybe tomorrow."

"Tomorrow's Thursday. We've got that thing at Gwyn's on Friday. Let's schedule the first session for Saturday morning."

Two days and three long nights.

"There's just one thing."

She looked up, puzzled by the catch in his voice.

"No more swimming alone."

She glanced out at the dark water beyond Devon's porch and nodded. Tonight's experience had destroyed all desire for solitary pursuits.

···· 31 ····

"**N**ever knew a lawyer with so much free time," Mid told Nicki as they wrapped sandwiches for a hastily assembled picnic lunch.

"He expected to be in court all day, but his case was rescheduled at the last minute."

The front screen door banged, and Lexie whirled into the kitchen.

"He's coming," she announced, darting back out.

"Stay off the dock till I get there," Nicki called. The door banged again in response. She shook her head. "You'd think we were going on a world cruise."

"I just hope you don't capsize," Mid murmured, bustling about the kitchen, sealing peeled carrots in a plastic bag and adding more cookies to the growing pile of food.

"Reed knows what he's doing. Besides, we'll have vests on."

"I know, but those kind of boats worry me." She glanced at Nicki and frowned. *"You* worry me."

Nicki looked up in surprise.

"Hard to ignore a wet swimming suit that wasn't hanging over the tub when I went to bed last night."

Nicki felt strangely comforted by the motherly concern. Renee had been an indifferent parent, warning her about obvious dangers but rarely displaying signs of the nagging anxiety Nicki felt about her own child's safety. She gave Mid a quick squeeze.

"I promise I won't do anything that foolish again. Okay?"

Lexie had done her best to obey her mother's command—only her toes were touching the dock when Nicki and Mid crossed the lawn. At her mother's okay, she raced ahead to meet the approaching craft. Reed waved and tossed the women a rope. A gray cloth rope, Nicki noted, standing back to study the small catamaran.

Reed held out his arms. Lexie stepped off the dock and settled where he told her on the mesh that stretched between two crossbeams and the dual hulls. Nicki followed gingerly. Mid handed Reed the lunch, and he stowed it in the small cooler lashed to the deck. Their tennis shoes joined his in a similarly attached waterproof bag. He grinned at his passengers.

"All set?"

Nicki tightened her legs about her daughter and pulled her as close as she could, given their bulky orange vests. She whispered to hold on and nodded that they were ready. Mid issued one last warning to be careful.

Moments later they were flying over the water. The wind whipped the sails, almost drowning the sound of Lexie's giggles. Spray soon drenched their swimsuits and T-shirts. The exhilaration was intoxicating. *And familiar.*

"Again! Do it again!" Lexie shouted as they slowed.

Reed reached up to adjust the sail.

"When he tells us, we have to duck and shift to the other side," Nicki told Lexie loudly.

"Thought you'd never sailed before," Reed shouted as they changed positions.

Nicki grinned.

By the time the sun hung directly overhead, they'd seen the entire shoreline and become familiar with the lake's various landmarks. The gusty morning breeze had calmed. Reed maneuvered the catamaran slowly along the bank, pointing out the houses and summer cottages of families he'd known since boyhood.

"I thought we'd picnic in one of the coves," he told them, slipping over the side to anchor the boat in the shallows. "We'll have to wade from here. Can't get in closer because of the trees. Grab the shoes, Nicki. Lexie, hang on to our lunch."

He swung Lexie onto his shoulders, ducked beneath the overhanging branches, and disappeared. Nicki held the three pairs of shoes above her head and followed.

The inactive fountain in the center of the cove sparked a flash of recognition Nicki had almost expected. She waded closer to the stone statuary. An industrious spider was busily spinning her web between the young woman's upturned urn and the rim of the fountain's basin. Dead leaves floated in the stagnant rainwater that ringed the figure's feet.

"Don't walk in that stuff," Lexie told her, pointing to a clump of reeds nearby. "You could get a leech."

"Do you know what leeches are?" Nicki asked.

"Mr. Verdell says they stick to you and hurt."

She scrambled down from Reed's shoulders and splashed over to a cleared place along the bank.

"This is moss. It's real soft to sit on."

"Apparently Mr. Verdell gives quite a nature tour."

"He taught me lots of stuff." She opened the lunch sack. "Can I have a cookie?"

After lunch, Lexie begged permission to walk a little way down the overgrown trail that wound into the woods. Nicki, her feet still dangling in the water, lay back on the bank. Overhead, branches formed a canopy that shaded the cove from the afternoon heat. Only a mixed chorus of chirps and twitters, the scratchy scurrying of the woodland's smaller inhabitants, and the rustling leaves disturbed the almost reverent hush.

"When did you learn to sail?" Reed asked, propping himself on one elbow beside her.

Omitting the previous night's terrifying experience, Nicki described her most recent flashbacks.

"Today isn't the first time I've been in this cove or seen that fountain. Renee and I had to have lived here when I was small, at least for a while. The sailboat I remember probably belonged to my father."

"The man without a face."

"Someone lobbed that ball back to me. And took us night sailing. Renee hung around the tennis courts when we lived in the condo, especially if a bunch of guys were playing, but I never saw her pick up a racket. Boats didn't interest her much either, and the closest she ever came to studying the stars was reading her horoscope in the daily paper."

Reed sat up and fished another cookie from the lunch sack. Nicki called to Lexie to be sure she hadn't strayed too far. Lexie's voice responded from some nearby spot.

"I took your advice," she said softly. "Clay and I are having some kind of session Saturday morning."

"Would you like me to be there?"

Nicki shook her head. The thought was comforting, but Clay had been reluctant enough about working with her. She didn't want him to construe Reed's presence as a lack of confidence.

Reed leaned down to kiss her. Lexie's giggle interrupted the moment.

"Come on," she said, tugging their hands.

Reed helped Nicki to her feet. They slipped into their shoes and followed Lexie along the twisted path as she pointed out an abandoned bird's nest, a massive spiderweb among a patch of lacy ferns, and the knarred stump that Lexie insisted looked like an old man. Proud of her position as guide, she cautioned both adults to move slowly to avoid startling the wildlife. Their vigilance was rewarded by the rat-tat-tat of a woodpecker.

"See. He's got red hair like me," Lexie whispered.

"Which way?" Nicki whispered back as the path branched in two directions. Reed started down the left fork.

"No!" Lexie pulled him back. The startled woodpecker took flight. "I don't wanna go that way."

"Why not?" Nicki frowned at her daughter's pouting face. The alternate trail appeared to be narrower and more overgrown.

" 'Cause this way's better," Lexie told her, tramping noisily down the branch to the right. Two squirrels darted up a tree in alarm. Lexie stopped and turned, hands on her hips. "Come on!"

"Someone's getting t-i-r-e-d," Nicki whispered to Reed as she followed. Stumbling over an exposed root, she glanced behind her. Lexie might be the expert, but it still seemed to Nicki the other path looked better used.

* * *

Mid was sitting in the yard when they sailed around the jutting point of Tarleton shore a short time later. She closed her book and hurried onto the dock to catch the rope and help them out.

"You have a surprise in the side yard," she told Lexie.

"My swing!"

She raced toward the metal frame.

"So much for her fatigue," Nicki said.

Reed cast off to return the catamaran to its mooring off his parents' dock.

"We had a great time," Nicki called.

"Be by about a quarter to six tomorrow," he shouted, reminding her of his promise to walk them to Gwyn's.

Mid took the trash from their picnic inside while Nicki walked toward the swing. Lexie was dangling by her hands from the rings, trying to imitate the male gymnasts she'd watched on TV. Clay was nowhere around, but Bob Stockton was digging in one corner of the garden. Lexie switched apparatus.

"Push me, Mommy. Please?"

Nicki got her started, then crossed the road to investigate the yardman's project.

"What are you planting?"

"Didn't think you'd want your little one to see this."

With his shovel, he nudged the body of a dead squirrel into a hole. Nicki turned and ran blindly across the road past Lexie.

Behind her, Lexie's plaintive demand barely registered.

"What did you do to my mommy?"

When the front screen door slammed behind her, Nicki stopped running, but her heart continued the race. She pressed her head against the door and gasped for air. A sound on the flagstone walk brought her head up. Lexie burst through the door.

"I hate him. He's mean."

Nicki dropped to her knees.

"Mr. Stockton's not mean, Lexie. Mommy just . . ."

Just what? What had sent her fleeing? Not the dead animal. Roadkill in Texas was a topic of jokes. Skunks and raccoons, coyotes and ranch dogs— even deer and wild turkey littered the highways. She'd never reacted to them in any way.

Lexie patted her face gently. Nicki took a deep breath.

"Mommy just had one of her spells. Mr. Stockton didn't have anything to do with it."

"You didn't fall down," Lexie noted with suspicion.

"Maybe that means I'm getting better," Nicki told her. She stood up, relieved to find her legs no longer trembled. "I'd like a swim. How about you?"

To her relief, Lexie pounced on the suggestion. Nicki grabbed two of the clean towels Mid had stacked on the stairway and followed Lexie outside.

32

Thursday night passed without incident—no nightmares for Lexie, no nocturnal wanderings or ill-advised swims for her mother. Friday morning and afternoon were spent in customary leisure. Getting ready for Gwyn's party, Nicki reflected that if her life continued along the same lines, she'd soon abandon all inclination to work for a living.

Being a full-time mom was great, but Lexie would be in kindergarten half days in the fall. Eventually she'd need to find a part-time job or decide about going back to school. She'd have to ask Reed if there was a community college or university branch within commuting distance.

The reflection brought her up short. Sometime in the past two weeks, she realized, she'd made a decision to remain at the lake when summer ended. Except for the Tarleton woodland, Trumpeter Lake's shoreline was fully developed. According to Reed her property was worth almost as much as the investments that were now supporting her and Lexie.

The thought of selling seemed as foreign as ownership of the house and grounds once had. Despite whatever had driven Renee from this place, Nicki felt no compulsion to leave. Not even the specter of

continued panic attacks was enough to make her
run.

She belonged here. This was her home. Clay
would help her deal with her terrors, and eventually
Reed would trace her paternal parentage. Lexie
would start school and make friends and have
slumber parties and giggle over little boys and . . .

How had she stumbled on this train of thought?
Nicki wondered. She ran a brush through her hair
one last time and went downstairs to wait for Reed.

Gwyn's patio furniture had been moved aside to
make room for several picnic tables. Much to
Lexie's delight the fabric of the tablecloths topping
each one portrayed an army of black ants marching
across red-and-white checks.

"Always prefer to invite my own guests," their
hostess explained with a wink.

Ichiro Tanaka, presiding over an enormous char-
coal grill, had exchanged his stiff chef's jacket for
jeans and a short-sleeved western shirt. In keeping
with the party's theme, a caricatured anteater
chased a swarm of retreating ants across his bib
apron. Miko wore a knee-length denim skirt, red
blouse, and short red cowboy boots. She circulated
among the arriving guests, taking drink orders.

People crowded the deck. Nicki was introduced
to the Nielsons and the Cravenses, who had missed
Gwyn's previous dinner party. Reg Craven, whose
run-in with the family pet had caused their last-
minute cancellation, stood stiffly beside his blond
wife and endured some good-natured ribbing from
the others.

Four other couples whose names Nicki couldn't
keep straight joined the party, as did Del Ferris and
Joel Lynch. Joel made the rounds to greet everyone,

then attached himself to Mid's side. Nicki caught Gwyn watching the pair with a calculating expression.

Though several of the couples exchanged updates on their children's summer activities, Lexie was the only child present. Nicki glanced around to see how she was coping with the crowd. Perched on the deck railing facing the lake, Reed and Clay on either side of her, Lexie was entertaining another half dozen guests with an account of her first sailboat ride. Clay caught Nicki's eye and smiled.

She tried to relax. Tonight was the first time she'd seen Clay since he'd rescued her. No one had spotted him hanging Lexie's swings on Thursday morning and, according to Devon, her messages on his machine had gone unanswered until an hour before he'd appeared at her patio door to escort her to Gwyn's.

With Clay's appearance, apprehension had settled like an icy hand on Nicki's shoulders. The panic attack that had sent her fleeing from the garden the day before faded in importance as the moment of their session neared. She'd learned to cope with some of her memories on her own; maybe in time she'd be able to deal with the rest. Maybe forcing her mind to give up its secrets too soon would make things worse.

"You'd enjoy this party a lot more if you'd stop worrying about tomorrow," Devon murmured beside her.

"I can't help thinking I'm making a mistake."

"You aren't," Devon said firmly.

The other guests had congregated by the deck rail, their attention drawn by something beyond Lexie and her companions.

"I bet that great blue heron's back," Devon said.

She caught Nicki's hand and drew her toward the crowd.

Devon had guessed correctly. The huge bird provided the predinner entertainment while Ichiro prepared their meal.

Foil-wrapped bundles of seasoned potatoes and ears of corn joined spicy glazed ribs, skewers of marinated vegetables and jumbo shrimp, and others of pineapple and papaya and green peppers on platter-size plates. French bread spread with garlic butter and warmed on a rack above the grill completed the feast.

Dessert consisted of fresh fruit and warm Brie. Compliments to their hostess and her chef flowed freely.

After-dinner conversation ranged from national politics to a positive assessment of the Rockwall educational system. Three of the couples whose names Nicki couldn't remember left early, one to hurry home to eight-week-old twins, the other two to watch teenage sons on opposite sides of a softball tournament.

Lexie had managed to behave herself for most of the evening, avoiding the spilled food and dribbled soft drinks Nicki had foreseen. Being the center of attention hadn't hurt, Nicki reflected, wondering if Gwyn had included Lexie for just that reason. Nicki herself appeared to be the only restless member of the group.

Part of her uneasiness could be caused by Clay. Every time she glanced in his direction, he was studying her. No one else seemed to notice his obsession, except perhaps Del Ferris who appeared to be watching her as well. When Lexie squirmed in her arms and whispered her need for the bathroom, Nicki gratefully excused herself from the gathering.

*   *   *

Reed patted the empty cushion beside him, away
from the others, when Nicki and Lexie returned
from inside. Someone caught Lexie's attention, but
Nicki sank down beside him. Two more couples
had gone, leaving only the Nielsons, Joel Lynch,
and the neighborhood residents scattered about the
deck.

"Worried about tomorrow?" Reed murmured,
feeling Nicki's tension as he dropped his arm lightly
about her shoulders.

"I can't seem to stop thinking about it." She
clasped her hands in her lap. "Renee always told
me only crazy people let a shrink mess with their
minds. Shrinks and head doctors. I used to have
this image in my mind of half-naked men with
bones through their noses sitting around a pot of
bubbling water."

She managed a nervous laugh.

"We had a housekeeper for a while whose father
had been a psychiatrist before they fled some South
American country. If I came home from school in a
funk, she tried to analyze my mood."

She opened her mouth as if to continue, then
frowned.

"What's the matter?"

"I just remembered. Renee caught the woman
questioning me about my father. The next week we
had a different housekeeper."

"Hey, you two. Stop whispering secrets and
come join the rest of the party," Devon said, crossing the deck to stand in front of them. She lowered
her voice. "You've put Gwyn in a feeding frenzy,
huddling over here with your heads together."

"I think we're secondary tonight," Nicki murmured, nodding toward Mid and Joel.

"Am I missing something?" Reed asked, looking between the two women.

"Nothing important," Devon told him with a laugh.

Reed moved their bench nearer the others. Clay and Del were discussing the merits of various fertilizer mixtures with Betsy Nielson. Lexie was curled up next to Mid, fighting to keep her drooping eyes from closing. Somewhere in the trees beyond the deck an owl hooted. Nicki turned toward the sound.

"I wonder if that's the same owl I hear late at night in the woods next to my house?"

"Could be," Gwyn told her. "This guy usually shuts up around ten or so and flies away. Probably nests in that Tarleton mess somewhere."

"Why has that property never been developed?" Nicki asked.

"It's been tied up for years in an estate," Reed explained.

"What's the problem?"

"Seventy-six heirs," Betsy Nielson said. "Each one tooting his own trombone. You knew some of them, didn't you, Gwyn?"

"Sonny Tarleton was number two on my matrimonial hit parade. His dear departed mother, Satan rest her soul, was a big part of the settlement problem."

"If that's not a setup, I've never heard one," Joel goaded her. "Come on, Gwyn. Tell them the rest."

Their hostess grinned wickedly, clearly in her element.

"The Tarletons were a prolific banking family—husband, wife, and eight proper children. Weathered the crash by some shrewd overseas investments. One muggy August afternoon, sweet-faced, even-tempered Momma attacked her stuffed-shirt husband with a meat cleaver. Chased him around the croquet court until one of the gardeners took her down with a blind-side tackle."

"I knew there'd be a scandal in this somewhere," Betsy Nielson said, pulling her chair closer.

"The family tried to hush up the incident, but barely a month later a maid found Mrs. Tarleton dead in her bed."

"Murdered?" Betsy asked eagerly.

Gwyn shook her head.

"Liver disease. Hastened, I'm told, by a secret penchant for Kentucky bourbon."

"How did that tie up the estate?" Mid asked as Lexie squirmed onto her lap.

"After his wife's funeral the family patriarch announced that for fifteen years he'd been supporting a second family in Montreal. He intended, he told his astonished brood, to legalize the relationship and change his will to include his Canadian off-spring and three stepchildren as well. His American family reacted predictably and promptly sued to protect their interests.

"By the time the old man was summoned to answer to a higher court, a third generation had entered the fray. The will had been altered a dozen times, and there was some question as to the validity of the most recent copy."

"Surprised they didn't have to sell the place to pay the damned attorneys. No offense, Reed," Reg Nielson said.

Reed grinned and shook his head. He was enjoying the tale as much as everyone else.

"Several of the children had already made their own mark or married money and vowed never to give in. In the fifties, after the lake house burned, . . ." Gwyn began.

"There was a house in the midst of all that?" Nicki asked.

"The Tarletons had one of the first summer houses on the lake. Huge, rambling place. The original Mrs. Tarleton was an early advocate of the wilderness movement and, except for the immediate area around the house, forbade clearing the land. She laid out the pine-needle paths that wound about the grounds and down to the coves herself. Secluded benches here and there encouraged quiet contemplation of nature's bounties. There was even a gazebo tucked away in a little clearing."

Lexie slipped off Mid's lap, her feet hitting the deck with a thud. Reed thought she looked out of sorts. He tried to catch her attention, but she was too busy scowling at Gwyn to turn her head. She was probably bored with adult talk, he decided.

"What caused the fire?" Nicki asked.

"Lightning. Old place was a tinderbox. Burned right down to the foundation. Wonder the whole woods didn't catch fire."

"Maybe the trees were too wet to burn," someone suggested.

"Probably. Anyway, after that, nature really took over. One faction of the original family was determined to honor their mother's convictions and refused to allow any sale of the property that didn't contain an antidevelopment clause."

"And therein lies the problem," Reed murmured.

"It's a natural sanctuary, but Kellogg's is too close for anyone to maintain it formally. So the estate pays the taxes and Mother Nature rules," Gwyn said. She smiled wistfully. "Sonny proposed to me on a swing in the gazebo. I've often wondered whether it survived in the midst of all that wilderness."

"I wanna go home," a pouty voice announced loudly, interrupting Gwyn's reminiscence.

Reed was surprised to find Lexie staring not at her mother, but across the deck toward the bench Clay and Del were sharing. Unshed tears glistened in her dark eyes. Reed felt a tug of compassion. It was late. The poor kid was worn out.

"Before you go, I want to show you something," Gwyn said.

She darted into the house and returned with a small cardboard box. Everyone gathered about one of the picnic tables.

"I thought you might like to see these. Most of them were taken at the club's July Fourth celebrations over the years."

She spread an array of photos on the table.

"This one shows Sonny Tarleton. It was taken a year or two after our divorce. That's me on the end with husband number three. We all look civilized, don't we?"

"Who's this trio?" Reed asked, picking up another photo.

Gwyn squinted at the picture.

"The girls are Ollie and Pip Sheridan."

"Let me see," Lexie demanded, pushing herself closer. She frowned. "She's supposed to be little, like me."

"This was taken when she was older. I don't remember the young man . . . oh, yes, I do. Ollie's one venture into romance. A med student. I don't recall his name. He spent several weeks with the family the summer before the parents died."

"Were he and Ollie ever married?" Devon asked.

"No, but there was talk of an engagement. The

Peace Corps had just been formed, and the young man announced his intention to sign up. Pip admired his dedication and wanted to know more. By the end of his visit, she and the boy were spending most of their time on her sailboat. Things were never good between the two sisters. After that episode open warfare described it best."

Nicki glanced at the snapshot of the three young people, then passed it to the Nielsons. Lexie whispered in her ear. She excused herself for another trip to the bathroom.

The photos made their way around the table. Del glanced at each with a professional's disdain for the attempts of amateurs, then handed them to Clay and Devon. Reed shifted his gaze to Clay, startled to catch an expression of raw anguish on his usually guarded face.

Del rose and joined the Nielsons, who were murmuring thanks to their hostess and gathering their things. Clay sat staring into the darkness beyond the deck, his expression now unreadable. Devon's hand rested on his arm. One of the photos lay between the pair. Curious, Reed slipped into the spot Del had just left.

"Something bothering you, Clay?"

Clay shook his head.

Nicki was about to entrust her psyche to this guy, Reed thought, suddenly sharing her uneasiness. He lowered his voice.

"Nicki told me about tomorrow's session. If you've got some sort of personal problem right now . . ."

"I offered her the name of another therapist," Clay snapped. "She wasn't interested."

Not a denial. Not even an answer, Reed noted.

Devon sat quietly beside Clay, not volunteering to join the conversation.

"I'm more than just Nicki's attorney, you know. I care about her and Lexie."

Reed picked up the photo. The Sheridan sisters and their hapless young medical student smiled at the camera. Behind them the branches of a willow drooped over the bank, leaves straining toward the water. A willow like the one Nicki insisted had been the original backdrop for a similar shot of Renee. Reed felt apprehension prickle the hair on the back of his neck.

"Something about this picture upset you, didn't it?"

Clay offered no response. Devon's hand tightened on his arm. She turned to look at him, her face an unasked question. Clay glanced at the photo, then nodded.

"Clay knew Pip Sheridan when they were students at Berkeley. The photo brought back old memories."

"Is that what's troubling you? A few memories? No personal hang-up that might jeopardize Nicki's therapy?" Reed asked, still unconvinced.

Lexie and Nicki came out of the house and started toward the group at the end of the table.

"That's what's troubling me," Clay said simply.

"She's almost out," Reed whispered as he laid Lexie on her bed.

Lexie opened her eyes and murmured something. Nicki bent closer to listen, then motioned to Reed to leave. She stripped Lexie's dress off and tugged on her pj's as Lexie murmured again.

"No, sweetie, no one saw your panties," Nicki murmured back. She kissed Lexie good-night and passed through the empty bedroom behind the sleeping porch into the hall. Reed stepped from the room with the nautical theme, startling her.

"I've got a knot plaque somewhere like the one in there."

"I don't like that room," Nicki said with a shiver.

"Do you think it was yours as a child?"

She shook her head.

"My father's maybe. Or his and Renee's. Whoever used it, it doesn't trigger happy memories."

Joel had driven Mid home while the rest of them walked. A thin line of light beneath her door was the only indication she was still up. Downstairs Reed kissed Nicki good-night, lingering over the embrace as if unwilling to end the evening.

"You know, you don't have to go through with tomorrow if you think it's a mistake. Nobody's holding your feet to the fire."

"What happened to that 'go for it' attitude you had earlier this evening?"

"I just don't want you to rush into anything."

"I wouldn't call the way I've been dragging my feet about getting help rushing into something."

"Sure you don't want me there?"

"I'm sure."

Later Nicki lay in bed, trying without success to sleep. She was tempted by thoughts of a relaxing swim, but recent experience and her promise to Mid made her reject the idea.

Lexie whimpered. Nicki held her breath, expecting the distress of another nightmare. Instead, Lexie relaxed once more. A woodland creature cried out, and Nicki heard the sound of beating wings. The owl was on patrol, perpetuating the original Mrs. Tarleton's edict that nature ruled supreme.

Nicki rolled onto her back. Bits of the party replayed in her head. She wondered if the off-and-on tension she'd felt could be blamed on her uneasiness about tomorrow. Everyone seemed to have had a great time listening to Gwyn's stories. Except maybe Clay and Del. Neither had had much to say all evening. Then again, both men had quiet natures.

Clay had probably been brooding about tomorrow, she decided. He'd made no effort to hide his reluctance to help, and she didn't hold the patent on second thoughts. Her eyelids began to droop.

When the nightmare came, it wasn't Lexie's, but her own.

She awoke in terror, pushing at an invisible weight on her chest, fighting for breath. Her ears seemed to ring from a crash of cannons. She looked wildly around her in the darkness.

The night was silent. No artillery boomed. No vague, dark shapes threatened to snatch her breath. Whimpering overrode the ringing in her ears. She started to go to Lexie, then sank back on the bed. The sounds had been her own.

The Tarleton owl hooted as if protesting some disturbance of his nocturnal pleasures. When dawn lit the darkness, Nicki was still awake.

┅┅ 33 ┅┅

When the party had finally broken up, he'd fled to the safety of the hidden room. He stared at the blank projection screen, hands clenched, shoulder muscles aching.

Damn Gwyn and her stupid parties. Pretending drained his strength. To be so close to Lexie, to smell her honeyed skin, hear her provocative giggle, almost taste her hidden sweetness and not reach out to her, had been unbearable.

Lexie and Nicki. One cried out for his love; the other threatened his existence. Twice he'd failed. His blundering first attempt had been an error in judgment, a panic-driven mistake, but he'd been sure of his plan the second time.

And he'd almost succeeded. To be so damn close . . .

Who'd have thought someone as slender as Nicki could have so much strength. He rubbed the tender spot on his chest where her thrashing feet had found a target, taking his breath. Nicki was no longer a child. She'd fought hard for her life.

Things were about to explode. Gwyn's damn pictures hadn't detonated the ticking bomb in Nicki's head, but they had surely fanned the slow-burning fuse. He'd needed all his control not to shred the snapshot or crumple it in his hand. Only Reed Jordan's watchful eyes had stayed his action.

Eventually, with the right catalyst, Nicki would remember. Sooner or later, if the Sheridan name kept cropping up, if she saw the right photo . . .

One hand strayed to the projector, caressing the ON switch. His eyes remained on the blank screen. Once the images began, it would be too late to turn back. Memories would gnaw at him like maggots at an open wound. There was only one escape, one way to eliminate the danger forever. What had started so long ago must be finished. He smiled grimly. Maybe he and Nicki should watch the film together. A controlled return to her forgotten past.

Control, that was the key. Monday was the Fourth of July. Just three more days to freedom and independence.

The irony broadened his smile. He'd succeed in getting rid of Nicki this time, and afterward . . . a very private celebration for two. Here in this room Lexie could be his for as long as he dared before he'd send her to join her mother in the lake.

He'd done a lot of reading as well as planning in the past few days. Tangled in some discarded fishing line snagged on some bottom debris, a small body might stay submerged for weeks before it was found. By then deterioration would mask the time of death as well as any signs of the things they'd done together.

The image of his beautiful Lexie like that brought a wave of nausea. But he mustn't think about that, only about the hours they'd have together in this soundproof refuge, every precious minute preserved on film to be savored again and again. Think about that . . . and about the elimination of Nicki.

He took a deep breath and flipped the projector on. The images sprang to life, ripping open a wound he'd thought long healed. By the tenth showing, an awed calm and eager anticipation had replaced his earlier dread.

▬▬▬ 34 ▬▬▬

"How's that?" Devon asked, massaging the knotted muscles in Nicki's neck.

"Much better, thanks."

Nicki's tentative smile failed to mask her apprehension. Devon patted her hand, then returned to her chair. Nicki sat stiffly on the end of the padded lounger Clay had moved in from the porch. She glanced nervously at the empty chair.

The makeshift office in Clay's small back bedroom was as Spartan as the rest of his house was cozy. A hollow-core door had been positioned atop two small file cabinets to form a desk. The desk, two chairs, and the lounger were the only furnishings. A steno pad and a pen lay at precise right angles on the corner of the desk. No other objects cluttered the surface.

Warm pecan paneling saved the room from austerity, but the walls themselves were unadorned. The air filtering through a duct near the ceiling was cool and crisp. Tightly closed vertical blinds covered the single window. A green-shaded banker's lamp on the desk provided the room's only light.

Clay's work environment was as unrevealing as the man himself, Devon thought, wrenching her gaze from the metal files. The cabinet's locks were pushed in, their contents as hidden as their owner's inner thoughts.

"All set?" Clay asked, returning with the glass of water Nicki had requested.

Nicki nodded. The apprehension in her eyes remained. She scooted back in the lounger, her hands gripping the arms as if they were anchors. Clay picked up the notepad and pen, then glanced at Devon.

"You'll have to wait in the other room."

"No, I want her to stay," Nicki protested.

"Nicki, what's said in therapy should remain between therapist and patient."

"I'll sign a release. There would be other people in the room if I was in group therapy. Devon's taken special courses to deal with traumatized students."

"I can't help you if you don't trust me."

"I *do* trust you," Nicki protested. She took a deep breath. "I just can't do this without a friend."

"Yesterday *I* was your friend."

"But today you're my therapist."

"I'm breaking enough rules doing this as it is."

Nicki's eyes pleaded with Devon to make him understand.

"You won't know I'm in the room," Devon said softly.

Clay looked at Nicki thoughtfully, then uncapped his pen.

"Therapy's a slow process, Nicki. Resolution rarely happens overnight. It may take weeks, even months to uncover what's causing your panic attacks."

"I don't care how long it takes. I just want them to stop."

"Even if it means facing something very painful?"

Nicki swallowed hard, then nodded.

"All right, then, tell me about your childhood."

"What do you want to know?"

"Was the world a frightening place as you were growing up?"

"Not frightening. Surreal. I felt as if everyone but me was living a normal life—mothers who were always around, fathers who gave encouragement and discipline in equal doses."

"Were your friends' lives really like that?"

"No. Some of their parents were divorced. A few kids had problems with alcohol or drugs, and we drifted apart. All of us had the usual teenage angst. But living with Renee felt unreal, as if it was all a game and I couldn't remember the rules."

"You told me once you didn't remember your early childhood. Describe the earliest memories you do have."

Devon could see a visible relaxing of Nicki's shoulders as Clay's quiet voice soothed and reinforced the connection between himself and his patient. She felt invisible, her presence fading into the surroundings as the questions and answers continued.

Lexie kicked at the grass beneath the swings. She felt hot and sticky, and the bite behind her knee was itching again. Mommy had told her last night not to scratch, but it felt better when she did. She twisted away from the house in case Miz Mid was watching and clawed the back of her leg. The swing's chains clanged as she kept turning in circles.

She threw back her head and held up her feet.

The swing unwound, then tightened again in the opposite direction. Above her, treetops and sky spun around and around.

"Looks like fun," a voice called.

She put her feet down and let the swing finish unwinding slowly. Mr. Ferris grinned as he walked along the road toward her. He was coming from the wrong way. A cobweb dangled from his shirtsleeve, and there were fresh grass stains on his pants. Lexie was sure he hadn't got them in the garden. She'd looked for him before she came outside.

"Where's your mommy this morning?"

Lexie scowled.

"She went somewhere."

Mommy always ate breakfast with her, but this morning she'd slept late, and when she came downstairs, Mommy had already gone. Miz Mid had acted like she didn't know where Mommy was. Lexie had decided Miz Mid knew, but wanted it to be a secret. She hoped that meant Mommy was going to bring her a surprise. Then they'd both have surprises.

"Are my pictures 'veloped?"

"Not yet." He stopped beside the swing and smiled. "Did you enjoy Mrs. Chamberlin's party last night?"

"Uh-huh." The back of her knee was itching again.

"Why are you scratching?"

"I got a 'skeeter bite."

"You shouldn't dig at it. It might get infected."

That was what Mommy had said. Lexie stopped scratching and pressed really hard on the bite instead.

"This itches, but I haven't scratched it."

Mr. Ferris stuck out his arm. Lexie could see a red bump just above his wrist.

"Did a 'skeeter bite you too?"

"No. I got stung by a bee. In there." He pointed toward the wooded area beside the house.

Lexie frowned. She'd hoped Mr. Ferris didn't know where the bees lived. Bees liked flowers as much as walking-sticks. She'd seen them darting in and out of the daylilies.

"Have you seen the beehive, Bunny?"

She nodded. Her leg was itching again. She tightened her hold on the swing chain so she wouldn't scratch.

"I hope you didn't go in there by yourself."

"Mr. Verdell took me."

"I suppose he showed you the gazebo."

Lexie glared up at him. The gazebo was supposed to be a secret. If Mr. Ferris knew about it, the secret was ruined. At least part of it was. Maybe he didn't know about the special part. Mr. Ferris stepped behind the swing. Lexie twisted her head to see what he was doing.

"Would you like a push?"

"I guess. But I wanna go real high."

If she got going really good, Mr. Ferris would have to stop pushing. Then maybe he'd go away. The swing climbed higher. Higher than Mommy or MarLynn or Miz Mid had ever let her go.

"You can stop now," she told him.

Mr. Ferris stopped pushing and walked around in front to watch. Lexie tried not to think about how high she was and pumped really hard so the swing would keep going. After a while Mr. Ferris went home. As soon as she was sure he was gone, Lexie let the swing die down and ran into the house.

⸺ 35 ⸺

Devon studied Clay as he made a notation and stared at what he'd written. For a moment the only sound was the soft whir of the fan on the air-conditioning unit. She shifted positions.

"I'd like to try something, if you'll let me, Nicki," Clay said finally. "We call it regression therapy."

"Hypnosis," Devon murmured.

Nicki's shoulders stiffened. Her knuckles whitened on the lounger's arms. Clay shot Devon an angry scowl.

"You promised to trust me, Nicki. Regression may be the best way to get at the truth. All we'll be doing is taking a journey through your past. A very cautious journey. If we come to disturbing memories, we'll skip over them for now and go on. We can explore them another time, when you're better prepared."

Nicki glanced at Devon, then back at Clay.

"And Devon can stay?"

"You're making it difficult for me to help you."

"I'm about to bare my soul. Can't I have some control of the process?"

Devon caught the flicker of something almost like admiration in Clay's eyes before he looked back down at the pad in his lap.

"All right, Nicki. We'll do it your way."

"What do I do?"

"Close your eyes and take slow, deep breaths. That's it. What's the most relaxing thing you can think of?"

"I used to have this tape—waves breaking on the beach, shorebirds, a babbling brook, flute music in the background."

"All right. I want you to imagine you're walking very slowly along the shore of a calm, peaceful river. The water's so clear you can see minnows darting about beneath the surface. Now and then a gentle breeze ruffles your hair. The sun is warm on your arms. You're barefoot, and you can feel soft green grass beneath your feet."

Clay's soothing voice continued, walking Nicki leisurely along the bank, reinforcing his visual descriptions with instructions to breathe deeply and relax. Slowly Nicki's earlier tension drained away, and her hands curled limply in her lap.

"Where are you, Nicki?" Clay asked softly.

"Walking by the river." Her voice had a strange, faraway quality.

"It's fall, and the distant mountains look red and gold in the sunlight. Here by the river some of the trees have begun to drop their leaves. They've landed on the water. Can you see them floating there?"

Nicki nodded.

"How do you feel?"

"Peaceful."

"Why don't you sit down on the bank for a little while and watch the leaves as they drift by?"

Nicki's head tilted slightly as she relaxed even more against the cushions. A small smile played about her lips.

"In a moment the breeze will rise, and the leaves will begin to float away. As they drift away, the years will go with them, and we'll move back in time. We're going to look for pleasant memories to-day. If we find an unpleasant memory, I want you to step back from the water and look toward the mountains. Do you understand?"

"Yes," Nicki responded in the same detached tone of voice.

"You're sitting on the bank, watching the leaves, and your adult years are floating away. We're going to go back until we find something special that happened when you were a teenager. Something pleasant. You're smiling. What do you remember?"

"I won freestyle at sectional. Coach says I'm the fastest freshman swimmer he's ever had."

"What does Renee think about your win?"

Nicki's happy expression faded.

"She's not home. Lupe says maybe she'll be back for the regional, but I know she won't."

"Who's Lupe?"

"The housekeeper. She's nicer than the last one, except she doesn't go out much. I don't think she's got a green card."

"Did Renee get back in time to watch you swim?"

"No."

"Did you win again?"

"No. I got a cramp and came in fourth."

As Clay moved her deeper into the past, Nicki's features began to soften, and her voice became that of a child.

"I'd like you to try to go back now to the week you started first grade."

Suddenly Nicki's lower lip began to protrude.

"Why are you pouting, Nicki? Tell me what you feel."

"Don't wanna go."

"Why not?"

"Don't wanna talk."

"Don't you like to talk?"

Nicki shook her head from side to side. Devon could imagine pigtails slapping Nicki's cheeks the way Lexie's did.

"Sometimes I talk to Mommy in my head."

"But not out loud?"

"Uh-uh."

"Let's move forward this time, Nicki. You've been in school a few weeks. Do you talk to people now?"

She nodded.

"Who do you talk to?"

"Teacher. Kids."

"Why did you change your mind about talking to them?"

"They don't ask scary questions."

Clay scribbled something on his pad. Devon wished she could peer over his shoulder.

"Let's move backward again, Nicki. The river's so peaceful and it's such a pleasant day. I want you to go back a few months before you started school. It's summer, and you and Renee . . ."

Nicki's face twisted into a mask of terror. She shook her head violently. Her body thrashed upward, arching away from the cushions. Clay leaned forward in his chair.

"Tell me what's happening?"

Nicki whimpered and pressed both hands against her mouth. The whimper stopped but her body continued to writhe.

"You can step back from unpleasant memories, remember? You don't have to face them today. Just look away from the river and focus on the mountains and feel yourself relax. That's it."

Nicki lay back. Her terrorized expression began to recede.

"I want you to move back again, as far back as you can go. Back to when you were a very little girl."

Instantly Nicki's face was transformed.

"You're having a happy memory," Clay said softly, his voice as gentle as if his words were his hand and he was stroking Nicki's forehead. "Tell me what you feel, Nicki."

"Not Nicki. Sky."

Devon glanced at Clay in confusion. His eyes had closed. Only the tremor of his mustache revealed his reaction to Nicki's revelation. He reopened his eyes. Devon could see moisture glistening along his lower lashes. She fought an urge to ask a few questions of her own.

"How old are you, Sky?"

"Five. And a half."

"What are you doing?"

"Digging." Nicki's smile widened.

"What are you digging?"

" 'Tatoes. Mommy's gonna make me french fries. Season says they're bad for you. But Mommy promised."

Devon looked at Clay again. His fingers had tightened on his pen, but he'd ceased to write.

"Who's Season, Sky?"

"She thinks she's boss, but Mommy says she's not. Nobody can be boss 'cause ever'body's the same."

"Everybody's equal?"

"Uh-huh."

"Where are you, Sky?"

"In the garden."

"Where is the garden?"

"Behind the house."

"Do you know where the house is?" Clay asked patiently.

Nicki's face clouded. She shook her head.

"Look beyond the garden, Sky. Tell me what you see."

"Trees and sky." She giggled. "That's my name."

"It's a very pretty name. What else can you see?"

"Tinker's under our bus. I can see his feet. He looks funny. Mommy says somebody's gonna have to buy a new carb . . . er . . . ra if we wanna go anywhere."

Devon felt as if all of Nicki's earlier tension had settled between her own shoulder blades. Clay began tapping the pen against the notepad.

"Sky, do you and your mommy ever take walks?" Nicki nodded. "Where do you go?"

"Down to the gate. It's a long way. Sometimes I get tired and Mommy has to carry me back."

"Do you go anywhere else?"

"The canyon. But we walk real slow so I don't get tired."

Clay smiled. He was more relaxed than he'd been only moments before, Devon realized.

"What do you see in the canyon?"

"Deer. And raccoons and possums. Tinker and Moonbeam say there's a lion in the canyon. One time I saw where he walked in the mud by the creek. Mommy says he won't bother us if we don't bother him. She says he just wants Tessa's chickens."

"What else can you see in the canyon? Are there birds?"

"Uh-huh." All of a sudden Nicki's voice sounded very small. "Mommy said not to look, but I did."

Her voice changed to a wail. "Somebody hurt the eagle!"

"Step back from the memory, Sky. Look away for a moment."

Nicki's distress faded once more as she followed Clay's reminders to breathe deeply and slowly.

"What do you think we should do about the dead eagle, Sky?"

"Mommy says we have to bury him and then sing a song and say a prayer. She says the eagle doesn't hurt anymore 'cause the arrow freed his spirit. Being free is real important."

"What does your mommy look like, Sky?"

Nicki frowned. "She looks like Mommy."

Clay glanced at his notes.

"Sky, have you ever heard the word commune?"

"Mommy says that's where we live."

He closed his notebook and recapped his pen.

"The memories we found this morning are yours to keep, Sky. Remember each one. We're going back to where we started now. When I count to three, I want you to take a deep breath and open your eyes. You'll feel rested and refreshed, and you'll remember the pleasant memories and how good they made you feel."

Devon listened as Clay reversed the process that had taken Nicki into her past.

"You can open your eyes now."

Nicki blinked several times, adjusting to the light.

"How do you feel?" Clay asked.

"Relaxed. Happy."

"You just came back from a very long journey."

Her eyes widened. She placed her hands on her temples.

"Everything was so real. I could feel the clods of dirt in my hands. They were warm from the sun. And the smells and the sounds. *I was there.* I was right there and watched it happen all over again. I saw the eagle. And I saw vultures overhead."

She shivered.

"We piled rocks up so they couldn't get to him."

"What else can you remember?"

"I was living in some kind of group home. A commune. And my name wasn't Nicki. It was Sky."

A flush of anger darkened her face.

"Why did Renee change my name? Why didn't she ever talk about my childhood? I wasn't terrified by things as a child. Those were *happy* memories. I shouldn't have blocked them out."

Clay's face remained impassive. Nicki sat up straighter, staring at him intently.

"I didn't remember everything, did I?"

"You remembered much more than I expected for an initial session."

"But pieces are missing. Memories I was afraid to face."

"I told you resolution takes time."

"But why do some parts of the past frighten me so?"

"You've gone back with knowledge of the future. It's important to go slowly and not overwhelm yourself."

Nicki stared at her lap, then looked up, her eyes wide.

"What if I start remembering the frightening parts on my own? Could that happen?"

"It's possible. If it does, I want you to call me."

"Even in the middle of the night?"

"Especially then, but don't worry about those memories right now. When you're ready to face them, you will. And I'll be beside you when it happens. I promise."

"It's just so frustrating," Nicki said with a sigh.

She looked at Devon as if suddenly remembering her presence. Devon smiled reassuringly, unsure whether she had Clay's permission to enter the conversation. She was certain of one thing. Once she had him alone she didn't intend to wait for his consent to voice her questions.

"What happens now?" Nicki asked.

"Let's wait a week or so before we try this again. Monday's the Fourth. Relax, enjoy the weekend, take Lexie to the club."

"We'll be able to see the fireworks from this side of the lake, won't we?"

"It's not just the fireworks," Devon protested, deciding the session was clearly over. "Everyone goes to the club on the Fourth. It's an annual tradition, the only day they're open to nonmembers. If you're a property owner or registered at one of the rental units, you're automatically on their guest list."

"According to Gwyn, pigging out is part of the tradition," Clay said. "Free hot dogs, corn on the cob, homemade ice cream. Lexie wouldn't want to miss all that."

"She could probably skip the stomachache."

"It's more than just the food," Devon explained. "There'll be clowns and a magician. Even a carousel. It's like stepping back in time. When I was a kid, going to the club on the Fourth was the highlight of the summer."

"All right. I guess we'll go."

Clay opened the blinds. Sunlight streamed into the room.

"Would you like one of us to walk you home?" he asked.

"No. I'll be fine. To tell the truth, I feel too relaxed to do much of anything. I think I'm going to spend the rest of the day lying in the sun, watching Lexie chase minnows."

"Sounds like the perfect way to spend a Saturday afternoon," Clay said, smiling for the first time.

▬▬▬ 36 ▬▬▬

Devon watched until she was sure Nicki had safely reached her own yard, then turned and walked back to Clay's door. He opened the screen door, somewhat reluctantly, and motioned her in.

"I don't suppose you want to discuss the weather or world politics," he said as they settled on the screened-in porch.

"That wouldn't be my preference, no."

He sighed in resignation, propped a foot on one knee, and folded one hand over the other.

"Regression is used with adults who were sexually abused as children, isn't it?"

"Sometimes."

"Is that what you think Nicki's blocking?"

"I doubt sexual trauma's an issue here."

She studied his impassive expression, exasperated by his detachment. His profession might demand objectivity, but he ought to feel *something*. And he had at one point, she realized.

"You know where Nicki was, don't you?"

"Devon, I let you stay because Nicki obviously wouldn't have continued if I'd gone by the book, but I can't discuss her case with you. Patient confidentiality . . ."

"Dammit, Clay. Stop trying to prove what great ethics you have. This isn't about Nicki. It's about you. The name Sky, her life in a commune, none of that was news to you."

He looked away, staring across the lake without answering. Damn the man. Did he think she was stupid?

"You said Pip Sheridan lived in a commune. Life's full of coincidences, but you'll never convince me this is one of them."

He continued to stare at the lake, his gaze unfocused.

"Were Pip and Renee friends?"

"Yes," he admitted, turning at last.

"Joel talked as if Pip died here, not in California. Did Renee and Nicki come back with her when she left the commune?"

"Devon, you don't realize what you're asking."

"Maybe I don't know the right questions, but I'd bet you have the answers."

"For right now that's the way it has to be."

Mid met Nicki at the door.

"Reed's called three times. The last time he said if you didn't call him in half an hour, he was coming out. That was fifteen minutes ago."

The thought of answering questions made Nicki want to curl up and hide.

"Where's Lexie?"

"I sent her up to her room. She's been slamming around here with a chip on her shoulder all morning. Didn't want to go back out to play on the swings. Wouldn't color or sit still for a story. Stomped her feet like a two-year-old when I asked what kind of bee she'd got in her bonnet."

"I'll call Reed, then see what I can do with her."

* * *

"I knew I shouldn't have let you go there alone," Reed fumed when Nicki tried to tell him she wasn't ready to talk about her session. "What did Clay do to you?"

"I wasn't alone. Devon was there. And he didn't *do* anything to me. We talked awhile, and then he took me through regression therapy."

"Hypnosis? My God, Nicki. You've been afraid of shrinks as far back as you can remember, but you let someone hypnotize you? What were you thinking?"

"It seemed like a good idea at the time. And it was. I remembered things, Reed. I remembered living in a commune when I was five. And I remembered finding the dead eagle."

There was silence on the other end of the line.

"Reed?"

"Nicki, therapists have been known to plant ideas in their patients' heads. There's even a term for it—false memory."

"Clay didn't do that. What I remembered was real."

"Are you going to let him do this again?"

"We talked about another session next week."

"Clay's treading shaky ground. He's not licensed here."

"This wasn't his idea, you know," Nicki protested. "I sort of bullied him into it. Besides, he's not charging a fee."

"Now I'm really concerned. How many doctors do you know who offer charity services to rich young women?"

Nicki couldn't help herself. She started laughing.

"What is it you find so hilarious?"

"I'm sorry. It's just that you sound like an out-raged parent lecturing a wayward child."

"Okay, okay. But I want to be there the next time. Now, how about dinner? The club has a trio on Saturday nights during the summer. Just college kids, but they're pretty good."

"All I want to do is loaf around here and go to bed early."

"Sure you won't change your mind later?"

"I'm sure. Why don't you come out for lunch to-morrow? We can stuff ourselves with Mid's fried chicken, then go swimming. I know Lexie misses you."

"What about Lexie's mother?"

Nicki grinned at the receiver.

"Her too. Does that mean you'll come?"

"I never miss an opportunity for fried chicken," Reed told her before he hung up.

Lexie flopped on the end of the lounge chair and hugged her mother's legs. Nicki opened her arms, ignoring the dripping bathing suit. Lexie snuggled closer, only to squirm down a moment later and return to the water. Her mood had shifted a dozen times since Nicki had coaxed her from her room. Lunch had been eaten in petulant silence. The afternoon had alternated between explosive energy and periods of clinging affection.

The effects of her own morning lingered, erasing any desire she might have had to join Lexie in play. She lacked the energy to carry her body from the lounge chair to the water. Physical exhaustion aside, she felt a more pressing need to relive the memories the therapy session had restored.

Small details of the scenes she'd remembered floated through her mind—a tire hanging from an old tree beyond the garden, another beside a metal carport, half buried and filled with flowers, a ramshackle chicken coop presided over by an aggressive rooster, a tumbledown horse corral somewhere deep in the canyon.

A butterfly settled for an instant on Nicki's knee, decided the flower beds near the house held greater promise, and flittered off. Mid, her weekly letter to her son and grandchildren completed, came out wearing a bright print swimsuit and initiated a game of water tag with Lexie. Momentarily relieved of lifeguard duty, Nicki closed her eyes.

As vivid as the new memories were, she could summon nothing further. She flipped onto her stomach. Another butterfly had joined the first in exploring the flowers. Nicki's thoughts drifted with them, landing for a moment among the dirt clods in the commune's vegetable garden, then moving on to the funeral service for the eagle.

She'd never read anything about canyons in the literature she'd studied about Michigan. Texas had canyons. Maybe Renee had raised her in a commune somewhere in Texas, brought her here for a time, then returned. That would explain one element missing in her memories of the commune— nowhere had she felt the presence of the third person who haunted her earlier flashbacks.

Where had her father been while she and Renee dug potatoes and explored the canyon behind the commune? Had the blurry figure returning her tennis serve and piloting the sailboat spent those years in Vietnam as Renee had once indicated? And why had Renee changed her name?

Sky. Season. Moonbeam. The kind of names sixties hippies had embraced in their disdain for the conventions of the establishment and the generation that bore them. Earth mothers returning to nature. The original Mrs. Tarleton would have felt right at home. Peace and brotherhood.

Nicki's eyes flew open.

Communal living. The sharing of thoughts and possessions. Mental and physical joining of lives and souls and bodies. *Free love.* Renee had given her conflicting stories of her invisible father. Could the truth have been as elusive for her mother as for herself? If Renee hadn't been sure whose seed had been sown in her womb, how could Nicki hope to discover her heritage?

A reassuring thought rose above the pounding of her heart. Some tie with Trumpeter Lake had brought her here with Renee. The Sheridan sisters' growths weren't the only ones charted beneath the new kitchen wallpaper. Another name had been added years later in a different hand—a short name that began with *S* and ended with *Y*. Her name. Sky.

Sky Prevot. Or was her last name as false as her first?

She'd come here with hopes of tracing her father, only to rush headlong into another kind of identity crisis.

Who was she really?

......37......

"You can unleash that wild pony now," Joel Lynch told Nicki just before noon on Sunday morning.

He winked as Lexie tore around her mother and Mid and raced into the side yard. Squeals of delight echoed back to them.

"Seems she's satisfied. How about you?" Joel asked as the group approached the newly erected playhouse.

Nicki smiled her approval, unable to put words to her emotions. Lexie waved from inside the structure, then darted back out to examine the empty flower boxes beneath the two front windows. Nicki stepped onto the narrow, child-size porch.

"Never was inside the original myself, but I think this one's pretty close."

"It's perfect," Nicki told him.

"I'm gonna go get my things," Lexie announced, racing back to the house.

Mid and Joel followed her, chatting about the July Fourth celebration. Nicki remained in the yard, drawn to the playhouse.

Any lingering doubts about her connection to the lake property had been erased. The image she'd formed of this structure in her mind had not come from some photograph Renee had destroyed. Nor was the memory a product of her imagination. The playhouse was a very real part of the past she'd buried.

Once she'd walked without stooping through the doorway of the original building, settled herself in a child-size chair at an equally miniature table, and poured imaginary tea for dolls of her own. *A wooden table and chairs.* The new image flashed so vividly she expected to see the furniture as she bent to enter. She knelt in the empty interior to look out the windows.

Lexie was returning, her arms filled with toys, a plastic sack, heavy with books, dragging on the ground behind her. She saw her mother at the window and wiggled her fingers in greeting. Nicki returned the wave.

Her breath caught in her throat. The motion brought back an image of herself as a child, pulling a red-checked curtain aside, waving to Renee and . . .

The image wavered and dissolved before the second figure could take shape. She closed her fingers as if trying to recapture the illusion. Lexie stumbled through the door, scattering the vision's shadowy pieces like the puppets that tumbled from her arms to the floor.

"When's Reed gonna come?"

"Soon," Nicki murmured, her thoughts still centered on the newest flashback. A happy memory. Not a sad or frightening one to be pushed aside or looked away from.

Lexie had settled cross-legged in front of her, a puppet on each hand, Mr. Flops and the third *Sesame Street* character propped between her legs. Sun streamed through the playhouse windows, warming the small enclosure. Nicki closed her eyes and imagined herself Lexie's size, playing with toys of her own in this cozy setting. Outside, a car door slammed.

"He's here," Lexie squealed.

She thrust her menagerie at Nicki and raced from the playhouse, calling Reed's name.

Nicki reached to clear the puppets away from the door. Bert's egg-shaped face grinned up at her. Without warning, icy fingers of anxiety clawed at her, robbing the playhouse of its warmth. She dropped the puppet and scrambled through the doorway, gasping for air.

In the sunlight her terror faded. Lexie and Reed were unloading something from his trunk. She pulled herself together and joined them.

"Joel tipped me off you'd built a second home," Reed said over his shoulder, his head still buried in the trunk. Two flat boxes lay propped against the car's bumper. "No home's complete without furniture. I hope you've got a screwdriver."

A large box joined the smaller two. Nicki took in the sketch on each one with a sense of déjà vu. CHILDREN'S DINING SET—MAPLE FINISH.

All she needed now were the red-checked curtains and one long-buried childhood image would be perfectly restored.

Muffled sounds from Mid's portable radio filtered down from the second floor. Despite an afternoon of water play with Reed and Lexie, Nicki was charged with energy. The day felt incomplete, as if she'd forgotten some important routine.

Reed had left about eight, shortly after an exhausted Lexie had been put to bed. Nicki had returned his impassioned kiss at the door, assuring him for perhaps the tenth time that she was all right. She'd found it impossible not to appear distracted during the afternoon. Confiding the details of her therapy session had increased her impatience to get on with the process.

The breeze from the open porch windows ruffled the paper in her hand. She ticked off the notations once more in her mind.

An aversion to fire or gas. The nautical bedroom. Worms. Puppets.

She checked her watch and ran upstairs to tell Mid what she intended to do.

"You're sure you want to do this?" Devon asked doubtfully.

"I'm sure. I just hope he's home."

Clay opened the door after the third knock. He was wearing khaki shorts and a black T-shirt and his feet were bare. His gray hair looked as if he'd raked it with his fingers. Despite the reserve that had sprung up between them after their last conversation, Devon found herself fighting an urge to run her own hands through the tousled locks.

"What's happened?" he asked, leading Nicki to the chintz-patterned sofa and waving Devon toward the matching love seat. Nicki perched on the edge of the cushions, hands clasped in her lap, thumbs pressing against one another until their nail beds turned as white as their tips.

"I don't know who I am anymore, Clay. My entire life's been a lie. Not even my name is real."

"That's an understandable reaction. Next week we'll . . ."

"I don't want to wait for next week."

Clay was shaking his head. Nicki handed him her list.

"Those things triggered panic attacks. I want you to regress me now and ask me about them the way you did the eagle."

"Nicki, therapy isn't a game. If we rush this . . ."

"I'm remembering more and more of the good memories by myself. Wouldn't it be better if I faced the frightening ones in a controlled setting before they came back on their own?"

"You don't realize what you're asking."

Devon stared at Clay, hearing the echo of the words he'd said to her. She added her own plea to Nicki's. Clay studied Nicki's face a few moments, then nodded in resignation.

Devon listened as Clay's voice droned on, walking Nicki beside the gently flowing river once more. He'd combed his hair and slipped a pair of worn loafers on his feet, but hadn't bothered to change from casual clothes. The three of them could have been sitting around discussing plans for tomorrow's holiday instead of probing the corners of Nicki's mind.

"We may find some unpleasant memories while we're walking this time, Nicki. If we do, instead of looking away, I want you to just step back from what you see. Step back and imagine you're watching what's happening on a movie screen. You'll be watching yourself on the screen. Do you understand?"

Nicki nodded. Once again her features relaxed and her voice grew childlike as Clay took her back to her life in the commune.

"Who do you play with, Sky?" he asked, switching without comment to the name Nicki had revealed in the previous session.

"Zane and Carlos. But they don't like dolls. Wren

says she does, but she'd rather read. She's gonna write her own books someday. Next year, when she's twelve. Mommy says when Moonbeam has her baby, we'll have a real doll."

"Who's your best friend?"

Nicki's forehead wrinkled in pain. She shook her head.

"You can step back and watch the screen, Sky. Remember?"

Nicki nodded.

"Tell me your best friend's name."

"Tani."

"Are you and Tani playing together?"

"Uh-huh." A tear traced its way down Nicki's cheek.

"I know you can do this, Sky. You can step back from the memory and tell me about Tani."

"Her clothes are on fire," Nicki blurted out as more tears coursed down her face.

"Go back to right before Tani's clothes catch fire, Sky. What's Tani doing?"

"Trying to make hot chocolate, but the little light won't come on."

"The pilot light on the stove?"

"Uh-huh. Tani says she's watched Season fix it lots of times with a match. Mommy won't let me have matches. Tani says that's 'cause I'm still a baby, and she's almost seven."

"What's happening now, Sky?"

"Tani turned the little knob and now the kitchen smells real funny. I don't like it when Season gets mad. I'm gonna go back outside."

Slowly the color drained from Nicki's face.

"What's happening, Sky? Step back and tell me what's happening."

"Tani's screaming! Her dress is on fire. Tinker's

rolling her on the ground, but she won't stop screaming . . ."

"Step away from the memory, Sky. Move ahead in time a little while. Is Tani all right now?"

"Mommy says she is. Mommy says the hospital made Tani better. But she never came back. They took her to the hospital and she didn't come back. And now Mommy says we have to leave."

Clay moved on to less traumatic memories, and Nicki's face relaxed once more. Devon massaged the tension in her own neck.

"Did your mommy tell you why you have to leave, Sky?"

"Tinker and Moonbeam went away 'cause he didn't want to fight the war. Mommy doesn't like the new people. She says we can't stay here anymore."

"Where are you going?"

"To the lake."

Devon glanced at Clay. Despite the cool air filtering through the air-conditioning ducts, perspiration lined his forehead.

"How are you going to get to the lake?"

"On a bus. It takes a long time, but Mommy's gonna read me stories."

"Let's move ahead now, Sky. Are you living at the lake?"

"Uh-huh. Renee's teaching me how to swim."

Something about Nicki's sudden use of her mother's first name jarred discordantly in Devon's thoughts.

"What does your room at the lake look like, Sky?"

"It's got a big bed with a roof."

"A canopy?"

"Uh-huh, but I like my bed on the porch better."

"Do you ever sleep in the room with the boat things?" Nicki shook her head. "Does anyone sleep in that room?"

"No."

"Tell me about your toys."

"I've got dishes and dolls and books and puzzles and a croquet set . . ."

"What about puppets, Sky? Do you have any puppets?"

Terror replaced Nicki's childlike exuberance.

"Sky, do you like sailboats?" Clay asked abruptly, changing the subject once more.

"You have to duck for the beam," she told him, her face relaxing into a smile.

"Who raises the sails?"

"Mommy. But she's gonna teach me when I get bigger."

Clay changed subjects again, asking about favorite foods.

"Renee fixes baby pancakes sometimes," she told him.

This time Nicki's reference to her mother as Renee brought Devon upright in her chair. *Mommy and Renee.* Interchangeable yet somehow different when Nicki said them. She glanced at Clay. His bland expression remained unchanged.

"What do you think about when you see a worm, Sky?"

"Worms crawl in," Nicki wailed, her voice rising hysterically as the blood drained from her face. "Mommy! Don't let the worms get Mommy!"

"Step back from the worms, Sky. Look away from them."

Nicki's cries dwindled to sobs, then trailed off completely as Clay's soothing words continued. Despite his emotional control, Devon detected a strain in his voice.

"Sky, when your mommy gets mad, what does she say?"

"Raspberries."

Clay's eyes closed for a moment.

"We're going to start back now, Sky. The years are passing and you're older now. Tell me your name."

"Nicki. Nicki Prevot."

"Nicki, when you get mad about something what do you say?"

"Raspberries."

"Is that what Renee says?"

"Renee says 'shit.'"

"Will you be all right?" Devon whispered, giving Nicki a hug. "I feel like I should stay with you."

"Mid's here if I need her, and I'll be able to sleep now. I'm really relaxed." She turned to Clay. "Tomorrow afternoon?"

In the moonlight Devon watched Clay's reluctant nod. Nicki slipped inside and locked her door. When Devon turned, Clay was already striding across the lawn, forcing her to sprint to catch up. At the touch of her hand on his arm he stiffened.

"Are you angry with Nicki or with me?"

"With myself. I shouldn't have agreed to another session so soon. I shouldn't have started this in the first place."

"But she's remembering more each time," Devon protested. "And she wants to remember the rest. She needs to remember."

"She *needs* a different therapist."

"It's you she trusts."

"Maybe she shouldn't."

Devon tugged on his arm, making him turn toward the moonlight so she could see his face. His anguished expression made her drop her hand to her side. Clay lowered his eyes, but not before her shocked recognition registered in their familiar depths. He twisted away and began walking again.

"Renee wasn't Nicki's mother, was she?" Devon asked softly, so softly she feared he hadn't heard, but he stopped without turning. The stiffness drained from his shoulders.

"No," he said hoarsely.

"She's Pip Sheridan's child?"

A nod, almost imperceptible in the moonlight.

"And you're her father."

Clay's response to the statement was to begin walking again, faster this time as if being pursued.

"It's the eyes, Clay," she called after him softly. "It skipped a generation, but Lexie has your eyes."

Still not turning, he entered his house and closed the door firmly. In silence broken only by amorous crickets, the snap of the dead bolt echoed like a slap. She waited a moment. One by one Clay's lights winked out, leaving her alone in the darkness.

┉┉ 38 ┉┉

"**T**hanks for coming," Clay murmured as Reed shut off the ignition and got out of the car. The electric door rumbled down, sealing them inside the garage.

"Is all this cloak-and-dagger stuff really necessary?" Reed asked, following Clay into the house.

"I need to talk to you before Nicki gets here."

"I thought her second session wasn't until later this week?"

"We had the second one late last night."

Reed fought to control his temper.

"I hope you've kept up your malpractice policy."

"Bear with me, Counselor. I'll put things in perspective as soon as Devon gets here."

"Why not invite Gwyn and Del and the rest of the neighborhood? I'm sure they'd love to hear the details of Nicki's problem. Hell, you could probably sell tickets."

"Dammit, Reed. We're both after the same thing. Why don't you just shut up till you hear what I've got to say?"

Devon's tap on the door momentarily diffused the moment. Clay fended off questions until they were settled in the small room Nicki had described as the site of her first therapy session. Reed glanced about impatiently.

"Okay, we're both here. Now what the hell's going on?"

Clay rubbed his hands together and stared at his fingers.

"I met Pip Sheridan at Berkeley the day JFK was killed. She invited me to a candlelight vigil she was organizing. A few weeks later we moved in together. We fought about everything except whether the sun would rise in the east, but somehow it worked."

Reed opened his mouth, then decided his question could wait.

"I lost my student deferment when I graduated in May of sixty-five. The protest movement hadn't gained its real momentum yet, but as usual, Pip was in the vanguard. She urged me to move to Canada. I'd been telling her for months I couldn't do that to my parents. She was so against our involvement over there, she blocked out what I said.

"Things were just beginning to heat up in 'Nam. Most of us didn't realize how bad it was going to get. I'm not sure anyone did at that point. I couldn't see putting off the inevitable, so I enlisted. The morning after I told Pip, she packed her things and disappeared somewhere in Haight-Ashbury. I spent my last two weeks knocking on doors and having them slammed in my face."

"Okay. You and a woman who once lived in Nicki's house were lovers. What's that got to do with what's happening to Nicki?"

"Let him tell it his own way," Devon murmured.

Clay flashed her a look of gratitude.

"I tried sending letters through people I thought might know where she'd gone. Every one came

back unopened. After my first hitch, I tracked down
the commune where she was living—an old ranch
back in a canyon."

"The same commune Nicki remembered?"

Clay nodded.

"I camped outside the locked gate until Pip
agreed to talk to me. She asked if I'd changed my
mind about the war. I tried to convince her none of
that mattered now. I'd done my duty, survived, and
come home. For a long time, she didn't say anything. Then she asked me how many babies I'd
killed."

He shuddered. Devon reached out, but he waved
her away.

"There was nothing I could say to bridge the gap
between us, so I left. I was angry and hurt. I know
it doesn't make sense now—hell, it didn't make
sense at the time—but I reenlisted. Pip's question
haunted me during that second hitch. Things had
gotten much worse by then, more troops, more car-
nage, more hopelessness . . . After I got out, I
stayed to work with the kids our guys had fathered
and then abandoned."

"What does any of that have to do with Nicki?"

Clay's mustache twitched. He looked at Devon,
then away.

"When I came back in seventy-three, I tried to
find Pip again. The commune had been raided a
couple of years before—one of the members had
turned up on Nixon's enemies list—but Pip's name
didn't appear on the arrest records. People had
scattered. No one knew anything; or if they did,
they weren't talking.

"I knew Pip and her sister didn't get along, but I
wrote Ollie anyway. I got back an impersonal letter

from a lawyer informing me Pip had drowned the summer before I returned."

"You still haven't answered my question."

"Nicki is Pip's daughter. Pip's and *mine*."

Reed half rose from his chair, then slumped back.

"You're sure about this?" Clay nodded. "Does she know?"

"Last night Nicki referred to her mother and Renee within the same time frame as separate people, but she didn't make the connection," Devon broke in.

Reed glared at Clay.

"Why wait until now to contact her?"

"I didn't know Nicki existed until eighteen months ago."

Clay rubbed his temples, then splayed his hands on his knees, staring at his fingers as if an explanation might be penciled on his nails.

"A woman who'd lived in the commune for a while brought her youngest child into the clinic for treatment. She spotted Pip in a group picture I kept on my desk and asked if I knew what had happened to her. When I said Pip had died, she wondered what had become of her little girl. She said Pip never talked about her baby's father, just that they split up because they couldn't see eye to eye about the war.

"The dates, the circumstances, everything fit. I managed to find out that Pip moved back here after a radical element took control of the commune. I wrote Ollie again, demanding to know what happened to my daughter. My letter came back marked 'DECEASED.' I moved here hoping to find some clue, *someone*, who could help me find my child."

"Then Nicki showed up," Devon said softly.

Reed, his thoughts swirling, stared at Clay's now tightly clenched hands.

"My God, Clay. This goes way beyond normal ethics. You're trying to treat your own child."

"Dammit! What was I supposed to do? Nicki was hurting. She wouldn't talk to anyone else, and she practically begged me to help her. Things have gone too far to hand her over to another therapist at this point. She's too close to the truth."

"I don't understand where Renee comes in and how she was able to make Nicki forget so much," Devon murmured.

"As best as I can determine, Pip met Renee on the bus coming home. Their personalities were exact opposites. Renee was materialistic. She came from a poor background, but she liked nice things and was looking for a way to get them. She'd been traipsing around the country as a groupie with a band that never quite made the big time.

"I imagine Renee's attitude toward money reminded Pip a little of Ollie before things got so bad between the sisters. But this time Pip was the older of the two opposites. She invited Renee to live with her in exchange for watching Nicki, or rather Sky, whenever Pip was out championing one of her causes. Pip liked having other people around. She probably considered it a challenge to convert Renee to her viewpoint. Renee, on the other hand, had always been an opportunist."

"She saw her chance to live the good life for a while and took it," Devon said as Clay nodded.

"After Pip died, Ollie stepped in to protect her precious social position from the scandal of her sister's love child. She cut a deal with Renee—a continuation of the comfortable lifestyle she'd had with Pip in exchange for reenforcing Nicki's own desire to forget. A child's natural urge to repress trauma just made Ollie's scheme easier."

"What trauma?" Reed asked warily.

Clay raised his eyes from his hands.

"Nicki watched her mother drown."

Nicki walked slowly down to the last terrace. Successful gardens demanded lots of attention, she decided, noting Del hard at work. Clay's patch looked pathetic in comparison to his.

Her restlessness of the previous night had returned. An hour sitting quietly beside the deserted tennis court hadn't sparked more memories as she'd hoped it would. Maybe she should ask Reed to take her sailing again. If she still felt as jumpy after today's session, she'd ask Clay's opinion of the idea.

"Taking your little one to the festivities tonight?" Del called to her.

"I haven't decided. We may just drive over later for the fireworks. What about you?"

"Never been much for celebrations," he said, collecting his things.

Nicki watched him walk briskly away, then hurried inside to spend time with Lexie before her session with Clay.

"What's going on?" Nicki asked as Clay ushered her into the small room.

Devon glanced at Clay for guidance. Both she and Reed had agreed to take their cues from him, although Reed had made clear his reservations about what Clay intended to do.

"I asked Reed to be here," Clay explained, taking Nicki's hands in his. "I think it's time we try to face those unpleasant memories you've kept buried for so long."

The color drained from Nicki's face.

"You can do this, Nicki. You'll be seeing whatever's there with the perception of an adult, not a child. I won't lie to you. Facing suppressed memories is painful. But you're strong, and you're surrounded by people who care about you very much. You won't have to handle that pain alone."

"You know what's been causing my blackouts," Nicki said, her eyes widening. "I don't understand. How . . ."

Clay shook his head.

"What I know or don't know doesn't matter right now. The only thing that matters is that you understand you can't change the past, but you *can* accept it and go on with your life."

Nicki closed her eyes and bent her head. Above the air conditioner's hum Devon could hear the muffled rumble of a powerboat on the lake. No other sound broke the silence. It was as if they'd each ceased to breathe. Finally Nicki nodded.

"The leaves are floating away, and so are the years."

Clay's voice continued, as gentle and soothing as always. Devon felt Reed shift uneasily. She touched his arm and offered what she hoped was a reassuring smile.

"Sky, is Renee your mommy?"

Nicki giggled.

"Mommy's my mommy."

"Who is Renee?"

"Our friend."

"Where did you meet your friend Renee?"

"On the bus."

"But she's coming with you to the lake?"

"She doesn't have anyplace to live and Mommy says the house is too big for just us."

"Let's move forward a bit. Do you know anyone named Ollie?"

"Mommy says she's a witch. She made Mommy sign some papers so we could live at the lake forever."

"Just you and Mommy and Renee?"

"Uh-huh."

"I want you to move forward again, Sky, to your second summer at the lake. Is Renee still with you?" Nicki nodded. "What's your mommy's name?"

"Mommy."

"That's what you call her, Sky. What does Renee call her?"

"Renee calls her Pip."

Devon glanced at Reed. He was clutching the seat of his chair as if anchoring it to the floor.

"I want you to think about the last day you lived at the lake, Sky."

Nicki drew her arms protectively across her chest.

"You can step back and watch this on the screen, Sky. Like you did the day Tani was burned, remember? Watching may make you very sad, but once you've watched what happened, the memory won't frighten you anymore. Tell me what happened that day, Sky. What happened the day your mommy went away?"

"Can't tell! The worms! The worms will get Mommy!"

"Step back and look at the screen, Sky. Tell me what you see."

"Can't. Can't! Finny fish! Mustn't tell! The worms!"

Nicki clawed the air, fighting a terror only she could see.

"Hide! Don't tell!"

Her cries continued, almost like a chant. Clay caught her flailing arms, but she shoved him away. He continued his calm instructions, telling her now to look away from whatever was feeding her terror. Finally she fell back against the cushions.

"It's all right, Sky. Deep, deep breaths. You don't have to remember today. You can walk away from the water. That's it. Deep breaths. Think about the pleasant memories you have of your mommy. Memories of the things you and Mommy and Renee did together. I want you to remember those things when I count to three and tell you to open your eyes."

Something nagged at Devon's thoughts. She tried to recapture Nicki's fragmented words and phrases, but nothing made sense. Only one thing was clear. Nicki was going to need all the support she could get when she returned to the present.

▪▪▪▪▪ 39 ▪▪▪▪▪

Nicki opened her eyes, but the enormity of her new discovery made her cover her face with her hands.

"Nicki."

Reed's voice, filled with concern. And something else. Anger? She opened her eyes and found him glaring intently at Clay. Devon's hand lay on Reed's arm, her fingers tightened as if in restraint.

"Renee never acted like my mother because she wasn't. It was Pip Sheridan. *She* gave me life. *She* brought me here."

Realization struck with an agonizing finality.

"And then she died," she whispered.

"Nicki, what do you feel?" Clay asked.

She shook her head to clear it. Was numbness a feeling?

"I don't feel anything." She looked at Reed. "That annuity Renee told me about was Pip's legacy, not my father's. And *she* must have left me the house and the money. But I still don't understand. She died a long time ago. Why did it take so long?"

"I think I might be able to explain," Clay said.

Nicki looked up, suddenly remembering. Clay had known where she was going. Known where she'd been.

"I knew some of your mother's story before you came to me for help," Clay admitted. "A little digging filled in the rest."

"Digging?"

"I talked to a woman who'd been the Sheridan family's cook for nearly fifty years. She stayed on with Ollie after the girls' parents, your grandparents, were killed. Elke's the perfect closemouthed image of the family retainer, loyal to her employer even though Ollie's been gone over two years."

"Two years is a reasonable period to probate an estate as complicated as Ollie Sheridan's must have been," Reed offered.

"Elke's in a nursing home now, pretty far gone. Coherent one minute, babbling the next. I finally caught her in a lucid moment and convinced her the truth had lost its power to hurt."

"You must have been very convincing," Nicki murmured, unwilling to voice the suspicion forming at the back of her mind.

"What did she tell you?" Reed asked.

"When the commune atmosphere began to change, becoming more militant than Pip liked, she brought Nicki . . . Sky, that is, back where she'd been the happiest as a child herself."

"I thought she and Ollie were always at each other's throats when they lived here?"

"Devon's right," Reed said. "Gwyn told us . . ."

"Gwyn repeated gossip. But there were good times, too. You have to remember the eight-year age difference between the sisters. They spent the biggest part of Pip's childhood pursuing different interests, almost in separate worlds at times. Pip's strongest memories were of fun and freedom, the same environment she wanted for her own daughter."

Clay smiled at Nicki. She lowered her eyes, afraid of what he might read in their depths.

"But Ollie didn't exactly welcome little sister home," Clay continued after a moment.

"Or her bastard. That's what Ollie called me. I remember hearing that the day she brought some papers to the house. Renee took me outside, but I could hear them shouting."

"Elke knew about the papers. Ollie agreed to buy back the house, arrange for its maintenance, and provide a generous allowance. In exchange, Pip would sever all contact with her sister, keep a low profile . . . and sign over her inherited interest in Sheridan Industries."

"She gave up a fortune," Devon protested.

"She gave up her investment in the decadent establishment as well," Reed said. "But she protected Nicki, or thought she did."

His eyes still on Nicki, Clay nodded.

"A place to raise you in peace and safety. Enough income to see to your needs and education. And no more guilt about owning a chunk of a company that was rumored—correctly, it turned out—to be developing guidance systems for missiles that would rain havoc on innocent children in faraway places."

"But the money came from the same source," Nicki protested.

"I'm sure it took some rationalization, but motherhood had softened some of Pip's fervor. And I imagine some of that generous allowance found its way into the protest movement. She probably considered it a reasonable trade-off. Freedom from Ollie's domination, security for you—what more did she need?"

"A closer look at the fine print," Reed suggested.

Clay nodded again.

"Pip hated the establishment, but Ollie was family. She couldn't believe her sister might have a loophole written into their agreement. The contract they signed, except for the clauses pertaining to Sheridan Industries, became null and void upon Pip's death."

"Gwyn was wrong about Ollie," Devon said. "The woman wasn't a barracuda; she was a piranha."

"You were born in the commune," Clay said softly. "If Pip ever recorded your birth, she didn't have anything among her things to prove it. In some ways you became a nonentity. Ollie stepped in and negotiated a similar deal with Renee, except this time she wanted you far enough away that her dirty deeds wouldn't come back to haunt her. She had access and clout. A false birth certificate, a new name . . ."

"And I ceased to exist," Nicki finished bitterly. "How convenient for her that I forgot my past life so completely."

No one spoke for a moment. Nicki looked up, suddenly wary.

"There's something you're not telling me. I was there, wasn't I? When Pip . . . when *my mother* drowned?"

"That's what everyone believes, Nicki," Clay said, returning to his professional voice. "Repressed memories are usually the result of some type of trauma."

"I can remember things now. Things we did, things she said, even the way her mouth curved up on one side when she laughed. I remember, but I don't feel any emotion—it's like something won't let me feel. And I don't remember watching her die."

Her voice broke. Suddenly Reed was beside her,

circling his arms about her, pulling her against his chest. And still she felt no emotion, had no vision of the horror everyone claimed she had witnessed. She looked at Clay, seeking some form of confirmation, and saw pain in the depths of his eyes. Pain and a different kind of confirmation. As quickly as their gazes locked, he looked away.

"Pip had been to a political rally. She told someone she was going home to take you sailing. According to what I could piece together from Elke, Renee came home, saw the boat capsized just offshore, and called for help."

His voice thickened.

"When they found Pip, they assumed you'd been with her, slipped out of your vest, and . . . They kept looking. Hours into the search Renee found you hiding somewhere. You were in shock and refused to speak.

"The dinghy Pip used to row out to the sailboat was filled with water, but still attached to its cleat when they righted the boat. Renee decided you must have been watching from the dock as Pip maneuvered in to take you on board, and you'd seen the whole thing. She called Ollie, insisting you needed professional help."

"Renee hated that kind of thing."

"But she did care about you, Nicki. Not the way Pip did, not the way you wanted or needed, but she didn't become your surrogate mother for entirely materialistic reasons. According to Elke, Renee went to see you every day.

"A few weeks after you began treatment, Renee stormed into Ollie's office and insisted the doctors' questions were making you even more withdrawn. The people Ollie sent you to had good credentials; I just don't think Ollie provided them with enough information to format the best treatment."

"So Ollie made an offer Renee couldn't refuse," Nicki said, pulling away from Reed's support and leaning back in the lounger.

"Elke told me Renee kept sending Ollie boxes of your school work, photos and snapshots, report cards, things like that. Ollie locked them in a closet, unopened. Near the end, when she was alone and knew she was dying, she went through each box and finally realized the enormity of what she'd done. She spent a week in conference with her attorneys trying to find a way to assuage her guilt, then destroyed every scrap Renee had sent."

"That's when they began transferring deeds through the dummy companies and blind trusts I've been trying to trace," Reed said. "Even in death she wanted to avoid any scandal."

"Part of Ollie's agreement with Renee was a large single deposit if Nicki reached majority without learning about her past. Elke swears she saw a copy of the certified check endorsed by Renee."

"The lump-sum payment she told me about. I never saw it."

"Could she have opened an account you never learned about?"

"Maybe, but it's more likely she converted the check to cash. It's the kind of thing she'd do. The dealership let her take the car she died in based on a ten-thousand-dollar cash deposit. She probably had the rest with her when she hit the gasoline truck."

For a long moment, no one said anything.

"I know what you're describing makes sense, but I still can't remember that day or any of the things you say came after."

"It's a lot to digest all at once, and you've kept it buried a very long time. When you're ready, the rest will come back."

"Where do the worms come in?"

"I don't know, Nicki. Children make connections adults might never think of. Maybe Pip was taking you fishing."

"Exactly when did all this happen?"

"The dates on the microfiche copies the library sent me were blurred. There's no headstone, no grave to visit. Ollie had Pip's remains cremated. I think it's the only time she made a decision Pip would have agreed with."

"You must at least know the year," Devon prompted.

"Summer, 1972. A few months after Nicki's sixth birthday."

"Lexie's nearly six," Nicki murmured. She rubbed her temples, trying to feel something, some physical connection to her body, if not her emotions.

"What about the puppets? And Lexie's loose tooth? Why did those things trigger panic attacks?"

"Nicki, I just don't know. Hypnosis isn't a cure; it's simply a tool. Identifying the problem's only part of the solution. You still have to learn to accept what you've found and to deal with your pain."

"But that's just it. I don't feel any pain. I don't feel anything at all."

"You will. That's why it's important you continue treatment with someone in active practice. Someone better trained in dealing with what you're going through."

Someone not so involved? Nicki longed to ask. She bit back the words and chose another question equally as dangerous.

"How did you know my mother?"

"We were at Berkeley at the same time."

He looked away before meeting her gaze.

"Someday, when all this has had time to sink in, we can talk about your mother. There's a lot you need to know. After you've talked to someone else, someone impartial . . ."

His words stopped short of an admission, but Nicki realized he was right. She wasn't ready for any more revelations this afternoon.

"I need to be with Lexie."

"Reed can drive you home and stay with you until it's time to go to the club," Devon suggested.

"I'm not exactly in the mood for a celebration right now."

"Why don't you get some rest and bring Lexie over later for the fireworks?" Clay said quietly.

Nicki offered him a weak smile, grateful he understood.

As Reed backed from Clay's garage, Nicki tried to summon some emotion for the new images that filled her head.

The figure gently lobbing balls back across the tennis net had been her mother, not her father. Her mother had hoisted the sails and taught her the constellations and waved to her as she waited in the playhouse for the milk and cookies that signaled the time for her afternoon nap. Pip had poured juice into the little orange-trimmed glasses and shared the dollar-size pancakes that were the specialty of their friend Renee.

Her mother's features came to her clearly now. Long, light brown hair, braided or swept into two ponytails like perky spaniel ears. Hazel eyes so like her own. A generous figure the braless fashions of the time had done little to conceal.

Pip's impish, crooked smile as she bent to exchange their good-night kiss was as vivid in Nicki's mind as if it had been etched in indelible ink on the tissue of her brain, but her heart remained untouched by emotion. The peculiar coldness was almost as frightening as the searing terror of her blackouts.

She'd just been given her life back. A large chunk of it, anyway. She should feel *something*. Anger, a sense of loss, joy at the recaptured memories—even the pain Clay had assured her would eventually come would be a welcome relief. At least she'd know she was alive. It was as if in bringing the memory of her mother's death back, some part of her had died.

"Nicki?"

She looked up. They were sitting in her driveway, Reed's car idling quietly, his eyes studying her with concern. He reached for her hand. A degree of warmth returned to her body as his fingers closed around hers.

"Thank you for being there," she murmured, offering him a quick embrace before she slipped from the car.

He started to get out, but she came around to his side of the car and shook her head.

"I meant what I said about being alone."

"I'll come back and drive you over for the fireworks."

"No. I'll bring Lexie when I'm ready."

"You shouldn't . . ."

"Reed, I need to be in control for once in my life. My decisions. My timing. Can you understand?"

His eyes denied his comprehension, but he nodded.

"But you'll be there when it begins getting dark? You'll bring Lexie to see the fireworks?"

Nicki placed her fingers on his lips.

"We'll be there. I promise."

For a moment as he pulled away, Nicki battled an overpowering urge to call him back. She shook off the feeling and went inside to share her newest discoveries. As with Renee, Mid shared none of her heritage, but Nicki had come to think of her as family.

Maybe such relationships were more precious than those of the flesh, she thought. At the least they might offer less pain when they were severed. Except she felt no pain. At this moment she still felt nothing at all.

"I don't like leaving you alone," Mid said, for perhaps the tenth time. "I could ride over with you when Lexie wakes up."

"Mid, I'll be fine. That's probably Joel in the drive right now. You two go on. Have a good time. And tell Reed I'll be there. I promised Lexie I'd wake her in plenty of time for the fireworks. She won't let me change my mind and stay home."

"If you're sure . . ."

A few more reassurances and Mid reluctantly gathered her things and met Joel at the door.

Nicki waved them on, shutting the screen and flipping the latch with relief. Lexie had fallen into an exhausted sleep about five o'clock. Only Nicki's reminder that the fireworks wouldn't start until after her usual bedtime had convinced her of the necessity for so late a nap.

The weariness that had accompanied the previous therapy sessions had crept up more slowly after today's. Nicki climbed the stairs and stretched out on the bed opposite Lexie's. Mid had lowered one blind to block the late-afternoon sun. The sleeping porch was warm and cozy.

Nicki lay on top of the ribbed bedspread and let reawakened memories flood over her. The images left her tense and edgy. She was still emotionally bereft. All her feeling seemed concentrated in her extremities and the hairs along her arms. Every nerve ending quivered like waiting antennae.

Waiting for what? Some kind of cosmic connection from the heavens? The ultimate return of childhood memory? Gory details of her mother's last few agonizing moments?

She rolled onto her side, away from Lexie, willing tears to come to banish the numbness broken only by the prickling sensation in her limbs. The tingling was a feeling of sorts, she decided. Probably some form of delayed reaction or shock. Whatever it was, it could never be as frightening as her panic attacks. Those should be over, now that she'd faced the truth.

Her eyelids began to droop as the warmth of the setting sun slanted across her legs. There were still unexplained images, she thought sleepily. Her reaction to the hand puppets. And to the worms.

She shivered despite the cocoon of sunshine and burrowed her face into the pillow. A vague sense of alarm made her twist away from the softness. Something about the sensation of the cushion against her skin flickered for an instant and was gone. Her eyes closed as exhaustion claimed her consciousness.

* * *

Lexie opened her eyes. She probed her front tooth with her tongue, nudging to see if it was any looser. Miz Mid had said the fairies might leave a quarter if she put the tooth under her pillow when it fell out. One of Russell's friends had explained all about the tooth fairy and the Easter bunny. When the same boy had taunted Lexie and Sharraye that Santa Claus wasn't real either, Russell had gotten mad and made him stop coming by after school.

A quarter would be nice, Lexie thought, but there really wasn't anything she wanted to buy. She'd decided the tooth belonged with her other special things.

Miz Mid had given her a cardboard box covered with pretty paper. In it she kept her favorite shells and the baby duck's feather and a bit of fur from the bunny's favorite spot and a rock she'd found that looked like a heart.

She rolled on her stomach and reached beneath the bed, but the box wasn't there.

Lexie frowned. A sound made her look over her shoulder. Mommy was lying on top of her covers, breathing the funny way grown-ups sometimes did while they slept. She slipped quietly off her bed and padded barefoot down the hall to the room with the canopy bed.

The box wasn't anywhere in that room either. She clamped her hands on her hips and twisted her face up the way she'd seen Miz Mid do when she couldn't remember where she'd put down her reading glasses.

The house was quiet. Miz Mid must have already gone to the party. Mommy had promised they could go watch the fireworks. She'd have to wake up soon or they'd miss them.

Lexie went to the window and looked out to see

if any squirrels were playing in the side yard. Her tongue worried the loose tooth once again. The playhouse drew her attention, and she smiled. That was where she'd left the box of treasures. On the table Reed had given her, next to her dishes.

She walked downstairs and pushed on the screen door, but it wouldn't open. The little knob was flipped over. Lexie pushed on it until she was able to twist the handle and step cautiously outside. The sun was starting to disappear into the trees across the lake. She peered into the twilight beyond the door.

Nothing moved in the yard. Even the birds had quieted. She glanced over her shoulder. Mommy would probably wake up soon. Then they'd have to hurry so they wouldn't miss the fireworks. She didn't want to leave her special things in the playhouse. If she woke up before her mother, she liked to have them near so she could lie in bed and look through her treasures.

It wasn't really dark yet. She could see the playhouse clearly and beyond that the swing, swaying gently in the breeze. If she ran real fast, it wouldn't be any darker when she returned. And Mommy was right upstairs.

Lexie darted across the yard and opened the playhouse door. The cardboard box covered with pretty purple-flowered paper was right where she'd left it. Her fingers closed around the container, then drew back as a shadow blocked the fading rays of sun slanting through the playhouse window.

She whirled around.

"Hello, Lexie. I'm so pleased you came out. It makes things so much easier."

Lexie backed away from the hands that reached for her. She'd made a mistake by leaving the house. An awful mistake. Mommy was gonna be really mad at her when she woke up.

▬▬ 40 ▬▬

"Who's that with Bob Stockton?" Devon asked Gwyn, indicating a teenager wearing slashed jeans, a too-tight tank top, and a generally bored expression.

"His youngest. Juvenile-court judge thought she needed a change of environment. Bob fetched her home one day last week."

"That's probably the reason he missed his regular day at Nicki's," Mid said.

Gwyn spotted other friends and excused herself. Devon glanced around at the milling crowd.

"Where did Clay wander off to now? He's been as edgy as a tabby in a rocking-chair factory ever since we got here."

"He's probably looking for Nicki," Mid murmured. "She should be getting here soon. I wish I hadn't left her alone. Maybe we should drive back over there to get her."

"You'd probably pass on the road or miss her going the other way," Devon said.

She turned her attention to some children about Lexie's age, several of whom she recognized as former or potential students. The group was clustered around a man in a stovepipe hat and a gaudily striped tailcoat. The performer plucked a coin from behind one boy's ear, then presented the bouquet of flowers that sprang from the end of his wand to a blond toddler with her thumb in her mouth.

The children clapped in delight. The magician twisted one corner of his pasted-on mustache with precise exaggeration and grinned. A memory flashed unbidden across Devon's consciousness. She turned to Joel.

"Does the name Finny Fish mean anything to you?"

"In connection with what?"

"A man, an older boy, really, who hung around us kids during the summers. Someone named him that because he kept bugging us to go fishing with him. It had something to do with his name, too. I just can't put it together."

Joel studied her closely.

"What made you think of him?" he asked.

"Something Nicki said this afternoon. And then, just now, I remembered an incident the last summer I spent here as a young girl. An encounter I'd forgotten all about."

"What happened?" Mid asked.

"It was so long ago. I . . . maybe it didn't really happen. Or I took it the wrong way or something."

"Tell me about it," Joel said quietly.

"I think he tried to molest me," Devon blurted out. "At first I was flattered. An older boy—he must have been close to twenty; he was living alone. Anyway, I thought his interest in me meant I wasn't the baby the other kids kept calling me. I looked a lot younger than I was."

She ducked her head, suddenly disconcerted.

"He put his arm around me, and I got kind of scared. Then he tried to run his hand between my legs. When I told him I was too young to do things like that, he laughed and asked me what I thought was too young."

Devon stared at the ground.

"This is really embarrassing," she said, lowering her voice.

"What did you tell this older boy?" Joel prompted.

"That I was only twelve. He pushed me away and then . . . this was what was so weird . . . he said he'd thought I was eight or nine. That didn't make sense to me at the time, but I've read enough about child molesters since then to know each one targets his own special age range."

"Did you report what happened?"

"He told me no one would believe me. That they'd think I was just trying to get attention. I didn't care. I ran home to tell my mom, but when I got there . . ."

She closed her eyes, remembering the different kind of shock she'd found when she burst through the door of the rental unit.

"My father had just come home and asked my mother for a divorce. In all the screaming and confusion, it just didn't seem very important that some older boy had tried to 'feel me up.' I guess I forgot about it over the years. The same way Nicki blocked everything about Pip's death all this time."

"What about Pip Sheridan's death?" Joel asked, looking pointedly between Devon and Mid.

"Clay's been treating Nicki for a childhood trauma," Mid explained.

"She's the daughter."

Both women stared at him in disbelief.

"You knew?"

"Suspected. All her questions about previous

owners, her insistence the playhouse be an exact duplicate of the original."

He looked away, probing the crowd with a practiced eye.

"Could your molester's name have been Finley?"

"I suppose. Why? What's he got to do with Nicki being Pip Sheridan's daughter? They didn't come back until . . . it must have been ten or twelve years after what happened to me."

"There was a young man named Finley Houghton living around the neighborhood off and on during those dozen or so years. Been on the outs with his family—one of those yours, mine, ours, and theirs tribes—from Chicago, Gary, someplace like that. Calumet, maybe. Never stepped over the line that anyone could see, but some of the guys had their suspicions."

"What did he look like?" Devon asked.

"Bushy blond, skinny. Always trying to grow a mustache."

"That sounds like the boy I remember, but it was all so long ago. And I'd really forgotten the episode until just now."

Devon spotted Reed coming through the crowd, scanning faces. She caught his attention and waved.

"Where's Nicki?" he demanded when he joined them.

"She hasn't gotten here yet. Did you happen to run into Clay? He wandered off about a half hour ago."

"He must be around somewhere. I saw his car parked out by the road when I got here."

"How long ago was that?"

"Fifteen, maybe twenty minutes. A client pigeonholed me inside the clubhouse when I was trying to make my way out."

Devon felt Mid pulling on her arm.

"Joel says that Houghton man was renting a house on our side of the lake the summer Pip died."

"What are you talking about?" Reed demanded.

"A man who tried to molest Devon as a child was living nearby during the summer Nicki blocked from her memory."

"I asked Clay when he first began treating Nicki if she could be blocking some kind of sexual abuse. He dismissed the idea," Devon protested. "He already knew her problem stemmed from watching Pip drown."

"He told you that?" Joel asked.

"Not until this morning. He wasn't ready to explain . . ."

"Explain what?"

The former sheriff's deputy had taken command of the conversation with a simple change of tone in his voice. Reed glanced at Devon and Mid, then shrugged.

"Clay believes he's Nicki's father."

"He *is* her father. Lexie has his eyes," Devon said.

"And he insists Nicki couldn't have been abused?"

"Not insists," she said defensively. "He just shrugged the idea off when I brought it up."

"Since he knew about her mother's death, maybe he just assumed that had to be the root of her problem," Mid suggested.

"Maybe," Joel said, sounding unconvinced.

"*Was* Nicki a witness?" Devon asked.

"Probably. We didn't get much chance to talk to her. Poor little tyke refused to speak, for one thing. Then Ollie Sheridan started wielding pressure up

the line, and no one could find out where she'd
been taken. The whole thing looked pretty cut-and-
dried. We had more pressing problems at the time.
That was a rough week around here."

"When exactly did Pip Sheridan drown, anyway?" Reed asked.

"Verdell didn't tell you?"

"He just said the summer of 1972," Devon murmured.

Joel's expression darkened.

"She drowned the night of the July Fourth celebration."

Reed slammed his hand against his forehead.

"Nicki's alone in that house with a daughter almost the same age as she was when her mother
drowned. Dammit, where's Clay? One of you try to
call Nicki. I'm going to have him paged."

"Have him meet us out front," Joel called over
his shoulder, taking the lead in their rush for the
clubhouse.

Nicki opened her eyes to a dusky twilight. A sound
drew her attention toward Lexie's bed. She sat up
and turned, and her heart leaped into her throat,
stealing the breath from her lungs.

"Good evening, Nicki. Or do you prefer Sky
again?"

Lexie stared at Nicki with saucer-shaped eyes,
her own breathing restricted by the right arm encir-
cling her chest.

"Please don't hurt her. What do you want?"

"It seems you've forgotten my warning."

"Mommy . . ."

Lexie struggled against the viselike grasp and the
left hand that kept stroking her leg. A single tear
hung on her upper lip. Nicki reached out her hand.

"It's going to be all right, baby."

"It *would* have been all right, if you hadn't come back to stir up what was buried. Did you think I wouldn't realize what you were trying to do? That I was so stupid I'd let you ruin things all over again? How much more have you remembered?"

His arm tightened about Lexie while his other hand continued its almost seductive caress. Hate-filled eyes bored into Nicki's.

"Please. I'll do anything you say. Just let Lexie go."

"It's too late for that now."

"Why are you doing this?"

"I never meant to hurt her, you know. She hadn't been around for a couple of summers. I'd never done that much with her anyway, but she remembered me and she'd gotten nasty. Threats didn't work. She wanted money not to tell. She said hateful things . . . just like Kathy. Kathy told, and they sent me away. I couldn't let them do that again."

"No, of course you couldn't," Nicki said, inching forward on the bed, her eyes locked on the tortured face before her.

He sidestepped to the far end of Lexie's bed, dragging his sobbing captive. His left hand pressed against Lexie's thigh, inching higher.

"Please, you mustn't do this. You can't."

"I can! I watched the film. You didn't know I had the camera running, did you, Sky? Her threats, my rage, your tragic walk-on appearance. I caught it all. That's why I know I can do it again. I've been reliving every moment planning for this."

He hugged Lexie to him, bending to rub his mustache against her auburn curls. She whimpered again, her dark eyes pleading with Nicki to intervene.

Tears blurred Nicki's vision. She blinked them away, her thoughts roaming, seizing, and rejecting approaches and actions. If she jumped him and failed, she might make things worse. But how do you reason with a madman who kept talking in riddles . . . about things you couldn't remember?

"Don't cry," he crooned in Lexie's ear, his voice as gentle as his hands as they turned her against him and cupped her bottom to draw her even closer. "I have a special place, Lexie. You'll like the things we can do there together. Midge and the others liked them after a while. And I love you much more than them."

I have to get her away from him, Nicki thought frantically.

"And when we're done, I'll send you to be with your mother. Just like I meant to do with her after I got rid of Pip."

Nicki gasped. He offered a twisted smile, one corner of his mustache inching upward, trembling as if with a life of its own.

"You should never have forgotten the worms, Sky. You should have remembered. But you didn't, so you left me no choice. The worms got Pip, and now they'll get you."

Nicki fought a rising wave of nausea and panic. Lexie! She couldn't black out now. Lexie needed her.

Mid and Devon hurried down the club's front steps as Reed's blue Cutlass careened up the circular drive.

"Clay didn't answer the page," Devon told him through the open passenger window.

"His car's gone," Reed said, glancing beyond her.

"Operator says Nicki's line's out of order," Joel

reported breathlessly as he joined the group around the idling car. He tossed a set of keys at the women and jumped in the front seat as Reed slammed his vehicle back into gear.

"To his pickup," Mid explained, pulling Devon with her in the direction of the club's crowded parking lot.

Nicki fought the blackness, clinging to the present with every fiber of strength. The past was gone. She was the mother now, not the child. Lexie needed her. Lexie was all that mattered.

"Coming back, is it, Sky?"

"They said she drowned. That the boom knocked her overboard, and her vest came off, and . . ."

He was nodding his head, smiling that same sickening smile, the twisted grin that filled her mind with fragmented memories too frightening to be real.

"The reports were somewhat accurate. Except *she* swung the boom. I caught her on the back-swing. The vest was lying on deck. The clasp was already frayed. A few firm tugs . . .

"I waited until I was sure, then let it float after the body. Everyone knew she couldn't swim. I didn't even have to hold her down. Capsizing the boat was harder. I forgot to untie the dinghy, so it sank. It didn't really matter. *I've* always been an excellent swimmer."

Lexie had stopped crying and now sagged limply against the arms that pinned her, her expression more detached than frightened. *A symptom of shock?* Nicki wondered as anger roiled through her, clenching her fists.

"You murdered my mother!"

He shook his head.

"You killed her, Sky. You tried to tell."

He glared at her, eyes narrowed once more.

"I came back for you, you know. Could you hear me searching? Did you think you were safe when Renee came home and frightened me away? She assumed you were already out there somewhere . . . bait for the fishes . . . just like your mother."

An acidic taste filled Nicki's mouth.

"Waiting was the hardest part. They said you never spoke, but the risk was too great. I loved it here, but I had to leave."

Nicki braced her hands to push away from the bed, but he sensed her intent and scuttled farther away to resume his gentle stroking of Lexie's limp body.

Night was settling around them. She'd switched on the hall light when she'd come upstairs. From the corridor it cast a grotesque glow on his twisted features. The faint pop of firecrackers drifted across the lake on the breeze.

Reed and the others would be wondering why she and Lexie hadn't come. Would they worry, maybe try to call? If she didn't answer, they'd come looking. But they might be too late. Maybe it was already too late. She fought another wave of nausea that accompanied a snatch of returning memory.

Run, baby. Hide. Hide till I come for you.

"When I came back, I heard you'd died, locked away in some sanitarium. After all this time I thought it would finally be safe. Nothing left to betray me but the film. And no one knew it existed. I wish we had time to watch it together, Sky."

Lexie whimpered again. Across the lake, a cluster of aerial bombs exploded, echoing over the water, demanding startled attention.

Nicki lunged, rage driving her forward. Her fist

caught him above the lip, jamming the delicate bones of her hand into her wrist. Something cracked. She felt a warm rush of blood. His hands flew automatically to his damaged nose.

Ignoring the throbbing pain at the end of her arm, she snagged Lexie up with her good hand and shoved her through under the bed out toward the farthest away of the two doors to freedom.

"Run, Lexie. Run fast. Hide."

Had she said the words, or were they yet another echo of her mother's voice?

"No!"

His cry spurred her on. She squirmed after her daughter, urging her forward. Lexie's bare feet disappeared through the doorway. Nicki scrambled after her, switching on lights and slamming doors as she fled toward the hall. Behind them their pursuer crashed against the feeble barriers, roaring her name.

A whimper, from the room to her left. The room with the nautical theme. Nicki froze on the threshold, fighting the darkness of remembered terror. Lexie stared up at her from behind the pillows on the big bed, eyes wide and pleading, bathed in the light from the hall.

A hand shoved Nicki violently into the room. She stumbled to the bed and gathered her trembling child in her arms.

"Shall we replay it all, Sky? Pip's not around to come to your rescue this time. Your friends will be so saddened when they find you in the water. So shocked your therapy drove you to relive and complete the tragedy you witnessed."

"They'll never believe that. Clay . . ."

"A professional misjudgment, leaving you alone like this."

"They'll find out."

"Who's going to tell them? You won't be around. And by the time they find you, neither will Lexie. I really regret that part of all this. Especially since it wouldn't be necessary if I'd succeeded the other night."

"It was *you* pulling me down, *your* rope around my ankles!"

"If you hadn't lashed out, it would have been over quickly."

A staccato burst of skyrockets rippled over the lake, followed by another round of aerial bombs.

"It's time to go, Sky."

Lexie whimpered again. Nicki stood up slowly, calculating the distance between them and their adversary. He dropped his gaze to Lexie, the twisted desire on his features sickeningly apparent. Nicki charged, head lowered, catching him in the chest, driving the breath from his body, staggering him to his knees. She swung Lexie in a wide arc toward the doorway.

"Downstairs!" she screamed. "Run, Lexie. Now!"

Instead of following, Nicki lashed out with both feet toward his crotch, landing not as squarely as she hoped but definitely on target. His agonized scream faded as she raced toward the stairs.

......41......

Lexie was huddled against the closed front door, watching the stairs with hollow eyes. Nicki's appearance sparked an instant of frightened relief before an angry roar and the thud of a body crashing against the wall in the hallway above drove the hope from her face.

Nicki took in the locked dead bolt, its empty key-hole a searing reminder they were still not safe. The lock's duplicate key, as well as the ones to the Blazer, lay in the bottom of her purse upstairs. As if punctuating the bleakness of their situation, another round of skyrockets flared and crackled across the lake.

Hide, baby. Hide till I come for you.

Nicki raked her hand across the light switch, plunging the stairs and entryway into darkness, and grabbed Lexie's hand, moving instinctively to the paneling that covered the dead space beneath the stairway. Fingers scrabbling at the grooves, she probed desperately for a half-remembered indentation.

The catch snapped open, and a section of paneling swung outward. She shoved Lexie through the opening and pulled it shut behind them as the first footstep sounded above their heads.

A layer of dust rose about them, tickling her throat, choking its way into her lungs. Nicki crabbed deeper into the blackness, feeling her way. Her hand brushed over an unexpected form. She closed her fingers about the object, drawing strength from its shape. They'd be safe now. Safe till someone came.

Wrapping her arms protectively about her daughter, she buried her face in the thick tangle of curls and pressed her lips against Lexie's ear.

"Not—one—sound," she whispered savagely.

Beyond their airless refuge, the Fourth of July celebration continued, each muffled discharge driving Nicki's consciousness further back in time, recreating a nightmare.

How could she have forgotten? The question battled with her desire to embrace the blackness, to curl up as tightly as she'd done a lifetime ago.

A thin line of light appeared beneath the bottom of the hidden door. He'd switched the entryway light back on. Nicki laid her fingers gently against Lexie's lips. She pressed her face once more into Lexie's hair, willing silence and strength from herself to her daughter with each muffled breath.

The sudden splintering of wood blotted out the explosions of rockets and star bursts. Light flooded their sanctuary. Lexie's screams burst free, filling the enclosure with sound, sending dust motes whirling about the sudden brightness in a feverish dance.

Hands jerked the paneling free. Nicki shoved Lexie behind her as a face appeared in the opening.

"You have no secrets, Sky. Renee told everyone about your refuge. I used it myself when you were searching the house."

Fingers clamped about her ankle, dragging her

forward. Nicki kicked at his face, clawing desperately for leverage against the walls and floor. Lexie's shrieks continued.

Hatred-filled eyes bored into hers as she blinked against the light. She raised her arms against his descending fist, steeling herself for the blow.

Instead of numbing pain or blackness, the night seemed to explode around her. Broken glass rained over the entryway. A whirlwind flung her attacker away. Nicki scuttled away from the shouts and muttered oaths filling the air and pulled Lexie's unresisting body from beneath the stairs. Shards of glass from the shattered window beside the front door tore at her clothing as she leaped through the opening and raced into the darkness.

Familiar voices and arms surrounded them. Shouts of authority rang out. Reed's reassuring voice. Devon's and Mid's arms. Joel's commands to use Mid's key to open the door and separate the men scuffling in the entryway.

A savage scream signaled the end of the struggle. Nicki forced herself to look up. Two uniformed deputies, supporting a third man between them, appeared in the lighted doorway. Fear and panic had replaced the rage on Del Ferris's face.

Reed lunged forward, but Joel stepped in his way.

"Assault charges should do for starters," he said, eyeing Del with disgust. "Probably add more once we sort this all out."

Del raised his eyes to the little group huddled in the yard.

"Bunny?"

Lexie pressed herself against her mother, trembling uncontrollably. Nicki tightened her arms about her child.

"Get him out of here," Joel told the deputies.

A shadow blocked the light from the doorway. Nicki's gasp brought everyone's attention from the retreating officers and their captive to the figure that filled the opening.

Scratches crisscrossed his face, and one eye had already begun to swell, but Nicki thought Clay had never looked as imposing as he did at that moment. His eyes sought hers, then dropped to Lexie's tear-stained face.

"I got here as soon as I could, Sunshine. How you doing?"

Lexie stared at him with solemn eyes.

"I'm feeling a bit shaky myself. Think you and Mid could find me some ice and a cold rag for my head?"

An engine roared to life. The patrol car's rotating lights swept the yard as the vehicle pulled away. Confusion-filled dark eyes turned to Nicki, seeking direction.

"He's not coming back," Nicki said, kneeling beside Lexie. "Not ever, I promise."

She led Lexie back into the house. Mid moved past them, murmuring something about ice cubes and coffee. Clay sank down on the stairs and laid his head against the newel post. Lexie left Nicki's side to stand beside him. She pointed to the puffiness around his eye.

"Maybe if you don't think about it, it won't hurt so much."

The others looked up as Clay and Nicki joined them.

"Lexie's asleep," Nicki said. "Mid said she'd call down if she needs me again."

Clay sank into a chair and leaned his battered

head against the cushions. Reed pulled Nicki down next to him on the sofa. Her vision clouded. Feeling had returned with a vengeance, replacing her earlier numbness with a kaleidoscope of emotion. Even breathing felt painful. Guilt, anger, despair— each fought the other, as she battled for control.

"How much of this is going to stay with her?" Devon asked.

"Most of it, for a while," Clay said. "We talked a lot about good secrets and bad secrets and how talking helps. Maggie Stein's probably the best person around here for this kind of trauma. I'll call her as soon as it's light."

Devon refilled coffee cups. Across the room the low murmur of Joel's voice on the phone was the only sound. He hung up and rejoined the group.

"I'll say this, the SOB's inventive. Claims he thought Nicki was suicidal and he was trying to protect Lexie."

"He murdered my mother!"

Joel's assurances that Del would remain in custody, at least till morning, had kept Nicki silent until Lexie's fears had been calmed and she'd fallen asleep. Now her control crumbled and the pain Clay had predicted sparked uncontrollable tears.

"It's after midnight. This can wait till morning," Joel offered once her sobs subsided.

Nicki shook her head.

"It's in bits and pieces, images that don't quite fit together." She turned to Clay, her question unspoken.

"Nicki, if I regress you now, knowing the true source of your trauma, anything you remember might be challenged by Del's attorney in court."

"Clay's right," Reed said. "He could claim Clay

planted or suggested false memories to incriminate his client."

"Maybe if I talk about it . . . Some of it came back while we were under the stairs. That's where I hid from him the first time. Tonight was like re-living it all again—the fireworks exploding, his stumbling around calling my name."

She shuddered. Reed's arm tightened about her shoulders.

"I think it all began to unravel that day I blacked out at Marquet's. When I saw Jenna's picture on their wall."

"Jenna Edgerley," Joel murmured.

"The girl who ran away?" Devon asked.

"Disappeared. On July fourth, 1972. The same night Pip Sheridan drowned," Joel said, shifting in his chair.

"Somebody wanted Mommy to speak at a rally. I'd been whiny and cranky all afternoon, and I needed a nap. She told them she'd come if she found someone to stay with me."

"Where was Renee?" Clay asked.

"She'd been gone for a couple of days. She did that a lot. Some guy would catch her fancy, and she'd disappear for a while. Somebody had told me about the club party. I wanted to go see the clowns and the magician, but Mommy said it wasn't right to celebrate while people were dying in an immoral war."

"You were too young to understand that con-cept," Devon protested.

"But not to hear the words. Anyway, she called around for a sitter, but everyone was at the club. Finally she put me in the car and started to town. That's when we saw Jenna walking toward the crossroads with her backpack."

"Running away," Devon murmured.

"I don't suppose she told Mommy that, but she jumped at the offer of a bonus to stay with me. Mommy dropped us off here and promised she'd be back in time to watch the fireworks from the end of the dock."

"Where does Del come into this?" Reed asked.

Nicki rubbed her forehead.

"I'd been trying to show Jenna that I could twist my loose tooth around backward, but she wouldn't pay attention. She stuck me in bed with my puppets and then left."

Nicki frowned and shut her eyes for a moment.

"This is where things get a little fuzzy. I know I heard the front door close and got out of bed and looked out the window. Jenna was running across the yard, yelling at the man who lived where Devon does now. They went into his house."

"Finley Houghton," Joel said.

"He had a camera and liked to take pictures . . ."

She turned to Reed.

"That photo of Renee by the willow. He took it. Mommy and I were in the original print."

"What happened next?" Clay asked.

"I took my puppets and followed. The screen door was open, and I could hear them arguing. I remember reaching for the door . . ."

Nicki shook her head.

"I'm sorry. The rest is pretty jumbled."

"You're doing fine. Stay with it," Clay murmured.

Nicki raised her eyes. The gaze that met hers was achingly familiar, so like Lexie's, that her thoughts tumbled into words before she could stop them.

"Are you my father?"

Clay nodded. Nicki felt something deep inside her shift.

"What did you see when you opened the door?" Joel asked.

"Jenna and the man were yelling at each other."

"Do you remember what they said?"

"Jenna wanted money for a bus ticket. She told him if he didn't give it to her, she'd tell about some pictures he'd taken. He said no one would listen if he tore them up. She said that wouldn't matter. She'd say he touched her and did nasty things to her. They yelled a bunch more and I got real scared."

"Why didn't you run back home?" Clay asked gently.

"The door wouldn't open. It snapped shut when I came in."

"What did you do?"

Nicki hunched her shoulders and pressed a clenched fist to her lips as the memory wavered and then stabilized with agonizing clarity. She fought back a new rush of tears.

"I made myself real small and crawled behind a chair. They kept yelling at each other, and then he screamed really loud and Jenna started making funny noises, and then she didn't anymore and I could hear him crying."

The words tumbled out like water from a broken main.

"I wanted to go home. Jenna was asleep on the floor. The man was still crying, but he got mad again when I stood up. He grabbed me and held me. He tried to take Bert and Ernie away, but I wouldn't let him. I asked when Jenna was going to wake up. He said never, and if I told anyone about what happened, he'd make Mommy go away and never come back."

Nicki abandoned her attempt to stanch the flow of tears. Reed leaned forward. Clay held up a hand, motioning him back.

"Stay with it, Nicki. Take deep breaths, just like in therapy. That's it. Try to tell us what happened next."

"He put Jenna in a wheelbarrow and put a big rug over her and made me lie down on top. It was getting dark, so he made me hold a big flashlight."

Nicki's tears had stopped. She squeezed her eyes shut, suddenly terrified of the memory hovering just beyond her consciousness. She couldn't do this. She wasn't ready.

"What were you feeling, Nicki?" Clay asked gently, his voice surrounding her, giving her strength.

"I was mad at Mommy. 'Cause she didn't come."

"Where did he take you?"

"To the garden. He made me hold the light."

Nicki gasped and opened her eyes.

"He dug a big hole and he sang about the worms! About how they crawl in and out and eat you when you die. He put Jenna with the worms! He said if I told, they'd get Mommy too. Then he made me touch them."

Nicki felt as if her skin were crawling. She hugged herself, rubbing at her arms, but still felt unclean. The horror was too terrible to hold in any longer. She had to get it out of her head and into the light.

"He threw Bert in the hole! He threw dirt on him and on Jenna and . . . she opened her eyes! Jenna opened her eyes! I had to run, had to find Mommy. Jenna didn't want to be with the worms."

She covered her face, trying to blot out the image of Jenna's eyes reflected in the moonlight so long ago.

"I ran in the house and hid in the room with the boat bed. But he found me and held a pillow over my face. I couldn't breathe. But then I heard Mommy calling my name downstairs, and he stopped pushing so hard, and I yelled 'help' real loud."

Nicki lowered her hands and raised her head, the pain too deep now for tears to flow.

"Mommy came and started hitting him. She yelled at me to run and hide till she came for me. I hid in our special hide-and-seek place, but she never came."

42

Outside, the sound of activity continued. Darkness hung over the lake, but the eerie glow from the searchlight mounted on a flatbed trailer cast a surreal spell on the night.

Nothing felt real anymore, Nicki thought. She wondered if she could have somehow invented the horror. By three A.M. she'd repeated her story a half dozen times—to deputies and officers from various departments, to an elderly professor of forensic medicine, and to a man from the prosecutor's office who'd listened attentively, then rushed off to wake a judge and obtain a warrant to search Del's house.

Sleep had never seemed an option, despite repeated entreaties for her to join Lexie upstairs. Tucked in Mid's bed, soothed by Mid's protective arms and Nicki's quick appearance whenever she woke, Lexie had slept through most of the confusion.

Devon refilled coffee cups once again and left to brew another pot. Nicki stared at the dust-covered puppet Joel had found beneath the stairs. The rubber head's painted features had faded. The brightly striped shirt had begun to disintegrate. Tufts of the synthetic hair were missing—mice, someone had speculated—but Ernie's gumdrop nose and grinning mouth were still recognizable.

Ernie had been her only comfort as she huddled beneath the stairs that terrible night. Abandoned when exhaustion claimed her, ignored by Renee when a sleep-induced whimper had revealed Sky's location, the disappearance of her second puppet had seemed further proof her mother had met the same fate as Jenna and Bert.

"How you doing?" Clay said softly.

"No one told me she drowned. No one told me anything. All they did was ask me to talk about what I'd seen. But I couldn't. I thought he'd made her go away like he'd threatened he would."

"Nicki, when Pip disappeared and no one would talk about her, wouldn't even mention her name, your guilt took over."

"I don't understand."

"You'd been angry at her for leaving you alone. Angry at Jenna, for the same reason. A child's logic is one-dimensional. You cried out. Pip responded, and you never saw her again. You'd been warned of the consequences, so you must be to blame. And there was always that fear that he'd come back for you. Survival meant denying the good things as well as the bad.

"Ollie provided a perfect environment to strengthen that goal," Clay continued, taking her hands in his. "The doctors she sent you to thought your trauma was caused by watching Pip drown. I made the same mistake. If I'd had any idea . . ."

"You couldn't have known."

"When I called to check on you and found the phone out of order, all I could think was I'd really screwed things up."

Joel and Reed returned from the yard, trailed by

one of the deputies. The officer held out a sealed plastic evidence bag, its contents all but obliterated by nature. Nicki's fear about the validity of her memories faded, replaced by an overpowering sadness.

Blackened and pitted by two decades of interment, the cone-shaped rubber mass was final confirmation of the fate of Ernie's partner. Bert had come home.

▦▦▦ Epilogue ▦▦▦

Sultry air offered little relief from the heat. Nicki and Reed and the two other couples had changed into swimming suits. Only Lexie's absence and the lassitude that accompanied late-August afternoons had delayed the after-lunch shift to the water.

"The little girl in those San Jose newspaper clippings identified Del from a picture in a photography magazine," Reed told Nicki as she settled beside him on the porch sofa. "Courthouse scuttlebutt says his attorney's ready to plead."

"Not much choice once the judge ruled that film they found in his projector was admissible," Joel noted. "With all the physical evidence, Nicki may not have to testify. We figure he planted the girl's backpack on some westbound bus once things calmed down."

"Didn't anyone think the freshly turned earth in the garden was suspicious?" Devon asked.

Joel looked embarrassed.

"Bob Stockton's father dug up a hedgerow in the garden on July third. It rained the morning of the fifth, so the whole row looked freshly dug. Someone had seen Jenna walking toward the crossroads. She'd just fought with her parents, and she had a history of taking off. No one was looking for a body."

Bare feet pounded down the hallway above their heads, and a bathroom door slammed. Clay glanced up at the sounds.

"She still having nightmares?"

"Not since her seventh session with Dr. Stein."

"Maggie was a good choice."

"She thinks I'll sleep better too, once I get beyond the trial. I finally took her advice and went through that box in the garage. I found this tucked between the pages of a book."

Clay studied the worn photograph she handed him.

"Lexie may claim this for her collection."

As if sensing the perfect moment for her entrance, Lexie raced into the room. A price tag dangled from the *Sesame Street* book bag she was dragging behind her, and her eyes sparkled.

"Is that another picture of Aunt Rita?" she asked, referring to a childhood photo Clay had given her of his younger sister. The resemblance between Lexie and her auburn-haired aunt had fascinated Nicki as much as her daughter.

"No," Clay said, drawing her into his lap. "This is a picture of your grandmother when she was a young girl."

"Grandma Verdell on the phone? In California?"

"No, Grandma Pip."

Lexie studied the picture intently for a moment.

"It's the 'zebo," she said, looking shyly up at Clay.

He whispered in her ear.

"Grandpa says I can tell now. When Aunt Rita and Grandpa and Grandma Verdell come for Labor Day, we can go see the 'zebo."

"Then it's still there," Devon said. "Gwyn won

dered if it had survived. Remember? She told us one of the Tarletons proposed to her in the gazebo."

"On a swing," Nicki murmured, glancing at the picture in Clay's hand.

According to the date on the back of the photo, Pip would have been seventeen. She was wearing a fifties-style halter top and shorts, her feet tucked beneath her on a wrought-iron swing. Her long hair streamed out behind her as if blown by the wind, and one corner of her mouth turned upward in laughter. Even in the faded sepia print, the mischief in her eyes was unmistakable.

"Grandpa bought a new swing like the one Grandma Pip's on," Lexie announced. "He's gonna hang it in the 'zebo and take a picture of me and Mommy in it."

"I don't understand," Nicki told Clay. "Why would you buy something that expensive for someone else's property?"

"Gwyn's been negotiating with her ex-husband's family for several years. They're very close to a settlement that transfers title to a trust that would develop the property as a retreat and rent it out to youth groups."

"What about all the dissension?" Mid asked. "I thought the family couldn't agree."

"Fervor lessens with each generation. The recent economy had a lot to do with things as well. Money in hand looks much better than idle property when interest rates go down.

"Gwyn's proposal guarantees the grounds will remain as the first Mrs. Tarleton had intended. She's had architects design a nature center to be built where the house used to stand. The trails will be restored, but the rest will be left undisturbed. She's dedicating all of it to her husband's memory."

"Which one?" Devon asked. "She's had four."

"The last one, Karl Chamberlin. Most of the funding is coming from a foundation they set up before he died."

Lexie squirmed off Clay's lap and began emptying her book bag. She positioned her newest acquisitions, a Barbie and Ken, against the wall. Big Bird and Mr. Flops joined Reed and her mother on the sofa. The bright perky faces of Bert and Ernie grinned up from beneath a table lamp. When she was finished, Lexie stepped back and nodded her head.

"Ever'body's got somebody," she announced.

"I see Gwyn's influence here," Devon murmured to Nicki.

"The woman's a menace," Nicki whispered back. "I'll bet if it rains for more than a week, she commissions an ark."

Lexie ignored the snickering adults.

"Big Bird goes with Mr. Flops, 'cause they're both animals," she explained. "Barbie's got Ken. And Bert has Ernie."

She moved to the similarly partnered adults in the room.

"Miz Mid has Mr. Joel. Grandpa's got Devon. And Mommy has Reed."

Her mischievous eyes reminded Nicki that Pip's genes were as much a part of Lexie's makeup as the auburn hair she'd inherited from Clay's side of the equation.

"Ever'body's got somebody," Lexie repeated.

Clay caught her in a bear hug.

"What about you, Sunshine? Should we start looking for some freckle-faced six-year-old to be your partner?"

"I don't need a boyfriend, Grandpa," Lexie said,

spreading her arms as if embracing the room. "I got ever'body."

As if commenting on Lexie's observation, avian voices echoed loudly across the water. Seven half-feathered ducklings swam around the jutting point of Tarleton land, following their conservatively adorned mother and brightly plumed father.

"This is the best place in the whole world, and I don't ever wanna leave," Lexie said, clapping her hands.

"We're not leaving," Nicki told her. She watched Lexie snuggle deeper into Clay's arms. "Someone very wise once told me: when you find a place that feels like home, you should put down your roots."

"Is this house our home?" Lexie asked.

Nicki blinked back a sudden prickle of tears.

"This house is going to be our home forever. Someday *your* little girl can sleep in the bed you're using now."

"I wouldn't like that," Lexie said, frowning.

"Why not?" Clay asked.

" 'Cause then I'd have to sleep somewhere else. Maybe she can sleep in the one on the other side of Mommy."

"We'll see what we can do," Nicki said, adding her laughter to that of the others.

It felt good to laugh, she thought. The past had been exhumed, its demons laid to rest. The present seemed secure. Reed's arm tightened about her. She laid her head against his shoulder and smiled.

The future wasn't shaping up too badly, either.

Match wits with the best-selling
MYSTERY WRITERS
in the business!